"But you see, Jim, you didn't have me."

Jim McGowan started as though struck from behind. It was Gwen's voice issuing from the tape recorder, repeating in poignant, husky tones her private words of the night before.

If someone had bugged her room while he was there secretly, what other clandestine meetings of executives were being overheard—and by whom?

Jim became conscious of a lust to fight, a ravenous hunger to smash and be smashed. Someone in the conglomerate empire was trying to transform him from king to pawn in a deadly game of corporate intrigue!

"Knebel is in fine form . . . a tricky plot that hits on the most relevant business issues of the day."
—*Publishers Weekly*

THE BOTTOM LINE
was originally published by Doubleday & Company, Inc.

Books by Fletcher Knebel

The Bottom Line*
Dark Horse*
Night of Camp David
Trespass*
Vanished
The Zinzin Road

*Published by POCKET BOOKS

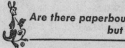

THE
BOTTOM LINE

Fletcher Knebel

PUBLISHED BY POCKET BOOKS NEW YORK

THE BOTTOM LINE

Doubleday edition published 1974

POCKET BOOK edition published November, 1975

L

This POCKET BOOK edition includes every word contained
in the original, higher-priced edition. It is printed from
brand-new plates made from completely reset, clear, easy-to-
read type. POCKET BOOK editions are published by POCKET
BOOKS, a division of Simon & Schuster, Inc., 630 Fifth
Avenue, New York, N.Y. 10020. Trademarks registered
in the United States and other countries.

Standard Book Number: 671-80136-8.
Library of Congress Catalog Card Number: 74-6990.

For Cecelia Bergquist

THE
BOTTOM LINE

Friday Evening

He checked off the last item on Katie's must list, swung back in his swivel chair and stretched. Long day, damn it, but now everything was buttoned up for the week away from the office. He had called Smitty again, finished his notes for the Waldorf meeting and composed the blast at the Polex people for the shabby quality of the last plastic shipment. Best to handle that one himself, much as he loathed paperwork.

The Lexington Avenue office was deserted now. Katie, the last to leave, had said her "good-by, have fun" a half hour ago. The electric desk clock showed 7:03. He had been here since seven-thirty in the morning, but now that he'd cleared his pad of the final niggling detail, he felt good, even if he was late for his drink with Meg before the NSGA dinner. He pushed back from the clean desk.

One of his three phones rang. It was the private line—unconnected with the Top Court switchboard—with the unlisted number. Probably Meg. He picked up the receiver with a feeling of annoyance.

"Hello. . . . McGowan."

"Hey, Jim." He recognized the familiar voice. "Tony Percevale . . . I figured you'd still be hanging around that sweatshop." American colloquialisms flowed effortlessly from the bilingual Argentine who had spent his prep school, college and early business years in the United States.

"How you doin', Tony? Where you calling from?"

1

"Here in New York. I just got in from Buenos Aires. How about buying you a drink?"

"Nothing I'd like better." He meant it. Seldom did he feel so relaxed as when trading business and personal chitchat over the glasses with his old classmate from Brown. "I'm tied up tonight—toastmaster at a sports goods industry dinner. But I'm meeting Meg right now for a quick one at the St. Regis. How about joining us?"

"Thanks. You know how much I'd like to see Meg, but I want to talk to you alone. How about after your meeting?"

"No can do, Tony. Meg and the girls are going out to the Island and I promised to get out there tonight. I have a session with Senator Ireland after the dinner, so I won't be able to clear the city until after midnight as it is. But what the hell, I'll see you Sunday in Acapulco."

Both men would be landing at Acapulco Sunday afternoon when executives of Arc-Horn International gathered for the conglomerate's twentieth-aniversary celebration. Percevale, who made his headquarters in his native Buenos Aires, was president of Gusto Más, S.A., the huge foods subsidiary whose ranches, farms, processing plant, and retail supermarkets spread throughout Latin America.

"This is business, Jim." Tony's voice took on an urgent note. "It concerns us both—and Arc-Horn. What about tomorrow? I'll come out to Westhampton to see you."

"No good. Honest. It's my one day in a month with the family. Sunday I take off early. What's up?"

"I can't tell you on the phone," said Percevale with uncustomary caution. "I've discovered some things about Arc-Horn that trouble me."

"What kind of things?" This was unlike Tony. His usual style with his old college friend was flippant candor.

"Incredible stuff, believe me." Percevale paused. "Well, let's just say it looks like Arc-Horn is involved in burglary and bribery. You're the only man in the outfit I'd trust to talk it over with."

"Burglary!" Hugo Praeger, Arc-Horn's flamboyant, domineering president, had hatched some peculiar capers in his time, but breaking and entering was hardly his manner. "Look, Tony, why not switch over and fly down in Top Court's new Falcon with me Sunday? My men will be playing cards anyway. We can talk up front."

"That's out too. Our team has to get squared away for that supermarket opening in Acapulco. We need the flight down to get everything set."

"We're missing all around." Jim eyed the desk clock. "Any other ideas?"

"Yeah. Let's meet in my room at the Mixteca as soon as you get in. We're scheduled in ahead of you, so I'll be waiting. It'll give us a couple of hours before that asinine early-bird fiesta."

"Okay, pal. See you then. . . . You in shape for some tennis?"

"Sure . . . Don't forget now. This is important to both of us. We need that nimble brain of yours."

"That's not what you usually call it."

"You know me. I only insult you when I don't need you."

Jim locked his private file cabinet, closed the door and walked through the empty Top Court executive offices, past the hooded typewriters, the yawning desks and the TeeCee wall calendars. What with the emergency trip to the Illinois plant, two nights with Smitty at the Doylestown factory and now the NSGA dinner, he had not been home all week. Yet, tired as he was, he loved this business and it did not occur to him to lament the fact that the last employee to leave the New York headquarters of Top Court, Inc., was President James Francis McGowan.

Meg was waiting at a booth in the King Cole Room. His first glance told Jim that she was seething. His second took in the Yves St. Laurent gray pants suit, the silver pendant, the new hair set, the slim figure, the empty martini glass.

"Sorry." He slid in beside her. "A couple of things

came up at the last minute; then just as I was leaving, Tony Percevale called."

"I've been sitting here for exactly one half hour." Her brown eyes flicked toward him, then away, a flash of reproach. "People were beginning to look at me like I was here for a pickup."

"I'm surprised you haven't been." He decided to play it light. "In that new pants outfit, you look terrific."

"New?" Meg bristled, then sighed. "Jim, you've seen this one on me at least a half dozen times."

"You still look great. . . . And I'm not a half hour late." He reached for her wrist and examined the oblong watch. In place of hands, two movable diamonds marked the time. Although Katie had purchased the watch last year as one of Meg's Christmas gifts, Jim admired the expensive timepiece and had come to believe that he had selected it himself. "Only twenty-four minutes."

"So I'm a liar for six minutes."

Jim felt it again, a sinking sensation like that during the swift drop of an elevator. Almost invariably now even commonplace conversations with Meg became a battleground. He tried a new approach.

"What's in the box?" A package rested on the cushioned seat beside her.

"A stack of new records for the party." Meg brightened. "Carol's crazy about some group called the Pilgrim Streakers. Connie, of course, wanted more Bill Withers."

Party? What party? Obviously he was supposed to know.

"The girls decided you and I will fade out about nine o'clock. Right after you do the steaks." Meg laughed and Jim felt the old tug of affection for her. In her radiant moments, no woman he knew could quite match her sparkle. "We eat and run."

Oh, so it was the twins' party. "That's okay with me. I can use a good, long sleep tomorrow sight."

"It's not tomorrow, Jim. It's Sunday night."

"Oh, that's too bad. I'll be in Acapulco, you know."

"Is that supposed to be a joke?"

"No. The Arc-Horn convention. Remember?"

She folded her arms and turned toward him. "You won't be home for the girls' bash?"

"Not if it's Sunday night. I'm flying down in the Falcon Sunday. . . . I told you a couple of weeks ago."

"You mean you forgot to tell me." Meg visibly sagged. "The girls will be awfully disappointed—again. The main idea was to show you off to their friends."

She toyed with her cocktail glass. A waiter appeared, hovered inquiringly at Jim's elbow.

"Nothing for me," said Jim. "Just the check, please."

A few minutes later, in the cab that would drop him at the Waldorf before taking Meg to the apartment on upper Park, Jim tried to melt the frosty silence. Meg sat apart from him, wrapped in herself. A chill March rain pelted the windows and traffic crawled through mid-town Manhattan with a petulant whine.

"Let's you and I go out tomorrow night," he said. "There's a dance at the club."

"I'm sick of the club."

The taxi stopped in front of the Waldorf. On the sidewalk umbrellas bent to the slanting rain like an army of turtles.

"Well, how about having the Rogerses over?"

"Forget it. I'm not in the mood."

He leaned toward her for a parting kiss, but she averted her head. As he stepped out, he slammed the door, a salute to the nineteen-year McGowan marriage. He fumed as he walked into the hotel, but by the time he had checked his coat and headed toward the ballroom, Meg could have been on another continent. His mind was fastened again on business, specifically on his upcoming chores as toastmaster of the eastern regional dinner of the National Sporting Goods Association.

Sunday

Jim stared down at the low cloud bank brooding over the Mexican shoreline, blotting out the city of Tampico. The Falcon 10 executive jet left the Gulf of Mexico behind and with a barely perceptible shift in heading began its final leg across Mexico.

"We estimate Acapulco in an hour and seventeen minutes, gentlemen." The intercom gave the pilot's voice a metallic rasp. "Acapulco temperature, ninety-one, not bad for March sixteenth. Wind at four knots. Unlimited visibility, natch. Gus says he'll mix a margarita for anyone who wants to get in the mood."

The news failed to deflect Jim's thoughts. He was in a curious psychic space, buoyed one minute and deflated the next as his tumbling images drifted back and forth between Top Court, Arc-Horn and Meg. By this time his mind should be centered squarely on business and the five-day round of meetings ahead, but Meg kept intruding.

Strange. When he dwelled on the business awaiting him, his mind clipped along, anticipating decisions, moves and counterploys in the clutter of scenes that, like those of some manic carnival, probably would mark the twentieth-anniversary celebration of Arc-Horn (We Nourish the World) International.

Hugo Praeger, that sybaritic yet half-primitive showman of the conglomerators, always staged Arc-Horn's annual gathering of the corporate tribes in some mammoth resort hotel where the sales staff of one of the subsidiaries paraded its new product line on the wings

6

of music, bombast, flimflam and corn. The louder and the more vintage P. T. Barnum the show, the better Hugo Praeger liked it. He would sit in a rear row, his great bulk stuffed into his special chair, and let his thin, cackling laugh mingle with the guffaws of his highly paid chieftains. Later in his lavish suite upstairs, Praeger would chew out a $200,000-a-year executive, chat with his young blond masseuse, who was once a Miss America contestant, plan a new business foray, hold a 10 p.m. board meeting or summon Arc-Horn's money man for a midnight chess game.

This year being Arc-Horn's twentieth birthday, Jim knew the scene would be wilder and more unpredictably bizarre than ever. Center stage for the customary outrageous sales presentation would be Summit, Inc., Arc-Horn's second-largest subsidiary, which manufactured and marketed television sets, radios, video cassette players, hi-fi equipment and audio-visual gear. It was as a Summit salesman that Praeger got his start three decades ago after immigrating from Switzerland and he had never lost his zest for the con man's pitch on his streaking rise to sales manager, president of Summit and finally the founder of Arc-Horn.

But what was all this about Arc-Horn and burglary? Tony's oblique phone call had nagged at Jim, especially when he recalled his own experience last week when the Columbia University biochemist called to say that his Manhattan apartment had been ransacked and his research notes on Top Court, Inc., stolen along with other papers. The Columbia professor, a frail, timid man, had interviewed McGowan and other Top Court executives several weeks earlier on a variety of company operations. Could this conceivably be linked to Percevale's incident which Tony said was important to both of them and to Arc-Horn? Was Hugo Praeger involved in some way? Hardly a credible ploy for a man charged with the demanding business of running a large multinational corporation. Well, whatever the facts, he'd find out from Tony in a couple of hours.

Unsettling too was that late talk Friday night, after

the NSGA dinner, with Senator Phil Ireland, who was determined to go for the Democratic presidential nomination next year. Phil disclosed that he intended to campaign on what he called "the great unmentionable" among rival politicians—what Ireland saw as the necessity to "wind down" industrial production lest the earth's resources become exhausted. Ireland offered Jim new figures on the swiftly accelerating depletion of vital resources and he wanted McGowan to enlist other "open-minded businessmen" in his campaign to halt "the plundering of the planet." Although he was no expert on the subject, Jim thought some of Ireland's figures might be more alarmist than factual. Still, Ireland was obviously sincere in his belief, for no politician powered by ambition alone would be such an idiot as to ask his countrymen to scale back a productive capacity that yielded them such a high level of civilized comfort. Ireland said members of the Group of Twelve would present some of the more frightening statistics next week in Geneva at a U.N. Conference on the Human Environment. Jim was torn. He'd like to help Ireland, a compelling, unpretentious man of conviction whom Jim implicitly trusted. And yet, it was difficult to buy the proposition that the good earth below this speeding plane would soon reach the limits of abundance that had sustained man for centuries.

Now through his seat window Jim could see the jagged mountainous sprawl far below, thin ribbons of trails and roads lacing the dusty hills and canyons like spider webs. Tampico's cloud bank had dissolved into scudding patches as Mexico's crumpled landscape heaved and dipped toward the horizon.

"Gin!" Behind him Jim could hear Al Bebout's sharp voice above the slap of cards. Jim's three-man executive team was playing gin rummy, loser out each hand, and drinking Beefeater and tonic. Bebout, Frankenheimer and Teigert were in a festive mood. Barring a rare summons from Praeger, theirs would be a week-long holiday with President Jim McGowan as Top Court's sole target of corporate heat.

And heat Jim expected when Praeger probed into the reason for this quarter's slump. But hell, the Doylestown, Pennsylvania, plant was off and winging now and soon might sweep all of Top Court into new highs. Besides, he had not a thing to apologize for. Top Court might be one of Arc-Horn's smallest properties, but in percentage of earnings increases it ranked No. 2 among all of Arc-Horn's nineteen subsidiaries. While Phil Ireland might raise an eyebrow at Top Court's growing appetite for the earth's metals, such hunger worried Hugo Praeger not at all. Anything that Praeger could dish out on the company's temporary lag, from sarcasm to biting invective, Jim could take. He even felt a flicker of excitement as he looked forward to the duel. What lay ahead, he could handle with no sweat. He would play his role and his hand and play them well.

It was that problem back in Westhampton—Meg, the twins, the party—that harassed him. He had chewed it like old cud all the way from the refueling stop in New Orleans, sitting alone, feigning sleep, while the other three men poked around the new Falcon, swapped stories and played cards.

Meg had raked him last night with her barbs dipped in that caustic mixture of drollery, amateur psychology and venom. She would prefer an open encounter with him, she said, but since he refused to fight back, a confrontation with him was like boxing with a blind man.

How had she started? Oh, yes. He had about as much regard for his family, she said with a dust of a smile, as Jackie Onassis did for photographers.

(Wrong, of course. So absurd it didn't merit an answer.)

His business always came first. And tennis second.

(Partially right. Would she rather share the salary of an eight-to-four postal clerk? . . . Or have a flabby husband who never exercised?)

He had spent the last three weekends at "drink tank" business conferences.

(Wrong. Only the last two. And this weekend he had been home all day Saturday, ducking an important huddle with Tony Percevale.)

He had known for a week that Carol and Connie had invited the teen crowd to a party Sunday and wanted to show off "their handsome six-foot-one father with those freaky freckles on his Irish map."

(Wrong. He couldn't remember anybody telling him about the party. Also Meg knew about Acapulco and the Arc-Horn conference weeks ago. He could swear that he had told her back in February. He had, hadn't he?)

What's more, if the twins had as little mothering from her as they had fathering from him, they'd either be orphans or strung out on drugs.

(Partly right, maybe, but Jesus, *that* old story again.)

And frankly, as a bedmate for the last few years, he'd make a good short-order cook.

(Right, he supposed, but did she expect a sex god after nineteen years of marriage? Also, the gibe showed a lack of understanding of the pressures he was under.)

And then in bed, just as he drifted into that fuzzy zone of wavering images, he heard her say, "Jim, I think I may have an affair." Startled, not sure whether the suggestion came from the wife beside him or from the fog of half-dreams, he mumbled something to the effect that she would probably do what she wanted to, as usual. But he remembered thinking, dimly but spitefully, that with the honey-haired twins, the apartment on upper Park, the home, pool and tennis court in Westhampton, the Mercedes, the Jag, the country club, the villa on Majorca, a husband soon to be worth about fifteen million and then a lover, Meg would have it all.

So you take the marital hassles of Jim and Meg McGowan and multiply them by about three million and you have most of the couples in corporate-office America in the same damn bag. Or maybe you threw in the British, the French, the Japanese, the Germans, the Brazilians, the Dutch and the Belgians and multiplied by ten million. Well, maybe not the Japanese and the Brazilians; they had their own customs. But he was sure of the Europeans because he'd heard some of the women talk. Any way you looked at it, the international brotherhood of business executives, the new royalty of the twentieth century, embraced countless couples around the world, all of them living high, all the men knocking their brains out to keep it that way and most of the women complaining that there had to be much more out there in that rose garden than they were getting from their husbands.

He sympathized occasionally with Meg's plight. The twins almost gone, off to Yale in September. Right now Meg had tennis, bridge and luncheons at the club. Fleeting avocations in the recent past had diverted her but briefly while leaving her vaguely dissatisfied. She had dabbled at antique collecting, served as a hospital gray lady, headed several charity drives, flirted with yoga and worked as a research volunteer for the League of Women Voters. . . . Sure, she had to find an absorbing interest, but that was her problem. If women's lib meant anything, and Jim was ambivalent about that, it meant a woman taking charge of her own life.

He thought he and Meg had pretty well settled the issue two years ago after their Mediterranean cruise with the Young Presidents' Organization which he revisited as an alumnus. They both had a swinging time aboard the *Queen Elizabeth II* and Meg even listened in on some of the "Odyssey of Knowledge" seminars. He and Meg talked far into the night after Mortimer Feinberg's talk on Corporate Bigamy. As usual, her ears heard a different talk than his did. As she understood it, they had to find a new, intimate, honest way of relating to each other. What he heard was, face it, a man who was any good was married to his job *and* his wife and they'd better start from that fact of life. In his case, the facts stood out in boldface long before that voyage on the *QE II*.

Fact One. Top Court, Inc., was his baby, his creation, just as live and pulsing as the twins who emerged from Meg's womb. Would Meg desert her own offspring? Never. And he would never abandon Top Court.

After intercollegiate tennis on a team that included Tony Percevale and after his B— average at Brown, Jim opened his own tennis shop in the summer of '48. Two years later, on a modest loan from his father, he began a couple of branch racquet-stringing operations. The next year, with a $50,000 loan negotiated through a trusting young officer, Hal Frascella, at First Merchants Trust, he launched into the manufacture of high-quality racquets. Soon he had spread to the making of balls, nets and tapes and the loans from First Merchants nudged $1,000,000. In 1955 he named the outfit Top Court and took it public. The underwriters offered the shares at $15. After costs and allowance for his own stock, Top Court suddenly had $5.5 million in equity capital and Jim took over a small garment factory and branched into tennis sportswear. The stock went to 21 over-the-counter until settling down at 18. That meant that Jim McGowan, with 200,000 shares in his own name, was worth $3,600,000 on paper—and damn good paper it was. Only he knew the fourteen-hour days, the nights, the Sundays, the ulcer, the aspirin and the pills during that one awful month in the '57–'58 recession when he thought the company might go under. Hal Frascella pulled him through with two extensions on the big loan when top brass at First Merchants wanted to call the paper and write off the loss. That call from Hal he would never forget: "I got you ninety more days. We're both in this together, Jim. If you don't make it, I'll see you on the welfare line."

Fact Two. The twins were born during that bad month in '58, two years after he and Meg were married. It's true he didn't take Meg and the babies home from the hospital, but Jesus, that day was one of the worst in Top Court's fight for survival. And he saw but little of the family in the first months after the birth of Carol and Connie, but again, who would have suffered most if he spent those nights at home and let

Top Court go down the drain? After the recession, things started coming up roses again, but success took as much time as near failure. And it *was* success: election to the Young Presidents' Organization, winner of somebody's Silver Stallion Award as "the most innovative young executive of the year," short personality takeouts in *Time, Forbes* and the trade press, an appeal from Jack Kennedy to help raise funds for the Senator's plunge into the presidential primaries. The point was that Meg knew when she married that she was joining a possible big winner with all that entailed in time and effort.

Fact Three. Top Court would soon dominate the tennis market from Australia to Russia. Five out of the eight quarter-finalists in the men's singles at Wimbledon last year swung TeeCee Championship racquets, three of them wore the new TeeCee Italian-designed jerseys and Bart Gatchell, the young American sensation from Oklahoma, took the court in a complete TeeCee outfit from shoes to headband. The surge was on, but he could rely on only one man, James Francis McGowan, to keep the boom alive—with a little crafty help, never to be trusted completely, from Hugo Praeger.

Son of a bitch though he could be, Hugo would never lose Jim's admiration. The big, hulking Swiss immigrant, for all his seventy-five-dollar custom-made monogrammed shirts, his falcon tactics, his capricious way of treating a person with disdain one day and outlandish generosity the next, his tastes of the voluptuary and the vulgarian, his midnight chess matches, his blond masseuse, hired out of a Los Angeles massage salon, well, Hugo was a genius. Back in '66 only two men sensed a vital commercial clue to the future. One was Top Court's Jim McGowan and the other was Arc-Horn's Hugo Praeger. As vivid as though it had happened yesterday was the memory of that 8:15 a.m. phone conversation.

"McGowan?" asked the voice. "This is Hugo Praeger. So you've been at your desk for a half hour already?" A bit of a challenge and a faint Teutonic accent.

"That's right to the minute, Mr. Praeger. How did you know?"

"I've been casing you. You see, I think we're the only two men in the world on to the same secret."

"What's that?"

"That ten years from now you'll be riding the fastest horse in the leisure-time derby." Praeger's laugh was high, thin. "By 1976 Hal Geneen will be wishing he'd been born with a couple of tennis balls in his crotch."

Jim grinned and at once became aware of a warm tingling sensation. It was as though he were walking down the street, proud to be carrying his first hundred-dollar bill in the wallet inside his coat, when a stranger accosted him and asked him if he would like five twenties for a hundred. Odd—and flattering.

"I agree," said Jim. "If I didn't, I'd have sold out long ago."

"How about selling and keeping it all at the same time? I've worked out a very sweet deal for you."

"No, thanks, Mr. Praeger. This is my baby and I'm staying with it."

"Call me Hugo. Everybody does. It's a beautiful deal, Jim."

"Not interested. Sorry."

"You're lying. You're curious as hell. What have you got against listening in person?"

"Well, I suppose I could always listen. My ears are good."

"All right then. My office in the Pan-Am Building at nine, what?"

"Make it ten. I'll be there."

And so the buccaneer conglomerator had set sail for him, the two-billion-dollar fleet ready to seize the eleven-million-dollar frigate. Jim turned to the stock tables in *The Wall Street Journal*. Arc-Horn closed the day before at 60⅛, or thirty times earnings. On the Amex, Top Court was selling at 22, or fourteen times earnings, no bargain unless one were privy to the secret. Jim was proud that a man with Praeger's supposed foresight shared the secret, or faith, or hunch, or vision, or whatever you wanted to call it. And to this day, despite Hugo's excesses and bravura, that initial sharing remained a bond.

Jim listened to the deal in the cream-colored office of Arc-Horn's president with its dominating view of upper Park Avenue. They sat on black leather chairs slung from brushed-steel frames on either side of a glass coffee table and were served coffee, for Jim, and bitter lemon, for Praeger, by an obsequious white-coated steward. Mobiles, one a replica of Arc-Horn's logo, twirled slowly from the off-white ceiling and the walls held three paintings, a Pollock, a Chagall and a Tamayo, then worth a hundred grand or more, Jim calculated. The coffee table held but three items, a copy of *Fortune,* an onyx ashtray and a red-tabbed manila folder marked TOP COURT.

Praeger's style reminded Jim of your friendly neighborhood loan shark, blunt, cynical, profane and yet withal not unappealing. He oozed warmth and sweat from the enormous body, perhaps two hundred thirty pounds on a five-eleven frame. His eyes peered from fleshy puff balls where beads of moisture appeared to be permanent inhabitants of the creases. He wore a blue denim sports jacket with white stitching and a wide, silk Italian-made tie. His voice boomed in a confident bass register, but the frequent cackling laugh, with a high, nervous pitch, seemed rented for the occasion from an Eighth Avenue crone. Jim had two quick impressions that firmed into convictions over the years: a fascinating man of power who was not to be trusted completely.

After the pleasantries Praeger handed him one of the three-by-five cards made famous by the recent two-part *New Yorker* profile. Everything the frigate captain needed to know before the seizure could be found on one side of the card.

Deal for Jim McG.
    McG gets: 1 A-H for 2 T.C.
          10-yr. mgmt. contract, 100

Gs annually, plus 1 G each
pct. point over prev. yr's
earnings.
100,000 A-H shares, vested after
10 yrs.
50 Gs annual retirement
policy.
200 Gs term insurance.
A-H jet, all expenses.
1 seat A-H board.
P. gets: All T.C. assets.

"A deal that makes music, what?" Praeger's tone
was that of the elderly admirer offering the young girl
a diamond clasp in return for unsampled favors.

"Lots of goodies, that's for sure." At the day's market, Jim calculated, one share of Arc-Horn for two Top
Court would yield him an instant paper profit of $1,600,-
000. With Top Court a cinch to increase earnings ten
percent a year, that meant a salary after years of,
let's see . . .

"You'd be making at least two-thirty the tenth year,"
cut in Praeger, the friendly telepathist. "But we both
know Top Court is good for more. . . . And don't
forget the stock the corporation gives you at the
end of your ten-year management contract. You'll get
a hundred thousand shares, worth six million now, maybe ten or fifteen a decade from now. Some gift, what?"

"Any strings on these hundred thousand shares?"

"Only one. You have to increase Top Court profits
each year. But hell, that's hardly worth mentioning.
You'll do that with your left hand."

Jim thought so too. Tennis had a cash future.

"Five, six years from now, they'll all be calling tennis a growth industry." The man was a mind reader.
"And right now only two of us know that." Praeger
beamed, whipped out a handkerchief and dabbed at the
sweat beads beneath his eyes. Then came that cackling laugh like piccolo notes out of a bass drum.

"Look, Hugo. Today I'm my own man, a father

with a fast-growing boy. If I sign with you, I'm just another piece of somebody else's property."

"Outdated attitude. You tell me we've got a deal and overnight you step into the big numbers. That's where the action is."

Praeger heaved himself out of his chair and stood beneath the Arc-Horn mobile, a bright blue circle trailed by four red lines indicating speed. The logo symbolized planet Earth, from the Arctic Circle to Cape Horn, being powered to its destiny by the streaking, multi-fold services of Arc-Horn on the longitudinal axis and embracing continents, nations and duchies of all latitudes.

"Ten years from now you'll be aboard the greatest vehicle of power and commerce since the Holy Roman Empire." Praeger reached up and touched the mobile, sending it spinning about in a shimmering dance. Then he walked to his black steel-edged desk and flicked the intercom. "Hold everything unless Sukit calls from Bangkok." He turned back to Jim. "We've got a nice Thai soft goods buy-in coming up."

For the next fifteen minutes Jim got the short-course wooing lecture. Arc-Horn, said Praeger as he surged about the room, would become the Rothschild of banking, the Prudential of insurance, the Sony of audio, the Volkswagen of wheeled transport, the Onassis of shipping and the Anaconda of copper. Arc-Horn products would penetrate more remote tribal villages than Coca-Cola. It would become the No. 1 multinational corporation of the world, its interests so interwoven and commingled across the seas and continents that no nation could possibly start a war without bombing its own industries.

"And by God, Jim," he concluded, "if wealth and power aren't enough to pull your ass out of that one-business rut, then the vision of peace on earth ought to be."

Praeger sank back into his chair and dabbed at his face again. "I've been called a megalomaniac. It's much simpler than that. I'm just a new-style idealist

who believes that peace and greed can go hand in
hand, what?"

Jim sat silent for a moment, awed by the display
of raw hunger. "And if I say no, I suppose you'll
go after Wilson or Dunlop?"

Praeger shook his head. "Nope. I'll put out a tender
offer for Top Court at thirty. You only own a piece
of the stock. Six months from now you'd be a poor
little rich boy with no place to hang your hat at seven
forty-five in the morning."

Though he suspected Praeger had a wider strategy,
the bald threat staggered Jim. In the gap of silence,
he also noted a Praeger mannerism that he would see
many times when the entrepreneur gloated over a profit
figure or choice commercial prey. Praeger slid a hand
across his chest in a caressing, circular movement
not unlike that of a narcissistic woman fondling her
own breast. His expression was one of erotic content-
ment.

"Actually," he said, "I'm already one of your mi-
nority stockholders. I picked up ten thousand shares
yesterday from the Mozart Fund at twenty-four. As
you probably know, Chick Reynolds, the fund manager over there, holds another fifteen thousand Top
Court he'll unload at a few premium points. Twenty-
six, say, ought to fetch it in."

So the raid was already on. Jim's flash reaction was
one of rage at monstrous injustice, like a householder
watching the state exercise eminent domain to seize his
home for a superhighway. A few seconds later he
thought of fighting back. Maybe he could hock everything he owned to Hal Frascella at First Merchants
and start buying in the publicly owned stock. But he
knew at once that battle would be foredoomed against
Praeger's vast resources. But soon came another feeling, a kind of grudging admiration for this bulbous
pirate with his knack for spotting the prize merchant-
men on the seas of tomorrow. Tennis a growth industry? So far as Jim knew, only two men believed

that today and one of them was this sweating hillock of flesh across the coffee table.

"Why not relax and enjoy it?" Praeger glowed with bonhomie.

"I'd like to think it over."

"Sure." Praeger gathered in the Top Court folder. "How about nine a.m. a week from today?"

Instead Jim surrendered by phone after only two days and papers for the Arc-Horn acquisition were signed a month later. As part of the deal, Jim swung management contracts for his three top men, Al Bebout, Frankenheimer and Teigert. Soon Jim had his first ride in the Arc-Horn jet assigned to Top Court and that fall he attended his first floating Arc-Horn directors meeting aboard the *Arc Hornet,* Praeger's yacht, cruising off Martinique.

The new family relationship worked out with remarkable, even miraculous, smoothness. Praeger, whose rule of thumb held that any subsidiary which increased profits five percent or better annually was not to be molested, had interfered but twice over the years. Once he asked Jim as a favor to hire a friend. Jim did and the man worked out well. Again Arc-Horn's accountants on Praeger's orders one year juggled Jim's inventory numbers, boosting his yearly earnings. In trouble on other fronts, Praeger wanted Arc-Horn's steady march of progress on the bottom line to remain unbroken. "Just a little of the old robbing of Peter to pay Paul," he said on the phone. But for the most part, Praeger seemed hardly aware of Jim's existence except at the quarterly board meetings, when Top Court's report became almost a ritual. Jim would estimate a profit boost of anywhere from eight to fourteen percent and Hugo would nod approval. "Thanks, Jim," he'd say. "No-problem McGowan, we call him. . . . Next we have Indo Deep Rig."

Arc-Horn itself was another matter. Despite the upward parade of book profits, the stock took a pasting during the big sell-off of conglomerates in the late sixties and early seventies. Arc-Horn, from 60 at the

time of the Top Court takeover, sank as low as 17
in the bear market of 1973 and at one time during
those months Jim found himself waking up $100,000
poorer every morning.

Now, with money markets stablizing, Arc-Horn had
climbed back to 48—a respectable figure since it happened to jibe with Jim's own age—and James F. Mc-
Gowan was a multimillionaire with a salary of $335,000
this year.

Top Court was the second-fastest grower in the whole
Arc-Horn empire. An average growth rate of 12.2 percent for eight straight years and a cinch to go higher.
Jim was sure of that. Yeah, he'd be down to only
three percent growth for this first quarter, but that
was partly due to the big switch in operations at the
Doylestown racquet plant, which would begin paying
off next week at the start of a spring season certain
to be the best ever for the tennis industry.

And Hugo had played it straight as promised. Top
Court was still McGowan's thriving son, untouched by
Praeger and acknowledged as McGowan's own by everybody in the industry. In fact, in his *Newsweek* interview, Praeger went out of his way to praise what
he called "Jim McGowan's smash serve on the tennis
courts of the world."

Jim even had his special political niche in Arc-Horn.
At the height of the Watergate and allied scandals,
when critics skewered Arc-Horn for its executives' cash
contributions to President Nixon just under the new
law's deadline, Jim called Hugo and told him of his
own $25,000 contribution to a Democrat, Ed Muskie.
Praeger welcomed the news as a lifesaver, leaked it to
the press and was soon publicly describing Arc-Horn
as "without political bias," a fact only if a ten-to-one
alignment in the Republicans' favor were not considered
evidence of bias. But McGowan's Muskie contribution
did help defuse the controversy, undoubtedly because
the Democrats feared losing such Arc-Horn scraps the
next time around.

But what stirred Jim's imagination this sixteenth of

March, flying over the arid mountains of Mexico, was the new bounce of morale at the racquet plant, kingpin of Top Court production. Hell, it was phenomenal.

Because of Dave Moyer—and he could thank Meg for Dave, he confessed somewhat ruefully—the coming success at the racquet plant might mean, just possibly, a new lift for all Top Court production, balls, nets, tapes, surfaces, togs, accessories, the works. Jim had caught a spark of Dave's flame now and he even permitted himself to speculate that Top Court might point American industry toward a revolution of method, a middle way between flabby, bureaucratic socialism and the hard, bottom-line numbers game played by today's corporations. Hold it, Jim, he told himself, drop that big dream stuff or you'll begin to sound like the poor man's Praeger. Still, first returns from Doylestown were heady wine.

He first met Dave Moyer, the low-key, wise, pipe-smoking behavioral scientist from the University of California at Davis—"my plant guru," in Jim's first skeptical, later proud words—at one of Meg's summer mixers at the Westhampton house. Dave and Fran Moyer were among some oddballs—a fag artist, a writer for *The Village Voice,* a stuttering Harvard anthropologist and his wife—who spent the weekend with the McGowans. Jim gravitated to Dave because the latter had done some industrial consulting and at least knew Jim's language.

It began late that June in 1973 when he and Dave were sitting beside the pool, speculating about Watergate and gazing at the star-dusted sky as they tried to sort out a few constellations.

"Do you have any fun at Top Court?" asked Dave idly.

"Sure. I'm one of your high-motivation guys who gets the hots every Monday morning. Hell, when I'm out here on weekends, sometimes I even go back to New York Sunday night so I can hit the desk early in the morning. I love my work."

"How about your employees? They like theirs?"

"Some do. Some don't. Usual story." Jim thought the question unworthy of undue thought.

"Everyone ought to have fun at his work," Dave said it with exaggerated slowness.

"Oh, come off it, Dave. You've been around. You know the score. That's impossible."

"Well, maybe for sugar-cane cutters," said Dave, "although even there I'd have some ideas. But in a tight production outfit like Top Court, the pleasure's there for the finding—for everybody."

If the talk were to center on Top Court, Jim was hooked. "Give me a couple of for-instances."

"Okay. Which of your operations do you suspect the workers enjoy the least?"

"I guess I'd have to say the racquet plant. It's near Doylestown in Pennsylvania. Nice surroundings, but a lot of routine, repetitive assembly work. No other way to make 'em."

Well, said Moyer, satisfaction with work wasn't so much a question of what one did as how one did it, with whom, under what conditions, with how much independence and responsibility, factors like that. He supposed Jim knew all about the motivation studies. Among job attributes desired by workers, pay almost never ranked first, usually fourth or fifth behind such items as pride, sociability, environment, self-respect, feeling important to the operation, etc. Some of Dave's ideas struck Jim as impractical and far-out, but they talked for several hours with ever-mounting understanding of each other. Jim liked Dave. He was no glib academic con man like some of the breed Jim had met and Dave confessed candidly that he had a lot to learn even though he'd been successful with some of his organization development theories at TRW, Inc. In the end, Moyer proposed a bet.

"Tell you what, Jim," he said. "You give me three days a month at the Doylestown plant for a year and a half. Expenses only. If you have a happy plant by then, you pay me twenty-five thousand dollars and write me a new contract, your terms, to study another division

of the company and work out a plan for it. You be
the sole judge of 'happy plant.' If you're not satisfied
in any way, you pay me nothing. All you'd be out
would be my expenses from California."

"What about production?" asked Jim quickly. If
happiness did not come down to the bottom line, who
needed it?

Dave fussed with his pipe. "I can't promise more
racquets, but if your costs aren't down, discounting inflation, you pay me nothing. And your accountants can
assess the inflation factor."

"You don't care much for money?"

"Big money for power, no. Good money for comfortable living, sure I do. The thing is, I'm pretty sure my
plan will work."

Jim spent a few days mulling over Moyer's offer.
Ever since the big employee rebellion at General Motors'
Lordstown plant, executives had been discussing the
problem of boredom on the automated assembly lines
and the demand of workers that their jobs yield something other than pay checks. Jim was embarrassed by
the high turnover at Doylestown and he had to admit,
whenever he watched the racquet assembly line, that he
wouldn't be able to stand more than a couple of days
at any of the dull, repetitive, unchallenging tasks. It
pained him to realize that people didn't like to work
at his plant.

Then there were those guilt strings that occasionally
twanged away somewhere inside him. On public policy,
Jim considered himself a moderate liberal. He custom-
arily favored Democratic candidates nationally and recently had had several talks with Senator Ireland, a possible Democratic presidential contender in '76. But Jim
divorced politics from business even though he believed
that the business executive had perhaps more power than
the politician to build the better life that Jim wanted,
at least in theory, for the mass of Americans. Jim
McGowan, he knew, didn't put his corporate money
where his political mouth was.

Perhaps Doylestown could be a beginning. By midweek, Jim began running a check on Dave Moyer. He found that both TRW and Alza Corp., where Dave had also consulted, were enthusiastic about him. Of course, unlike Top Court, they were both high-tech operations. In the end, after several weeks, Jim decided intuitively, as he usually did. The Doylestown plant needed help and Moyer was the man who wanted to supply that help. Jim liked and trusted Dave. Moyer might be wrong, but he believed in himself and that, thought Jim, was half the game. He telephoned Moyer in California and accepted the wager. Dave, in turn, started at the Doylestown plant the next week.

At first, Oscar Smith, the plant manager, raised hell. Smitty didn't like the idea of "some screwball professor with a lot of nutty ideas" coming in to mess up his production schedule. But six months later, to Jim's amazement, Smitty was chanting Dave Moyer's praises and gabbling about the "team concept," "up-and-down learning" and "process observation."

Dave worked with employees throughout the plant, learned their job skills and gradually gained their confidence. After initial suspicion faded and mutual respect began to form, together they worked out functional teams of fifteen to twenty people. Team bonuses replaced individual bonuses, although each person could earn additional pay if he learned to perform more complex and diverse tasks.

Each team included almost every layer of the plant hierarchy, from management to janitor and including secretaries, purchasing officials, bookkeepers, shipping clerks, maintenance men and assembly-line workers. Smitty himself became a member of Team Skyreach. Every team member was encouraged to seek help from any teammate, to learn the problems and know-how of other jobs within the team, to complain, suggest and advise within the team.

People at first groused that authority had been severed, but gradually under Dave's patient guiding hand the system sorted itself out. A coordinating group was formed with one member elected from each team. The coordinators met once a week to deal with plant-wide problems, but primary responsibility rested with the teams. Every person in the plant, with the exception of a few malingerers, now had a voice in the decisions of production and planning.

By the summer of 1974 strange things were happening in the Doylestown racquet plant. Absenteeism and sick leave declined by half, the switchboard operators were being praised as the cheeriest and most helpful in Bucks County and one team spent several weekends repainting the drab factory walls a vibrant yellow. Team Fast Ball offered a fairly detailed concept for a new press machine that would boost the output of the molded plastic handles. Originated by an electrician, the idea had been worked on by team members during and after hours. The concept was now being refined to the blueprint stage by Warner & Swasey, whose engineers estimated $1,000,000 for two presses. Jim calculated a possible production acceleration of thirty percent and a lowered cost of about forty-five cents a racquet. Barring unforeseen hitches, the machines should be installed next fall. Team Fast Ball, which already had received $20,000 against a probable total $200,000 bonus, had voted half of the front money to the electrician.

Other benefits, reflected Jim, included a sharp reduction in padded expense accounts, better food in the cafeteria, less unproductive paperwork, stiff penalties against drugs or liquor on the premises and an all-team vote against nepotism up to and including first cousins. This amused Jim because he knew Smitty was considering hiring his young brother-in-law, a kid chiefly distinguished for goofing off in five colleges without squeezing out a degree.

But the biggest change in Doylestown was the atmosphere. Morale was soaring. Jim felt good just to be inside the place and he found himself dropping by a couple of times a month. In fact, word had spread and recently the *Philadelphia Inquirer* asked Smitty's permission to tour the factory for a story on "Pennsylvania's happy plant." Smitty stalled the reporter on the ground that not enough time had elapsed yet. Actually Smitty was not about to disclose morale secrets to the competition. Thank God for Dave Moyer, thought Jim. Dave didn't know it yet, but next week Jim intended to hand Moyer a $50,000 contract to duplicate his feat at the Illinois tennis-ball plant.

Just one thing bugged him right now about Top Court. When Hugo Praeger went around the horseshoe table tomorrow, quizzing his subsidiary managers on first-quarter forecasts, Jim would have to report, for the first time in nine years, that Top Court's earnings increase over the previous year's first quarter had slipped below five percent. There were several causes, including the wildcat strike in the tennis-wear division, but the major reason was the switch on the assembly line voted by the teams at the Doylestown racquet plant and approved by Smitty. That had caused confusion and delays, anticipated by both Smitty and himself. Now the last bugs were out, as Jim had seen for himself this week, and Jim felt confident production would zoom upward in the second quarter. But Hugo Praeger looked only at the numbers and those would read: "estimated Top Court earnings up three percent," thus sinking Jim below the magic "up five" level and making him a vulnerable target for Praeger's falcon-like attack. Maybe, he thought, he could blame it all on the wildcat strike, but if Hugo's shrewd eye happened to light on the Doylestown production figure, Jim would be in for a rough skirmish. Well, tomorrow's hassle tomorrow.

The thought of hassle brought him full circle back to Meg. Just what the hell was he to do about Meg? Divorce was out of the question. He wouldn't do that to Carol and Connie and he wouldn't let Meg do it, even if she was so inclined. Anyway, unraveling their lives would be a God-awful mess. The old, common memories, their friends, the comfort, those moments, although rare now, of wordless intimacy, all knit them together. He was fond of Meg even if she increasingly irritated him, and he believed that she was fond of him. Love? He wasn't sure any more just what the word meant, but he felt that it might be re-explored if they had the time. Love needed time, time, time, but Top Court soaked up that commodity like a sponge. Well, face it, whatever the next few months might bring, he was not going to let some high-priced lawyer start fiddling around with his Arc-Horn stock in a settlement with Meg or anybody else.

Jim usually avoided self-scrutiny, probably because he was so inept at it. His vaunted decisiveness and intuition at the Top Court desk dribbled off into a fog of uncertainty when he turned to his personal life. He'd gone around and around on the home front and come up with only one absolute about himself. If it ever came to a choice between Meg and Top Court, he realized reluctantly, then Top Court would win. Top Court was his baby, his son, his flesh and blood. Meg was his wife. Without a wife, he'd suffer. Without his creation, he'd flake away like old, dried skin. It was that simple.

But, of course, he hoped he would not have to face that choice. Much as he detested the thought of an encounter with Meg, he would brace himself and go through with it, point by point, next weekend. . . . Wait a minute. . . . No, next weekend, he had to fly to the Coast for a conference on that new tennis-ranch acquisition. Well, Friday night then. He'd listen to Meg without flaring up in angry retorts; he owed her that much, even if she got into sex again. That sex bit . . . lucky she didn't have Hugo Praeger for a bedmate. Why couldn't she understand . . . ? Oh, goddam it, Friday was soon enough for all that. . . .

Suddenly, beyond the brown, wasted mountains of the state of Guerrero, he saw the Pacific unroll like a misty carpet. Not a cloud stood in the sky as the jet began its letdown toward Acapulco. Buckling his seat belt, Jim twisted away from the window to escape the blaze of the western sun.

"That's sailfish country." It was Al Bebout's voice behind him. "I figure on getting me one."

Jim looked back up the aisle. The gin game had ended and his three executives, coated with the cheerful glaze of expectant travelers, were strapped to their seats.

"Listen, you guys," he said. "You're on your own until we take off at seven a.m. Friday. Praeger'll have me on his midnight pan, I guess, but that's my problem. Have a ball, get laid, anything. Just don't bore me with the details."

"How about Summit's show?" asked Bebout. "It's listed at ten for three straight mornings. Praeger going to insist as usual that everyone show up?"

"Beats me." said Jim. "Hope for the best and plan for the worst. Maybe you can hire some innocent tourist to sit in for you."

"Fat chance. Jesus, three mornings of TV sets and pitchman crap on top of a hangover."

And that, thought Jim, was exactly Praeger's sly game plan for the perfect Arc-Horn convention: plunk his men down in a luxury resort hotel, stroked by moonlight, beach, surf, palms, music, tennis, golf, and then order them to keep on minding the store.

Sunday Afternoon

As the young tribes trek to rock fertility rites at their Woodstocks and Watkins Glens on tens of thousands of rubber-sheathed wheels, so the elder chiefs and warriors make annual pilgrimages to their sacred convention grounds on wings of fire. They leave their lodges and their homes by the million, salesmen and surgeons, purchasers and purchased, draftsmen and bankers, automatic car washers and makers of missiles, embalmers and publishers, insurance agents and computer programmers, all flying the friendly, fattening skies of United, American, TWA, Eastern, Braniff and Pan-Am and all flocking toward the hallowed hostelries where they spend eleven billion dollars annually to feast, pray, chant, palaver, commune, copulate and render up thanks for another year of good business.

Those blessed by many bountiful harvests forsake the commercial airways, where the great contrails weave feathery murals on the blue wall of the sky, and speed to their mercantile Stonehenges, Monte Albáns and Tikals by private jetcraft that thunder pagan hymns of rejoicing to the bottom line and the gross national product.

As Top Court's Falcon 10 fled smoothly down the runway, Jim McGowan could see the long, sparkling line of executive planes near the terminal. He counted eighteen of them, Grumman Gulfstreams, Aero Commanders, Westwinds, Merlins, Falcons, Cessna Citations, Rockwell Sabre 60s, Lockheed Jetstar IIs, each at the command of an Arc-Horn International subsidiary and all bearing the blue-and-red logo of the conglomerate. Bernard Hirsch, vice-president for public relations, had protested that such prodigality in an era of fuel shortages would tarnish the corporate image, but Hugo Praeger decreed that for its twentieth-birthday celebration, Arc-Horn would appear in all its finery. Near the planes stood several trim, blue-and-red jet helicopters, flown down from New York to service the recreational and sightseeing whims of the conventioneers. One of them, Jim knew, was for Tony Percevale's own uses attendant upon the gala opening of a new Gusto Más supermarket in Acapulco. Apparently Top Court's plane was the last to arrive save for Praeger's own swank Gates Learjet, scheduled for lone, regal put-down at four-thirty. When the chief of chiefs landed, he wanted all the astral steeds of his warriors tethered in silent homage.

Jim glanced at his wristwatch. Three twenty-seven Acapulco time. They were three minutes ahead of the ETA assigned the Top Court jet a month ago by the conference manager.

"Nice timing, Bish," he called forward to the open cockpit door. The pilot signaled his thanks by circled thumb and forefinger.

The plane halted, the engines died with a long whistling sigh and the fuselage door opened. A flood of humid, tropical heat poured in and with it entered a short tubby man whose buttery features reflected both the Angst and disciplined merriment of the tour guide. Along with his harried grin, he wore a blue manta cloth shirt, cut low on the chest to reveal a thicket of curly black hair. Affixed to the shirt above the heart, an Arc-Horn badge proclaimed him to be: CAL. In smaller print below: Silliman . . . Conference Manager . . . Arc-Horn Staff.

"Where's Jim McGowan?" The bustling manager invested the question with the breathless quality a rescue worker might use when nearing a half-buried miner.

"Here, Cal." Jim extended his hand, which Silliman pumped eagerly but clumsily. His arm was laden with more sports shirts.

"Got a message for you." The manager offered an envelope with his free left hand.

Jim extracted the note on Mixteca Hotel stationery. "Jim: Waiting for you with a rum collins in Room 740. Tony."

"Okay, men. Off with the jackets and ties," commanded Silliman. "Strip to the waist, please." Noting the blank stares of the four executives, he added: "Hugo's orders."

Sheepishly Jim and his associates shed their clothes above the belt, revealing a trimly fit McGowan, a surgical scar below Bebout's concave chest and several square feet of pale, soft flesh on the other two. Silliman, prattling like a busy blue jay, slipped the shirts over the heads of the four men. Jim's was a rich gold in color, the others red.

"All presidents gold, subsidiary execs red, Arc-Horn staff shirts blue," the manager explained. He took four name badges from his pocket and pinned one over the heart of each man. In the shape of the Arc-Horn emblem, Jim's read: JIM . . . McGowan . . . President . . . Top Court.

Two luscious, black-eyed girls glided into the plane. They wore translucent blue shirtwaists, cut to the bosom in deep V's, and loose trousers of matching fabric. Jacaranda blooms nestled in tumbling black hair and their bare, mahogany-hued arms bore gifts of welcome. One girl carried four Arc-Horn flight bags, the other a wooden tray planted with six salt-rimmed glasses of margaritas.

"María and Felicia, two of our conference hostesses," said Silliman. "Where are the pilots? . . . Everybody drinks to beautiful Mexico." Silliman pronounced it "May-hee-ko." Felicia giggled, but María's smile was edged with faint scorn.

The pilot and copilot came aft and the six men raised glasses, toasting the host country where the vigor of an eight percent annual economic growth rate was rivaled only by the zealous, human reproductive labors of more than fifty million Mexicans.

Silliman unzipped one of the flight bags, drew out a chain and draped it about Jim's neck. Bright silver links coiled down to a silver-mounted turquoise medallion shaped like the circular Arc-Horn logo. Copper streaks replaced the four red lines which traditionally marked the orbiting thrust of the conglomerate.

"Taxco silver. Every president gets one," explained the self-harassed manager. "Present from Hugo. . . . The rest of the stuff's for everybody."

He dunked into the flight bag, pulled out the contents and handed them one by one to McGowan. Like most conference managers, Silliman operated on the theory that his clients were most impressed by welcom-

ing largesse and parting grandeur. "Always give 'em
what they'll first and last remember" was Cal's favorite
quote from his first convention of convention managers.

"Your room key, Number 1023," he said to Jim.
"Your suite's right under Praeger's. The other guys are
scattered around. Good rooms, though. Every one has
a balcony. And of course all Top Court men get the
ocean view."

Each executive knew that Silliman's pattering mono-
logue cloaked an event of significant protocol. Suites
were always allotted to company presidents on an
inflexible basis of latest annual earnings. The high-
netters rated the three-room luxury suites, mediocre
earners got the large two-room suites, while losers
wound up in smaller quarters. Two years ago the president of Sea Routes, Inc., the freighter and tanker line
that dropped millions, found himself in territory that
could be termed a suite only by exercising a mariner's
vivid imagination. The auxiliary room was actually a
closet-like economy kitchen. As for vice-presidents, con-
trollers, treasurers and secretaries, those from flourishing
enterprises drew the mountain or ocean vistas while the
losers often looked down on garages and trash cans.

The tropical Santa Claus ticked off his gifts with
relish.

"Conference program." A handsome, hard-bound,
blue-and-red volume, slick paper, color phootgraphs
and page after page of advertisements from Arc-Horn's
suppliers from across the seven seas.

"Tickets for all events." A thin trail of blue paste-
board. "Including the final banquet when yours truly
is going to spring the surprise of the century right after
the Golden Globe Award."

"What are you going to do?" asked Al Bebout.
"Cut Hugo's throat for not giving the prize to you?"

The winner of the annual Golden Globe Award, be-
stowed on the executive who exhibited the most "initiative and enterprise" on behalf of Arc-Horn, was picked
by an outside management consultant firm, but the

troops suspected Praeger sometimes dictated the result.

Silliman ignored the remark. "For the wife when you drag ass home." A gray felt case in which rested four exquisite crystal bottles of Trespass, one of the world's most expensive perfumes, compliments of Fragrance, Inc. Jim thought fleetingly of Gwen Piggott, the lively if driven president of Fragrance, with whom he had feasted and flirted last year in Boca Raton.

A copper-plated paperweight from Magna Mines. . . . A polka-dot eyeglass cleaner, packed in a white leather case, thanks to Hi-Western Corp. . . . The can of tennis balls from Top Court. . . . A gaucho doll from Tony Percevale's Gusto Más, S.A., of Argentina. . . . A metal savings bank, shaped like a small ten-gallon hat, contributed by Six Flags Insurance, the big Dallas-based company. . . . Goodies from Brazil, France, Ohio and Denver. . . . And finally an eight-digit pocket calculator, shining with red buttons and blue housing, from Nakamura, Ltd., the great Japanese subsidiary.

"That little beauty is going to retail in this new seventy-six model at only thirty-nine ninety-five," said Silliman with proper awe.

"And maybe wholesale Arc-Horn right over to Tokyo," added Al Bebout. In merging into the conglomerate three years ago, Nakamura's negotiators had finished with so many shares of Arc-Horn stock that the *Business Week* story had been accompanied by a cartoon of a nude, bloated Praeger captioned: "Prisoner in a Japanese Bathhouse?"

The remark forced a feeble smile from Silliman as he extracted two last items from the flight bag, a large, sealed manila envelope stamped "Confidential" in red print and a small blue envelope, also sealed.

"The big one contains the agenda for the annual board meeting at four p.m. Thursday," said Silliman. "The little one has the combination to the wall safe in your room. Every board member gets one. Only you and the hotel manager know your combination, so don't blame yours truly if you lose something." He hurriedly crammed the loot back into McGowan's flight bag. "And so, let's get going, men."

Led by the graceful, black-haired hostesses, the party filed out of the Falcon 10 into the hot Mexican sunlight—to be welcomed by a cascade of music.

A ten-piece mariachi band, solemn-faced under towering sombreros and attired in gorgeous vests and peg-legged pants with silver buttons flashing down the seams, raced into the rippling "El Cascabel," replete with high tenor cries, *"Arriba muchacho,"* blasts on the trumpets and stringed frenzy from the guitars, violins and the single *guitarrón*.

"Olé!" shouted Silliman with the perfunctory ardor of a man who has raised the same clamor nineteen times during a long, torrid day and who has spent a month in the Latin tropics readying the conference.

He motioned the pilots toward a waiting station wagon, gave baggage instructions to a Mexican attendant and hurried his Top Court charges across the concrete apron to a black Mercedes. The hostess Felicia sought shelter in a blue-and-red pavilion where a white-coated bartender reigned over a battalion of bottles. The proud María, it appeared, would escort them to the hotel.

The Mercedes flew a small Mexican flag on the right front fender and a cluster of national ensigns, United States, France, Thailand, West Germany and Brazil among them, on the left. A cloth hood bearing the Arc-Horn logo covered the Mercedes symbol crowning the radiator grill.

"I have to wait for Praeger," said Silliman. "You're all pre-registered. Your bags will be delivered to your rooms. Any questions, ask María. See you at the early-bird fiesta."

The limousine, driven by an uncommunicative Mexican who divulged little but his name, Miguel, purred away from the terminal, Jim and María in the front seat and the others in the rear. They rode in air-conditioned comfort along the low, flat tidal plain south of the hills of Acapulco. Palm trees straggled over the sandy loam, heat waves shimmered on the highway and Jim felt pleasantly tired and unstitched. In the distance he could see the Mixteca Hotel, a great looming structure vaguely resembling an ancient Indian pyramid.

"Are you from around here, María?" Jim asked.

"From the hills of Guerrero, señor." María's smile masked a private look, not quite contempt, Jim thought, but certainly patronizing. "Now and then I work in Acapulco when the tourists come."

Before them they could see a solitary figure walking along the shoulder of the highway. As they drew nearer, Jim noted a backpack, ragged blue-jean shorts, hiking boots and a pair of bronzed, hard-muscled legs.

"Oh, I know that man," said María. "Could we stop please?"

"Sure." Jim nodded to the driver and Miguel slowed the car to a halt. Jim lowered his window. The hiker was lean, tanned, with wiry brown hair, in places bleached a pale yellow by the sun. The face was weathered but young. Hazel eyes flooded directly into Jim's with peculiar intensity, then switched to María, who sat in the middle.

"María!"

"Steve!"

They traded a few rapid sentences in Spanish before María reverted to English.

"Where are you going now, Steve?" she asked.

"South to Puerto Angel and then just keep on going toward the Canal. What are you doing in that freaked-out costume?"

"I'm working a convention at the Mixteca. Why don't you stop off for a few days and earn some money with your drawings?"

"Not a bad idea, María. I could use some bread." Steve's eyes centered on Jim. "What's the convention?"

"Arc-Horn International," said Jim.

"Oh yeah. That fat old pirate I've read about who travels around with a massage girl. What's the matter, can't he get it up?"

Jim laughed. "We wouldn't know about that. We work for him. . . . Come on. Climb in the back. We'll give you a lift to the hotel."

"No, thanks." The accent was American Midwest. "I haven't been inside a car in seven years."

"How's that again?"

"I said I haven't ridden a car in seven years." A grin, cracking tiny grooves in the tanned face, offered quick friendship. "I tell that to all of them. They don't believe it, but it's true. I've been walking."

"For seven years, for Christ's sake?"

"Yeah. Around the world." He leaned deeply browned forearms on the window frame. His look was bold, in-quisitive, but without arrogance. "I earn my way doing caricatures at a buck a throw."

"You'd be wasting your time at the Mixteca," said Bebout from the rear seat. "Most of the types around Arc-Horn are caricatures already."

"Mine are different. I try to show the inner guy too. . . . Thanks for the suggestion, María. They ought to have plenty of spare bills. I'll pitch my tent on the beach. . . . See you at the hotel then."

He straightened, shifted his pack and walked ahead, the heavy boots beating the pavement in short, easy cadence.

The car moved off and passed the hiker. Jim turned to watch him. "Something about that guy . . ."

"It takes all kinds," said Bebout.

The Mercedes soon turned off the highway. They headed toward the sea on a wide avenue stretching to the hotel, which overwhelmed the flat landscape like a skyscraper in a cornfield. Golf fairways framed the avenue and ahead palms bent before a steady ocean breeze. Beyond, whitecaps of the Pacific glinted under the lowering sun.

The limousine glided to a halt before the broad steps of the Mixteca. Another hostess in diaphanous costume opened Jim's door and greeted him in soft, lilting Spanish. A jacaranda petal fluttered from her hair like a flake of purple snow.

Above the portico stretched a long metal sign: "Bienvenidos Arc-Horn."

Led by María, the Top Court crew trudged up the steps to the great open foyer, a tunnel for the wind, moist, warm and languorous, that swept in from the ocean. A half dozen security guards, wearing blue uniforms and prominent black holsters, surveyed the new arrivals with that alertly hostile stare so characteristic of the breed. An odd welcoming note, Jim thought, for a peaceful week of work and play.

Blue, red and gold manta shirts striped the lobby, a hum of voices blended with the scuffle of feet and in the distance Jim heard a fevered "Hey, Bill, when'd ja get in?" a male bonding cry that would be repeated ad infinitum during the 75,000 American business conventions being held that year.

The twentieth-anniversary celebration of Arc-Horn International was under way.

Sunday Evening

Antonio Percevale lowered the venetian blind in the balcony doorway, diffusing the glare of the western sun as it dropped toward the Pacific like a swelling balloon of fire. An ocean wind, warm and salty, curled into the room, rattling the blinds seven floors above the wide beach with its collar of surf.

"Want another one, Jim?" Percevale held up a high-ball glass.

"No, thanks. I'll stand. It'll be a long night at the fiesta."

Percevale slouched back in the heavy mahogany arm-chair, upholstered in crimson, which harmonized, more or less, with the room's curious decorative motif of mingled Indian symbolism, Mexican colonial and United Express impromptu, United Express being the conglomerate that owned the Mixteca along with containers, sports stadia, tobacco, contraceptive devices and floor wax.

Jim thought again how comfortable and secure he felt with his old friend. No barriers stood between them. A common Catholic boyhood helped mute the difference in cultures and racial stock. Jim was American Irish, Tony Argentine Italian with some Spanish blood from a grandmother. Jim knew that no confidence, excluding perhaps a sudden confession of plotted murder, would rend the fabric of their understanding.

Tony had changed physically of course. The youthful patrician, once lean and supple with muscles nourished by the Argentine protein diet, was fleshier now and the wavy brown hair was speckled with gray. But Jim could sense scant change in attitude. Antonio Percevale's world was one of discovery, of exploration, of intense curiosity about the "how" of things. The great philosophical whys seldom bothered him, centered as he was in an aristocratic family tradition amid a set of absolutes decreed by an inscrutable higher power. The question of why the earth forever circled the sun with a cargo of disputatious, pullulating human beings, lizards, wolves and shellfish interested Tony not at all, but the mechanics of orbit intrigued him.

Percevale's Gusto Más, S.A., once largely confined to Argentina, had expanded throughout Latin America as far north as Mexico since Jim persuaded him to join the Arc-Horn empire six years ago. Fueled by Arc-Horn financing, Gusto Más retailed the fruits of its plantations, ranches and farms in seventy-nine Latin supermarkets. The eightieth would open in Acapulco Wednesday night with a gala ceremony, complete with marching bands, portable saints, a local Gusto Más queen and Hugo Praeger snipping the blue-and-red ribbon at the portals of canned and packaged abundance.

Aside from his inherited respect for the siesta hours, Percevale shared with all Arc-Horn executives a drive, an intensity and a voracious hunger for work that marked them as a class apart as indelibly as though they had been branded with the corporate emblem. Whatever their goal, and the uninitiated might view it as obscure or perhaps even a mirage, they were eager to labor fourteen-hour days to reach it.

The two friends had skipped through the opening banter, made fun of their gold shirts, exchanged cursory bulletins of families, tennis and health, and now, Jim sensed, they were about to come to the point of the urgent meeting in Room 740 of the Mixteca Hotel.

"As I told you on the phone, Jim, some peculiar things have happened with Arc-Horn down in Argentina since I last saw you." Tony stretched his legs, a flash of green. He wore lime-colored linen slacks and canvas beach loafers. "I need some help."

"I'm your man. Shoot."

"Well, let me start at the beginning—that Gusto Más slaughterhouse in Rosario that you've heard mentioned a couple of times at board meetings. It's an old-fashioned manual operation and Praeger has been after me for some time to tear it down and build a modern, automated plant. That makes sense, but there've been difficulties. The union wants the place as is and the union has influence with the government. We walk a narrow political line down there ever since the second Perón era and I'm careful not to offend the powers that be. At our December meeting, Hugo got after me again about it. So I decided to play for time. I had an acquaintance named Eugenio Portilla, a former professor of geology at the University of Córdoba, who set up an outfit called Environment Impact Center. He did studies on resources, pollution, population, that kind of thing.

"I got hold of Portilla and talked to him about the proposed new plant. Did he think there'd be any significant harm to the area if we went ahead with it?

I didn't think so, but it was a way of delaying Hugo. Portilla said he'd do me a free study on environmental impact, chiefly because he'd like the data himself. It would fit right in, he said, with some kind of study he was doing for a North American group.

"So I turned our rough plans over to him and he went to work on them in his shop in Buenos Aires with a couple of trips to Rosario. Then he called me in early February and said he'd be finished in about a week. He added that some of his tentative figures showed there might be 'considerable adverse impact' in Rosario. Privately I welcomed the news because of the union's objections and I called Praeger in New York right away and advised him of the upcoming report and the fact that it didn't look good from the standpoint of Gusto Más and Arc-Horn. Praeger, annoyed that I'd commissioned the report in the first place, didn't give me much time. Just said he'd turn the matter over to Davidson."

Chalmers Davidson, Arc-Horn's vice-president for international operations and communications, was an imposing, self-contained Boston Brahmin. A dean of the American establishment, he had labored at the State Department and the World Bank before pioneering in the profession of "overseas management consultant." His decision a few years earlier to join Hugo Praeger, the corporate buccaneer, proved a surprise to friends, who remarked on the sharp difference in life styles and attitudes of the two men.

"Do you know a young guy in Davidson's shop named Ron Jeffers?" Tony asked.

"I think so." Jim frowned. "Super-efficient, talks to the point, chop, chop, plays it cool?"

"That's the one. Well, he shows up in Buenos Aires three days after my call to Praeger. He says he's there to check up on the report of the Environment Impact Center. So I brief him on what little I know. He spoke Spanish with me and I must say he speaks fluently for an American. That afternoon he goes around to call on Portilla. That was a Monday. On Thursday, Jeffers calls me, says he's on his way to the airport to go back to New York. There won't be any report, he says. The figures were off, Portilla had made some errors in calculation, I don't know what all. Anyway, he said to forget about the study and he'd report to New York that there wouldn't be any environmental roadblock to the Rosario plant.

"Naturally I was surprised, after what Portilla had told me, so I put in a call to Portilla at the E.I.C. to find out what cooked. When my secretary put me on —she said later the phone rang for a long time before being answered—it turned out to be the custodian of the building. He said Portilla and his two assistants moved out that morning. No, he didn't have any idea where to. They left no forwarding address. Sounded weird to me, so I sent my secretary around to investigate. The information was correct. No sign of Portilla or his stuff. The two-room office on Calle Florida was bare as a bone. And Portilla had moved out of the hotel on Calle Reconquista, where he'd been staying, we found out."

"No trace at all?" asked Jim.

"None. We made a few more inquiries and then I got busy on other matters, chiefly this new supermarket we're opening in Acapulco Wednesday night. That'll be our fourth retail outlet in Mexico and we had some problems with the Mexican government. The Mexicans can be tough on Argentines—we're the southern racists, you know. Anyway, Portilla dropped from my mind until the next week when Sukit Sukhsvasti came to Buenos Aires on business."

Jim smiled at the mention of the Thai businessman who headed one of Arc-Horn's most consistently profitable enterprises, Thai-Tex Corp., which made and sold printed fabrics around the world. Sukit Sukhsvasti also occupied a niche in Arc-Horn lore for an amorous adventure with another executive's wife during one of the annual meetings.

"I had dinner with Sukit one night," continued Tony, "and I told him about the strange case of Señor

Portilla. Sukit said the story had a familiar ring to it.
It seems he had given a Thai academic type permission
to do some research on Thai-Tex's production and mar-
keting methods. The guy was working away, asking a
lot of questions, when the Arc-Horn controller team
from New York moved into Bangkok for the annual
cost-control inspection. Suddenly, the research man came
to Sukit and told him he was abandoning his work because he'd just been offered a job with another Arc-
Horn subsidiary, Indo Deep Rig, at a fancy salary. He
left the next day for Jakarta, bang, like that. Sukit
called Charley Holloway in Jakarta and Charley confirmed the hiring of the man, but said he knew very
little about it since the orders had come out of New
York.

"Naturally, Sukit and I wondered whether the Thai
and Argentine incidents had any connection. We chewed
it over some, then just left it that we'd talk some more
here at the Mixteca."

"I don't understand," said Jim. "Was the research
man on Sukit's payroll?"

"No, no. This was an outside study of Thai-Tex,
supposed to be a scholar's look at company operations.
Sukit got the idea the man was collaborating with some
academics in the States."

Percevale left his chair and began to pace the room.
The sun had touched the horizon now, setting the sea
aflame and licking the venetian blinds with rosy tongues,
but Tony seemed unmindful of his surroundings.

"Sukit's story bothered me," he said, "and after he
left, I decided to make a real effort to locate Portilla.
I put out a lot of feelers through mutual acquaintances
and a young hot-shot in our office spent a week on
the case. No sense going into details, but we finally found
Portilla. He was living in a boardinghouse in Carlos
Paz, a lakeside town not far from Córdoba. I flew to
Córdoba myself and drove over to see him."

Tony slid back into his chair, stretched his lime slacks
and began drumming restlessly on the armrests. "Here's
where the story gets peculiar. First, I ought to explain

about Portilla. He's a man who runs scared—and with reason. He served two stretches in prison on political charges under the military regimes, accused of being a leftist, and was tortured once. Bad raps, by the way. If anything, Portilla is apolitical. Anyway, at this time of his life—he's about fifty—trouble is the last thing he wants. I had a tough time getting him to talk, took all one morning to win his confidence. Finally, he told me that Ron Jeffers came to see him in his office on the Calle Florida in Buenos Aires, questioned him about the Rosario study and other work he was doing, then offered to buy out the whole Environment Impact Center for fifty thousand dollars—in cash American. What with the black market in foreign exchange, fifty thousand dollars cash American is an awful lot of money in Argentina right now. Portilla declined the astonishing offer and after some more talks, Jeffers left, he said."

Percevale paused, reached over and tapped Jim's knee. "The next morning when Portilla came to his office, he got an excited call from the head of the computer company where Portilla leased time for his calculations. He was told that during the night someone broke into the computer company's offce and stole the magnetic tape that held all of Portilla's data on it. The burglars also took Portilla's backup tape, so he was wiped out—completely. The official said whoever did the job knew a lot about computers because it appeared Portilla's tapes were the only ones missing out of some twenty or thirty projects leasing time.

"When Portilla asked if the computer company had reported the robbery to the police, the official said not yet, that they were still checking the staff to see whether it was an inside job. Well, Portilla was badly upset, you can imagine. He'd hardly recovered from the shock when he got an anonymous phone call, man's voice, speaking Spanish with an Argentine accent. The caller said that he'd heard of Portilla's 'misfortune' and that he and his 'friends' wanted to help out. Therefore, if Portilla would go to the front door of his office, just inside the door by the water cooler he would find a black leather bag with a 'contribution' in it. The caller said that in return for this 'contribution,' his 'friends' hoped Portilla would see his way clear to close up shop, get out of the research business and not inform the police of his 'misfortune.' If he refused, the 'friends' would contact Portilla again—a clear threat. The man hung up before Portilla could answer. The black bag was indeed there beside the water cooler and when Portilla opened it at his desk, he found it crammed with American currency, all twenty-dollar bills—a total of twenty-five thousand dollars."

"That's incredible," said Jim. "The obvious question. Did Ron Jeffers know . . . ?"

"About the computer company?" Tony broke in. "Portilla thinks he may have mentioned it in their talk, he's not sure. . . . But let me finish, Jim. Ordinarily a man of Portilla's stature would have gone to the police with the whole story, but Portilla's two terms in prison had given him a police record, and what with the memory of the torture on a political frame-up, he wasn't about to go to anybody in authority. Without going into the ins and outs of his psychological state at the time, let's just leave it that he was scared as hell. So he paid off his two assistants, took the money and went off to Carlos Paz, where he is right now. He lives by feeding out the American currency through black-market sources, an easy thing to do anywhere in Argentina.

"Now the other angle of the story. Data on our proposed new Rosario plant occupied only a small space on the stolen tape. Most of the material on it concerned natural resources throughout South America, ore deposits, soil composition, forests, crops, rainfall, that kind of thing. Much of it involved Brazil, where Portilla spent a lot of time during his years as a university geology professor. He made a specialty of the Amazon Basin. Portilla was gathering the data for some North American people. He was very cagey about his connection, didn't want to reveal names, etc. He did say he had informed the parties in North America that he had been forced to cease his active participation. The only clue he dropped was a reference to something called the 'Group of Twelve' and when I picked him up on it, he became vague and secretive again. At any rate, I got the clear idea that Portilla believed whoever stole his computer disks was more interested in the general data than the Rosario plant."

"Group of Twelve." Jim pondered as he repeated the phrase. "That's funny."

"Why?"

"I just heard the name for the first time Friday night from Senator Ireland. Remember, I told you I was to see him after the NSGA dinner? . . . But look, Tony, what about the computer company? Didn't they go to the police about the robbery?"

"No. And that was a bit strange too. My secretary knows a junior exec over there and she found out that the boss decided to keep the break-in quiet. His excuse was that any publicity would just give ideas to any business rivals who might want to steal some of his clients' trade data. Seemed rather a lame excuse to me. . . . Well, that's it."

The breeze was dying with the sun and Jim found himself perspiring beneath his absurd golden shirt. Tony looked at him inquiringly. "What do you make of it?"

"I've got a number of ideas," said Jim, "including the fact that I've a story that matches. Last week, believe it or not, a Columbia University professor named Russell Kirkland called me and told me that somebody broke into his Manhattan apartment, ransacked it and made off with a lot of research material about Top Court." Jim described Kirkland's interviews with him, Al Bebout and other Top Court officials after McGowan agreed to cooperate with the study.

"For God's sake," said Tony. "The same thing in the U.S., Argentina and Bangkok."

"Right. So I have to conclude that somebody is doing a study on Arc-Horn that Praeger wants to suppress. If you add the three incidents, you have a pattern. Three cases of academic studies being made of

Arc-Horn operations and three cases of trying to break up the studies."

"The question is who's making the investigation and who's trying to stop it."

"On the last, I'd say Praeger, of course." Jim shook his head. "Very little happens in Arc-Horn that Hugo doesn't have his finger on."

"I'm not so sure. In my case Ron Jeffers works right under Chalmers Davidson. And Jeffers is here now. I saw him crossing the lobby." Tony thought for a moment. "You know, Davidson has one hell of a lot of power in this company."

"Not unless Praeger delegates it to him. Face it, Tony, Arc-Horn's a one-man show, and now and then a side show. . . . Let's look at the other part. What's this "Group of Twelve'? Your man Portilla mentioned it and so did Ireland."

"Beats me." Tony shrugged. "Probably some university people in the States."

"Right. As I get it, they're going to present some statistics to the U.N. Conference on the Human Environment next week in Geneva that Ireland thinks will prove 'frightening.' Figures on the depletion of resources. Now maybe this Group of Twelve has tapped other experts, such as Portilla and Kirkland, for supporting information, or hell, maybe they've commissioned a study of Arc-Horn International to use as a horrible example."

"They'd talk about looting the earth and make us the scapegoat, huh?"

"Sure. Why not? It happened to ITT on the political scene."

"So what do we do?" Tony left his chair again to light a floor lamp. The room was darkening swiftly, the tropic night settling like a black hood.

"I think you and I ought to have a frank talk with Praeger about it," Jim said. He was quiet for a moment. "You know, I'm in the switches on this whole thing about resources and production. Phil Ireland is convinced that we're going to run out of minerals in a damn short time if we don't cut back on production.

But every Arc-Horn subsidiary, with the exception of you and Hi-Western and a couple of others, is in the business of taking irreplaceable stuff out of the ground and changing it into consumer items or else machines to make the items. Now, how the hell does a company quit producing without going broke? . . . On the other hand, we're all on this planet together and if Ireland's right, we'll just have to face it. The thing is, we need a lot more facts, but we're not going to get them if Praeger or somebody acting for him goes around suppressing reports by bribing people and breaking into offices and apartments. That's very heavy-handed business that I don't care for at all. What's more, it's criminal. Hell, I think we ought to lay all our cards on the table and cooperate with anybody responsible who's after the facts."

"Of course, I agree with your last point." Percevale, restless, walked to the balcony doorway and raised the blind. The sun disappeared, leaving billows of mauve, streaked with pink, on the distant edge of ocean. From the beach below could be heard the shouts of some late bathers. He turned back toward Jim. "We're in a delicate situation in Argentina and I just don't want to operate with somebody out of headquarters using extralegal methods. . . . But on the broader question of ecology, my hunch is that a lot of people are crying wolf too soon. God, South America is loaded with minerals that we couldn't use up in hundreds of years."

"Are you sure about that?"

"Well, I don't have any figures, no, but some of the stories of what lies under the soil are phenomenal. . . . All right, let's make a date to see Praeger later in the week. In the meantime, let's pick up what we can from other Arc-Horn people around the hotel. Maybe somebody has a handle on what's up."

"A little detective work might liven up the week," said Jim.

"Maybe we could hire Cal Silliman to snoop around for us. He's got his nose into everything. Order him to unshred the shredding machines." They both laughed.

Jim stood up and stretched. "I'm tired. I ought to lie down for a while before that screwball fiesta."

Tony walked with him to the door, his arm around Jim's shoulder. "Take all the rest you can get, Jim. They have indoor and outdoor courts here and I intend to take two out of three sets from you."

"From what you've been telling me, we may not have time for tennis. . . . See you later."

Jim took the elevator up three flights and walked down the carpeted corridor toward his room. He was turning the key in the lock when he heard a shout down the hall.

"Hey, Jim! When'd ja get in?" Walter Lowdermilk, Arc-Horn's foremost advocate of revelry as a cure for middle age, waved a glass at him. "Come on over and hoist one."

"Later, Walter. Thanks. Right now I'd like some shut-eye." Jim quickly let himself into the room.

The living room of Jim's suite, larger and more opulent than Tony's, as decreed by Arc-Horn protocol for high earners, dripped with the same pseudo-elegance of mingled Indian, Mexican colonial and United Express décor. Richly figured Indian rugs were strewn about the terrazzo floor, heavy furniture squatted like ingots and vivid blue upholstery matched the floor-length drapes. A gilt-framed mirror dominated one wall while the others held azure tapestries and prints of cowled Spanish monks and blandly happy Indian children. Near the open balcony door was a long mahogany bar and near it a massive, dark Mexican chest, laden with more welcoming gifts, courtesy of Cal Silliman. Bottles of rum, scotch, gin and vodka, all bearing Arc-Horn tags, rested beside a basket of flowers, Thai-Tex beach towels, a tourist's guide to Acapulco, the flight bag of goodies and the beautifully bound conference program.

Jim fumbled in the flight bag, found the manila envelope marked "Confidential" along with the little blue envelope containing the combination to his wall safe. He kicked off his shoes, turned on a reading lamp beside the blue velveteen couch and lay down facing the bal-

cony. A few early stars pinned the dark sky, the surf
rolled smoothly on the beach far below and the warm
night air had an indolent texture. Jim yawned as he
leafed idly through the pages of the conference program,
then opened the manila envelope bearing the agenda
for the final board session Thursday afternoon, the official annual meeting of Arc-Horn directors. What new
ventures did Hugo have in store for them? Jim liked
to keep ahead of the pack.

The first item involved the Arc-Horn pension fund
and the second a French patent suit. He scanned other
subjects, then paused at Nos. 8 and 9, where the wording caught his eye.

*8. Proposed resolution: "Resolved that execu-
tive officers of Arc-Horn International are hereby
authorized to utilize the services of Magna Mines
Corp., Gusto Más, S.A., Hi-Western Corp. and such..
other subsidiaries as may be necessary for development of Uni-Land Corp.'s Project Green Tree."*

No. 9 contained somewhat similar wording:

*9. Proposed resolution: "Resolved that executive
officers of Arc-Horn International are hereby authorized to utilize the services of Magna Mines
Corp. and such other subsidiaries as may be required for development of Project Neptune West."*

Jim puzzled over the phrasing for a moment, then
reached for the telephone resting on an occasional table
beside the couch. He dialed Tony's room number. Tony
answered.

"Jim. Have you looked . . . ?"

"I thought you were going to take a nap."

"I am, but I believe in being prepared. Have you
looked at your agenda for the Thursday board meeting yet?"

"Yes. I just glanced through it."

"Well, what's that Project Green Tree? I see

Gusto Más is in it along with Magna and Hi-Western."

"I don't know much about it, Jim. Hugo mentioned it when he called last week on other business. He just said he was cooking up one of his 'sweet deals' and he'd tell me about it at the conference. It's some kind of joint development by the three companies, but just what, I don't know."

"Could it have any connection with the reports we were talking about?"

"Portilla's stuff? I hadn't thought of that. I doubt it."

"Well, when you find out, let me know. I don't like to go into that annual meeting cold."

"Will do, Jim. . . . Go to sleep."

Jim placed the agenda back in the envelope, then looked around for the wall safe. Probably in the bedroom, where huge double beds, each one large enough to sleep three persons, rested beneath yellow-and-tan headboards of Indian design. He found the wall safe located over the squat mahogany table between the beds, slipped the envelope into the open metal-lined box and wondered what else he ought to put there. He could think of nothing. He closed the door and twirled the dial.

Jim shook his head. He always felt foolish with Arc-Horn's security precautions. Hugo ran the corporation as if rivals lurked behind every bedpost, bus and vine, ready to snatch the secret formula and run it up into a billion dollars. Well, there weren't any secret formulas and competitors were too busy with their own wares to man the bedposts and bushes.

He glanced at his watch. Little more than an hour before the fiesta began. He stripped, climbed into the bed nearest the balcony and soon fell asleep to the beat of cresting waves, the rattle of palm trees and, from the corridor, the muffled cries of greeting by Arc-Horn warriors gathering for the annual rites of power, commerce, carousal and, not infrequently, betrayal.

Sunday Night

A frail, sickle moon floated on a sea of stars as more than five hundred men and a scattering of women gathered on the great patio on the ocean side of the Mixteca Hotel. Waves crested and spilled on the beach with metronomic regularity, the sultry Pacific breeze, a steady insect repellent, nuzzled the palm trees and flames of the high torches fled inland.

The program misnamed the first event of Arc-Horn's jubilant anniversary. "Early-bird fiesta" implied that the Sunday-night diners had arrived by choice in advance of the Monday-morning conference opening. Also hinted was a volunteer's eager anticipation coupled with the unspoken rewards awaiting those who appeared first on the scene. In fact, the celebrants appeared on the terrace by Hugo Praeger's command and most had napped to muster stamina for the night's alcoholic exercises after deplaning throughout the afternoon according to the timetable decreed weeks earlier by Calvin Silliman.

Praeger himself was the final self-bidden early bird, sweeping up to the Mixteca at the head of a motorcade which disgorged top Arc-Horn officers, Nina Robbins, the masseuse from Rock Island, Illinois, via Hollywood, official greeters from the city of Acapulco and the state of Guerrero, several conference hostesses with their provocative décolletage and twenty-two pieces of Praeger luggage, including one document-crammed dis-

51

patch case for each of the nineteen subsidiaries and their components.

Jim McGowan groomed himself after an hour's nap by showering, shaving for the second time that day and donning one of the nine golden shirts, courtesy of the Thai-Tex Corp., that he found hanging in his closet. The one tagged for Sunday night, an elaborate creation, had ruffles tripping down the shirt front, intricate embroidery on the long sleeves and an Arc-Horn emblem snuggling near the bottom like an artist's signature.

Resplendent if self-conscious in his president's uniform, Jim sauntered through the tropic night on an exploratory tour of the Mixteca. He toured the lobby, the conference rooms, the shops and the communications center in the Toltec Room, where executives could find direct phone lines to Arc-Horn headquarters in New York, news and financial tickers, newspapers and business periodicals. He walked through the "cavern tavern" beneath an artificial waterfall, past the swimming pools and tennis courts. A solitary, red-shirted figure occupied a stool at the circular, thatch-roofed Tarascan Bar.

"Hey, buddy. When'd ja get in?"

A man shaped vaguely like a ketchup bottle, slight shoulders and wide rump, swiveled toward Jim with some difficulty. Peter Quigley, a vice-president of Meersdorf Welding, the metals fabricating company, had an affinity for bars and banalities. Jim had last seen him on a bar stool at Boca Raton in Florida at the close of last year's Arc-Horn convention. Quigley, grandson of the founder, had sold to Praeger, then been dumped into the executive scrap heap while Arc-Horn's own crew whirled Meersdorf into a carnival of new ventures—some of them profitable. Praeger treated him with the surface respect due an owner of several hundred thousand Arc-Horn shares and the thinly veiled disdain Praeger had for those he rated as incompetent. But Quigley refused to fade away. He attended every Arc-Horn convention, lapping at the fringes and weaving fantasies of daring commerce. Jim understood.

Meersdorf Welding lingered in Quigley's blood even as Top Court sang through McGowan's.

"What'll it be, Jim?" The casual use of the first name followed a close inspection of McGowan's badge through Quigley's bifocals.

"Rum, lime juice and soda." He stood beside Quigley, ignoring the stool, in good stance for a quick getaway. "What's new, Pete?"

"Another day, another dollar. . . . Hate this hot weather." Quigley flipped dew from his brow with a snap of his fingers. "Praeger goes south every year just to torture me. . . . How's the bride? Mine's got arthritis. . . . Gave my grandson a TeeCee racquet for his birthday. . . . Where'd Silliman find those hostesses? They're beauts. . . . You hear the one about Brezhnev and Nixon? Nixon asks Brezhnev if he thinks history would have been different if Khrushchev had been assassinated instead of Kennedy. Yeah, says Brezhnev, he doubted that Onassis would have married Mrs. Khrushchev." Quigley shook with stage laughter. "Okay, huh?"

"Not bad." Jim had thoughts of flight.

Quigley plucked at Jim's sleeve, drawing him closer. "Hey, Jim, what's going on, are the feds after Arc-Horn or something? A guy who claimed he was on the faculty at Kansas State came around to see me a couple of weeks ago, asking questions about our fabricating processes, our suppliers, how much steel and copper we used, stuff like that."

"Did you tell him anything?"

"Not me. I'll bet he was out of Justice or Infernal Revenue. I told him to take the plane over to New York and talk to Hugo. You don't catch me spilling my guts to some stranger. Do you blame me?" Without waiting for a reply, Quigley rambled on. "Say, Jim, you hear the one about the nigger who . . . ?"

"Later, Pete. I've got an appointment." McGowan finished off his drink. "See you at the fiesta."

"Not me, buddy. I got this spot rented for the duration." Quigley winked at the bartender. "Right, José?"

José's okay. When he got up this morning, it looked so good out, he left it out all day." Under cover of Quigley's second blast of laughter, Jim back-pedaled to safety and walked on toward the dining area.

The clans were mustering in force. Gold, blue and red shirts clustered about three portable bars and a swell of voices vied with the skittering melodies of a Vera Cruz trio, harp, marimba and guitar, and the occasional falsetto plaint of the tenor soloist. Waiters bustled impatiently through a snowy field of round linen-draped tables.

At the edge of the covered passageway ringing the patio, Antonio Percevale, flashing the lime slacks beneath his ornate gold shirt, stood beside an aluminum frame which held a pad of drawing paper. On a low box squatted the hiker of the afternoon, sketching with a black marker crayon. He was barefoot now, but he wore the same pair of ragged blue-jean shorts and a short-sleeved denim shirt.

"Have a go at it, Jim," said Percevale. "The guy's not bad for a buck."

"Hi again." Steve looked up from his sketch, locked on to Jim's eyes for a brief, intense moment, then resumed his drawing. "So your name's Jim?"

"Yep. Jim McGowan. . . . You're Steve what?"

"Just Steve." He scrawled something at the bottom of the drawing, ripped off the sheet of paper and handed it to Percevale.

Tony shared his inspection with Jim. The caricature aptly depicted the sprinkle of gray in Percevale's hair, the handsome patrician look. The thick eyebrows, however, arched upward like question marks, lending the sketch an air of startled apprehension. Steve's caption read: TROUBLE?

Jim and Tony looked at each other in shared recognition. "Pretty close," said Tony. He handed Steve thirteen pesos.

"How about you?" asked Steve.

"Why not?" Jim posed beside the easel and tried to relax as he looked out toward the crowded terrace. Cal

Silliman was circulating among the drinkers, ringing a cow bell and exhorting his charges to move to the tables.

"You're easy, man." Steve's gaze shifted from Jim to the easel and back again. He drew rapidly. "I see you got one of those gold shirts. What you president of?"

"Top Court."

"It's a leader in the tennis industry," added Tony.

"That figures . . . with Jim running it." Steve stroked quick, heavy lines. He finished within three minutes, scribbled something and tore off the sheet.

Jim's first glance brought dismay. The drawing had his curly hair, the long, freckled nose and faint smile, but the head was enormous, dwarfing the body except for oversized feet encased in tennis shoes. On the left side of the chest prison bars enclosed a tiny, throbbing heart. A line looped away from the heart to a cartoonist's balloon containing the words: LEMME OUT!

"So you're an amateur shrink, huh?" Jim did not try to hide his irritation. He fished a dollar from his wallet.

"Wicked," said Tony.

"I draw what I see." Steve's eyes fastened on Jim's. "Sometimes I'm off target. You think I blew this one?"

"I sure do." Jim's words carried a truculent assurance that he was not sure he felt.

"Well, let me try again Thursday—a freebie. I may see something else."

"You're hanging around all week?"

Steve nodded. "Might as well make a buck, man, like María said. I'm heading south and there won't be many paying customers between here and Puerto Angel."

"How'd you get a room?" asked Tony. "The Mixteca is sold out to Arc-Horn."

"A room?" Steve's laugh was low, easy. "I can live for a month on your room rent for one night. No, I pitched my tent down the beach." He pointed to the south. "Come see me. Rappin's my hang-up."

Jim folded the sheet and tucked it in his shirt pocket. "A lot of freaky ones roaming around the world these days," said Tony as they walked away.

But Jim took no comfort from Tony's remark. Big head and small heart, huh? Same line Meg handed out last night in different language. Well, Meg and the walker missed the whole point. His problem wasn't lack of heart. It was how to find the time and energy to cope with the demands, the pressures, the decisions. In business, a man either fought to win or he dropped out. How could Meg and this Steve possibly understand that daily grind of competition? Jesus! . . . Jim bristled defensively as he threaded his way through the noisy throng toward table No. 1.

Buoyed by alcohol, the early birds flocked to the acre of flower-decked tables, jostling, joking, greeting. Flushed masks of conviviality hid a few joyful moods and whole battalions of frog-eyed devils that hopped through five hundred psyches, croaking of lost sales and souls. Like the millions of conventioneers who would swarm that year across hotel lobbies and exhibit halls from the Sheraton-Waikiki in Hawaii to the Dorado Beach in Puerto Rico, the managers and minions of Arc-Horn obeyed the Ten Convention Commandments: (1) Fix thy smile. (2) Belt down thy booze. (3) Reveal not thyself to thy neighbor. (4) Profit by what thou hearest and lose not by what thou sayeth. (5) Protest not the litanies of thy commercial society lest ye be scorned and cast out. (6) Covet thy neighbor's mate. (7) Tell thy newest and oldest joke. (8) Make profitable commerce where thou canst, for the bottom line is thy salvation. (9) Call thy friends and thine enemies alike by given names. (10) Hold thy liquor, for ye know not who ye are.

The flaming torches illumined the faces of hundreds of white males, a few white females and a sprinkling of men of the darker races. There was but one black, Lucy Jenkins, a vast, mobile uninhibited vice-president of Fragrance, Inc. The diners spanned such nationalities as American, British, Japanese, French, Thai, Argentine, Venezuelan, Belgian and Brazilian (We Nourish the World) and embraced every known managerial skill from engineering to cost accounting. Pilots of the Arc-Horn executive fleet occupied five tables. At least a third of the assemblage were salesmen and officers of Summit, Inc., whose new TV, radio and audio line would be undraped the next day for the delectation of all. Uninvited to the fiesta, but garnishing the premises, were a dozen elegant, busty call girls flown in from Miami's fading season by Cal Silliman.

Gathering near the stage where the Vera Cruz trio held forth were employees of Jake Apple's Convention Dynamics Co. Apple, an impresario who had deserted the dwindling showman's pastures of Hollywood for the more lucrative field of entertaining business conventions, had lavished almost a half million dollars on Arc-Horn's twentieth anniversary. He had written, composed, designed, orchestrated and choreographed the entertainment that would snake through the Arc-Horn week from the opening fiesta to the final Thursday-night formal banquet, including Summit's entire three-morning sales presentation. His crew included a seven-piece New York orchestra, stage hands, electricians, sound men, a stand-up comic and an eight-girl chorus line from Manhattan headed by Gilda, the red-haired Lesbian whose wild, flaming dances had turned several mediocre off-Broadway musicals into hits.

Hugo Praeger's table for six always stood front and center at the annual early-bird dinners. For some years he had been flanked on his right by Nina Robbins, the Rock Island beauty plucked from a Los Angeles nude photography and massage salon to become Praeger's traveling companion since his divorce. To his left sat John Lindquist, a solemn numbers genuis whom Praeger had lured away from General Mills and installed as Arc-Horn's financial vice-president. The other VIP slots went to the chief executive officers of the three subsidiaries with the best growth records the previous year.

Tonight that meant Jules Amarel, board chairman of the Dallas-based Six Flags Insurance Co., Gwen Piggott, president of Fragrance, Inc., and Jim McGowan.

Praeger, a genial host in his special blue-trimmed golden shirt, was busy with the amenities when Jim arrived. He introduced Amarel, a tall, dark-visaged man with the pained look of an aging diplomat as "this year's newcomer." "Nina . . . John . . . Gwen Piggott and Jim McGowan you know from opening night at Boca Raton. This is Gwen's second year with us and Jim's, let's see, third, what?"

Jim found his place card, stamped with the inevitable Arc-Horn emblem, near a fruit cup huddling in a silver bowl of cracked ice. He was seated between the taciturn Lindquist and Gwen Piggott, a break, thought Jim. Since Lindquist hoarded words like sapphires, Jim could center his attention on Gwen, a small, galvanic woman who crackled with good will and fashion prattle of famous personages. Last year, Jim recalled, they had danced, flirted and even hinted at a later rendezvous that wilted in memory when Hugo ordered all hands to his suite for a nightcap that turned into a three-hour business session.

"Gwen, you look smashing." Jim meant it. She wore a clinging gold jersey dress with scooped neckline.

"Presidential color." Her laugh was warm, self-deprecating. "Made by Thai-Tex naturally. And, a miracle, it fits."

"Your hair's different this year. I like it." At Boca Raton, he recalled, she wore her hair fashionably short and cropped like a boy's. Now the brown, wavy hair hung loose and full.

"So you noticed." She showed her pleasure by squeezing his hand. "Hair's the least of it. I've gone through a lot of changes, Jim. I'm different . . . I hope."

"What kind of changes?"

"Head stuff."

"Sounds interesting. Like to hear more about it."

But he was merely making conversation now. That caricature in his pocket still bothered him. Across the table Praeger was zestfully spooning up the cornucopia of melon, pineapple, orange and mango.

"Okay," said Gwen. "If you're really interested, I'll tell you more later."

To Jim's left, a surprising sound. John Lindquist spoke. "Top Court will be up as usual this quarter?"

The question hit him like a dart. Did Lindquist suspect? Jim wanted to retort: "None of your business." But of course it was Lindquist's only business. While waiting for his stomach knot to unkink, Jim said: "Things look good. I'll have the estimate ready for the first board meeting." He had never liked Lindquist, the gourmet of numbers who neither knew nor cared about the ulcerous toil required to produce the numbers he fed upon.

When Lindquist made no reply, Jim turned gratefully back to Gwen Piggott. "Sorry, Gwen. All I caught was one word—later."

"Later I'd like to go walking barefoot on that big, wide beach. If you care to come along, you're invited."

The waiter was pouring a white wine. Jim clinked his glass against Gwen's. "Deal," he said. They both drank and Jim noted fleetingly that the prospect of a beach stroll with Gwen aroused flickers but no quick flame.

"Ladies and gentlemen!" Cal Silliman's feverish voice burst from the amplifiers hidden in the palm trees. He adjusted the stage microphone downward. "Please stand for the invocation by Monsignor Jaime Morales Ortega of Chilpancingo."

"Where's Chilpancingo?" asked Jim.

"About two hours by car on the highway to Mexico City." Gwen waved toward the east. "It's the capital of Guerrero."

Chairs scraped and heads bowed as the monsignor beseeched the Almighty in unfettered Spanish to guide the Arc-Horn galleons to a safe and profitable harbor. Jim surmised that for later blessings and benedictions

Silliman had imported Catholic, Jewish and Protestant clerics, from Mexico City and from perhaps as far north as Texas. Arc-Horn needed all the spiritual succor it could entice by liberal honorarium and expense account.

"And now, gentlemen and a few ladies." Silliman was obviously happy to put his ecclesiastical chores behind him. "Your early-bird show is timed to go along with each course of this colorful, gourmet spread. Act One is coming up, but first the man who can take credit for anything that moves on every stage from now through Thursday night. I give you Arc-Horn's old friend, Mister Show Biz himself—the one and only Jake Apple!"

Apple, a man of restless, febrile energy, waved his baton to the crowd and promptly began jigging his foot, setting in motion a tide of music from the dinner-jacketed orchestra. On stage danced the chorus line, eight leggy young hoofers clad in red hot pants and blue bras. Gilda, her red hair flashing, took the mike and sang while the dancers pranced and whirled.

> We're here tonight to welcome you,
>   Arc-Horn, Arc-Horn.
> We wear your colors red and blue,
>   Arc-Horn, Arc-Horn.
>
> From the Arctic Circle's blinding white
> To wild waves curling 'bout Cape Horn,
> Nourish the world from morn till night,
> The old, the young, those yet unborn.
> Empires built and proud ships sailing,
> Your crest adorns rail, tower and mast.
> You're into everything but whaling,
> And that will come. Your harpoon's fast.
> Your commerce floods the seven seas.
> Your salesmen march through every land.
> Bankers love you, float loans to please,
> And castles rise at your command.

We're here tonight to welcome you,
Arc-Horn, Arc-Horn.
We wear your colors red and blue,
Arc-Horn
Arc . . . Arc . . . Horn!

Gilda flung the last word, along with a kiss, toward Hugo Praeger. The conglomerator, beaming with pride, led the applause, which, while not deafening, was loud and raucous. Behind her hand, Gwen whispered to Jim: "If only we didn't have to suffer all of Hugo's cornball inanities."

"Think of it as camp. It's easier to take that way."

Waiters fanned swiftly over the patio, whisking off the fruit cups and replacing them with wooden bowls of turtle soup. Silliman brooded over his wristwatch, timing the change of courses like an Olympic coach clocking his sprint men. Off stage, glinting in the thin moonlight, breaking waves beat a cadence for the changing of the calories. Nina Robbins stroked the back of Praeger's huge hand with a single finger. John Lindquist drew a ball-point pen from his pocket and jotted digits on his napkin. Jim wondered idly what Meg was doing with herself during the twins' party.

A fanfare from Apple's band fetched six girls from the wings. The chorines danced across the stage with plastic smiles, crimson shirts and cropped blue jeans that barely covered the crotch. They waved tiny flags beneath white ten-gallon hats while the orchestra swung into "The Eyes of Texas Are Upon You." At the close of the number all pennants dipped toward Table One. Jules Amarel, as president of Six Flags Insurance, stood up to receive the plaudits due the subsidiary with last year's highest earnings growth. A spotlight fingered Jake Apple, who held aloft a blue sign lettered in red: "No. 1 . . . Six Flags . . . Amarel Up 19.7%." Praeger waved his napkin to lead the dutiful applause. Jules Amarel wore the look of a dental patient bravely facing the drill.

"And now," cried Silliman as the dancers faded to

the wings, "thanks to Jake and his worldwide booking talents—he too nourishes the world—we bring you the original Boston bean boy, Frankie Fee. Frankie was born in a three-decker, went to Holy Cross and would have entered the priesthood except, he says, he didn't like the looks of the Vatican's bottom line. And so, for some comment on our life and times, the pride of Boston, Frankie Fee."

Fee, a sated veteran of the night-club and convention circuits, heaved on stage, shook hands overhead like a boxer and throttled the center mike. A vast man who looked not unlike an Irish Hugo Praeger, Frankie wore a crimson dinner jacket with pleated blue shirt. He patted his abundant stomach.

"I feel right at home," he said. "All us growth industries here together. . . . You know, I just flew in from a date in L.A. Rough ride up there. In fact, the turbulence was so bad, the hijacker got off in Guadalajara. . . . Speaking of airplanes, I know all you wage slaves were herded aboard the company jets with hardly enough room left for the martini pitcher, but . . ."

Praeger's high cackling laugh split the balmy air. Frankie, who played his routine deadpan, looked down at his host.

"Thank you, sir. Now if you'd just order a couple of vice-presidents to crack a smile, we'd be in business." Fee's gaze took in the lusterless John Lindquist. "Say, you look like a controller who's just come from the company funeral where the undertaker was guilty of padding the bill." He thrust out his jaw in mock belligerence. "Okay, if you're the money man, I'm a stockholder and this quarter I want earnings of a dollar seventy-nine a share." At last Fee fetched his first stout round of applause and laughter. Arc-Horn's earnings had risen steadily for twenty-nine straight quarters amid wide suspicion that often the figure was less accurate than arbitrary.

"So back to airplanes," said Frankie without a smile on his whisky-veined face. "There was this inbound jet that asked the tower what time it was. 'Identify yourself,' said the tower. 'Why?' asked the copilot. 'Well,' said the tower, "if you're American, it's fifteen hundred. If you're Eastern, it's three p.m. And if you're Allegheny, the big hand is pointing to twelve and the small hand to three.' "

Frankie gunned through his airborne repertoire, then switched to the religious scene where priests, ministers and rabbis alternated as his dupes. His favorites were those good friends the Boston priest and rabbi. Once the rabbi agreed to substitute for the priest in the confessional so his friend could take a well-deserved vacation. The rabbi squeezed into the stall with the priest to learn the ropes. The first woman to appear confessed that she had committed adultery that week. "How many times?" asked the priest. "Three, Father," replied the woman. "Go out and say five rosaries," ordered the priest. When the rabbi took over for practice, another woman confessed to adultery. "How many times?" asked the rabbi. "Twice," said the woman. Advised the rabbi: "You might as well go out and do it again. This week we're offering a three-for-five special."

Frankie swung from theological capers to the in-house jokes that seldom failed to convulse the customers at business conventions.

"I suppose you're wondering why we have so many security police around this ancient United Express temple? Well, we have some lovely lady guests here from Miami and they need protection. You don't believe it, look at the guy next to you. He's drooling, right? . . . Seriously, the Latin guerrillas, Arab terrorists and American Mafia have their own conglomerate now. A friend of mine in Boston, Hymie (the Duck) Giancotti, is the chief executive officer. He's split the world into territories and established a minimum ransom and fair practices act. Down here, to be kidnapped, you've got to have an impeccable Dun and Bradstreet rating, be listed in the Social Register, hold a master's degree from the Harvard Business School and have served at least two years in Danbury for price fixing. Hymie runs a prestige operation for a select clientele, so don't waste time hoping to be snatched unless you can meet his exacting standards."

Fee wrapped up several more kidnapping gags, then closed with the disclaimer: "No encores please, folks. I'm late for my date at the Tarascan Bar. I'm playing gin rummy with one of the bar's oldest inhabitant's, a guy named Pete Quigley. He's been there since the Spaniards landed."

As Frankie yielded the stage, rivers of waiters poured from the kitchen, bearing platters of choice filet mignon flown in that morning by cargo jet from Texas. High above the dun hills and gullies, where peasants scrabbled a bare living from the dusty soil, rode the cuts of fattened beef at 35,000 feet, courtesy of Jules Amarel's high-earning insurance spread.

Silliman gauged progress of the serving by his watch, Apple's orchestra played "The Yellow Rose of Texas" and Praeger, still chortling, dabbed at his cheeks with a handkerchief.

"Great comic, Frankie," Praeger proclaimed. "Jake pays him twenty-five hundred and expenses for the week and he's worth every dollar. Did you catch those Arc-Horn gags? Deft, what?"

"About as subtle as a hog," said a rich, throaty voice. Lucy Jenkins, table hopping, laid a large black hand on Praeger's shoulder. "Hugo, honey, if I didn't know better, I'd think you was from right off the farm. That man Fee has more corn to peddle than the Chicago Board of Trade. Twenty-five hundred! You pay me half of that and I'll come up with some fresh material. I heard those tired rabbi and priest stories long before people stopped calling me nigger—to my face."

Praeger reached out an arm and encircled Lucy's ample waist. The Fragrance vice-president was one of two people in the Arc-Horn empire who could play the jester to the king. The other was Walter Lowdermilk, star salesman of the Summit wares. Praeger loved good salesmen and Lucy had come up through sales and now presided over the array of special Fragrance beauty aids that glistened in the slick advertising pages of *Ebony* and other black publications.

"You just a patsy for any so-called comic who does his homework and picks up some Arc-Horn gossip," said Lucy. "Hi, honey." She waved to Gwen Piggott, her boss, across the table.

"No, Lucy," said Praeger. "You'll notice there was no blue stuff. Fee lived up to his contract. He has a dirty mouth sometimes, but tonight he kept it clean."

Praeger upheld ambivalent censorship standards. While he banned what he called off-color stories on stage, the entire entertainment and sales presentations swirled in sexual allusions, including prominent displays of the female bosom and frequent rotation of the pelvis.

"I do believe you're down on pleasuring, Hugo." Lucy winked at the other diners around the table while favoring Nina Robbins with a broad smile that belied the charge.

"And I think you're trying to take over Walter Lowdermilk's act," Praeger replied.

"Well, let's see how Walter does tonight. Then next year, Hugo, you call me." She moved away on the chords of another musical prelude from the orchestra.

This time the chorus line danced on stage to the rock beat of a Santana number. The girls, dressed in tennis miniskirts, churned the air with TeeCee Championship racquets. It was obviously Jim McGowan's turn. The dancers swiveled hips, racquets and breasts in his direction. The spotlight probed Apple again and his new sign: "No. 2 . . . Top Court . . . McGowan Up 12.9%." Jim stood up and bowed. He drew more applause than had the suffering Amarel, but he noted that Praeger's hand clapping was just a shade less vigorous. Faced with a choice between personalities and numbers, Hugo knew where duty lay.

Gwen too caught the difference. "You get more points from this crowd than Jules," she whispered. "That's a good feeling."

"Wait'll they get to you." Jim knew she was right. The spontaneous approval gave him a lift. Strange, he thought, no matter how much recognition he got, he always thirsted for more.

Hardly had the tender filets been ingested than a prolonged fanfare ushered Cal Silliman to the center mike. "Arc-Horn leaders," he called with breathless exuberance, "we now come to the feature attraction of the early-bird fiesta, the spot you've all been waiting for. I give you, without further ado, that salesmen's salesman, that favorite of many an Arc-Horn night, the unbeatable Walter Lowdermilk!"

Lowdermilk burst to center stage as though shot from a cannon. He was a tall, portly man with graying hair and the ruggedly handsome features once seen by millions on the sports pages when he played fullback for Ohio State. Fleshy now, he emanated an aura of the good sales life from the two-martini lunch to the palming of the check at 21 after a Broadway musical. Someone once calculated that Walter's sales of Summit TV, radio and hi-fi sets to retail chains matched, in any given year, the combined exports of Haiti and the Dominican Republic.

Walter tugged at his embroidered maroon shirt, nodded to Jake Apple, waited while the orchestra swung through the prelude to "Hello, Dolly," then sang slyly and satirically:

> *Hello, Nina, well, hello, Nina,*
> *It's so nice to see you here where you belong.*
> *You're lookin' swell, Nina,*
> *I can tell, Nina,*
> *You're still strokin', you're still pokin'*
> *At our grand King Kong.*
> *He feels the room swayin'*
> *When your hand's playin'*
> *Upon his old weary limbs from toe to thigh,*
> *So:*
>> *Rub that back, Nina,*
>> *Let him blow his stack, Nina,*
>> *Just like he used to do in days gone by.*

Praeger's broad smile froze on his lips like a grotesque mask.

Good Christ, thought Jim, Walter's drunk.

Gwen gasped and beneath the table she brought her heel down on Jim's loafer.

Jake Apple, directing the orchestra with his head straddled by earphones, looked stricken. He shrugged weakly, a gesture of helplessness plainly intended to indicate that he had no forewarning of the lyrics Walter would sing. The musicians, obviously prepared for more verses, paused and looked questioningly at Jake.

The silence on the patio was broken by several inebriated laughs, quickly choked off.

The jester had, at last, committed lese majesty. He had alluded in public to a topic about which the gossips only dared whisper in secluded alcoves—the purported impotence of the king.

Only the deceptively wholesome Nina appeared unperturbed. A smile flickered for a moment, then vanished. A portrait of artful innocence, she continued to survey her fellow diners from the haven of her long, blond hair.

If Walter Lowdermilk was aware of the bomb he had dropped, he gave no outward sign. Hands caressing the mike, his face a wreath of impish joy, he awaited his next musical cue. My God, thought Jim, there's more. When no note sounded, Walter began singing anyway. Apple, astounded, shook his head with the air of a man unjustly condemned. His baton slowly waved the band into accompaniment. Walter switched from the bawdy insouciance of the first verse into the hearty baritone of a man who might be rendering the national anthem.

Hello, Hugo, well, hello, Hugo,
Arc-Horn's glad to have you here where you belong.
The quarter's great, Hugo,
Like your mate, Hugo,
You're still leadin', you're still feedin'
You're our grand King Kong.

We feel the cash flowin'
From the loans owin'
To First Merchants, Chase and Chem and Guaranty,
So:

    Let 'er rip, Hugo,
    One more ego trip, Hugo,
    And we will own both Ford and ITT.

There was a long, hushed moment. A great wave crashed and a gust rattled the palm fronds. All eyes turned toward Praeger. He stared up at Walter. Slowly the hillocks of flesh crinkled into a grin and the monarch waved a salute to the minstrel. A freshet of relief washed over the patio. Laughter sounded. Walter spread his arms beneath the star-sprinkled sky and cried: "Come on, everybody!" Jake Apple, as ecstatic as the condemned man abruptly reprieved, flung his baton upward for the encore.

Led by Walter and Jake, the crowd started hesitantly, gained confidence as the familiar melody unfurled and finally devoured Ford and ITT with gusto. "One more time," yelled Walter triumphantly. On the second reprise, Praeger himself joined in. Nina beat a tattoo with her table knife and the noise overwhelmed the sound of surf.

"Okay, one last time," implored Walter. Now everybody stood up. Lucy Jenkins plowed over to Praeger, kissed him soundly and raised his right arm high. The music took wing. Jake's earphones bobbed like the antennae of some electronic creature from space. Even John Lindquist mumbled the words. And when Ford and ITT were swallowed once more, a piercing rebel yell from a Six Flags executive stabbed the night and from the Tarascan Bar came a wavering, drunken cheer. Walter left the stage with the aplomb of a star while a hum of frenetic conversation filled the void of song.

"What gall!" Gwen spoke into Jim's ear. "But he got away with it."

"I'm not so sure." Jim recalled the look on Hugo's face after the first verse. A smile congealed in hatred?

No, not quite. Hugo usually hid his emotions behind bluster and jubilation. This time Jim thought he detected something else, a sadness perhaps, a vulnerability as if Praeger were asking himself, in wonderment, why a jester would want to wound his old friend the king.

The filets were snatched away to make room for the dessert, mint ice cream afloat in crème de menthe. Apple's men boomed their way through a medley of college songs which evoked ragged cheers from nodules of alumni from Cornell to Stanford. Conversation at the first table took a bizarre turn as though every early bird had joined a conspiracy to launder the memory of Lowdermilk's first stanza.

"Walter's a happy-go-lucky pirate." Hugo set the pace. "And believe me, anything he can dish out, I can take."

"Very honestly, I don't know what to think." But Nina Robbins did not appear displeased with the commercial.

"A little of that goes a long way." Humor, the dour Jules Amarel implied, was a drug to be taken sparingly lest the side effects sap a man's zeal for productive labor.

"Best salesman in the world," said Lindquist. "His one deal with Korvettes added three cents a share to earnings in seventy-two."

"I like Walter," said Gwen, "but sometimes he's hard to take. He's always playing games."

That was near the truth, thought Jim. Walter treated life as one enormous game in which men competed only because it was the only one in town. If God ordained the rules, then God was either a moron or a prankster, for Walter acted as though the rules were incredibly silly. He delighted in ridiculing Hugo every year because with power as a measure of success, he would show the Arc-Horn hierarchy that he had as much power as Praeger, for Hugo would not dare fire him. This year he honed the barb of challenge to the sharpest point of all, the master's sexual capacity. High risk? Not at all. The $200,000-a-year celebrity,

No. 1 salesman of the worldwide television industry, ran risks only when there was no other way to play. If Hugo failed to order his dismissal, Walter rolled merrily along, awash in stock options, a huge salary, liquor, friends, women and long sailing cruises in the Caribbean. If Hugo zapped him, he merely flew over to Magnavox or Admiral on the wings of Hugo's humiliation and continued the game from there.

"Do you envy him?" The question from Gwen surprised Jim.

"I was just thinking about that. No, I don't. I'm not made that way. My work is no plaything. I live twenty-four hours a day with Top Court."

"Uh-oh. I'm about to live with Fragrance again."

The dancers returned to work, this time somewhat awkwardly, for they were costumed as bottles and boxes of a cosmetic line, Etoile facial cream, Persian Twilight bath powder, Trespass perfume, Mountain Mist flavored douches and the famous My Touch lipstick, flagship of the Fragrance beauty fleet that dropped anchor in all ports of the free world and now threatened the shores of the Communist powers and their satellites. The girls clustered center stage at the finale and bowed toward Gwen while Jake held up his sign: "No. 3 . . . Fragrance . . . Gwen Piggott Up 11.4%."

"And Lucy Jenkins too," said Gwen as she stood up for her applause. "Come on, Lucy, take a bow."

"If you can't get it at Saks," shouted Lucy, "bring your Afro up to Harlem and we'll drown you in sweet stuff. That's a promise, honey."

Jake Apple, with a professional's sixth sense of audience mood, knew he was in prime milking time. He whipped his musicians into the rushing notes of "Smackwater Jack" while Gilda, bobbing, hunching and flailing her arms in staccato rhythm, led the Broadway dancers on stage once more. The girls wore white bikinis and their full mops of hair, swooping and swinging in cadence, spelled out a color scheme, brunettes on each end, flanking four blondes with Gilda's red blaze flaring in the center. The girls jived into a semi-circle, clapping in unison as Gilda began working faster and faster. She pulsed, she throbbed, she strutted, grinding first her shoulders and then her hips. The audience joined the hypnotic beat, Hugo Praeger marked time with his palms on the table and Apple's trumpet man fought a duel with the electric vibes. Gilda kept accelerating the pace, using her glistening white body first like a cracking whip, then like a frenzied mechanical doll, through two fast numbers. Then, during a lull while the girls snapped fingers and rocked in place, Gilda beckoned to men in the audience to join up. Her gestures drew enthusiastic promptings, but no takers, and finally Lucy Jenkins filled the breach.

The big black woman proved almost a match for Gilda. Her crimson caftan swirled, her breasts heaved and her bare feet stamped out the cadence on the boards. The two women faced each other to the music of "Come, On, Baby, Light My Fire" and danced slowly closer, narrowing the gap with each lurch and wriggle. "Now don't get me wrong, honey," Lucy shouted. The crowd, afloat in after-dinner cognac, roared. Gilda's sexual penchants were as well known as her mop of fiery hair.

Suddenly a figure vaulted to the stage from the seeming dark wings of nowhere. Bronzed and lean, he wore frayed blue-jean shorts and he tore off his denim shirt as he landed before the footlights. Within seconds he merged smoothly into the dance of the two women. Steve, the hiker, was also a dancer. Like Gilda, he started fast and boosted his body tempo higher and higher. He danced fiercely, pounding his bare feet, grinding his pelvis toward first one woman, then the other, flinging his arms and rolling his shoulders. Soon his bare chest sparkled with sweat. His look was one of wild intensity. Jim McGowan watched in fascination.

"Who is that man?" asked Gwen. "He's got my blood zinging."

"Guy named Steve." Jim felt a touch of resentment

toward him. "He does caricatures. He also claims he's hiking around the world."

"He knows where it's at."

"Oh, he does?" Gwen's phrase irritated Jim as much as Steve's abandon, unseemly, Jim thought, for a grown man.

"Every man here would like to let go like that, but they're afraid of looking ridiculous. That one doesn't give a damn how he looks. It's how he feels up there that counts. And why should he get any less of a kick out of dancing than the women? That's what I mean."

"Oh." Jim did not think the explanation, even if valid, accounted for Steve's exuberant abandon. "If you ask me, he's high on something."

Lucy Jenkins began to puff. Although Steve's dancing fired both women, Lucy's weight was telling and Gilda, perhaps tiring of sharing the spotlight with an unknown amateur, scanned the crowd for new game. At Table One Nina Robbins tapped her foot in time to the music. Gilda saw the movement and beckoned to her. Praeger's woman shook her head. Gilda insisted. Slowly, as if involuntarily, Nina rose from her chair and walked to the stage. She wore a long, white knit dress, slit halfway up the thigh, and as she mounted the steps, lights shimmered on tanned flesh.

The dancers paired off. Gilda with Nina and Lucy with Steve, and almost at once the dance tempo slowed to half-time with the music. Whatever Nina's skills, acquired over her twenty-eight years in beauty contests, bit movie parts, nude modeling and massage, they did not include dancing. She did her own thing, hardly moving her feet, wriggling her arms and shoulders somewhat less than gracefully and thrusting her hips forward just a shade off the beat. Still, the ripe, full figure in the close-fitting dress apparently aroused in Gilda what the Supreme Court would classify as "prurient" interests. Gilda circled her hungrily, never taking her eyes from Nina's body. Nina's smile was small, knowing, responsive. At times her shoulder-length blond hair swung in fortuitous rhythm with Gilda's loose auburn mop. Jim glanced at Jake Apple. The impresario was growing nervous again.

But Praeger seemed to relish the scene. If he were aware that a mating dance was in progress on stage, he gave no clue. Instead he kept time by swaying from side to side like a bull before the cape.

Jim felt uneasy. "I don't like to see Hugo's nose rubbed in it twice in one night," he said to Gwen.

"Oh, everybody knows Nina's double-gaited." Gwen was cheery. "Or maybe triple, depending on how you count Hugo. Don't worry about it. Hugo and Nina have an understanding. Whatever it is, it works."

"I've had enough. How about that walk on the beach?"

"Right now that's a lovely idea. I have to go to the john first. I'll see you down on the sand." She pointed to the southwest. "Right about there."

They both made excuses for their early departure, complimented Praeger on the entertainment and bid their good-nights. Jim walked off to the passageway leading past the Tarascan Bar. Pete Quigley, a lone customer, still occupied the same stool. But Pete was busy telling José a story and Jim slipped by unnoticed.

A glimmer of moonlight brushed the surf, which seemed heavier now in the darkness. A single cloud floated eastward, lending the masses of stars the illusion of marching west across the Pacific. Jim wriggled his toes in the warm, loose sand. He felt unhinged. Percevale's tale nagged at the back of his mind and tomorrow, he knew, Top Court would face the fire on estimated earnings. But that, somehow, was the real world, the world in which he could cope, take the ups with the downs. But out here, alone with the sea and the night sky, he felt unsettled, ill at ease with himself. That crazy fiesta didn't help, Walter jabbing cruelly at Hugo, Steve flaunting his sexuality, the red-haired Gilda eying Hugo's woman like a cobra. It was all unreal, as remote as the sound of drums drifting across the beach from the patio.

"Hi!"

He turned to see Gwen plodding through the sand, holding her shoes in her hand. The moonlight stroked her. She looked happy. Jim didn't feel at all happy. What he felt was an unusual malaise.

Monday, 2 a.m.

Jim stirred and opened his eyes. He must have fallen asleep, but apparently for only a few minutes, for Gwen still stood in the doorway of the ocean-side balcony, her nude figure dimly framed by pale moonlight. She was leaning against the wall, smoking a cigarette and gazing out at the Pacific. Smoke fled over her shoulder against a splash of stars. The night breeze blew steadily up here in her tenth-floor suite.

"What do you see?"

"Oh." She started but did not turn. "I thought you were asleep."

"I guess I did doze off." He glanced at his wristwatch as he swung his legs from the bed: 2:05. Not so bad. He could manage a decent sleep before the grand opening of the Summit sales extravaganza. But damn Hugo for commanding attendance as if they were school children fated to be ruled forever by clanging corridor bells. He started to retrieve his shorts from the nearby chair.

"Jim, I want to talk." She sensed his movement. "If you're not too tired."

"Sure." But he thought of his own bed only a few doors down the hall. He felt heavy, drowsy, and the combination of the pre-dinner drinks, three French wines and the cognac had left him with a mild headache, the merit badge of the proper conventioneer.

He dragged two armchairs to the wide doorway and found a smaller chair for their feet. They settled naked into the cushions. Late revelers or insomniacs on adjoining balconies would have seen only four bare feet protruding from the room.

They sat in silence while Gwen smoked. Waves broke far below them and out on the Pacific lights on a ship faded and reappeared on the swell of the dark horizon. Jim felt the air lave his body like a cool hand. On the beach to the left a single light winked.

"That's the hiker's tent," said Gwen lazily. "I saw someone dive into the breakers a couple of minutes ago. It must have been him."

"Steve's some kind of a head. A guy's got to be hyped up to let loose on stage like he did."

"You think so?" Gwen's tone was low, musing. "Wouldn't you like to be able to cut loose and go with the music?"

"No. Frankly I wouldn't. Not the way Steve did."

"Why not?"

"Oh, I don't know." As a tribesman of conventions, Jim observed the customs carved from American lore. Firewater, yes. Savage fertility dances, no. "A grown man doing the bump-and-grind looks ridiculous."

"That's bad?"

"What is this, a psychological quiz?" Jim bridled. "But the answer is yes, for me anyway. If I've learned anything in forty-eight years, it's that if you start losing control, you're on the way to losing the ball game."

Gwen drew on her cigarette. The breeze seized the smoke and hurried it back over her bare shoulder. "I used to buy that, but no longer. Too many brakes on the emotions are as bad as none at all."

"You're a woman."

She swung quickly toward him. "I'll let that pass, Jim. I'm in no mood for one of those dreary male versus female rap sessions. But you missed my point.

I told you at dinner that I've changed and I have—
a lot since we saw each other at Boca Raton last
year."

Gwen padded into the bedroom, found an ashtray
and ground out her cigarette. He admired her small,
compact figure, the soft breasts and the sway of her
rump when she walked. How old was Gwen? Forty-
four or -five, wasn't she? He also thought, almost at
once, of Praeger's reaction at the first 5 p.m. board
meeting tomorrow when he heard Top Court's quarterly
estimate and his mind veered again to Percevale's
extraordinary story of apparent Arc-Horn sabotage of
an academic study. He had to be alert later today
and every day this week.

Gwen eased back into her chair. "How do you feel,
Jim?"

"Great." He ran his hand lightly down her arm.

"I don't believe you."

He was about to protest when Gwen withdrew her
arm and turned to face him. "Please. Let me explain.
The simplest things become so damn complicated in
words. I've got a dozen thoughts boiling away inside
that I want to get out. I don't know where to start.
Will you just let me talk?"

"Sure." Now what's coming? he wondered. He
tensed despite the silky feel of the warm night air.

"Well, it's true. I don't believe you. That was the
automatic response of the gentleman who doesn't want
to hurt the feelings of the woman he's just had. But
you see, Jim, you didn't have me. You didn't have me
because you weren't there. You were off somewhere else,
probably with Top Court or Arc-Horn. You weren't
with me, with you, with us. And neither was I. I
wanted to, but every vibe from you said, 'No, I
won't let go. I won't be exposed and vulnerable. I'll
keep control.' Except at the end where nature took
over. . . . Now don't, for God's sake, say you're sorry
you weren't a good lover for me. I'm talking about
both of us and what I wonder, Jim, is whether any
man or woman, married to the job as we are, can

make love the way I want it. . . . Oh damn. Am I making any sense at all?"

"I'm not on your wave length, Gwen. But I'm trying to understand."

"Then do me a favor." Rays of the frail moon, brushing her softly, seemed in odd contrast to her intensity. "From now on, please don't bullshit me. Don't worry about my feelings. I can take care of them." She laughed. "Just level with me, Jim, please."

"All right." He braced himself. "I guess I was preoccupied tonight. I've got four different things bugging me, two about business and two from the personal bin. I can handle Arc-Horn and Top Court, but personal problems. . . . Well, let me show you something. Come inside a minute."

He found his ruffled gold shirt, fished the caricature out of the pocket, lit a lamp on the dresser and spread out the drawing paper. Gwen stood beside him, their bodies touching lightly.

"Steve drew it just before the fiesta." Jim stared again at the outsized head and the captive heart. "Funny thing. He only met me once before, for a couple of minutes while we were driving up to the hotel. You've known me for six or seven years, and as I get it, Steve said about the same thing you've been trying to tell me."

She glanced again at the drawing, then nestled against him. "Hold me, Jim." He put his arms around her and they embraced while her hair caressed his chest.

When they parted, she shook her head. "It's all so sad. We're so hungry and rapacious, all of us, and yet so vulnerable."

They walked back to their chairs. The air was cooler now. Out on the black rim between ocean and sky, the cluster of lights had moved to the south. A freighter, Jim guessed, heading for the Panama Canal or South America. From a balcony somewhere below came a burst of drunken laughter. One more convention joke had been buried with honors.

"Then there's the thing with Meg," Jim said. "It's so common it's boring to talk about. Still, it bugs me."

"Tell me. Try."

"It's the old story. Meg thinks I'm married first to my job and second to her. It's true. I can't deny it. It's no use reassuring her over and over that I love her, which I do. What she knows is that I'm not home much and, when I am, there's the office briefcase, my 'guilt bag,' she calls it. On weekends I finally get restless and bored, 'the Sunday-evening executive's depression,' as some psychologist termed it."

Jim shifted uneasily in his chair. "Also, frankly, I can't, well, you know, I don't get turned on with her. It's either too late, or I'm tired, or our kids are around, or I'm on the horn for some Top Court emergency. . . . You could multiply us by millions, in corporate families from Berlin to L.A., and you'd have the same story you could print in the women's magazines and Meg would make me read it, and I'd say to myself tough titty, knowing there wasn't much to be done about it."

Jim shrugged and suddenly felt his nakedness. He seldom revealed his inner conflicts, except occasionally at long intervals with Tony. Despite the murmurs of the soothing tropic night, he wished he'd put on his clothes.

"And so ten years from now, instead of the Praeger syndrome," said Gwen tartly, "they'll be calling it the Jim McGowan syndrome."

"That's a hell of a remark."

"But deserved. Sure, you'll be traveling with your masseuse or some chorus girl equivalent." Gwen was biting now. "And the story will be out that McGowan's impotent and another Walter will be throwing it in your face, and physically maybe it'll be true and maybe it won't, but deep down it'll be true because you'll have lost the capacity for the involvement of love—just able to handle the one-night stands."

"Thanks a lot." He could feel himself drawing into a shell. Who needed this?

"I'm sorry, Jim." Quickly contrite, she touched his arm. "That came out of my own frustrations with other ambitious men. I didn't mean to lay that trip on you. I'm surprised to find myself attacking you like this." She gentled her voice. "Actually, we're all in this together, men and women. . . . Give me another chance, huh?"

"Okay." Jim felt the need for movement. "How about a nightcap?"

"Oh, please. You'll find all of Silliman's free booze on the bar. A weak scotch for me. There's bottled water in the fridge."

He returned with two drinks in tall glasses and they sipped in silence for a while, listening to the waves splinter on the beach and then suck back across the sand, drawing strength for the next lunge.

"Advice is worthless," she said, "but it might help if I tell you about me. I said I've changed a lot since last spring. Well, it was already under way by then. Two winters ago, I was on the edge, all ajangle like a lot of bracelets clanging together. Fragrance wasn't my baby as Top Court is with you. I came up through the company and it was already part of Arc-Horn when Hugo picked me to run it, a woman yet—Hugo has a lot of good instincts inside that strange bag of bombast, by the way. I loved the work, the status, the money, the woman president bit, and I got a big thrill out of seeing my ideas and my decisions put Fragrance right up there with Revlon, Estée Lauder and the other biggies."

She paused, frowning. "Let's face it, in cosmetics, the competition is fierce. But I've always been competitive, and running Fragrance gave me a chance to outdo the opposition. So all right, most of the industry is a big con game. Women need all those moisturizers, skin astringents, dusting powders, under-makeup creams, and iced-milk masks like they need three feet. It's a fast put-on, really, and horribly expensive for the women who fall for the whole line. Still, I know the game, I was good at it, I was the boss, my own woman.

I faced the challenge that Hugo gave me and I made it. Shoddy business or not, I was proud of myself. . . . Yet something was missing. The divorce from Stan was three years in the past, Phoebe was in her last year at the George School and I was having a really destructive affair with a young man who wanted a mother, a tart and a psychological nurse all rolled into one. So there I was at forty-two, riding high in business and feeling absolutely shitty."

Gwen tasted the scotch, then lit another cigarette. "About that time a friend, who knew how I felt, told me of a group-therapy thing she was into. She urged me to join up. I resisted at first, but finally went to the once-a-week group, led by a psychiatrist, out of curiosity. Surprise, I liked it! No point going into details but ever so gradually I began to get a fix on myself. I also started smoking marijuana now and then. Both things helped in different ways. Soon I shed the child-lover and told him to find himself someone else to mother him. By last fall, I had myself pretty well together and I began to enjoy life again."

"Sounds good but vague. How did you change?"

"Believe it or not, I found out what I *wanted,* not next week or next year, but right then. And what I truly wanted, I discovered, was just what I had at Fragrance, but less of it. That is, I realized the job owned me instead of the other way around. Anyway, I turned the company over to our executive vice-president, Frank Morrison, for the whole month of December while I went to Morocco. I played, I swam at Agadir, I read a lot and one night, by serendipity, I even came up with a new packaging idea for My Touch. And, of course, the company didn't collapse. Frank and Lucy made a couple of mistakes, but no worse than some I'd made, and on the whole things went as good as ever. This year I'm going off for six weeks while Frank takes over. What I'll want to do two, three years from now, I have no idea. But right now, I've come to terms with Fragrance. I run the company. It doesn't run me."

"Hell, I'm not made that way." The thought of turning over Top Court to Al Bebout for six weeks disturbed him. "The company's in my blood, part of me. It's mine. I built it up from a goddam tennis shack."

"The twins are yours too. And you helped mold them. But do you intend to hang on to them for the rest of your life? Of course not. They are their own persons. Someone said it just right: 'You can't have anything unless you learn to let go of it.'"

"I don't get that."

"It takes some thinking first, and lots of feeling with a good deal of pain. Just remember someday that you heard it the last week before spring on a balcony over a Mexican beach from a woman who is very fond of you."

"That I'll remember." Jim was feeling easier now. The drowsiness had evaporated, the intimate talk no longer alarmed him and Summit's morning show seemed light-years away. He took another tug at his drink.

"So much for Fragrance and me," said Gwen. "But how about the rest of my life? Well, it finally hit me, like a big, solid truth that couldn't be denied, that I wanted to love a man deeply and fully and I wanted to be loved that way. Lots of bed life, sure—I dig that now more than ever—but within a whole aura of loving where each person folds into the other in every kind of way, head stuff and spiritual, the good with the bad, pain and joy, everything, everything." Gwen dipped her glowing cigarette toward the ocean. "Like the sea, sort of, heaving and flowing, taking and giving, making it all one." She paused and smiled. "I don't want much, do I?"

"Do you think you'll ever find it?"

"I think I may. I hope I do. . . . The sad thing is that there are millions of women like me, including Meg. And sadder yet are the millions of men who feel as we do except they don't recognize it, and if they do feel a deep stirring inside, they tramp on it, hard, for fear they know not what."

"The little heart behind the bars?" asked Jim.

"Yes, in cartoon terms. And only you can rip off the bars. Nobody can do it for you." She sipped at her drink again. "Does any of this make sense, Jim? I mean in terms of you?"

"Yes and no." He thought for a moment. "I feel that emptiness sometimes. Earlier tonight, for instance. But I don't see any way out. It's either Top Court all the way, or it's nothing. The kind of love you're talking about takes time, hours and weeks of it, and in today's world a man doesn't have that kind of time. Any total commitment is all-absorbing. Business gets a bad name, but it's no different than art or teaching. To be good at it, you have to work like hell . . . and the rest of life suffers."

"I used to think so too, Jim. Not any longer. Last year I met a couple here in Mexico who teach health care to the Mayan Indians in Yucatán. They're wrapped up in their work, but they have a full, intimate life with each other. What they do enriches what they are as persons and vice versa. Now, much as I'm hooked on my work, I don't kid myself that opening up the Yugoslav market to My Touch is the same thing at all. And I don't think the world would stop revolving if you sold five thousand fewer TeeCee racquets this year."

The mention of TeeCee racquets triggered a thought sequence, the Doylestown plant, Dave Moyer, the new assembly plan. "Business isn't all production and sales," he said. "Listen, we've got something big going at our racquet factory. You want to hear about it?"

"Of course."

He plunged into the story of Moyer's team concept at Doylestown, the new morale and his determination to expand the ideas through all of Top Court. He said industry was in trouble all over and he believed a revolt of the workers might come unless management evolved some plan to give employees more initiative and responsibility. Before he realized it, Jim had talked for almost half an hour.

"I didn't mean to beat your ear so long," he concluded, "but you can understand now. No matter how much flak I get from Hugo, I'm going through with this one."

Gwen's smile was a wry one. "Jim, do you realize that you've been more vibrant and alive in the last thirty minutes than you've been since we met at dinner?"

"Well, as Dave Moyer says, work can be fun for everybody—from the boss down to the sweepers."

"Yes, it can. And I'm all for your new scheme at Doylestown. The reason you've got a happy plant is that people are involved with the whole operation. That's wonderful. And I guess the reason you like it so much is that something beyond profits carries you inside other people, into their pride and hopes. Actually, Jim, you *are* like me. You do want something more than just what the balance sheet tells you. Am I right?"

"Of course I do. I'm human." Their legs were propped on the chair and Jim rubbed his foot against hers. On a balcony below they heard a glass splinter, a curse, then laughter.

"We can't separate work from the rest of living," she mused. "To make life sing, I've found, I've got to get wrapped up in all of it. You too, I'll bet. Not just you and work, but you and Meg, you and your children, you and friends, you and everything."

But now that he was back on the familiar terrain of plants, products and processes, Jim was reluctant to be steered again through psychological shoals.

"Listen, Gwen, let me switch the subject. There's something going on in Arc-Horn that could be bad news for both of us. I heard a story today that floored me." Without mentioning Tony's name and disguising the locale, he told her of the burglary and bribery apparently aimed at blocking an Arc-Horn study in two countries, then of his own call from Russell Kirkland in New York and finally of Pete Quigley's reference to questioning by a Kansas State professor.

"That's a lot more than coincidence," he concluded. "Obviously some kind of major research is being done on Arc-Horn subsidiaries and somebody inside the company is trying to derail it."

"Now I understand." Gwen tapped his arm. "Let me join the club. Somewhat the same thing happened to me."

"What?"

"A young graduate student, a woman, wanted to interview me and other execs about Fragrance production. I checked with Bernie Hirsch's p.r. office to see if it was okay. They asked me to hold up a few days, then somebody called and said to nix it. Damn it, I can't remember who called me back from Arc-Horn, but I don't think it was anybody in p.r."

"When was that?"

"A few weeks ago. Say early February."

"Did you ever hear of something called the Group of Twelve?"

Gwen reflected for a moment. "No. Never heard the term. Why?"

Jim told her what little he knew. "Phil Ireland says the Group of Twelve will report some alarming figures next week to a U.N. human environment conference in Geneva."

"Another round of oil shortages?"

"No." Jim frowned. "If the Group of Twelve represents Ireland's thinking, this is a lot more serious than temporary shortages. Ireland thinks we're nearing the danger point on depletion of many resources and that we have to trim back all production, private, government, military."

"Oh, I've been in that space for a long time." Gwen placed both hands on her head. "I'm always wearing two hats, one for president of Fragrance and one for Gwen Piggott, member of the human race. Neither one fits very well any more." She smiled. "Funny, isn't it? Do you realize that Arc-Horn's emblem represents the earth—and most Arc-Horn people spend all their waking hours drilling, mining and gouging that same earth? Sometimes I think the old planet will just collapse one night."

Jim shook his head. "I don't go that far. But I have been thinking about another paradox. With one ear I'm hearing the good news from the Doylestown plant, where they're all steamed up about involvement with their jobs. Soon, instead of just a few managers trying to step up production, we'll have three hundred people racing around gung-ho to churn out more of everything. . . . And at the same time, with the other ear, I'm hearing Ireland's warnings."

And while an early-morning stillness settled on the Mixteca Hotel and the stars lost their luster, they talked of ambiguities and dwindling certainties. A half hour slipped swiftly away.

"Crazy," said Gwen. "Here we sit, like a couple of naked kids, trying to puzzle it all out. And later this morning, Summit will blast us back into the real world. . . . Real? Uh-uh. I don't buy that any more."

"One thing's real. My friend and I are going to talk to Praeger soon. Whatever's up, we want Arc-Horn to face it openly. How about joining us?"

"Any time, Jim."

"Okay." He felt fatigue welling over him at last. The black sky was fading to gray now and the horizon's dark blur had an edge to it. "It'll be dawn soon. I've got to hit the sack."

After he dressed, he returned and stood for a moment, kneading the back of her shoulders. "It's been quite a night. And who knows? Maybe I've learned something from you."

He looked down on the beach and saw the shape of the hiker's tent growing more distinct against the silent gray reaches of early morning.

"Do you think Steve has it together?" he asked.

"Maybe. A man who's walked the world for seven years should know something of himself. I want to talk to him before we leave. I'm curious about him."

She walked Jim to the door, padding on bare feet, unaware of her nudity beside the fences of his clothing. She raised her face for a parting kiss.

"I hope you find what you want," he said.

"Or learn to want what I find." She smiled. "Despite all my running off at the mouth tonight, I'm not all that sure about what I do want. Maybe I'm ready for a bigger change than I suspected. . . . Good night, Jim. Don't be afraid to look inside yourself. What you'll discover may be beautiful."

He was halfway down the hall to his own suite before he realized the implication of her final lines. He had an impulse to go back and argue. He afraid? But he was tired. Today would be a long day of business —and nonsense—and business.

Monday Morning

A drill bit into Jim's skull, grinding without pain, causing his head to vibrate like a drum. He rolled over sluggishly, failed to shake the assault, came awake gradually and heard the insistent ring of the telephone. He fumbled at the bedside table, scraping his elbow, and uncradled the receiver.

"Jim? . . . Cal Silliman."

"Who?"

"Cal Silliman. You awake now?"

"I guess so. What time is it?"

"Seven-twenty Acapulco time, nine-twenty Praeger time."

Jim winced. He could guess what was coming. Some order from Hugo, who, regardless of the time zone in which he found himself, marked the hours by a watch set in New York. Once in London, Jim recalled, he had been summoned to a 2 a.m. dinner.

"Hugo's called a seven forty-five board meeting with breakfast," Silliman continued. "Arc-Horn conference room, eleventh floor. I'll have coffee at your door in a minute. Sorry, Jim. Orders."

"Where's that again?" His head throbbed.

"Conference room, next to Hugo's suite, floor eleven. Seven forty-five sharp."

Jim swung out of bed, stumbled to the bathroom and turned on the shower. What day was this? Oh yes, Monday. A gush of images, Gwen, Meg, Tony, Hugo, red-haired Gilda, that crazy fiesta. Goddam Hugo and his capricious commands. For all his genius, sometimes the man acted like a two-bit dictator. The first board meeting wasn't scheduled until 5 p.m. Jim let needles of cold water jab at his body, then stepped from the tub and rubbed himself vigorously.

He had pulled on his light-blue cotton trousers and slipped into the beach moccasins when the coffee arrived in the adjacent living room. María, the escorting hostess of yesterday, was wearing the same transparent blue costume. She placed a silver tray on the coffee table and favored him with a somewhat curt *"buenos días."* The fresh jacaranda bloom in her ebony hair failed to soften her guarded stance. She left after declining Jim's proffer of a five-peso note. No tips, señor, she said sternly.

The *Arc-Horn Anniversary Daily,* Cal Silliman's eight-page mimeographed digest of world news and commercial items of interest to Arc-Horn executives, rested on the tray. The New York public relations staff transmitted the news at 2 a.m. each day on the special leased wires connecting New York with its temporary corporate nerve center south of Acapulco. Jim glanced over the bulletins, culled from news tickers, *The Wall Street Journal* and early editions of *The New York Times,* but found nothing to hold him.

Several envelopes were tucked beneath the silver coffeepot. Jim poured coffee, skipped the cream, and sugar, and took a swallow of the steaming liquid, then opened the top envelope, a pale, grainy paper of

the Mexican telegraph system. It was a night letter from
Westhampton, Long Island.

> *Flowers arrived with your sweet card. Please
> thank Hugo for me. Party went well. Love from
> Carol, Connie.*
>
> *Also Meg.*

He frowned. Oh, sure. Every year Hugo sent bou-
quets to the wives of convention-bound Arc-Horn
husbands—in the name of the husbands. The earlier
custom of having wives attend had ended abruptly four
years ago after Mrs. Peter Quigley was discovered nude
on a Montego Bay beach at dawn enmeshed with Sukit
Sukhsvasti, the diminutive president of Thai-Tex. Meg
was not fooled by the card and Hugo's gesture grated
on Jim. Corporate floral tokens were not what was
needed in the McGowan household.

A second night letter from Doylestown, Pennsylvania,
made him feel better.

> *We go to two shifts tomorrow. Spirits high
> thanks to Dave Moyer. Kiss the senoritas for me.
> Good luck.*
>
> *Smitty*

But he felt unsettled again after opening the hotel
envelope. It contained Steve's caricature of him and a
note.

> *Something you forgot. Freudian? I vote with
> Steve. Time to saw those bars away. Love, Gwen.*

He had enough trouble, Jim thought, without amateur
psyching from Gwen. Still, he understood her yearning
and his own deficit in the lover department. But what
he needed wasn't what Gwen needed. And right now,
what he needed was a clear head.

The row of gold shirts hung in the closet like a
parade of de luxe scarecrows. The first hanger bore a

tag, "Monday." Helpful Cal. No executive need burden himself with wardrobe decisions. Jim slipped on the shirt, pinned on his name tag and headed for the elevators.

Gold shirts and blue shirts streamed along the eleventh-floor corridor leading to the Arc-Horn conference room, located on the ocean side just short of Hugo Praeger's luxury suite. Early-morning coughs punctuated the muted drip of conversation. Jim fell into step beside Tony Percevale. "Praeger time," grumbled Tony. "Helluva thing to do."

Banquet tables had been arranged to form a large horseshoe with a bend near open balcony doors through which poured blinding sunlight. The Arc-Horn emblem hung from the center of the horseshoe, Praeger's place. Signs indicated the seats for Arc-Horn executives. To Praeger's right were John Lindquist, executive vice-president, the numbers man, and Nicholas Calabrese, legal vice-president and Italy's renowned expert on international law. To Praeger's left sat Chalmers David-son, vice-president for international operations and communications, and Bernard Hirsch, vice-president for public relations.

Chief executive officers of the nineteen subsidiaries ranged along opposing prongs of the horseshoe, ranked by size of gross revenues. The arrangement permitted Praeger to question his subordinates with the sunlight at his back while they would have to squint into the glare when addressing him. Top Court's seat was third from the end on the right, between Meersdorf Welding ($107,000,000) and Indo Deep Rig ($88,000,000).

Waiters wheeled in room-service carts and distributed breakfast trays at the twenty-four places around the horseshoe. The men of commerce would start their day on orange juice, melon, bacon, eggs benedict and coffee. By 7:44, the waiters had hurried off along with an anxious, hovering Cal Silliman, who closed the hall door and posted two security guards, one outside the room and one at the bend of the corridor.

The generals who awaited the entrance of their field marshal commanded one of the crack mercantile armies

of the world. While Arc-Horn had not realized Hugo
Praeger's dream to duplicate the glories of the Holy
Roman Empire, and while it could not match muscle
with such powers as General Motors or Exxon, it could
and did boast that, like Britain of yore, the sun never
set on its domain. Arc-Horn's annual revenues were
climbing toward $8,000,000,000 and in a recent mixed
list of the gross national products of nation-states and
the revenues of multinational corporations, it ranked
fifty-seventh, behind Colombia, Egypt, Thailand, ITT,
Texaco, Portugal, and New Zealand, but ahead of
Peru, Western Electric, Nigeria, Taiwan, Gulf Oil,
U. S. Steel and Cuba. It labored on all continents,
employed more workers than the combined civil-servant
rolls of Australia, Norway and Spain, could borrow
more money from more banks than either Greece or
the Philippines, quartered offices in forty-seven countries
overseeing 678 profit centers and in any logical world,
in Praeger's opinion, should rate at least a rotating seat
on the United Nations Security Council.

Arc-Horn's board of directors had once had a dash
of outside spicing in the persons of Nick Calabrese,
Italy's legal star, and Chalmers Davidson, a vestryman of
the American establishment, but Praeger swept both
men into the operating fold with huge salaries and visions of world peace through commerce. Now, like the
nations in which it produced and sold, Arc-Horn regarded itself as a sovereign entity.

The board bore the stamp of white masculinity with
three exceptions. Gwen Piggott, the lone woman, wearing a simple cotton dress tie-dyed with a mix of golden
hues, greeted her male colleagues breezily as she skirted
the horseshoe. She waved to Jim and took her place
opposite McGowan and between Jules Amarel of Six
Flags Insurance ($331,000,000) and Antonio Percevale
of Gusto Más, S.A. ($204,000,000).

Of the two dark-complexioned males, Sukit Sukhsvasti,
the five-foot-three former world badminton champion
ran the prosperous Thai-Tex Corp. ($445,000,000), pro-
ducing vivid textile prints in plants scattered about the

world in regions where wage earners had yet to covet the kind of buying power that fetched television sets and indoor plumbing.

Masuo Sugimoto, a sleek commercial politician from Japan and the only officer in the Arc-Horn empire who owned more of the corporate shares than Hugo Praeger, headed the No. 1 subsidiary, mammoth Nakamura, Ltd. ($2,085,000,000), whose computers and calculators now rivaled IBM's in some markets and whose annual take comprised twenty-seven percent of Arc-Horn's total revenues.

Praeger, moving with remarkable swiftness despite his bulk, walked into the room from a side door at precisely 7:45. His twenty-three generals rose in place while the field marshal fitted himself into the wide custom-built oak armchair flown down from New York in the Learjet. Praeger, sporting a fresh gold shirt trimmed in blue, was already perspiring and a moist smile paid a brief visit to his facial mounds and gullies before vanishing as if snatched away by the early-morning breeze. Nowhere in this mountain of industry could be seen the jovial host of the fiesta who had unflinchingly borne a jester's barbs and roistered with his fellow playmates until 1:30 a.m. If Jim McGowan knew Hugo E. Praeger, Jim was sure that Hugo had risen shortly after dawn to pore over corporate figures. The "E." might nominally stand for Edward, but to Arc-Horn insiders, it was an E for energy.

"All right. Our first meeting of the week's in session." The multilingual Praeger spoke in English, the official Arc-Horn language, although native tongues scattered about the table included Italian, Japanese, Thai, French, Spanish, German and Portuguese.

Praeger downed a swallow of orange juice. "If we eat while we talk, we can be out of here by nine forty-five in time for the Summit sales presentation."

The executives fell to with a clinking of silverware and china. Praeger offered no apology for the sudden summons to a meeting not scheduled on the conference program until 5 p.m. and his aides, inured to such whimsies of iron, expected none. He finished his juice, then attacked the eggs benedict while simultaneously riffling through papers in his manila folder.

"There are just fourteen days left in the quarter," he said. "Of course, I'd like to see earnings hit a dollar seventy-nine a share as contrasted with last quarter's dollar seventy-seven." The numbers rolled out of his deep bass like church chimes. He peered at a paper as though to remind himself. "Yes, that's it."

Charles Holloway of Indo Deep Rig whispered to Jim. "The faker. Frankie Fee nailed the figure last night. Hugo's already told the accountants that's the figure he wants."

"One seventy-nine," intoned Praeger once more. He slid his right hand across his great padded chest in that curiously erotic motion that Jim had first seen nine years before in the Pan-Am office building. To few men did mere numbers bring such tactile pleasure. "So let's just go around the table and lay down our first-quarter estimates and see where we stand. . . . Masuo?"

Sugimoto nodded politely and eyed a slip of paper. "I'm missing the sales figures for Taiwan and Belgium, but Nakamura will be up about nine percent over the last quarter. I can say that with confidence, Hugo. That would make our gross earnings about forty-five million—in dollars." In Sugimoto's studied English, the last phrase dipped deprecatingly, implicating the dollar as still suspect in comparison with more robust currencies. John Lindquist punched the number into his new Nakamura pocket calculator.

Hugo nodded. "Right in line with my projection, Masuo. Thank you. No problem, as usual, with Nakamura. . . . Nate?"

Nathan Berger, the living ulcer who presided over Summit, Inc., Arc-Horn's original and second-largest operating company ($1,150,000,000) wielded his knife like a pointer. "We'll turn in just under twenty-nine million profit. That's almost eleven percent over the fall quarter." He blinked rapidly behind his spectacles. "The hi-fi line is very strong. We may be number one in the industry by next winter."

"No-problem Nate, we call him. Right on." As Lindquist stabbed at his calculator again, Praeger washed down the compliment with coffee, then sighed as he turned to his third commercial venture. Sea Routes, Inc. ($725,000,000) was in perennial trouble. Praeger had fired two managers in recent years, but the Liberian-registered freighter and tanker fleet had never once sailed out of the red. After vainly attempting to unload the property, Praeger last fall hired Admiral Joyce Boke-Milgrim, retired logistics chief of the British Navy, prompting *Fortune* to remark that Arc-Horn's board now consisted of "twenty-three millionaires and a sailor."

"What's the bad news, Admiral?"

"We'll be up three percent, but that still means a loss of six million." The admiral, a lean, weathered man with the kind of British accent that dismissed any world tragedy as the predictable result of human frailty, looked not unhappy over his report. "With old bottoms, you know, we pick up the leavings."

"We have a talk on the books?" Praeger asked rhetorically. "Six p.m., what?"

"Six o'clock, Hugo. I've canceled my cocktail date in Acapulco." This time Admiral Boke-Milgrim did appear unhappy.

Good news promptly followed bad. Damon Kimball of Magna Mines Corp. reported he would be up nineteen percent, thanks to a leap in the volatile world price of copper. A foreign academic group had tried to persuade Zambian officials to cut production quotas to conserve copper, but Magna Mines had effectively thwarted the effort.

Healthy increase estimates came from the next four ranking companies, Princess Beverages, the worldwide soft-drink enterprise, Thai-Tex Corp., Six Flags Insurance and Gwen Piggott's Fragrance, Inc.

Tony Percevale was next in line. To colleagues other than his friend Jim, Señor Percevale, when not wearing a conference gold shirt, was a walking Te Deum to the almost religious devotion his London tailor brought to the fashioning of his suits and casual attire. Percevale regularly made the list of the world's ten best-dressed men.

"Gusto Más will be down about ten percent." Percevale shrugged and extended his palms in a gesture of helplessness. "The retail supermarkets are showing a fine profit, with one or two exceptions. The trouble is beef. When the world price falls, what can be done?" After months of soaring meat prices, beef recently had turned downward, to the delight of the world's housewives and the chagrin of ranchers and processors.

"One thing that can be done is get going on that new Rosario slaughterhouse," said Praeger sharply. He drew a sheet of paper from the manila folder and brandished it like a writ of doom. "The old one is the most inefficient lash-up in South America. When will you break ground on the new one?"

Percevale flushed. "I'm not sure. We still face opposition from labor and the union, of course, has its influence with the government." Board members knew that ever since the return of Perón and the new Argentine attitude toward multinational corporations, Gusto Más had skated on fragile ice and that only Percevale's diplomacy had thwarted calamity. "In Rosario, the union and the government are united."

"Goddam it, Tony, I've told you time and again to close out that monstrosity."

"And I've explained the difficulties in detail." Percevale spoke in measured phrases, but the long fingers of his right hand drummed on the breakfast tray. In Argentina no one would dare level such a bald rebuke at a fifth-generation Percevale whose family's private holdings included estancias that covered three hundred square miles of lush pampas.

"It was a tactical error to ever commission that professor's report. It just delayed things and besides his data was faulty."

"In view of the political climate, I thought it only

proper and prudent to order the study," replied Tony.

Praeger turned to Lindquist on his right. "What are the numbers on the Rosario plant, John?"

"We can write it off, build the high-tech operation and recoup the investment in three years." Lindquist's tone was as somber as his visage. "I estimate the obsolescence factor is costing us one point two annually." Unless otherwise stated, Lindquist always spoke in millions.

Praeger swiveled to his left. "Make a note, Chalmers. Tony needs help."

In Arc-Horn custom, whenever Chalmers Davidson, the technician of "operations," made a note, it signified the possible veiled grafting of the budding branches of commerce and statecraft. Few were quite sure precisely what Davidson did, but his duties carried him on constant jet missions to various white, black, brown and yellow foreign and trade ministers on all continents. Only one clue had surfaced from the subterranean hothouses where Davidson nurtured his operational seedlings. Several years ago a trade deputy in Bulgaria, impaled in a Communist purge trial, testified that Chalmers Davidson offered him an Arc-Horn bribe of $100,000 to approve a favorable contract with Meersdorf Welding. Davidson indignantly denied the accusation, the press noted the suspect nature of the deputy's "confession" and history, aside from references in *The New York Times* index, apparently forgot the incident.

Davidson, a suave, well-groomed man in whom affability and restraint mingled in equal measure, carried himself within that aura of mission which enfolds certain statesmen, divines and university presidents. Looking at him, Jim McGowan wondered whether he had a hand in sabotaging the Portilla study in Argentina. Whatever the facts, Jim suspected that Davidson had carried off other assignments of international intrigue with finesse.

Now Davidson made his note with a gold fountain pen while Praeger rattled the paper dappled with Gusto Más statistics.

"It should be noted, Hugo," said Percevale, straining to keep his anger under control, "that regardless of the Rosario situation, the expanding supermarket division will soon have profits on the up curve again."

"But that doesn't make today's numbers any bigger, what?"

"True, but the board is entitled to a glimpse into our future." Percevale was stiff and proper now, an indication of his hidden ire. "For instance, when we open the new supermarket in Acapulco Wednesday night, that will mark our fifth entry into the Mexican retail market. The other four are proving very profitable."

Praeger nodded, then leaned back in his custom-built armchair. "That reminds me of something Tony knows, but I'm not sure the board does." The conglomerator's tone quickly became benignly folksy. "When the American and Mexican presidents met at El Paso in October, their agenda included Gusto Más, thanks to some astute work by Chalmers. An expansion of Gusto Más in Mexico was one of several secret understandings not touched upon in the final communiqué. The Mexican agreed to further expansion provided Gusto Más maintained a minimum of fifty-one percent Mexican equity money in the operations in this country. Then he reportedly wondered aloud why an Argentine headed Gusto Más and got off that old Mexican saying: '*Es buen negocio comprar a un Argentino al precio que vale y venderlo a lo que cree que vale.*'"

Praeger's quotation in fluent Spanish, one of four languages he handled with ease, brought snickers from several men about the horseshoe table. Praeger roared and gestured toward Tony.

"Translation, please," asked Masuo Sugimoto.

Percevale obliged with a tight smile. "'A good business deal is to buy an Argentine for what he's worth and sell him for what he thinks he's worth.' It's true that it's an old Mexican taunt, proving that Mexico's deserved feeling of inferiority toward us dates back many years. . . . Well, I'm honored to be the butt of international humor between two, er, politicians who'd like to sell themselves to each other as statesmen."

"Well said, Tony." Praeger admired the executive who could retort under pressure. "I think our Argentine will prove he's a match for the Mexicans in the retail groceries game. By the way, I want everyone to attend the grand opening of the newest Gusto Más store Wednesday night. It'll be a fine show, what?"

Praeger radiated good will like a kindly grandfather. Then, after another swig of coffee, he turned abruptly stern again. "All right, supermarkets are one thing, but an inexcusable loss on a slaughterhouse operation is another. Anybody got any ideas for Tony on his Rosario plant?" He swept his glance around the table.

No one replied. After upbraiding an erring executive before his peers, Hugo invariably besought aid for the victim in saccharine tones. Praeger had no truck with B. F. Skinner, the behaviorist who favored the carrot over the stick as the tool for producing meritorious acts by rabbits and human beings.

"All right, then." Praeger, allotting a bare ten seconds for his general staff to proffer wise counsel, glared at Percevale. "I want action on that fuckin' Rosario plant, Tony. I want ground broken on the new project within ninety days." He buried the Gusto Más paper and scooped up another one. "Next we have Deutsche-Mannheim. . . . Helmut?"

Helmut von Weise estimated the West German drug company would show advances of seven percent. He thus put himself above the "five percent increase" danger line. Similar safety-zone improvements were estimated by the next two ranking subsidiaries, Biggers & Sons, sugar, and Hi-Western Corp., lumber. Paul Chesterfield, Hi-Western's chief executive officer, noted, however, that the size of future profits would depend on the outcome of the new venture projected "on the agenda of our final board meeting here Thursday."

"Yes," said Hugo. "I'll refer to that a little later when we get to Uni-Land. . . . Okay, next is United."

United African Motors, producer of rugged vehicles

for the dark continent's terrain, estimated a profits increase above the safety barrier, as did Eurofact, Ltd., a factoring concern for Europe's common market enterprises, and Meersdorf Welding.

"That brings up Top Court," said Praeger. "What's the good word, Jim?"

McGowan had been dreading the moment. He had suffered with Percevale and had slowly tensed as the generals who followed him dropped one pleasing figure after another.

"We'll be up three percent," he said. It was the first time in thirty-four consecutive quarters that he had fallen below the hazard line.

"You've got to be kidding." Praeger, in the midst of drinking more coffee, brought the cup down with a clatter. He stared at Jim in disbelief.

"I wish I were, Hugo." Jim's fingers tightened on the armrests of his chair. "This is a spot situation only. Barring natural disasters, we'll be flying again next month."

"Now just a goddam minute here. You mean to tell me that with the tennis industry booming and everybody and his sister playing that stupid game, all Top Court can manage is a stinking three percent? That's incredible, what?"

Praeger's eyes roved the room as if soliciting affirmation for his incredulity. The glare through the balcony door forced Jim to blink as he faced the Arc-Horn chief. John Lindquist leaned over and whispered to Praeger.

"Yes. John reminds me that some of the sports goods analysts are predicting that tennis lines will jump fifteen to twenty percent this spring. What the hell is going on at Top Court?"

"If you'll look at your sheet," said Jim, "I'm sure you'll see that the wildcat strike in the tenniswear division hurt us badly." The unfairness of Hugo's attack galled him. Sea Routes' whopping loss of six million evoked only a summons to conference. Top Court, with probable earnings of more than two million for the quarter, rated a tirade because the sum wasn't larger.

Then he realized once more that Praeger could take almost anything from a subordinate except surprise.

Hugo's glance whipped up and down the sheet of type-written figures. Had he missed the culprit Doylestown numbers in his advance scrutiny? Jim wondered.

"Ha!" Hugo's forefinger stabbed the paper. "That's not the whole answer," he said with quick ferocity. "The Doylestown racquet plant is off."

"Do you want a full explanation of that?" Jim was seething now. It was one thing to watch others being grilled and quite another to become the target of Praeger's inquisition in front of the Arc-Horn hierarchy.

"You're goddam right I do. Wilson's way up. Head's way up. Spalding's way up." Praeger flung his huge arms aloft. "General Tire's tennis line is way up. Even Yoneyama Racket is hitting new highs and here we have Top Court, a leader of the industry, falling on its face."

At another time Jim might have admired Praeger's machine-gun enumeration of the competition, but today the feat impressed him less for Hugo's knowledge of the business than for his showmanship.

"I'll need some time."

"Take five minutes. Anything more amounts to a filibuster."

"Well, we tried an experiment at Doylestown that I'm convinced will pay off big in the future." Jim described, as briefly as he could, his deal with Dave Moyer and the changes that Moyer had made in plant operations and employee relations. As he talked, he realized that Hugo's attack had forced him into a more optimistic defense than he would have mounted in any ordinary discussion of the project. Well, he'd make Moyer earn the praise. Jim noted that Smitty, the tough production man, was at first reluctant to let Moyer in the plant, but now hated to see him leave. "Smitty wired me last night that the plant is going to two shifts today," Jim concluded.

Praeger glared at McGowan in silence for a moment,

then asked sarcastically of the room at large: "Anybody ever hear of a psychological grand master named Moyer?"

"Yes," said Masuo Sugimoto. "I understand he did a good job at TRW."

The prompt answer of the Nakamura chief, delivered in matter-of-fact textbook English, surprised Jim and astonished Praeger.

"I don't know about TRW," Praeger growled. "That's a whole different operation from Top Court."

"But," insisted Sugimoto, "there are similar employee involvement plans under way in a number of American companies—Monsanto, Texas Instruments, Procter & Gamble, Eaton, McCormick. Spalding has a golf-club factory in Arkansas where they've made a success of a plan like McGowan's. Employees in America and Europe are restless with routine bit jobs, as experts like Herzberg and Drucker keep reiterating. In Sweden some of the largest companies are giving employees wider and wider latitude. In Japan, it is still enough to work for the nation—but who knows of the future?"

"I appreciate that rundown from our leading mercantile scholar." Praeger bowed without irony toward Sugimoto, his occasional chess foe and Arc-Horn's chief foreign shareholder. "Someday perhaps we could entertain a full board discussion of the subject. But right now we're dealing with a curious phenomenon. Subsequent to the ministrations of a certain Mr. Moyer, production fell off at Doylestown despite an industry boom. Whatever the employees may think of his bottle-feeding, it doesn't come down to the bottom line." He surveyed the room. "Any other comments?"

"Yes," said Jim. By God, he wasn't going to take this. "Hugo, I don't like your—well, violent overreaction, let's call it. We've been pouring steadily rising profits into Arc-Horn for nine years. The Doylestown changeover is just as sound an investment as buying the latest machinery and it's going to pay off. I guarantee that."

"Objection noted," said Praeger. "Any other views on

our friend's social experiment at a time when tennis has become a glamor buy for funds from Tokyo to Berlin?"

Gwen Piggott broke the small silence. "I have one, Hugo. I don't care for your last crack and I don't think Jim McGowan deserves this kind of treatment. He has as much regard for profit as you do and he's proved it over the years. If he says the project will pay off, he ought to be given at least another quarter to make good on the promise."

Jim flashed a look of thanks to Gwen across the table. Her unexpected intervention, coupled with Sugimoto's surprise endorsement of Moyer and his ideas, marked a sharp break in Arc-Horn liturgy, somewhat as if a few bars of a jazz mass suddenly intruded on ancient Gregorian chants in St. Peter's.

"I agree," said Tony Percevale. "I think it's unfair to Jim. Give the man a chance. He knows more about the tennis business than anyone in the industry."

There was an uneasy stirring around the big horse-shoe table. Not within memory had a group of executives challenged the prince of conglomerators in such personal terms. Open, even strident, disagreement had flared sporadically at board meetings, but always over tactics, never over Hugo's personal style. John Lindquist and other Arc-Horn vice-presidents looked perplexed. Percevale's defense of his old college friend, they could understand, but why had the buoyant Ms. Piggott suddenly accused the notoriously bad-mannered Praeger of bad manners?

Praeger himself was taken back. He stared first at Tony and Gwen, then at Jim. But if the marshal suspected a secret alliance among his generals, he did not reveal it.

"There are no sacred cows—or bulls—here, Gwen and Tony," he said with exaggerated care. "Personally, I love everybody, including Mr. McGowan and Señor Percevale, but we're here for business, not to stroke one another." He paused, eyed his aides in the manner of a commander about to favor them with a light remark. "Nor do I think Mr. McGowan deserves special consideration because of his personal popularity with the sporting public or his friendship with such notables as Senator Ireland." He paused again before asking: "Jim, how long is your Mr. Moyer under contract to Top Court?"

"No set date," Jim replied, "but I imagine he'll phase out of Doylestown sometime this summer."

"Any other commitments?"

The man's a mind reader, thought Jim. "Well, I haven't mentioned it to Moyer yet, but Doylestown has gone so well, I intend to hire him to repeat at the Illinois ball plant. And if that's a success . . ."

"Let's leave the future to the future," Praeger cut in. "I want Moyer terminated at the end of this week."

"Christ, Hugo, that'll disrupt the plant."

"If these figures mean anything, that plant is already disrupted. If your Moyer is such a howling success, we'll read it in the numbers at the end of the second quarter. Time enough in July to decide the next step."

"I'm to tell Moyer he's through after this week?"

"Right."

"That's a big mistake, Hugo.

"It won't be my last one. When they write the history of Arc-Horn, they'll say our key to victory was the fact that we were only wrong thirty-five percent of the time." Praeger yielded a brief smile. "Okay, time's awasting. Let's move on. . . . Charley?"

While Charles Holloway took his turn for Indo Deep Rig, the company that leased its drilling gear and expertise to oil companies searching for fuel beneath the waters around Indonesia, Jim McGowan stewed in anger. Here was Top Court, representing less than one and a half percent of total Arc-Horn revenues, being treated as a big gun like Nakamura or Summit. And the racquet plant produced only about a fifth of Top Court's income. He had to concede that this was but Praeger's third interference in Top Court's business in nine years, but what an intrusion. Ordering him to fire a tested consultant on the brink of success. And Praeger's method left a bitter taste. Jim's first experience at being humiliated in open council brought Hugo's highhandedness into personal focus. He thought of just how he'd tell Dave and Smitty, imagined their disappointment and already anticipated his own feeling of frustration. Hugo's lavish salaries, stock options, expense accounts and perquisites carried their own shackles.

Holloway, after estimating that Indo Deep Rig would be up six percent for the quarter, was expatiating on the company's rosy future.

"Fine, fine." Hugo had less interest in hopes than in concrete numbers. "So that brings us down to Uni-Land, our final report. Take over, Paulo."

Praeger glowed with satisfaction as he waved theatrically toward Paulo Hochschild, the slim, supercharged Brazilian who presided over Uni-Land Corp. For years Uni-Land had been quietly buying up patches of earth in remote corners of the globe. The unheralded purchases, often through cloaked intermediaries, began shortly after the advent of the jet airliner. Hochschild, who envisioned a world real estate boom once the jet traveler spied the pristine beauty of faraway beaches, isles and bluffs, tried to sell his dream to a number of unimaginative investors before coming to Praeger, who took less than a week to come to an understanding with the Brazilian dreamer. The company started with $50,000 from Hochschild and $5,000,000 from Arc-Horn. Hochschild's acquisitions over the years from Sardinia to the Society Islands centered on unspoiled coastlines in warm climates, but he also bought large tracts in such inhospitable areas as Australia's interior, the Amazon Basin and the African jungle. Few acres ever went up for resale and Arc-Horn's total investment reached $80,000,000.

Every year Uni-Land showed an operating loss. When some Arc-Horn executives grumbled at the continued red ink, Praeger would say, "Wait until we start cashing in during the mid-seventies." Now the mid-seventies, brimming with investors who wanted land as a haven from the ravages of worldwide inflation, had arrived. Last year Uni-Land showed its first modest earnings of $750,000, but only the most astute of security analysts picked up the scent of Hochschild's spoor in the wilderness of Arc-Horn's annual report.

"I think you'll all be interested in this," said Praeger as he gestured down toward Hochschild, who sat at the very end, the last nail in the horseshoe.

Paulo Hochschild leaned forward as though mothering an unseen microphone. "Uni-Land will report earnings up more than six hundred percent over the last quarter," he said proudly. "We'll turn in $1,225,000. And that is only the beginning. At a rough guess, I'd say we may hit ten million this year on land that cost us an average of about fifteen percent of that amount."

Jules Amarel did an unusual thing. The Six Flags president began to applaud and soon the whole Arc-Horn board joined in. Not since the ouster of Pete Quigley from the helm of Meersdorf Welding had the generals been so united in their approbation of a single event.

"I don't have to remind you that all figures stay inside this room," said Praeger. "The quarterly report will be made public Monday, April twenty-first. I think we'll see some action then."

The tip was welcome if gratuitous. No one needed to be told that if he were in a mood to buy Arc-Horn stock, now was the time. Regardless of the Security and Exchange Commission's strictures on use of insider information, no one could be blamed for exercising prudent judgment as to his company's prospects. And besides, in addition to its listing on the New York Stock Exchange, Arc-Horn was traded in a dozen markets around the world where wives, children, cousins and nieces could buy with scant visibility. Ah, it was a world of ever-unfolding wonders.

"You'll note on your agenda for the four p.m. Thursday meeting that Uni-Land figures in a new venture with three other subsidiaries," said Praeger. "Good years ahead for Uni-Land."

"Just what is that Resolution Eight?" asked Percevale. "I see that Gusto Más is involved, as you mentioned to me, but I'm not clued in."

Praeger smiled. "Let's leave a few surprises for Thursday. Items Eight and Nine, Projects Green Tree and Neptune West, will take financing, but the outlook, I can tell you, is very big. . . . Okay, meeting adjourned. You've got fifteen minutes before the Summit show blasts off in Maya Hall."

As the golden shirts spilled into the corridor, joshing and jostling, McGowan was pressed against Masuo Sugimoto. "Thanks for the assist, Masuo," he said. "I didn't realize you were such a student of these employee experiments."

"I listen and read the literature," said Sugimoto. "What surprises me is that Hugo is so backward in the field. We'll have to teach him." He moved off down the hall.

Gwen slipped to Jim's side. "Nice going. You stood up to Hugo and dished it back."

"And lost. . . . But thanks for the help, Gwen."

"Any time. You haven't lost yet. Hit him again in June."

"Got a seat partner for the Summit show?"

"I have now," she said. "We rebels got to stick together."

"Can we make it a threesome?" It was Tony Percevale, elegant this morning in tan slacks that proved a match for his presidential shirt.

"Sure thing," said Jim.

"Welcome to the club," said Gwen.

The men each hooked an arm of Gwen Piggott as they swung off down the hall. And while an ideologue of the third world or a disciple of Fidel Castro's 26th of July movement might have derided the trio as hierarchical slaves of monopoly capitalism, the three presidents walked with the light-footed tread of insurgents. Jim felt better.

As they disappeared around the corner, the impassive blue-shirted security guard who had overheard their conversation near the conference door took out a pad from his pocket and jotted down some notes.

Monday, 10 a.m.

The power and glory of the Arc-Horn empire filled the hotel lobby and corridors. Hundreds of men in fresh red, gold and blue manta cloth shirts milled toward Maya Hall, the big conference auditorium, focal point of a hotel that lived or died by the number of conventions it attracted. From a distance the blend of voices sounded like the roar of a waterfall. Nearer at hand could be heard snatches of conversation and hearty swapping of first names advertised in billboard print on the chest badges. Executives, managers and miscellaneous officers queued up outside the hall, waiting to be checked off at a blue-and-red booth manned by Cal Silliman, at once agitated and apologetic, and an assistant. The line moved forward slowly.

Jim, ahead of Gwen and Tony, found himself waiting behind Damon Kimball, the stocky, brush-haired, truculent president of Magna Mines.

"I heard you mention some foreign academic group operating in Zambia," said Jim. "What's that all about?"

"Oh, the usual ecology crap. Some nuts from the Group of Twelve tried to frighten the cabinet. Said Zambia would run out of minerals soon if production quotas weren't cut." Kimball had a way of talking over a man's shoulder as if addressing an invisible but eager audience. "We fixed their wagon. Hell, there's plenty of copper for a couple of generations—not counting probable discoveries still to be made."

"I've heard of the Group of Twelve. Just what is it?"

"Bunch of professors who throw a lot of scare figures around and try to prove the world's running out of resources. They call it the Group of Twelve, as I get it, because they have fellows in twelve countries cooperating. Christ, they ought to be shut down. Shows you what kind of things we pay taxes for—to support university faculties who figure out how to ruin our business."

"Damon, what are those Green Tree and Neptune West projects on the board agenda for Thursday? I notice Magna Mines is involved in both of them."

Kimball put a finger to his lips. "Hush-hush stuff until Thursday. Hell, I wouldn't mind telling you, Jim, but Hugo told me to lay off the talk until then. But it's goddam big for Arc-Horn, believe me. . . . Sorry you got that rough going over from Hugo. You didn't deserve it. . . . These goddam lines. Helluva way to treat the hired help, if you ask me."

The moving line at last brought Kimball, then Jim, abreast of the booth. Jim handed over his blue ticket. "James McGowan," said Silliman to the assistant hunched over a tally sheet. The man made a check with a red pencil.

"Cheer up," said Jim to the worried Silliman. "It's not all that bad."

"You just don't know, Jim." Silliman appeared appreciative of the concern. "Details, details. But wait until Thursday night! I'm going to spring a surprise at that final banquet that'll make Arc-Horn history."

"Give me a hint."

"Nope." Silliman shook his head. "But if I can pull it off, it'll be the biggest coup of my career."

"Good luck, Cal."

Jim, Gwen and Tony found three center seats a few rows back from the stage. An overhead banner—"Summit's Glorious Scene and Sound of Seventy-Six"—indicated that Summit's new TV and radio lines would anticipate the next calendar year by a full nine months. White stars, bearing the message "Summit '76," glimmered from the folds of a red-white-and-blue stage curtain. Jake Apple, his head straddled by earphones, trailed a wire through his band as the musicians, dazzling in star-spangled jackets, tuned their instruments. The hall filled with expectant, discordant noises that once again merged into that roar of tumbling water.

More than five hundred missionaries of the merchant Gospel according to Adam Smith, Jubilee Jim Fisk, J. P. Morgan, Henry Ford and Hugo Praeger awaited the latest wares incubated by the doctrine of free enterprise as refined by such government-hallowed blessings as subsidy, tax charity and monopoly.

The foremost missionary of modern commerce, escorted by John Lindquist and Chalmers Davidson, swung into the hall at one minute to ten. Praeger took his accustomed place in the rear row and waved his handkerchief in the traditional signal to Jack Apple. The show was on.

A decorous sound, less a fanfare than a solemn bleat, issued from the orchestra, a spotlight laved the left of the stage and the Reverend Dr. Blair Payne Trowbridge, who, according to the program, was an Episcopalian divine servicing the spiritual needs of the American colony in Cuernavaca, stepped to a lectern. "Let us bow our heads," he intoned. He was a young man with a shiny nose and wavy blond hair that lapped at his clerical collar.

He solicited forbearance and initiative—two qualities that many in his audience seldom found compatible—in the unknown years ahead. He asked forgiveness for any inadvertent peccadilloes that might be charged to those who plowed the broad furrows of business, besought the Almighty's benediction for Arc-Horn's longing to nourish the world and prayed that peace and profits might attend the fulfillment of corporate visions. All in all, thought many in the audience, a celestial plus for

Arc-Horn in these days marred by the scoldings of religious activists. Dr. Trowbridge exited by a side door, leaving the auditorium in the embrace of the Arc-Horn missionaries.

Trumpets blared. The curtain rolled back and a film projector threw a realistic battle scene onto a huge screen. British redcoats exchanged musket fire with a ragged band of New England farmers, apparently on the sod at Concord. Actors played their warlike parts with relish, blasting away at one another and falling to the ground with stricken expressions. A voice boomed from the amplifiers: "Then: the shot heard round the world. And now, Summit: the sound heard round the world." The movie screen vanished upward, Apple's band bustled into an original martial tune and on stage marched Gilda, ablaze in an Uncle Sam costume that fitted her as snugly as a peach skin. She doffed her red-white-and-blue top hat, shook out her hair and began to sing. Behind her danced the chorus of eight girls, bare except for blue bras and red-and-white G strings.

> As they fought and won our liberty,
> So Summit earns integrity.
> The picture's bright, the sound is right,
> And one year runs the warranty.
> A triumph new, a magic mix,
> The Summit scene of seventy-six.
> From Concord and from Lexington
> Freedom called George Washington.
> So Summit's hues, reds, whites and blues,
> Will conquer markets every one.
> A triumph new, a magic mix,
> The Summit sound of seventy-six.

Gilda belted out three more verses that settled all historical doubts about the nature of the visions that inflamed the rebels who bled and died at Valley Forge and Yorktown. They fought not alone to free the colonies of British rule, but to realize the distant dream of a

Summit panchromatic, instant-audio, auxiliary video cassette, remote-control television set in every home of the brave.

Gwen Piggott, who sat between Jim and Tony, matched Gilda's final peal with a small groan. "If it weren't for that proud look on Jake Apple's face, I'd swear Hugo wrote that blasphemy himself."

Tony, whose own national lore evoked the ghosts of the 1812 liberators and Martín Fierro, the legendary gaucho folk hero, looked puzzled. "I've forgotten. Who," he asked, "was Betsy Ross?"

"The first of the sweatshop seamstresses," Gwen said.

"Come on, Gwen," Jim protested. "The man wants information."

"Can't wade to it right now. It's getting hip deep in here."

Another musical blast sounded as Gilda and her girls fled the stage. The spotlight swung to the left to reveal Nathan Berger, Summit's ulcerous president, standing at the lectern with a black loose-leaf notebook. The mercantile wars had ravaged Nate, leaving him with feverish eyes, sunken cheeks and a shoulder that twitched whenever ominous bulletins arrived from the field of battle.

"Hugo, brothers and sisters of the Arc-Horn family. Except for my brief explanation at this moment, the show you are seeing is identical with the one that will be presented to three thousand Summit distributors next month at McCormick Place in Chicago." Berger gulped from a water glass like a man who has just staggered in from the desert. "We have tied our new line to the patriotic motif of America's bicentennial celebration next year. Although our distributors come from many lands, we make no apology for the tie-in. We are proud of the United States, soon to be in its two-hundredth year, and we're proud of Summit in this its thirty-fifth year. And so, take it away, Jake Apple."

The band sounded the opening bars of "Yankee Doodle" and the spotlight went out, only to flash on again almost immediately, framing Nate Berger at the same lectern in the same posture of devastation.

"Good morning, all you Summit distributors! Today we at Summit bring you the most beautifully styled, the most carefully engineered new line it has ever been our privilege to unveil. Two hundred years ago, so Emerson tells us, our embattled farmers fired the shot heard round the world. And this year, from the magnificent new color television sets of Summit will come the scene and sound to be heard round the world. In a few minutes, we will give you each and every unit of this complete new line in all its elegance, but first just a brief word as to where Summit stands in the worldwide color television industry."

Berger pressed a button of Summit's new $50,000 dual-control, five-color, instantly positioned, automatic-feedback S-100 audio-visual system and the large screen dropped noiselessly from the stage ceiling. Red figures on a light-blue background proclaimed that Summit led such competitors as Admiral, Sony, RCA, Zenith and Motorola in the dramatic race to station one or more color symbols of the electronic age in every mansion and hovel from Kankakee to Karachi. "Atta boy, Nate," yelled Hugo Praeger. He beat his palms together to spark the applause.

Berger responded with a stricken smile. Click. Now yellow on black heralded Summit's leadership in penetration of the world's one hundred prime urban markets. Click again. Summit led the hordes in a yellow-on-red invasion of the underdeveloped countries. Click. As for the purely rural areas of the developed, or perhaps surfeited, nations, Summit fought a thrilling neck-and-neck race with GE, Sylvania, Magnavox, Motorola and Zenith. Viewers might think this forecast a photo finish in the country precincts, but no. Click. The ten-year, black-on-green historical perspective disclosed that Summit, far back a decade ago, had closed in the stretch. The implication of this dip into the thoroughbred annals of color TV was clear: Summit would wear the garland in the winner's circle.

"I could fix Nate another slide," said Gwen, "showing that Summit, in its brief lifetime, has chewed up more of the earth's insides than the ancient Greeks, the Incas, the Egyptian pharaohs and the Ming dynasty put together."

But Berger's thoughts were far from the ecological verities. "And now, before we introduce the most seductive new line ever to come off the Summit drafting boards, I want to present the famous two-man design-engineering team that made it possible. I give you those greats of Summit design, Ted Kramer and Alex Rosinski!"

The spotlight plunged to the front row center and a red-shirted figure, his black hair bobbed like Prince Valiant, bowed to the audience. In Arc-Horn's unwritten tonsorial code, hair dripping below the ears might be worn by artists, designers and inventors, never by salesmen, managers or executives. The spotlight wavered and probed, futilely seeking the second great man of design.

Cal Silliman hurried up the side steps of the stage and whispered to Berger, promptly contaminating the Summit chief with new anxiety. Gossip flew along the rows. Percevale cocked his head toward the man beside him, then relayed the rumor to Gwen and Jim. "They say he went into Acapulco with one of the Miami chicks after the fiesta last night and hasn't been seen since."

"I understand," announced Berger, a sculpture of pain, "that Alex Rosinski is unavoidably ill this morning."

Gwen leaned toward Jim. "As contrasted with Summit's regular line of avoidable ailments, I suppose."

"And now," cried Berger, "that glorious new scene and sound of Summit in seventy-six!"

Jake Apple waved his musicians into a slow, sensual melody and the patriotic curtains parted to reveal a luxurious bedroom scene of vivid greens. Muted lights played on jungled wallpaper, a king-sized bed with aquamarine headboard and matching bedside table. The coverlet evoked memories of rain forests. At the foot of the bed stood a handsome television set housed in a cabinet the color of jade.

In the bed lay Gilda, her flaming hair strewn over a bright green pillow. The music modulated to a whisper. She roused herself gradually, as if coming awake, sat up and stretched her arms, thus exposing an abundant bare bosom. She rubbed her eyes, yawned and reached to the bedside table, her arm as sinuous as a serpent. She pressed a button on the remote-control box and a picture quickly formed on the set at the foot of the bed. A lone horseman rode on a hilltop while a golden sun sank toward a distant horizon. "Oh!" Gilda's squeal was one of girlish delight. With a coy glance at the audience, she pulled the coverlet up over her breasts and leaned forward to absorb the miracle of Summit's panchromatic, instant-audio television.

Gilda and the bed slowly disappeared on the revolving stage while another rotating mechanism brought the jade TV set front and center. A burst of applause ended in one of those strange but not infrequent instants of complete silence when nobody coughed, sneezed or grunted.

Into the void from backstage came Gilda's husky voice: "Well, I'm finished with that male pig shit for another hour."

Jake Apple, a man of lightning reaction, produced a fanfare so quickly it seemed full-blown before Gilda's last word died amidst the scenery. Almost as quickly, Walter Lowdermilk, holding a hand mike at the end of a coiling wire, strode across stage to the television set.

"Good morning. . . . This is show-and-tell hour. Gilda did the showing and I'll do the telling." Lowdermilk, the salesmen's salesman, carried a collapsible pointer which, by the flick of an unseen button, he extended into a glistening aluminum rod with phosphorescent tip. He stood contemplating the television set with the mingled awe and lassitude of one who gazes upon the wonders of the Grand Canyon or the Taj Mahal after a night of revelry. "Ladies and gentlemen, last year at this time, when we revealed Summit's T-1001, we let your eyes feast upon a masterpiece. So naturally, this morning the question arises, how do you improve upon a masterpiece? Who can better the sheer perfection of a Michelangelo, a Dante or a Beethoven? Well, believe it or not, there is one place in the world where the miracle is wrought and that place is the workshop of Summit, Inc. Our master designers labored for a solid year on the seemingly impossible task of fashioning a product that would surmount perfection itself."

Lowdermilk walked to the set, placed one hand on the cabinet and stood for a moment of proud, if hung-over consecration. When he spoke, his voice had dropped an octave. "Here is the result, ladies and gentlemen, the finest, most gracious and subtle piece of workmanship in the entire color television industry—Summit's set for all seasons, the revolutionary T-1002. I use that word 'revolutionary' advisedly, for next year is the year of Washington, of Adams, of Patrick Henry, of Jefferson and Hamilton. Here, in the painstaking, inspired craftsmanship of the T-1002, is the proud successor to those noble spirits who founded a new nation. Revolutionary? Of course it is. Look at the color of that cabinet, an exquisite, subdued wonder. Pale green, you say? Ah, no. That is the color of jade, the stone prized by the ancients of the Orient as the most precious of all gems. Who but Summit would have dared to march out on that harshly competitive retail floor with a television cabinet reeking of jade?"

Having successfully linked the T-1002 to the Renaissance, the American Revolution, Oriental antiquity and the jade mines of the world, proving that benefits of a liberal arts education had not been wasted on an old Ohio State fullback, Lowdermilk raised his voice to normal power. "That cabinet is pure, unadulterated, one hundred percent Early American, and I don't need to remind you that this year your Early American will be the hottest item in the furniture game, and, gentlemen, let's not kid ourselves, we're selling furniture as well as televised images.

"All right, let's get down to sex and price because

that's where the action is out on those retail show-room floors. Okay, you take your T-1002 and you compare it sex-wise with the competition. Look at it. That sensuous styling, that finish that brings desire to the touch." Walter slid a loving hand across the cabinet, caressing the corners. "That smoothness, that sense of ripe indulgence, that thrill of seeing it stand there in all its natural, unspoiled splendor. My God, men and women, this is a product you can make love to!"

Gwen leaned against Jim. "With the T-1002, who needs Masters and Johnson?"

Walter suddenly tensed. He thrust his phosphorescent-tipped pointer at the audience. "But now we come to the gut question. How much will this Early American jade beauty sell for? Well, we've made some discreet inquiries, men, and we can tell you that the main rivals in this world leadership model will probably be Sony, Motorola and Zenith. The Sony leader, we're reliably informed, will be priced at $599.95, the Motorola at $598.90 and the Zenith at $596.85. Now I want some suggestions out there on what the Summit T-1002, the super-masterpiece of the line, will go for? All right, let's hear some numbers!"

"Five ninety-five," shouted a voice from right center, where executives and top salesmen of Summit were bunched.

"Wrong!"

"Five ninety-two." The Summit claque was well primed.

"Wrong again." Walter shook his head. "What I'm about to reveal now, I can hardly believe myself. Friends, despite a world hunger for the product, despite rising wages, despite the roars of inflation and in the teeth of advice from some of the top economic brains in the United States, the T-1002 will go out on that display-room floor with a suggested retail price of only $589.95!"

A roar of wonder leaped from the Summit crowd. Hugo Praeger led a round of hand clapping. Before the applause could prove itself short-lived, Walter nailed his truth to the ramparts. "Yes sir, an incredible $589.95. And who says that's not revolutionary?"

Walter strode to the wings, the music crashed into fast rock, the revolving stage whirred, the jade TV set vanished and in its place came another bedroom suite, this one with striped black-and-white wallpaper and a bedspread that resembled a zebra hide covering the king-sized bed.

Three people reclined against the headboard, two of the chorus girls in loosely tied white terry-cloth bathrobes and a bare-chested man who turned out to be a saxophone player from Jake Apple's band. He had an arm slung over the shoulders of each girl and all three inhabitants of the bed gazed fixedly at a creamy television set of supple modern lines. The screen showed the same horseman silhouetted against a dying sun. The trio nuzzled one another and stared at the set for almost a full minute before being swung from view by master controls of the stage machinery.

"So for singles who know where it's at," cried Walter, again commanding the stage, "Summit's swinging singles model, the understated, chic, with-it T-902. Another masterpiece of design, another bicentennial revolution." He advised the unseen Summit distributors that the T-902 would "hit the buyer's hot buds" at the amazingly low price of . . . ? The Summit claque guessed $350, then $335, finally $330. Walter, ever loath to yield his secret, finally uncorked the "revolutionary, bargain-basement retail price of only $328.95."

For ninety minutes, while the revolving stage spilled its cornucopias of boudoirs, interspersed with an occasional patio or game room, Walter strutted as the virtuoso of sales. Summit, he counseled, had answered distributor "demands to build a little more profit into the system" and had risen supreme on the peaks of "hot pricing."

And each and every model, Walter advised in his peroration, came equipped with a device for plugging in the most colossal advance in the history of mankind since the invention of holidays—the V-50 ultrasonic, super-fidelity video cassette player. This marvel, which would retail at only $489.50, would project onto the television screen old films, old football games, favorite commercials, home movies "or the kind of erotic dramas you'll hunger to see after the kiddies are all safely tucked away in bed and the Supreme Court's on vacation." The V-50 video cassette auxiliary unit would vie with such rivals as Sony's video player and MCA's laser-beam Disco-Vision and while no man could foretell the outcome of the looming titanic struggle for the "video library" market, Lowdermilk would bet a year's salary that this fall Summit's entry "will ring the cash registers like early jingle bells." So saying, he slipped a cassette into the unit, flicked a switch and on the screen of the T-902 "swinging singles" set flashed a shot of Gilda, tossing her cardinal mane and grinding her hips at Sunday night's early-bird fiesta. Arc-Horn's merchant missionaries responded with cheers and whistles.

"Talk about your seventy-six revolutions," shouted Walter. "Summit's in the business of revolution."

But long before Summit's patriotic rebel harvest had been reaped and stored away for the Chicago show, Jim, Gwen and Tony had wearied of Walter and his wares. In Jim's mind, cabinets, consoles and portable models blurred into a single TV screen where Gilda danced and a lone cowboy gazed vacantly at a lifeless sun that never set.

"I wish Hugo wouldn't inflict this juvenile crap on us," said Gwen.

"He came up through sales," said Jim. "He loves the corn."

"Sure he does," said Tony, "but that's no reason to make the rest of us suffer."

"Tomorrow I'm going to boycott the sales show," said Gwen, "even if the great man raises hell with me."

"Great man?" Jim let the question float.

"On and off," said Tony.

And in low tones they discussed the virtues of a leader whose faults and eccentricities provided corporate gossip from Rome to Tokyo. Hugo could be generous, said Gwen, in times of one's illness or personal tragedy. Tony thought Praeger often showed rare skill in financing Arc-Horn ventures, that he had a keen eye for the future. Jim recalled the clarity of Hugo's vision nine years before when he forecast that tennis and Top Court would become commercial high flyers.

"And I believe that he's at least partially sincere," said Jim, "when he makes his grand speeches about multinationals paving the way to world peace. But his blind spots are awful. One is the precarious situation right now with Sea Routes. If we don't get rid of that shipping line soon, investors will start dumping Arc-Horn stock. The drain's too big. Also, Hugo's autocratic methods belong to bygone days. Aside from inflating his ego, what good did it do to jump down our throats today? International factors now are far too complex for a corporation to depend so heavily on one man's judgment." Jim paused. "And there's that other matter we talked about, Tony."

Jim nodded toward Gwen, "I told her about our talk. She knows something that fits the pattern and she wants to help."

"Okay," said Tony. "Let's meet tonight. The only thing scheduled is Jake Apple's night-club show."

Nathan Berger now supplanted Lowdermilk on stage. While Walter had used neither note nor cue in a performance honed by night after night of home rehearsal before a full-length bedroom mirror, Berger needed his black notebook.

Berger took the lectern for the final quarter hour after Gilda and the chorus line went through a high-kick routine to illustrate just how far Summit's international advertising budget would soar in the coming fall season. Summit's color TV models would bloom from TV screens in Brazil, double-truck ads in West German magazines, movie houses in France and billboards in Guatemala, but the bulk of the war chest, a sum slightly larger than the gross annual income of Mauritania, would be lavished on media in the United States.

While the audio-visual system popped its omniscient charts, Berger clicked through the autumn advertising schedule. Final click: the apogee of Summit's conquest of the minds and hearts of a nation. Out scampered the Broadway chorus line in shimmering football costumes. They huddled, blocked and passed in psychedelic pantomime while Gilda kicked a series of field goals that triggered flashing lights, drumbeats and trumpet flourishes like some giant pinball machine.

"And that means," said Berger in a voice croaking with pride, "that for the first time in its history, Summit will be advertising on Monday-night football! . . . Yes sir, as incredible as it may seem, Summit will not only dominate the media in its highly visible fall campaign, but it will blanket Monday-night football each and every week. And that's what we mean by the revolution in color television: Summit, the sound heard round the world. Summit, the glorious scene and sound of seventy-six."

Cheer leaders in the Summit territory touched off a final fountain of applause. In his enthusiasm, Hugo Praeger rose from his seat and called: "Great job, Nate!" Berger, an island of desolation, closed his notebook on the stirring words conceived weeks ago by the omnitalented Jake Apple.

"That ends our color television presentation," said Berger as the cheering faded. "Tomorrow morning our black-and-white TV line and Wednesday morning some striking innovations in radio and high-fidelity equipment. But this afternoon we have an extra goody for you. You'll note in your program that Monday, two to four p.m., is listed only as a 'Summit surprise.' Well, the surprise is this: Summit has installed here in the Mixteca our brand-new executive closed-circuit television system, especially designed for large corporations.

"In the Arc-Horn conference room, Hugo Praeger will be interviewed informally by four Arc-Horn vice-presidents. Executives of the nineteen subsidiaries—there are a hundred and seventeen of us present—will gather in groups of six to watch and hear the interview in rooms scattered about the hotel. After watching for fifteen minutes, each group will shut off its set and candidly discuss what it has just seen and heard. Then each group will elect one of its number to go to the conference room and quiz President Praeger again for an hour while the rest of us watch on our closed-circuit sets. In consenting to do this, Hugo has asked that we all be as open and frank as we can, so that Arc-Horn profits by a candid exchange of opinion on problems facing our corporation."

Berger, who looked as though his ulcer might be aching again, pointed to Calvin Silliman at the rear door. "Cal has a fish bowl with a hundred and seventeen slips of paper. Each slip bears a group number and the name and location of the room where you'll watch Hugo's initial interview. If you're a subsidiary executive, take one and don't lose it. Remember, this is a high-security operation, so only subsidiary officers will be admitted. We want the utmost in candor this afternoon. That's it. Good luck and happy interviewing."

A voice cut through the rumble of departure. "Anybody who's interested, I'm buying at the Tarascan Bar." Pete Quigley waved from a middle row.

In the press of bodies crowding the rear exit, Jim brushed against Praeger. "Lots of razzle-dazzle this morning, Hugo."

"That it was, Jim. . . . I suggest you make your call to Doylestown during the noon break."

Damn the great man. He was unrelenting.

Monday Noon

Jim elected to make his calls from the privacy of his suite rather than through one of the six lines in the Toltec Room's communications center that were linked to Arc-Horn headquarters in New York. Now, because of the difficulty of getting a line through the hotel switchboard to either Doylestown or New York, he moved the telephone and long extension cord out to the balcony, where he munched a roast-beef sandwich and cooled his hangover with iced tea while waiting for the connections.

On the terrace far below him Arc-Horn executives and assistants lunched beneath varicolored beach umbrellas like the hosts of some desert legion feasting in their pavilions at an oasis of palms. The tinkling music of the Vera Cruz trio wafted upward. The sun rode high in a sky of cloudless perfection. The Pacific spread westward like a sparkling carpet. Jim could see tubby Cal Silliman cruising the terrace on one of his infinite errands and Steve sketching a caricature at a table. Nate Berger and Walter Lowdermilk circulated among the diners and Jim could catch faint traces of the cries of "Great job, Nate! . . . Great job, Walter!" echoes of the ritual encomia that would cosset the egos of tens of thousands of convention orators that year.

The call to the Park Avenue apartment came through first. Jim knew that Meg and the twins would have driven back to the city from Long Island early that morning.

"Hello, Jim. How's the weather down there?" Meg did not seem particularly interested.

"Outside, great. Inside, the corporate weather is stickier."

"Oh?" It was less a question than a refrain. Business problems, Jim learned long ago, did not quicken her. "It's rainy-cold up here. But the party went off well."

"Connie and Carol okay?"

"Fine."

"Thanks for the wire. Listen, hon, I don't want to leave it the way we did Saturday night. I want to try to talk it out Friday night after I get back."

"All right, Jim. I'm available all weekend."

"Well, it'll have to be Friday night. Saturday I'm flying to L.A. on that tennis-ranch deal I told you about."

"You did?" A touch of acid now. "Okay. We'll stay in town Friday night and talk. . . . Oh, by the way, I'm having dinner tonight with a friend of yours."

"Oh? Who's that?"

"Dave Moyer. I called him yesterday. . . . Remember, when he came to dinner a couple of weeks ago, I dropped some remarks about us that he picked up on? He said it sounded as if we were having problems, and if so, he'd be willing to help if we wanted him to."

"I remember. Dave mentioned it to me later. He's done some work with couples."

"I know. It seems a lot of you businessmen have more problems at home than at the office. Anyway, I told Dave I wanted to talk to him about us and he agreed. . . . Do you mind?"

"No. It's a good idea. If Dave can help us as much as he did the racquet plant, we'll be in business."

"Darling, business is the only thing we're ever in. Call me again if you get time."

As an antidote to Meg's tartness, Jim would have preferred an exchange of good news with Smitty in Doylestown, but he knew his coming chore would be as disagreeable as commanding Hugo Praeger to swear off chess, profits and self-indulgence. He tuned himself to the unpleasant business ahead and in a few minutes Smitty was on the line from Doylestown.

"How're those señoritas, boss?" To Smitty any place south of the Rio Grande quivered with exotic delights of the flesh.

"Everything fine here, Smitty. I got your wire. How's it going up there?"

"You wouldn't believe it. The first two-shift operation was supposed to start at five a.m. Well, Christ, some of the gang was here a half hour early. You remember Hank Marks, that old sourballs in the machine shop? Damn if he wasn't whistling on the job."

"That's great. . . . I'm sorry, but I've got some bad news." He described the scene at the board meeting, giving Smitty a good glimpse of the exchanges between himself and Hugo. He owed his plant manager that much.

"Well, if that ain't a swift kick in the ass." Smitty, a man who gave himself up freely to pessimism, had seldom sounded so bitter. "Tell me, just what good does that fat slob do for Top Court? Whatever it is, it's not worth it."

"We've had some easier financing because of Arc-Horn, but that's about it. You're right, Smitty. I've had those thoughts myself. But we're hitched in tight. Nothing we can do about it. . . . Look, keep the bad news about Moyer to yourself for right now, will you?"

"Oh no." Smitty's voice could have filed metal. "That's not the way we do things around here any more. We all lay it on the line with each other. I don't know what you want to call it, democracy some say, but whatever it is, that's the way we like it. No secrets. I'm going to have to pass the word around right off. And believe me, Jim, they'll be pissed off. Hell, Moyer's a big hero around this place."

"Where's Dave now, by the way? I owe it to him to tell him as soon as I can."

"He's over in the cafeteria. I wish to hell I was down there. I'd chop that fat Praeger down to size and bang

that massage girl of his in the bargain. . . . Okay,
I'll get Dave."

The midday sun crowded shadows on the balcony as
Jim waited. Several fishing boats, shiny dots on the
distant sea, vanished and reappeared with the rolling
curve of the ocean. Nearer to the beach frigate birds
floated the air currents on immobile wings and a pelican dove into the sea for its prey like a crumpled box
kite. Jim's headache was slowly dissipating.

"Hi, Jim." Moyer's greeting was as sunny as the glint
of the waves. "What's the good word down there?"

"All bad this morning, Dave." He gave Moyer as
many details as he could remember, including his as-
sists from Gwen, Tony and Masuo Sugimoto.

"That's tough to take right at this time. Any chance
of luring Praeger up to Doylestown to see for himself?"

"Hugo visit a production plant! That'll be the
day. . . . This is tougher on me than on you. I'd
intended to sign you up next week for the Illinois ball
plant."

"Well, it'll work out. This place is winging now.
They'll make it on their own. Actually I was going to
pull out in another month or so anyway."

"I know." But Jim also knew how critical Moyer's
guidance would be in these final days of trial. "Look,
can you stay there through this week? Praeger's at least
given us that much breathing space."

"Sure, no problem. . . . Jim, I'm having dinner with
Meg tonight and. . . "

"Yes. She told me a few minutes ago. If you can
help in that department, you're a genius."

"There are no geniuses in love and marriage. . . .
I've watched you two for some months now and, frankly,
neither of you knows how to listen to the other."

"Meg wants it all her way. She has no idea of the
time pressures of this job."

"But it's a two-way street. There's a possibility, you
know, that some of your pressures are self-generated.
Tell you what. I'll talk to Meg tonight and then how

about letting me sit in with the two of you this weekend and see if we can't get an honest dialogue going?"

"Okay, but it will have to be Friday night, as I've already told Meg. Saturday I'm flying to the Coast on a tennis-ranch acquisition."

"Whose idea was that—to do business on the week-end?"

"Why . . ." Jim hesitated. How had that come about? "Oh, yeah. The ranch partners suggested the date and I just went along."

"Can't you call them and reset the talks for next week?"

"Jesus. I'm away from the office all this week. I ought to be at my desk next week."

"Jim, I'll put it to you straight. If Meg isn't worth one weekend to you, then there's no use my wasting my time either. If I'm to help, I'll need a little give from both sides."

"Well . . ."

"I mean that."

"Okay, okay, I'll call Los Angeles and try to re-schedule."

"Good. I've got an idea. Why don't the three of us hole up at a motel near Doylestown? That way we can talk in a neutral atmosphere, away from the associations of home. Also I'd like Meg to get the flavor of just what you're doing at Doylestown."

Jim brightened. "Now you're talking. I like that."

"And Meg will appreciate your postponing the Coast trip. We want to try to build some bridges between you two."

"Okay, sold. . . . And, Dave, don't get too heavily committed. I'll have another go at Praeger. I'm deter-mined to put you to work at that Illinois plant."

Twenty minutes later Jim had connected with Cuth-bert & Siegal in Los Angeles and reached agreement to talk there Wednesday, March 26, about the proposed purchase by Top Court of the Desert Grove Tennis Ranch, twelve courts and a lodge.

Jim hung up with a feeling of surprised satisfaction.

Why had he assumed the deal could only be discussed Saturday? Because he'd be away from his desk all this week. But wasn't his desk wherever he was? Maybe Gwen had something about running the company and not letting it run her. And besides, it would be fun to show Meg the Doylestown operation and let her get a feel of the new spirit around the place. And then it hit him. Son of a bitch. How about that Moyer? He'd thrown in that Doylestown bit as bait for Jim and Jim had swallowed it, bait, hook and all. He'd been had. He grinned. Strange. He didn't mind it a bit.

On his way to the Olmec Room, his station for watching Praeger's closed-circuit interview, Jim crossed the open lobby. The warm, tangy wind blew off the Pacific, tugging at the red, blue and gold shirts, nipping at the sheer blue blouses of the Mexican hostesses and rumpling the hair of Cal Silliman, who looked more agitated than usual.

"Now what, Cal? Something gone wrong?"

"You better believe it." Silliman's eyes sought heaven's succor. "This job is the living end. That Summit designer, Alex Rosinski, is in jail. He went into Acapulco with one of the Miami broads last night, got into a fight over her in some joint, and now they're holding him for assault. Anybody who's seen a Mexican jail knows what that means. So that shoots the afternoon for me."

Silliman pointed across the lobby to a spot where Steve was folding his collapsible easel and putting away his drawing paper. He was chatting with María, the hostess. "And that guy's another problem," said Cal. "I suspect he's really an Internal Revenue agent."

"Oh, come on, Cal. That's ridiculous."

"Well, at the least, he's a hippy gate crasher." Silliman turned and strode across the lobby. Jim followed.

Silliman faced Steve with folded arms. "Young man, you're not wanted around here. This hotel is sold out to Arc-Horn."

Startled, María aimed a quick, derisive look at Silliman, then walked away. A haughty one, that girl, thought Jim.

"I just schlep around like any other tourist." Steve continued to stow his gear. "Don't tell me Arc-Horn owns the hotel too."

"No. However, this is a closed convention." Silliman's manner could be fussily effeminate at times. "All I have to do is take it up with the hotel manager."

"You just do that little thing." Steve challenged him with a glare. "And then come down on the beach and try to throw me off public property."

"Hold it." Jim stepped between the two men. "What's the matter, Cal? Has somebody been complaining about Steve?"

"Well . . ." Silliman looked uncertain. "Last night he barged in on a private show."

"Private, hell," said Steve.

"Look, Cal," said Jim, "why not let him do his cartoons? Apparently they're popular with the crowd and he's not hurting anybody. Time enough to take it up if you get some beefs."

"Okay, as a favor to you, Jim." Silliman looked relieved. "Just don't make yourself obnoxious," he said to Steve. "Now I've got to go into town to that damn jail." Silliman plowed off toward the portico on his rescue mission.

Steve grinned. "Thanks, Jim. Always some officious bastard trying to ruin a guy's business."

"Did you make much this noon?"

"Ten bucks. Not bad. I did your fat boss. He wasn't easy. A very complicated man." Steve looked Jim full in the eyes as he talked. "You know, you got a lot of flesh at this convention, including that guy Silliman. You're one of the few who isn't about thirty pounds overweight."

"I keep it down with tennis."

"The fat ones bug me. I thought business was supposed to be so tough?"

"It takes lots of calories to feed the nerves."

"You got all this booze and rich food while twenty

miles away, up in those hills, you see kids who don't get one decent meal a week." He waved eastward toward the mountains of Guerrero. "Man, the contrast really gets me. I spent two months wandering around and through those mountains, on the way down from Taxco. Good people, but God, they gotta scratch to live."

"I hear there are some guerrillas up there."

"Yeah. Man, a guy can hide for years up there. I rapped with some of them. We got along okay once they found out I was that rare specimen, a Spanish-speaking gringo without money. Of course, you get two kinds up there, guerrillas for a cause and then just plain bandits. You have to figure out who's who."

Jim's thoughts turned back to the fiesta. "Tell me, were you high on something last night?"

Steve laughed. "You mean the dancing? Naw, that was just old me, doing what I felt like. Oh sure, I smoke dope and drop some mescaline now and then, but around here, I'm careful. These Mexican cops would love to bust me. But the dancing . . . You see, I like to let it all hang loose, man. No boss, no company to keep me uptight. I do what I want."

"How much longer do you plan to hike?"

"Aw, I don't know. Right now I'm heading south to the Canal and then down through South America to Tierra del Fuego. I figure about eighteen months from here to the Strait of Magellan. Then after telling myself I've walked all around the world, big deal, I can sit down and figure what next. Who knows? No sweat. . . . Hey, why don't you walk along with me? You'd have a ball."

Jim shook his head. "Thanks, but I've got work to do."

"Yeah, there're all those gadgets to make that no-body needs, all those convention speeches to make that nobody wants to hear and all that good land to pave over so everybody can go faster getting nowhere. Shit, man, I've been in and out of that bag. You call it the GNP, gross national product. I call it the RTG, raping the globe. . . . Me, I hope to live simple and die like the Indians, leaving the earth just about the way I found it. . . . Well, I guess that's not the space you're in. So be it. But if you feel like rapping sometime, come on over to the tent."

Steve strode off toward the beach in his frayed shorts and faded denim shirt. The president of Top Court, heavy with his millions and the cares of two corporations, walked toward the air-conditioned room where he would hear the prince of conglomerators boast of new and daring forays into a commerce that fed on the gristle and the marrow of the planet. And for the moment, Jim wasn't sure which man, he or Steve, was headed in the right direction.

Monday Afternoon

Six high-backed rattan armchairs crouched in a semi-circle about the television set like brown cats around a bowl. The Early American walnut cabinet, mounted on small hidden wheels, held a placard proclaiming it to be one unit of Summit's new X-20 panchromatic, closed-circuit executive television system for company-wide decision making."

The luck of the draw had given Jim McGowan a fair cross section of Arc-Horn's executive fauna to share the viewing of Hugo Praeger's interview. With Jim behind the locked doors of the Olmec Room were Lucy Jenkins of Fragrance, the somber Jules Amarel of Six Flags Insurance, Tony Percevale of Gusto Más, Joyce Boke-Milgrim, the proper and somewhat jaded president of Sea Routes, and Meersdorf Welding's vice-president in charge of nothing, Pete Quigley, complete with two bottles of Mexican beer to tide him over the afternoon.

Amarel seized the small chores of leadership, perhaps by virtue of Six Flags' stature as the company with the best 1974 growth record. He dimmed the lights at the appointed hour, seated himself in one of the high-backed chairs and switched on the set via the remote-control box in his hand.

The twenty-five-inch screen came into focus, showing Hugo Praeger at the center of the horseshoe table in the conference room. He was sandwiched among four Arc-Horn vice-presidents, all bathed in scarlet as if suffering from some rare pigmentation disease.

"You got too much red, Jules," said Quigley, dean of the obvious.

Amarel pressed a button, quickly achieving a sharp picture of natural flesh tones. Praeger could be seen hunching forward like an amiable professor about to shed enlightenment on his students.

"Good afternoon, members of the Arc-Horn family." Praeger was pleased to be cast in the starring role of his corporation's latest drama. "Thanks to Nate Berger, we're privileged to try something unique in Arc-Horn executive communications. I'll be interviewed here for a few minutes, then each group will take a half hour for candid discussion of what you've seen and heard. Then each group elects one person to come up here and join in an hour-long give-and-take session with me. Okay, first question."

John Lindquist, the numbers minister, led off. He wanted to know what earnings per share might be this quarter, based on reports at the morning board meeting.

"A good starting point, John," said Praeger with the look of a man following a script. "Somebody must have given Frankie Fee advance information last night because he hit it right on the nose." Praeger slipped a hand inside his jacket and caressed his chest. "Yes sir, one seventy-nine, a new Arc-Horn high."

Bernard Hirsch, public relations vice-president, asked whether Arc-Horn was in good financial shape. Indeed so, replied Praeger. Most subsidiaries were up handsomely and steps would be taken at once to turn Sea Routes around. Heavy losses of the Liberian-registered freighter and tanker fleet would not be allowed to continue. Praeger slapped the table as if commanding the seas of red ink to recede.

What was the outlook for the international economy? asked Chalmers Davidson. Praeger supplied a succinct overview, worthy of a Paul Samuelson or a John Kenneth Galbraith, embracing Mideast oil, anchovies off the Peruvian coast and the vigor of Colombian coffee shrubs. Economic weather forecast: Mostly fair with possible scattered thunderstorms. Praeger adroitly fielded a question from Nick Calabrese about a patent-infringement suit in France and another from Hirsch on the status of Arc-Horn pension funds. The fifteen minutes fled by without any alarming addition to the explosion of human knowledge which, according to savants, was now doubling every seven years.

"Well?" asked Jules Amarel as he clicked off the set.

"Nice picture once you got the red out." Quigley finished off his first bottle of beer.

Boke-Milgrim yawned. "Nothing new."

"No hits, no runs, no errors," said Jim. The stagy performance, failing to deal with any vital corporate problem, left him with a feeling of having been cheated.

"Bullshit!" Lucy Jenkins gripped the arms of her chair and glared at her colleagues like an avenging prosecutor. "Why don't you say what you're thinking? Nothing but bullshit. Admit it, Tony. Am I right, Jim? Gwen told me you two got a going over from Hugo this morning. Did he say anything just now about interfering with your companies? Not a word. If you ask me, he didn't say nothin' about nothin'."

The big black woman, who could switch her syntax as readily as her coiffure, waved her arms as if banishing Hugo Praeger from the premises. Jim was never sure how much of Lucy's high-octane displays to allot to honest feeling and how much to showmanship. But whatever the issue, she was seldom neutral about it.

"What do you think Hugo should have talked about, Lucy?" In the face of spirited emotion, Jules Amarel acted like a health officer about to impose quarantine.

"About what's eatin' us." Lucy waggled a finger at Jules. "About treating Tony and Jim like they were kids. About Sea Routes dropping twenty-five million a year. About where the hell Arc-Horn is going and why. About Nader attacking us. About those stockholders who claim the accounting is phony. Man, anything you can name, Hugo didn't talk about it."

"Mrs. Jenkins is right about Sea Routes," said Boke-Milgrim. "Hugo didn't face the issue. Either we spend about a half billion on new carriers or we prepare ourselves for a huge write-off. The fleet will never make a profit against the modern competition. Hugo knows that as well as I do."

Jim and Tony Percevale both started to talk at once. Jim yielded.

"Hugo has no understanding of the situation in Argentina," said Percevale firmly. "We are there by the skin of our teeth. One false move by Arc-Horn and we could be banned. It's a great mistake to meddle with the Rosario plant now." Percevale briefly described the slaughterhouse problem for the benefit of Lucy Jenkins and Peter Quigley. "And it would be a greater mistake to have Chalmers Davidson take any part whatsoever in Gusto Más operations right now."

Jim moved in when Percevale finished. "Same with Top Court. Here I've got the highest morale at the Doylestown plant in the company's history, and this noon I had to call off the psychologist who's done such a great job there. Hugo acted in a highly arbitrary manner on something he knows nothing about, and believe me, that burns my tail."

"Same old story," said Lucy. "We could make the best perfume in the world and have workers as happy as angels and if it doesn't come down to the bottom line bigger than last year, Hugo and that numbers creep Lindquist will ax it."

"What's wrong with making a buck, for Chrissakes?" asked Quigley with unexpected belligerence.

"Nothing," said Jim. "But the point is, Pete, sometimes you have to live with a problem like Tony's. Or in my case, I need time to translate morale into production. But it'll come, don't worry about that. What Hugo did set us back instead of helping us."

"I'd like to bring up something else," said Amarel. He extracted a note pad from his shirt pocket and eyed it soberly. "I used my Nakamura calculator this noon to do some figuring. I estimate that this twentieth-birthday party, what with travel, food, the hotel, gifts, the communications center, visiting clergymen, Jake Apple's show, the works, will cost Arc-Horn a shade better than two million dollars. That's about four cents a share. My question is: who needs this kind of extravagance?"

"Now just a goddam minute," protested Quigley. "You want to take all the fun out of this lash-up?"

"Yeah, Jules," said Lucy Jenkins. "You take the partying out of Arc-Horn and what's left that's good for us? Not much, honey."

They argued the point with the avidity of supermarket shoppers until Amarel, with a glance at his watch, said it was time to decide just what matters the group's representative would take upstairs to the second Praeger interview. Amarel called for a vote on his proposal to forgo extravagances at the annual meeting. The result was a deadlock, Amarel, McGowan and Percevale voting for thrift, Jenkins, Boke-Milgrim and Quigley for munificence. Jules agreed to shelve his protest for the time being. A motion by McGowan to ask Praeger about the interference with Gusto Más and Top Court carried unanimously as did another by Amarel calling upon Praeger to explain the financial dilemma posed by Sea Routes' continuing heavy losses.

"And now the question of who represents us," said Amarel.

Jim nominated Lucy.

"Second the motion," said Admiral Boke-Milgrim.

"Any other nominations?" There were none and Lucy Jenkins was elected unanimously, five votes plus Quigley's belch.

"I accept the honor," said Lucy. "I guess the idea is that since I'm black, I can get burned up there without it showing." She walked to the door, then turned. "Hang loose, men. I'm goin' give that fat boy some kind of hell."

In the ten-minute recess allowed for gathering of the second panel, the five men in the Olmec Room traded banter with a slowly flowering realization that an event unusual in Arc-Horn's hierarchical history might be in the making.

"We may be in for a bit of a show," said Boke-Milgrim, "if the other representatives are as outspoken as Lucy."

"Nobody else is that feisty," said Quigley.

"I wonder if the other groups talked as frankly as we did?" Amarel looked perturbed as if his own candor now merited reconsideration.

When Amarel again turned on the television set, Praeger could be seen beaming at the center of the horseshoe table. Behind him like uncles posing stiffly for a family photograph sat the four Arc-Horn vice-presidents. Interviewers from the subsidiaries occupied twenty chairs, arranged in two rows facing Praeger. The camera cut from the side so that all participants could be seen clearly. Jim noted that no Top Court executive had been selected. Fragrance had two people, Gwen Piggott having been chosen by her group.

"All right, shoot." Praeger had a fatherly smile for the corporate talent in front of him.

Lucy stood up at once. "I've been instructed by my group to ask two questions. First. Why are you interfering with operations of Gusto Más and Top Court instead of letting Señor Percevale and Mr. McGowan handle their own business like they always have?"

"Fair enough, Lucy." Hugo was indulgent. "Both men fell below expectations for the quarter. Tony Percevale will lose money this quarter and Jim McGowan will be up only a couple of points. In my book, anybody who fails to increase earnings at least five percent needs help. And help is what I offered both men this morning."

Lucy was still standing. "But McGowan says it wasn't help. You ordered him to fire a guy who's doing his racquet plant a lot of good. Why?"

"Because McGowan and his friend were undertaking a social experiment that hurt production. We're in the business of making money, Lucy, not that of trying to mold human character—a mission we leave to the family, churches and schools."

"But why mess with something you haven't seen?" Lucy was dogged. "Why'n't you go up there to Doylestown and have a look yourself before you crack down?"

Watching the screen, Jim was delighted to hear Lucy propose exactly what Dave Moyer had on the telephone at noon.

Praeger's smile evaporated. "This corporation has six hundred seventy-eight profit centers, Mrs. Jenkins, and even if I traveled constantly, I could only visit each one at intervals of two years. It's impossible to cover my post at headquarters and make many visits."

"But this one is different," Lucy insisted. "To hear Jim tell it, he's got a real happy plant at Doylestown and there aren't many of them around, honey, in the U.S. 'n A. or any place else."

"I'll take your advice under consideration." Praeger's voice still boomed, but it had lost its warmth. "Did you say you had a second question?"

"Yeah, although I'm not sure you answered that one. The second is what is going to be done about Sea Routes? Are we facing a big write-off, selling the old ships for what they'll bring, or spending a half billion to build a new fleet?" Lucy sat down.

"I covered that subject in the original interview." Praeger cast his answer in a mold of finality and looked elsewhere for less thorny inquiries.

"But you didn't explain it." Lucy refused to let up. "My men want to know what's cooking."

Praeger said nothing and a hard look came into his eyes as they avoided Lucy to rove along the two rows of executives. Sukit Sukhsvasti stood up.

"I think we all want an answer to Lucy's question, Hugo." The Thai-Tex president was deferential but firm.

"It would be unwise to go into details before such a large group." No sooner had he dropped this evidence of mistrust of what he fondly called the Arc-Horn "family" than Praeger realized his error. "It's not a lack of confidence in any of you, you understand, it's just, well, this is a cumbersome forum in which to handle complex problems. But I assure you, Sukit, we're working hard on the matter. Of course Sea Routes is a severe drain on our resources. Put it this way. If we had a shipping line that broke even, Arc-Horn would be in clover, what? Now, er, Mrs. Jenkins indicated that there are but two choices—junk the fleet and write down our assets or build modern ship replacements at enormous cost. I believe there may be some other possibilities that I intend to explore with Admiral Boke-Milgrim this evening. However, the nature of these possibilities does not lend itself to wide discussion. I think you can appreciate that." Praeger for once did not appear to be in absolute command. "At any rate, I assure all of you that we'll take a very hard look at the future of Sea Routes, Inc., in the next few weeks."

As Sukhsvasti sat down, three men immediately rose to their feet. Praeger whipped out his handkerchief and dabbed at his face, then nodded toward Helmut von Weise, the president of Deutsche-Mannheim, the West German drug firm.

"How do we justify the enormous expense of this conference at a resort hotel with parties and bands and show girls?"

Praeger quickly reverted to his role of jovial host. *"Ich bin überrascht, Helmut, was ist los? Magst Du die Mädchen nicht?"* Hugo grinned. "But come now, all work and no play make Helmut and Hugo dull boys, what?" His sly look was not unlike that with which Lyndon Johnson once made fellow conspirators of his

televiewing countrymen. "I assume there are no Internal
Revenue agents listening. . . . Of course, we're only
talking about a penny or two a share here since convention expenses are deductible. And the expenditure
is fully justified by the renewed vigor and morale that
executives and managers of the great Arc-Horn family
will take back to the job on Friday."

Listening to Praeger's answer, Jim McGowan wished
he were on the panel. Couldn't the same argument be
made for Doylestown? New vigor and morale among
the workers?

"That's exactly what Jim McGowan says for his new
methods at Top Court's racquet plant." Gwen Piggott
was on her feet and speaking. Jim felt like cheering.
"But you ordered the psychologist fired."

"The two aren't the same, Gwen. A case of trying to
compare oranges and elephants, what?" Sweat now glistened in the folds of flesh. Praeger shifted uneasily in
his special oak armchair. "For the benefit of those not
present this morning, I should say that this was all
thrashed out and settled at the board meeting."

Masuo Sugimoto stood up. "Also for the benefit of
those who are not board members, we should explain
what's at issue here. Under the guidance of a Mr. David
Moyer, a reputable industrial psychologist, Top Court
is trying a new system at its racquet plant that aims
at involving the workers totally in their jobs and encouraging them to participate in decisions about production and planning. Jim McGowan is not a maverick,
in your American term. Many large companies have
similar plans under way."

Sugimoto talked for a full five minutes in his precise, school-book English while Praeger looked on
gravely. Even the monarch of Arc-Horn hesitated to
interrupt a merchant lord who could rally a quarter of
the corporation's shares through Japanese holdings in
funds, banks, trusts and individual accounts. "Some call
it industrial democracy," said Sugimoto in conclusion. "I
prefer the term 'full employee participation.' But however we phrase it, gentlemen, this is the wave of the

future and I would like to see Arc-Horn ride the crest and not be smashed to pieces by it someday."

In the Olmec Room, McGowan cut loose with involuntary applause. "Atta boy, Masuo," he called toward the screen. And Jim realized that the Nakamura president had articulated concisely many of the less-ordered thoughts that Doylestown and Dave Moyer had stirred in him in recent months.

"Why's that goddam Jap rocking the boat?" Pete Quigley had a sour look.

In the Arc-Horn conference room heads bent and a gush of conversation could be heard. "I'm with Masuo a hundred percent," said Gwen loudly. Several panelists nodded agreement. "Better go to Doylestown, Hugo," said Lucy.

Praeger cleared his throat, a peremptory rumble that served as a gavel. "In view of the considerable sentiment, perhaps a reconsideration of the Doylestown situation is in order. So Jim McGowan, wherever you are, we'll meet—let's see—Wednesday morning at nine in my suite and go over the pros and cons again. . . . Next question."

My God, thought Jim, maybe he's surrendering. Up Jenkins, Piggott and Sugimoto! And he intended to thank Nate Berger later for conceiving this closed-circuit wonder that somehow forced the fat one to reason with his managers.

"Could you explain corporate policy relating to ecology?" It was Paul Chesterfield of Hi-Western Corp., the lumbering enterprise. "We have a good program of reforestation, but the environment people still pick on us."

Praeger nodded and smiled. He was obviously well prepared for this one. "Arc-Horn will spend every dollar necessary to comply with anti-pollution regulations. We favor them. But as for cutting back production, as Senator Ireland and many well-intended innocents are advocating since the Club of Rome report, well, we just won't do it. The good earth can keep supplying us for hundreds of years yet and nobody's going to frighten me into falling back to the Stone Age—or damning automobiles like that crazy hiking cartoonist who's wandering around the hotel. Also, I'd like to say right here that I'm no hypocrite and you won't find Arc-Horn buying institutional ads to weep crocodile tears over the plight of the environment like Atlantic Richfield and some other companies. We're in the business of producing and selling goods that people want to buy and that's where we're going to stay." Praeger slapped the table with both palms.

It was perhaps a footnote on the ambivalence of the times that no one applauded this paean to man's right to gut the foundations of his only home. While no Arc-Horn executive had yet publicly challenged the glories of unlimited production, a few of them had occasional guilt pangs and collectively they spent millions of dollars to build private hideaways on the fringes of the rapidly contracting wilderness.

Sukit Sukhsvasti of Thai-Tex rose to his feet. "Is some group making a study of Arc-Horn operations and, if so, are officers of this corporation trying to sabotage that report?"

In the Olmec Room, Jim and Tony exchanged surprised, half-hidden smiles.

Praeger reacted to the question like a batter to a wide-breaking curve. He started to speak, checked himself, then looked at Sukhsvasti with a puzzled frown. This was one surprise too many for the man who detested surprises. Moments passed before he answered.

"Well, of course, somebody is always making a study of some kind on Arc-Horn, what? . . . Nader, a Senate committee, doctoral theses. you name it. Your word 'sabotage' is a peculiar one. We don't deal in that commodity at Arc-Horn. Naturally, we're not too cooperative when the clear thrust of the research is inimical to business. I'm sure you get the idea, Sukit, and in the best interest of Arc-Horn, I'd prefer to let the matter rest there."

"I would like to pursue it." Once the troops tasted the fruits of candor, they could be stubborn in demanding more.

"I won't be interrogated further on that. If you have a specific problem, Sukit, come see me and we'll discuss it. And I'd remind all hands that anything said on this closed-circuit, er, experiment is not to be mentioned outside."

Four men rose simultaneously, but a controller of United African Motors spoke out first. "What are these projects Green Tree and Neptune West that the corporation is considering?"

Hugo blinked. "Since you're not a board member, it's apparent some director has violated confidentiality. I'll only say this: Both projects will be considered by the board at its final Thursday session and both hold great profit promise for Arc-Horn."

Masuo Sugimoto was on his feet again. "Does Arc-Horn have any agents of the Central Intelligence Agency on its payroll?"

Praeger looked startled. "That's an odd question, Masuo." He leaned forward and grinned at Sugimoto. "Well, now, I suppose we'd have to consider that a possibility. We're both men of the world and we know that corporations like ours are the true internationals of our age, while nation-states still cling to their out-moded notions of sovereignty. Now in these circum-stances, it wouldn't surprise me if some minor executive of Eurofact, for example, reported to the CIA. Nor would it surprise either of us if, unbeknownst to you, one of your Nakamura functionaries reported to Japanese intelligence." He paused. "That's the way of the world, what? The national governments are far behind inter-national business, Masuo, and until they gain some of our wisdom about the interdependency of all continents and races, I guess we'll just have to put up with their stupidities. But Arc-Horn's no nest of spies, believe me."

Sugimoto's place was promptly taken by Charles Hol-loway of Indo Deep Rig. "What's the status of our big loan with First Merchants Trust? Are we well above the cash-reserve requirement?"

"Indeed we are." Hugo beamed. He loved favorable numbers even more than John Lindquist did. "To refresh memories, Hal Frascella at First Merchants gave us three hundred million at five point seven percent back in the spring of seventy-one when interest rates were low. That was looking forward to our needs for the Nakamura, er, acquisition. The loan runs five years, until the spring of next year. We've met all interest payments on time and we'll be in good shape to renew or perhaps even retire some of the loan next year. First Merchants stipulated that we had to maintain one-fifty in cash reserves at all times. We've never been in danger there and right now we're about thirty above the requirement. . . . Of course, First Merchants would like us to slip below, so they could saddle us with more interest and maneuver Frascella onto the Arc-Horn board. But I guarantee that won't happen. I don't want any damn banker telling us how to run our business."

Lucy Jenkins was back again. "Politics, Hugo. Which party are you going to favor for President of the U.S. next year and do you mind if I vote Democratic?"

Praeger joined the laughter. He seemed at ease again. "I intend to vote Republican, Lucy. The Republican administration has been good to Arc-Horn and I believe in rewarding our friends. You, of course, will do as you please, but among your Democrats, I'd warn you against that fellow Ireland, who appears to be out front at the moment. Senator Ireland wants to slash defense spending, trim down on civilian production to save resources and energy fuels and 'refocus U.S. foreign policy toward the peoples of the earth,' as he puts it. Now I'm all for eliminating waste in the military, but I'd remind the Arc-Horn family that our defense contracts amount to about thirteen percent, I believe it is, of our total revenues and . . ."

"Fourteen point two," corrected John Lindquist.

"Yes, fourteen point two, and I'd be very wary of some politician who'd come in and just hack away blindly without careful attention to just what weapons systems he might be endangering. Now on that second point, curtailing consumer production to save energy and stop 'heedless plundering of our natural resources,' as Ireland says it, well, that's the kind of idealistic hogwash that can bring on another depression. I've already stated Arc-Horn policy in that area in answer to Paul Chesterfield's ecology question. As for Ireland's call for a foreign policy directed toward people instead of toward dictators and exploiters, that sounds fine, but beware of fancy language. If he means he'd quit dealing with military governments like that in Brazil, then I'd say nobody in business can afford that kind of nonsense. . . . I didn't mean to devote so much time to Ireland, but I do feel strongly that the business community is heading toward disaster if we don't stop him."

Sukit Sukhsvasti stood up again. "Doesn't Ireland also advocate stripping the CIA of all its black operations and just confining its job to intelligence gathering?"

"I think he does, Sukit." Praeger nodded toward the Thai executive. "I'll let the experts in Washington debate that one. What concerns me is Ireland's fuzzy-minded idealism."

Hugo leaned forward with palms spread, again as if embracing his viewers in a secret fraternity of attitudes. "You know my definition of an honest idealist —a man who holds that peace and greed can go hand in hand, what?"

Praeger's chuckle fetched a few smiles from the panel of questioners. In the Olmec Room, a lone guffaw from Pete Quigley broke the silence.

"This one is about Mexico and Arc-Horn," said Helmut von Weise. "Does Article . . ." The ruddy German faltered, groping for words, then finished in his native language.

Praeger grinned as he translated. "Helmut wants to know if an Arc-Horn executive could be 'thirty-three'd' during this convention. Indeed he could. For those of you who may not know it, this beautiful host country of ours has a very convenient statute known as Article Thirty-three covering undesirable aliens. Any foreigner can be deported within hours, even minutes, without court proceedings, if the authorities conclude he has transgressed Mexican law or custom. Ordinarily it's used for hippies, drug addicts and political agitators, but it's wide as a barn door and can be invoked to get rid of any alien. . . . I'm glad you brought that up, Helmut. It behooves us all to conform to the local customs. We don't want expensive talent thirty-three'd this week for seducing the mayor's daughter or streaking across the golf course at high noon."

After a pause, a vice-president of Princess Beverages asked why Princess did not have a "peace and greed" soft-drink monopoly at the Arc-Horn birthday celebration. Praeger pleaded guilty to the oversight, vowed he never touched Pepsi-Cola or other hostile tonics and would ban their consumption at future corporate gatherings.

The questions came at him now like buzzing yellow jackets. Why wasn't there parity on executive salaries geared to earnings progress? Because of management contracts at the time of acquisition.

Would the United Nations inquiry into multinational companies damage Arc-Horn? No. He'd expressed his views publicly before the U.N. committee in '73 and Davidson had pursued personal contacts in the right U.N. quarters.

Were any new acquisitions contemplated? No, but like the madam of the house, he never refused to consider the merits of any spirited girl who wished to lose her virtue.

Was it true that he made recommendations to Freer & Mayborn, the management consultant firm, on the winner of the annual Golden Globe Award? Absolutely not. He had never once dropped even a hint to the firm on his personal choice.

Did he favor a new world court to adjudicate disputes between nations and multinational corporations? Yes.

Why couldn't intercompany memoranda clearly set out earnings of each subsidiary and its components? Because snooping security analysts might misjudge the total picture and unwisely recommend a sell-off of Arc-Horn.

Would Arc-Horn be up for the whole year? Yes.

Any antitrust action in the offing? Not under this administration.

Did he mind individual contributions to Democratic candidates? No. In addition to the open Democrat, Lucy Jenkins, Arc-Horn had a number of the closet variety. Jim McGowan for one.

"I'll take two final questions." Praeger apparently hoped to close the heavy going on a light note.

"My group wants to know," said Gwen Piggott, "whether the security guards around here are to protect us or to provide information to someone on the Arc-Horn staff?"

Color rushed up Praeger's puffy cheeks. He gripped the edge of the table and stared at her. "If we weren't such good friends, Gwen, I'd take that question as an insult. For those of you unaware of the facts of life, the nearby Sierra Madre del Sur provides haven for a number of guerrillas who'd love to grab some high-priced Arc-Horn executive and hold him for ransom. As you know, the public policy of this corporation, stated unequivocally four years ago, is that no ransom will ever be paid by Arc-Horn to anyone. Furthermore, we don't have a penny's worth of that secret kidnapping insurance that some multinationals hold. In the light of these facts, we deem it prudent to protect our own. You ought to be thankful for every single security guard you see, what?"

Paulo Hochschild of Uni-Land stood up. "I would not ask this question for myself," the Brazilian said hurriedly, "but I've been instructed by my group. . . . Will Walter Lowdermilk be fired for singing that first verse last night?"

Praeger's astonishment quickly bloomed into fury. He had had enough. "No, he won't," he half shouted, "but if I ever find the man who prompted that question, I'll kick his ass from here to Mexico City." And with that, Praeger pressed a control button beside him, snapping off the picture.

In the Olmec Room the vanishing scene showed Praeger turning angrily away from his interviewers. The last shot before the fadeout caught the dampened back of a blue-trimmed golden shirt.

"We'll never see that kind of interview again," said Jules Amarel. Worry was his soulmate.

"I almost felt sorry for him at the end," said Percevale.

"I wouldn't like to be in Nate Berger's shoes now." Admiral Boke-Milgrim voiced a common thought. "The double interview was his idea."

In the great lobby, where the Arc-Horn warriors congregated, the growl of voices vied with the warm afternoon wind sweeping in from the Pacific. Would Hugo retaliate and how? Who put Hochschild up to that last sticker? For once, nobody had a joke to tell and even Pete Quigley preferred the titillation of executive gossip to another trip to the Tarascan Bar.

Jim spotted Nate Berger hanging up one of the house phones. The Summit president looked as bleak as ashes.

"That was Praeger," he said. "He wants to see me in his suite pronto."

"Chin up, Nate. Once the storm dies away, he'll get over it. Hell, your idea is liable to become an annual feature."

"My idea!" Berger's voice was feverish. "Oh, no. The guy who sold me on the damn scheme was a psychologist friend of your man Dave Moyer. Thanks a lot." He marched toward the elevators, his shoulder twitching.

Monday Night

"Over here, Jim."

Gwen's voice drew him toward a table at the edge of the terrace where the outdoor fiesta had taken place the night before. Thousands of stars studded the vaulted sky like aimlessly scattered jewels and a lone cloud drifted past the quarter moon. The surf was gentle, the air balmy and fragrant. Shadows laced the round table, half hidden beneath a palm tree, where Gwen Piggott and Antonio Percevale waited.

"Sorry I'm late." Jim eased into a chair pulled out for him by Tony. "Hugo made good on his promise. He found out it was our Al Bebout who inspired the question on Lowdermilk's verse. Hugo called him to the big suite, chewed him out and told him he was finished after his contract expires in December."

"What are you going to do?" asked Tony.

"Wait until Hugo cools off and then have Al make a formal apology. It may work. I don't want to lose Al. Of course, he had no business suggesting a question like that, even in jest. Well, that's my problem. . . . Where are we?"

"I just got through telling Gwen what I told you yesterday," said Tony.

"Incredible story." Gwen lit a cigarette and leaned back in her chair. Tonight, like the conference hostesses, she wore a jacaranda bloom in her hair. "I'd love to hear what Ron Jeffers, our little Mr. Efficiency, has to say about it. Why haven't you asked him, Tony?"

"I'd rather go to the top. Since arriving here, I've learned there've been more incidents than those in Argentina and Thailand. . . . Papers about Top Court stolen in New York. The Fragrance study turned off by headquarters."

"And Meersdorf Welding," added Jim. "Peter Quigley refused to answer a Kansas State professor's questions. . . . Of course, I'm fairly sure now that this outfit known as the Group of Twelve is making a major study of Arc-Horn—use of resources, ecology, that kind of thing."

"The one you told me is making a report to the Geneva conference next week?" asked Gwen.

"Right. But I gathered from Phil Ireland that would be a general report on worldwide depletion of mineral resources. Maybe there are two studies under way. I tried to reach Phil this evening to nail it down, but he's away from Washington tonight making a speech. I'll try again tomorrow."

"And somebody at Arc-Horn is going to an awful lot of trouble to block the study," said Gwen.

"Praeger," said Jim. "You remember how Sukhsvasti's question startled him this afternoon and then how he ducked it? Obviously he knew a lot more than he let on. Peculiar, by the way, that Sukit should ask him."

"Not really," said Tony. "Sukit and I discussed the thing down in Buenos Aires last month."

"I know. Still . . ." Jim considered a moment. "I wonder why the devious, not to say illegal, maneuvering by Hugo? Of course, he looks on Arc-Horn as his personal property and usually suspects all inquiries from the outside, but I'd think he would either cooperate or tell the questioners straight out to go to hell. That's more his style."

"Don't discount Chalmers Davidson's influence," said Gwen. "I hadn't realized until recently how much power the man has in Arc-Horn."

"Such as?"

"It turns out that whenever something a bit shady happens, Davidson's shop is connected with it. Look at Ron Jeffers in Argentina. Ron is Davidson's No. 1 boy. And why all this elaborate security over Chalmers' private message center up on the eleventh floor?"

"I thought all the communications were centered in the Toltec Room off the lobby."

"No, no, Jim." Gwen shook her head. "Those news tickers and direct lines are for everybody's use. But Davidson has his own private complex on the eleventh floor. You know María, one of the conference hostesses?"

Jim nodded. "The feisty one with the chip on her shoulder. She was our escort from the airport."

"Well, María asked me today what all the machines in Davidson's suite were for. She said that last week they moved in Telex equipment, coding machines, shortwave radio, gear for private lines, all kinds of stuff. It's in the room just after you turn the corner of the corridor that leads to the big Arc-Horn conference room. Notice the sign on the door next time you go by: 'No Admittance. Authorized Personnel Only.' And there's always one of those blue-shirted guards on duty."

"But that figures," objected Tony. "They need sophisticated equipment for company business. And I know that some messages go in code. Always have."

"But security like we were the Pentagon or something? . . . Listen, Tony, how do you get a Telex message from your office in Buenos Aires?"

"Through Jeffers or Davidson. Jeffers tears it off the machine, puts it in an envelope and has it delivered to the room. I got one this noon."

"Right." Gwen pointed her glowing cigarette at Tony. "So that means Chalmers knows everything going on in this corporation. If you ask me, that gives him lots of advantage. Suppose he decides to act on some emergency without telling Hugo?"

"That's possible, sure," said Jim. "But if Hugo let anything important slip by him, I'd be damned surprised."

They debated the relative power nuances between

Hugo Praeger and his vice-president for international operations and communications while thin rays of moonlight, filtering through the palm fronds, traced dancing patterns on the table top. From the Cihuacoatl Room, the cavern-like night club named for the "woman serpent" of Indian myth, came sounds of merriment. They could hear Frankie Fee's whisky voice, Praeger's high cackle above a flood of laughter and Gilda's husky tones as she began a song.

Across the terrace a figure walked toward them, threading his way through the deserted tables. It was a blue-shirted security guard with holstered revolver. Gwen rose and took a few steps in his direction.

"Everything okay over here?" asked the guard.

"Fine." Gwen stood in his pathway with her hands on the back of a chair. "We're enjoying the fresh air."

"Nice night for it." He hesitated, scanning their faces, then walked away.

"Well, maybe he's patrolling." Gwen returned to her place. "And then again, maybe he's snooping. Anyway, I'm glad we decided to meet out here."

They turned from the tempting subject of Davidson and secrecy to a review of Hugo Praeger's interview. They discussed his autocratic behavior, the constantly shifting material shortages that beset all Arc-Horn subsidiaries, the apparent sabotage of an academic study of Arc-Horn, the upcoming U.N. conference in Geneva and the latent power of Masuo Sugimoto of Nakamura, Ltd.

"I was surprised the way Masuo helped me this morning and again on the closed-circuit show," said Jim. "That man's on the ball."

"And his question about whether there were CIA agents on the Arc-Horn payroll," said Gwen. "What's that all about?"

"Search me." Tony looked perplexed. "But I've been thinking we ought to talk to Masuo before we confront Praeger. Talk about clout. In this outfit, Sugimoto's got it."

"Right," agreed Jim. "In any kind of showdown, I'll

bet Masuo could come up with maybe a quarter of Arc-Horn shares when you count what's held by Naka-mura, by Sugimoto himself, Japanese investors and funds, suppliers, friends."

"You never catch Hugo getting off one of his smart cracks at Masuo's expense," said Gwen. "Hugo treats him with more respect than anybody in the organization."

"I like the guy," said Tony. "He's smart and he levels. I've never had cause to doubt his word. He's just the opposite of the stereotype of the devious, in-scrutable Oriental."

And so it was decided that they would include the president of Nakamura, Ltd., in any future councils of insurgency. They talked for another hour while the palms rustled softly, music and laughter floated across the terrace from the Cihuacoatl cavern and the fountain of light over the bay of Acapulco, a few miles to the north, began to lose its glow. In the end, they re-solved to gather more facts looking toward a conference with Praeger on Thursday, the final day of the anni-versary celebration, when they would urge that Arc-Horn deal openly and frankly with any responsible study of corporate operations and that Praeger agree to yield some authority to an executive committee on formulation of broad Arc-Horn policy.

Tony arose, yawned and stretched, then cupped an ear to the sounds of Jake Apple's jazz combo rolling out from the Cihuacoatl cavern. "I think I'll see what's going on in the den of the lady serpent. How about it?"

"Not me, thanks." Gwen slipped off her sandals. "I'm going to walk barefoot on the beach. Dig that moonlight."

Jim was about to ask if she wanted company, but Gwen already had turned toward the ocean, shoes in hand. He sensed her desire to be alone.

"I'm going to turn in," he said. "Not much sleep for the last two nights."

Jim strolled across the terrace while Gwen plodded

south through the sand and Tony headed for the night club where Gilda sang to the beat of drum, guitar and piano.

Entering his room, Jim found a note beneath the door from the hotel switchboard: "Please call Oscar Smith, Doylestown, Pa., USA. Urgent." He tried for ten minutes to return the call, but Smitty, elusive tonight when lines to the United States were clear, could not be located at either his home or the factory. Jim made a mental note to call first thing in the morning.

He shed his golden shirt and stepped to the balcony rail to let the cool air wash over him. It was another spectacular midnight, moonbeams playing on the ocean in a narrow, shimmering roadway, waves cresting and thrusting far up on the sand, the sky lighted by legions of stars shining from the recesses of the universe, thousands of light-years back in the depths of time.

He felt better tonight despite the perplexing Arc-Horn dilemma and Al Bebout's dismissal, permanent or temporary as it might be. Thanks to Sugimoto, Hugo had given ground on the Doylestown issue, no doubt about that. And perhaps this weekend, with Dave Moyer's help, Jim and Meg might reknit some of the old understanding. For one thing, he'd get a charge out of showing Meg around the Doylestown plant with its new morale. All in all, things were looking up.

Down below he could see the dim figure of Gwen, walking along the beach at the tide's edge, letting the retreating waters swirl about her feet. She was, he surmised, headed toward a clump of light on the sand where Steve's tent stood. Well, he thought, Steve's not exactly my style, but he's a candid, challenging sort of guy and I like him. And I hope restless Gwen finds whatever it is she's looking for. Jim grinned. My, what magnanimity tonight, McGowan. Credit the soft, benign night and those highways of stars stretching to an infinity of time and space.

Tuesday, 12:16 a.m.

Some four thousand miles southeast of Acapulco, at a point where the Paraná and Uruguay rivers flow together to form the broad, silt-laden headwaters of the Río de la Plata, the weather was turning cool with the approach of the Southern Hemisphere's autumn. A brisk wind cut the humid night air.

The S.S. *Aquarius,* an ancient coastal tanker of 10,000 tons capacity, moved cautiously through the Canal de Martín García, one of a score of channels fingering the Paraná's wooded delta a few miles above Buenos Aires. In the summer season now ending, hundreds of pleasure craft cruised the waterways. Summer houses, inns and boathouses lined the grassy banks. Sports-loving Argentines, using the canals like highways, moored their boats in front of rustic restaurants where Sunday crowds dined on grilled beef from the pampas and Mendoza wines from the slopes of the Andes.

Tonight the *Aquarius* alone plowed the Martín García Channel, her running lights glowing beneath a tumbled black sky and her Liberian flag standing out stiffly in the quickening wind. The tanker's home port was Monrovia, according to the legend visible under the stern lights. Both sides of the broad diesel stack bore the black letters of ownership, "Sea Routes, Inc.," above the blue-and-red logo of Arc-Horn International.

On the bridge Captain Cletus Tanner stood near the wheel, watching his helmsman steer the ship carefully in this waterway. The *Aquarius* made little more than four knots against the heavy current. Tanner, a veteran merchant mariner who hailed from the island of Saba in the Caribbean, was worried. For one thing, the stuttering radio, tuned to the weather information band, brought reports of an unexpected gale blowing in from the South Atlantic. Storm warnings were now up along the Argentine and Uruguayan coasts from Mar del Plata to the south to Punta del Este to the east. For another thing, Tanner was uncomfortable with the *Aquarius*'s old hull plates, especially on the port side. Two months ago he had told Admiral Joyce Boke-Milgrim, the boss of Sea Routes, that the old tub was nearing her end. Boke-Milgrim agreed she ought to be scrapped, but in these days of fuel hunger even the most senile of tankers continued to sail. In her old age, the *Aquarius* would be limited to the easy "milk run" from Venezuela to the Argentine coast, thence 240 miles up the Paraná River to the industrial city of Rosario. Tanner and the tanker had made the round trip at least fifty times.

This voyage should be as painless as the others—and yet Tanner worried. In his tanks he carried the equivalent of 70,000 barrels of crude oil destined for a Rosario refinery. The tanker rode low in the water, moving sluggishly up the waterway that the captain knew as well as the veins on his weathered hands. With a blow on the way, he wanted to clear the delta waters and anchor in the Paraná itself before high winds hit him. While the channel afforded some protection, the delta islands hugged the waterline and Tanner knew from experience that a storm sweeping across the wide, shallow, open Río de la Plata often gathered amazing force by the time it struck the Paraná delta, where strong currents and tides, coupled with twisting channels, complicated navigation even in fair weather.

The winds were increasing steadily now and when Captain Tanner heard that peculiar strumming sound off the big diesel stack, a sound not unlike the whining of early hurricane winds off the rocks of his native Saba, he knew that he was in for foul weather. The easterly wind picked up speed and volume by the minute. Then it began gusting and the waves slapping at the *Aquarius* quickly donned whitecaps. The vessel was heading northwest, so that the bursts struck the tanker full on the starboard quarter, forcing the helmsman to throw the wheel lest the screw snag the channel bank. Right now a sheared prop blade was a handicap to be dreaded.

Suddenly the storm invaded the *Aquarius*'s watery highway with a fury that even Tanner did not anticipate. Within seconds, it seemed, certainly within a minute, the waterway became a howling battleground of hostile elements. Waves crashed against the aging hull, the wind sang wildly through cables and housings, rain pelted the decks and a single stab of lightning lit nearby delta islands like noonday. Then an uncanny blackness enveloped the *Aquarius* and rain drummed against the bridgehouse with a harsh ferocity. Water streamed over the glass windshield so swiftly that wipers working at top speed could not compete.

Tanner shouldered his helmsman aside and took the wheel himself. The storm blotted the next navigation light from view and even the tanker's bow lights could be seen only at rare intervals. The only thing he could rely on now was luck.

But luck, a commodity he'd known in plentiful supply over the years, failed him this time. At 6:16 a.m. Greenwich time, 2:16 in Buenos Aires or 12:16 a.m. in Acapulco, the S.S. *Aquarius* came to a shuddering, groaning halt. On the bridge Tanner was thrown rudely against the binnacle, gashing his arm, while the helmsman beside him spilled on the deck. Down below dishes flew across the galley, men were hurled against bulkheads and in the engine room a pump was torn from its foundation and sent smashing across the vessel.

The tanker had rammed into the left bank of the channel. Now the quartering wind swung the stern against the same bank and the fusillade of waves pounded the *Aquarius* against the combination of mud, blocks and boulders that made up the channel bank. The tanker heeled slightly to port.

Captain Tanner, righting himself with a bloodied arm, ordered engines full astern in an effort to free the ship, but the propeller had sheared off on the rocks. Orders were futile. The *Aquarius* lay against the land like a beached whale.

Frantic activity continued on the bridge for half an hour, but finally and reluctantly Tanner gave up the struggle. The radioman sent out the first of a series of SOS's on the marine emergency band. On ship-to-shore telephone, Tanner himself raised the night duty officer of the Prefectura Naval Argentina in Buenos Aires. In his labored Spanish he described the tanker's plight and asked for immediate aid, fixing the location in the Canal de Martín García by the numbered navigation lights on the chart. While the Prefectura officer promised help, he doubted that a rescue ship could reach the tanker in less than two hours. The gale was blowing with great force now, heaving the shallow, muddy waters between Buenos Aires and Montevideo into hills and gullies that imperiled all but the sturdiest crafts.

The *Aquarius*'s old plates on the port side cracked under the incessant pounding about two hours after the tanker ran aground. Soon a huge rent opened in the hull, salt water poured in and oil flowed out. While the vessel itself was in no danger of breaking up yet, the oil stain spread slowly from the fractured hull like black ointment on wounded flesh. At first the crippled tanker yielded only the petroleum from one tank, but as time went on the storm's intensity crumpled other tanks and soon much of the oil, the equivalent of 70,-000 barrels, was free to mingle with the roiled, dun waters of the delta.

The storm spent itself soon after dawn, but by the time the black overcast turned to a smear of gray and the rescue cutter arrived to take off the crew, a scum of oil covered the Martín García passage from shore to shore. The tanker had run aground just a few hundred yards from a spot where one of the many watery fingers of the delta joined the ship channel. This smaller canal was flanked by grassy banks on which rested several dozen summer homes. The largest of these, a rambling wooden house situated on five acres of land precisely where the two waterways intersected, belonged to Señor Rudolfo Betancourt, Argentina's Deputy Minister of Public Works and Services.

When the sun rose higher, a ruddy glow behind the tumbled clouds, the oil smear licked at Señor Betancourt's shorelines, blackening the pilings of the white dock, staining the wooden boathouse and lapping with a thousand gummy tongues at the roots of shrubs and the slopes of the manicured lawn. It was now high tide. When the tide fell, Señor Betancourt's six hundred meters of waterfront would be a black, viscous, lifeless bog.

Tuesday Morning

Jim McGowan was sleeping soundly in the huge bed of his Mixteca Hotel suite when, for the second morning in a row, he was awakened by the clamor of the bed-side telephone. He groped for the receiver and cradled it to his ear. Through cracks in the venetian blind he could see ribbons of bright sunlight.

"What the hell are you trying to do to me?" Hugo Praeger's angry voice blasted Jim's eardrum. "Is this Doylestown ruckus your idea?"

Jim sat upright, shaking his head to clear the fog of sleep. "Hugo, I have no idea what you're talking about."

"You don't, huh? Well, read the goddam story in

the *Daily* and be up here in thirty minutes. This thing's an outrage!"

Now what? Jim massaged his face with his palms, dialed room service for coffee, then shuffled to the bathroom to wash and shave. Could this be connected with Smitty's urgent call last night? He had just pulled on Tuesday's golden shirt, a fresh duplicate of yesterday's when the coffee arrived with a copy of the *Arc-Horn Anniversary Daily* tucked beneath the silver pot.

María said her *"buenos días, señor"* this morning as though it pained her. Her thin smile had a touch of defiance with no trace of a servant's false obsequiousness.

"What's the matter? Can't you stand that outfit in the mornings?" Jim could see her dark skin through the translucent blue mesh and the bare valley of her breasts.

"I never like it."

"Well, that's convention work for you. . . . Thanks for the coffee."

"De nada. It's my job," María said bluntly as she strode from the room.

He gulped coffee and looked at the mimeographed news sheet. The first item stood out in boldface: TOP COURT STRIKE. ARC-HORN SUBSIDIARY DOWN.

(This story is reprinted in full from this morning's New York Times, *March 18, where it appeared under a two-column head at the bottom of Page One.)*

Doylestown, Pa., March 17—A novel strike shut down a tennis racquet plant here late today, idling 300 employees and halting production of 20,000 racquets a week.

Second-shift workers walked out at 5:45 p.m. in protest against management's dismissal of David A. Moyer, a consulting industrial psychologist, who devised a new work system for the plant. No differences over wages, hours or fringe benefits were involved.

The non-union factory is a division of Top Court, Inc., a major producer in the booming tennis industry and a subsidiary of Arc-Horn International. The Doylestown facility turns out various models of the TeeCee Championship racquet line popularized by the No. 1 ranked professional, Bart Gatchell.

"There has been an unfortunate misunderstanding which we hope to iron out as soon as we can," said Oscar R. (Smitty) Smith, plant manager. He declined further comment.

It was learned from other sources that the walkout followed a telephone call from James F. McGowan, president of Top Court, notifying plant management that the services of Mr. Moyer, a psychologist on the faculty of the University of California at Davis, would be terminated at the end of this week.

The racquet facility has gained a regional reputation in recent weeks as a "happy plant" where workers participate in production decisions and help plan work assignments. Under Mr. Moyer's guidance, the plant is run by teams of employees who recently modified the assembly line by eliminating some repetitive jobs and shifting employees about so that no one person spends more than a few hours a week at the unpopular one-task posts.

"We just decided we wouldn't take this," said Henry Marks, a veteran machinist. "Management put Moyer in over our protests and then, just when he helped us work out the best plant system in eastern Pennsylvania, management fired him."

The strike was thought to be precedent-setting. Labor circles could recall no other walkout staged in an effort to save the job of a consulting psychologist.

Top Court's President McGowan, a well-known figure in the tennis world and a friend of Senator Philip Ireland, probable Democratic presidential contender, could not be reached immediately. He is

*in Acapulco, Mexico, attending a twentieth-anniver-
sary convention of Arc-Horn International.*

Jim stared at the paper. For Christ's sake! So that
was why Smitty called. And Jim sensed at once that
his first feelings were mixed. He disliked the halt in
production, but his sympathies were with Hank Marks
and the other striking workers. In their place, he
guessed, he would have done the same thing.

He finished his coffee, then hurried down to the
Toltec communications center. A news ticker carried a
condensed version of the *Times* article. Jim squeezed
into a phone booth beside one occupied by Nate
Berger, who shook his head dolefully. The intricacies of
commerce seldom brought joy to the suffering Summit
president. No sooner did Jim lift the receiver off the
hook than an operator in Arc-Horn's New York headquarters answered on the direct line. Within a minute
Jim reached the Doylestown plant and soon he was
talking to Smitty.

"It's out of my hands," said Smitty. "I asked them to
go back to work, but hell, they knew I didn't mean
it. I feel just like everybody else around here."

"What's the situation right now?"

"No pickets. Just people milling around outside."

"Where's Dave?"

"On his way out from New York with Mrs. Mc-
Gowan. We're having a mass meeting at noon to decide
on the next step. Any orders, boss?"

"No." Jim told him of the exchanges about Doylestown during Praeger's closed-circuit interview. "So, despite Hugo's anger right now, it looks as if he's softening
up and may be ready to change his mind about Moyer.
Anyway, I'm seeing him in a few minutes and I'll get
back to you soonest."

"Okay. My guess is that nothing short of rehiring
Moyer will satisfy them. Once you start this democracy stuff, Jim, it's hard to stop."

Praeger was eating breakfast on his balcony with Nina
Robbins when Jim arrived. He wore a purple dressing

gown and a threatening scowl, which, Jim knew of old, might or might not accurately reflect Praeger's actual mood. The buxom Nina, all innocence and eye shadow, left after the exchange of amenities.

Praeger dabbed at his lips with a napkin. "Pour yourself some coffee and tell me just what the goddam hell is going on up there in Pennsylvania and just what you had to do with it." The scowl, it appeared, was not faked this time.

Jim told what little he knew, speaking as slowly and calmly as he could. "I'm to get back to Smitty after you and I talk."

Praeger lit a Cuban panatela, managing to frown and savor the cigar simultaneously. The ocean-side balcony was in shadow, but the early-morning sun already streaked the long rollers of the Pacific.

"This strike catches me at a lousy time," said Praeger, "what with that goddam oil spill."

"Oil spill?"

"You're slow on the news this morning, friend. A Sea Routes tanker ran aground last night somewhere near Buenos Aires and is donating oil to the fuckin' shoreline. It looks like we've lost her for good, to say nothing of seventy thousand barrels of crude."

"That's a tough break."

"Yeah. A freak storm." He pointed his cigar at Jim. "Disasters caused by nature are part of the game, but man-made conspiracies are something else. . . . Now just what the hell gives with Top Court?"

"There's a strike on, but I can't see what that has to do with a conspiracy."

"You don't, huh?" Praeger's booming voice swelled in volume. "Well, how about this? Top Court's Mr. Bebout prompts the most insulting question ever asked me in the history of this corporation. Top Court's Mr. Moyer's friend, an industrial shrink named Elliott Sheddington, cons Nate Berger into testing that damn closed-circuit inquisition on me." Praeger used his cigar to stress counts of the indictment. "Top Court's Mr. McGowan prods Masuo Sugimoto and others into pressuring me on the Doylestown fiasco and now a whole damn Top Court work force walks out on me. If that's not prima facie evidence of conspiracy, I don't know what is." Praeger's anger brought a tomato flush to his face.

"Now, Hugo." Jim kept his voice low. "Conspiracy is one of those paranoid words for coincidences."

"Damn long string of coincidences."

"But that's just what they are. I had no idea Bebout was behind that question. Al is often too flip for his own good, but he's a top-flight executive and I need him." Jim had intended to press for Bebout's reinstatement, but another look at the glowering Praeger told him this was no time to argue the case. "I know nothing about any psychologist friends of Dave Moyer. Never heard of anybody named Elliott Sheddington. As for the Doylestown matter, I didn't prod Sugimoto or anybody else yesterday. Lucy Jenkins brought it up in our group. . . . Nor did I know a single thing about the strike until I saw the *Daily* just now after your call."

"All right, all right." Praeger waved his cigar as though to brush aside his own accusations. "Instead of conspiracy, we'll settle for a string of startling coincidences. I'll take your word for that."

"You sound as though you don't."

Praeger flared like a torch. "What the hell is this, Jim? Are you doubting my word now?"

"I just want to get things straight between us."

Praeger pointed his slim cigar at Jim. "I intend to talk straight. That's why you're here." As frequently happened when his bluster was challenged, Praeger turned down his volume several notches. "Now, after I saw the sentiment yesterday for your, er, experiment at Doylestown, I decided to give you the benefit of the doubt and let you keep Moyer on through another quarter. It was my firm intention to tell you that when we met tomorrow." He paused, staring at Jim. "But today, no. Now the situation is completely different. The workers are holding a gun to your head, and when the issue is who runs the plant, McGowan or the employees, there can be no compromise, what? Management calls the shots."

"That's not quite right, Hugo. The issue here is who runs Top Court, you or me."

"You mean you're in favor of the goddam strike?" Praeger looked as if Jim had blasphemed Holy Scripture.

"No. But I could settle it in one minute. All I have to do is announce that Moyer's staying on as long as he's needed."

"Then you'd be surrendering to the workers. And once you do that, you're buying endless trouble from now on in."

"I'll take my chances on that, Hugo. The employees know I'm for Moyer and his system, so what it boils down to is not them against me, but you against me."

Praeger waved his cigar dismissively again. "You put it however you like, but I'm not going to allow any subsidiary of Arc-Horn International to be run by the son-of-a-bitchin' workers. That's anarchy."

Jim thought "anarchy" a poor word to describe the determination of employees to protect a system that would boost both morale and production, but he let it pass. "That may mean a costly strike at a plant where we make you a buck a racquet or about twenty-thousand dollars a week."

Praeger shook his head. "It'll all be over in a few days as soon as they start getting hungry."

"I doubt it. This strike isn't over money, you know. They've walked out over a principle."

"That makes it even more intolerable. A strike over principle is the worst kind, what?"

They argued the issue for another quarter of an hour, Jim insisting that he could insure resumption of production by a phone call and Praeger reiterating that only management, and by management he meant himself, would ever set policy in his corporation.

"Look, Hugo," said Jim at last, "we're not getting anywhere. I can end the strike by announcing that Moyer stays on. You refuse to let me do that. So just what do you want me to do?"

"I want you to get on that horn and order your employees back to work, period."

"You know they'll refuse. How does that help?"

"It'll show that you and I are united." Praeger studied the ash of his cigar. "And it'll tell me something about your loyalty to Arc-Horn."

Jim hesitated, then said quietly: "I won't do that."

"I could fire you, you know." Praeger also spoke in low key.

"I have a management contract with almost a full year to run."

"So did Bebout. . . . And Pete Quigley, what?"

They eyed each other in silence, measuring, calculating, waiting. Jim saw a pelican skim the waves, plunge clumsily, then hoist his beak in triumph. A small fish disappeared down his gullet.

"But, of course, you're no Pete Quigley," said Praeger. Had he retreated or had the threat been a ruse? Hugo's unsmiling face masked the answer. "We're not going to break up a sound partnership over a single disagreement—however important it is."

Jim breathed deeply. "I think I'd better fly up to Doylestown and see for myself." He tried to sound casual. "Maybe Moyer and I can come up with some kind of compromise you'd buy."

"No. You're not to do that." Praeger's veto was abrupt. "That would dignify the strike out of all proportion. You just stay down here with the sun and the sea and the sand and let events run their course. It'll be over in a few days."

"What am I supposed to tell the press when they call?"

"Leave that to us. I'll have Bernie Hirsch's people get out a statement for you."

"The media won't buy that canned crap. They'll want to know where I stand and what I propose to do."

"And that's just what we're not going to have you tell them." Praeger arose and stubbed out his cigar. The session was over. "I'll see that Bernie gets you the statement within an hour."

"This is a big mistake, Hugo."

"Not this one." A quick, sly grin spread over his face. "But even if I were wrong, you know my motto: If I can keep my errors to thirty-five percent, I'll die a big winner."

"In death we're all even."

"We might discuss that sometime." Praeger's hand on Jim's elbow propelled him toward the door. "It's one of those philosophical clichés to which I've never subscribed." His tone hinted that there was a good chance the Praeger ego, an entity no less sovereign than Arc-Horn, might go spinning into space, radiating, bleeping and vibrating down the long bright halls of eternity.

Jim's own frustration was a finite presence as he walked from the suite and trotted down the steps toward his room on the floor below. He found slips from the hotel operator, asking him to return calls to NBC, the Associated Press, the *Philadelphia Bulletin* and Dave Moyer in Doylestown.

Moyer took the news calmly. "Praeger's reaction was to be expected," said the psychologist after Jim related highlights of his meeting with the Arc-Horn chief. "Don't worry about it, Jim. It may take a few days, but we'll work out some solution."

"Damn it, Dave, we're losing four thousand dollars a day up there." Sometimes Moyer's undiluted optimism grated on Jim. "On the other hand, if they go back to work, that'll just confirm Praeger's belief that he knows more about running Top Court than I do."

"There may be a way to avoid that. In the meantime, I'm enjoying the honor. This is the first time anybody ever gave up a pay check on account of me." To the struggle of egos between Praeger and McGowan, add a third, Moyer's. "As far as you're concerned, Jim, there's a bright side. Meg's outside the plant now talking to people. We may have another convert before the day's over."

"I like that." If a strike was the price of Meg's sudden interest in Top Court, it was almost worth it.

"She's counting on our weekend session here. We

had a good talk last night and I think you'll find her ready with some new ideas for the McGowans. A little more give, let's say."

"That's fine. I can use some good news today. Tell her I'll call her this evening. I'll see you and Meg Friday night then. . . . Fill in Smitty on the Praeger talk and tell him that privately I'm with him a hundred percent."

Jim walked slowly to his balcony and sank into a deck chair. Although the western, ocean flank of the Mixteca still stood in shadow, the morning was already hot. The sky arched overhead like a great flawless blue bowl. Fishing boats, white specks on the horizon, trolled for sailfish, and from the Maya Hall below came the beat of Jake Apple's band as it primed the audience for Summit's new black-and-white television line, another revolution, another glorious scene and sound of '76 for the glutted consumer.

More bathers than usual strolled the beach and Jim guessed that some of the troops, stirred by the closed-circuit interview yesterday, had chosen sunlight over Summit this morning. To the south, in front of Steve's pup tent, he saw two figures romping at the water's edge. He thought he recognized them. Yes, Gwen and Steve. So Gwen was playing hooky. Truancy, it seemed, was a popular sport today.

Had Hugo actually considered firing him a half hour ago? Jim wondered. There was that one instant when he thought so. It was as though the tepid air had chilled momentarily between Jim and the ash-deep end of Hugo's cigar. . . . He had intended to ask Hugo for time on Thursday when he, Gwen and Tony could confront Praeger with their evidence of sabotage of an academic study and their demand for less autocratic rule. But this morning was no time for that. Hugo would merely have seized on the request as confirmation of a conspiracy against him. Three insurgent presidents stalking him with complaints would stretch the fabric of coincidence to the rending point.

The encounter this morning, following Praeger's out-

burst at Jim in yesterday's board meeting, left Jim with
a bitter taste. Was his relationship with Hugo eroding?
He recalled Smitty's question yesterday noon. Just what
good did "that fat slob do for Top Court?" Jim's answer about easier financing through Arc-Horn had
been a feeble one. . . . God, how he'd like to be
out from under Hugo and on his own as in the old
days. But how? No way. Hugo held all the weapons.

And while the sun climbed higher, thrusting the Mixteca's seaside shadow back toward the patio and the
thatch-roofed Tarascan Bar, Jim McGowan brooded and
pondered.

Tuesday Afternoon

All over the world that afternoon 677 of Arc-Horn International's profit centers hummed, pounded and ground
away, spewing out computers, calculators, TV sets, radios, hi-fi equipment, video cassettes, eight brands of soft
drinks, flowered shirts and dresses, printed fabrics, lip-
sticks, skin moisturizers, flavored douches, colognes, dusting powders, perfumes, beef, wheat, rice, barley, refined
sugar, millions of board feet of lumber, plywood, twenty-
seven varieties of machine tools, pills, salves, medicines,
vitamins, heavy-duty vehicles, metal extrusions, tennis
balls, nets and toys. Only the 678th profit center, the
tennis-racquet factory at Doylestown, Pennsylvania, failed
to join the disciplined stampede to cram more and more
goods into the maw of the human consumer.

Arc-Horn ships sailed the seas, loans were floated in
Europe, insurance policies signed in a hundred Ameri-

can cities, real estate hawked on four continents, cans and bottles sold off the shelves of Latin supermarkets, cattle slaughtered in Argentina, oil sucked from the ocean floor off Indonesia and a dozen minerals, from copper to cobalt, clawed from the earth.

And across the world that afternoon of March 18, events occurred that touched the outposts and nerve center of the Arc-Horn empire. Some of them were known within minutes at the Mixteca Hotel, thanks to Chalmers Davidson's eleventh-floor classified communications hub and to the elaborate complex of news and telephone wires funneling into the Toltec Room off the public lobby. In the Mixteca and in cities and towns thousands of miles away, events formed, expanded and dissolved, hour by hour, many of them directly affecting the lives of the five hundred Arc-Horn anniversary celebrants.

12 noon. Doylestown, Pennsylvania. Three hundred striking employees of the Top Court racquet plant crowded into the brightly painted cafeteria to deliberate on the next move in their contest of wills with President Hugo Praeger of Arc-Horn. Standing on a bench at the rear of the hall were David Moyer and Mrs. Margaret Chesley McGowan, the chic wife of Top Court's president.

12:20 p.m. Delta of the Paraná, Argentina. Elena Betancourt, wife of Argentina's Deputy Minister of Public Works and Services, stood on the veranda of their rustic summer home and surveyed the damage done to the property by oil still oozing from the crumpled hulk of the S.S. *Aquarius,* aground three hundred meters away in the Martín García Channel bank. The sight sickened her. The Betancourt shoreline, fronting on two waterways, looked as if it were clutched by some evil, nauseating plague. Oil from the receding tide clogged the shrubs, blackened the lower lawn and sucked at the pilings of the boathouse and dock. Two mallard ducks, their glossy green necks fouled by petroleum, sought futilely to lift wings trapped in the viscous fluid, and Elena sensed that they would die there.

She felt both disgust and an inner rage, and after a final look at the black swamp which glistened in the sun with a kind of corrupt beauty, she went into the house and telephoned her husband at his government office in Buenos Aires.

12:45 p.m. Mixteca Hotel, Acapulco. The convention army dined on terrapin sprinkled with sherry at the terrace tables shaded by gaily colored beach umbrellas. At the long table shared by Jake Apple's Convention Dynamics crew, Frankie Fee traded jokes with Walter Lowdermilk, who considered it only his due to sit with professional entertainers. The two comedians twitted Cal Silliman, accusing him of taking a twenty percent cut on the earnings of the voluptuous Miami women. Cal, whose broker's charge was only ten percent, was able to demolish the charge with honest outrage. One of Gilda's dancers chafed over an affront to her dignity. Admiral Boke-Milgrim had confused her with a tall Miami blonde and offered her two hundred dollars for a night's solace. "I wouldn't sleep with that British creep for five grand," she protested to Silliman. The convention manager confined his solicitude to a sigh of regret. Cal had other troubles. Alex Rosinski, the Summit designer, was still in jail and the chief of police seemed to be out of the office whenever Silliman called.

1 p.m. New York City. Five university professors, the executive committee of the Group of Twelve, lunched in a private room of the Harvard Club with Senator Philip Ireland, who had consented to render political advice for a cause he championed. The academics faced a problem.

On Monday they would read two papers to the second U.N. Conference on the Human Environment in Geneva. The first paper, entitled "Winding Down," bristled with facts and figures on the increasingly rapid exhaustion of the earth's resources and stated that the continuing petroleum shortage and the sporadic gaps in the supply of other vital materials were but mild forerunners of a barren, desolate future unless mankind drastically reduced its output of goods.

The second paper dealt with Arc-Horn International as an illustration of the drain on the earth's diminishing irreplaceable juices and sinews of just one large multinational corporation during a single working day. Since Arc-Horn's Hugo Praeger and Chalmers Davidson had refused cooperation, the study went ahead without corporate sanction. There was no question, said Russell Kirkland, a Columbia University biochemist, that top Arc-Horn officials had tried to sabotage the study by such techniques as burglary, bribery and theft.

"Give me a sample of what you mean by a drain on resources," said Ireland.

"On any single eight-hour working day," said Kirkland, "Arc-Horn International digs, sucks and drills or molds, extrudes, bends, shapes, squeezes and transmutes more of the earth's vitals than did all the people living on the planet during the four centuries from the birth of Plato to the death of Christ.

"Or, a reverse look. If someday we could pile in one dump all the obsolescent, non-recyclable articles from this one day of Arc-Horn extraction and production, the mountain of rubbish would be higher than would that made by the artifacts of all North American Indian tribes over a span of five thousand years."

Ireland learned that the Group of Twelve had evidence that Arc-Horn directors Thursday would be asked to approve two projects that would most certainly, the panelists believed, damage the environment irrevocably. One, called Project Green Tree, involved logging off a huge area of the Amazon Basin jungle, mining its resources and planting its thin, hot soil for crop production and cattle pasturing. Shorn of its trees, the Amazon soil would yield bountifully for a few years, then, leached by tropical rains, it would waste away into sterility. And since the Amazon jungle supplied more than twenty percent of the world's oxygen, Green Tree and other ambitious developments sure to follow it would mount the ultimate hazard to man and beast—depletion of the oxygen necessary to life.

The other proposal, Neptune West, would link Arc-Horn with the Mexican government in mining the ocean floor off Baja California for a variety of minerals. Recent data showed this would disrupt the delicate balance of marine life and threaten the existence of the oxygen-producing phytoplankton. Ocean mining already under way had thrown off pollutants injurious to these tiny aquatic plants floating in the upper levels of the seas and if phytoplankton vanished, all ocean life would perish.

Group of Twelve members believed it imperative that Arc-Horn directors either abandon or indefinitely delay these plans. If that were done Thursday, they would be delighted to announce the fact next week in Geneva, thus providing powerful leverage to persuade other companies and nations to begin at once the urgent task of "winding down." Question: how best to approach the Arc-Horn board?

"How about Jim McGowan of Top Court?" asked Ireland. "He's a friend of mine and he's down at the Arc-Horn convention. Could somebody fly down to Acapulco with copies of the reports for him?"

"Of course," said Kirkland. "McGowan would be fine."

"Let me get him on the phone," said Ireland. "I'm not sure what Jim can do for us, but he's a receptive guy with an open mind."

1:20 p.m. Mixteca Hotel. Jim McGowan, chatting with Tony Percevale, in Jim's suite, received a phone call from Dave Moyer in Doylestown. Employees of the racquet plant, said Dave, had just voted to send Moyer down to Acapulco with instructions to lay their case before Hugo Praeger in person.

"Okay," said Jim. "Maybe you can make him see the light. I sure as hell couldn't. When are you coming?"

"We take an Eastern flight out of Kennedy at six p.m., arriving ten-thirty tonight your time."

"We?"

"Meg's coming with me. She's as fired up as your workers. And I thought we could use any spare hours down there getting the dialogue going between you and Meg."

"Okay," Jim was enthusiastic. "I'll meet your plane at ten-thirty then."

1:30 p.m. New York City. Chick Reynolds, manager of the Mozart Fund, walked back to his office in the Chase Manhattan Plaza building after lunching in the financial district of lower Manhattan. A biting wind whistled through the narrow, gloomy streets threading the gaunt towers where slips of paper, representing hundreds of millions of dollars' worth of mines, factories, ranches and fleets, changed hands every hour. Chick Reynolds pondered as he walked. His Mozart Fund had been in and out of Arc-Horn International ever since he sold Praeger his first block of Top Court stock nine years ago. Currently the fund held 335,000 shares of Arc-Horn. This morning Arc-Horn had slipped to 47½, off a half, on news of the foundering in Argentine waters and the bizarre strike at Doylestown. But Reynolds thought the stock would go lower when word got around that the $16,000,000 insurance on the wrecked *Aquarius* was held by Six Flags Insurance, another Arc-Horn subsidiary, thus forcing Arc-Horn to absorb the loss. Arc-Horn was basically sound, Reynolds believed, but it might drop to perhaps 45 in the next few days. Why not sell now and buy back later? After shucking his topcoat in his office, Reynolds called a third-market broker and offered 335,000 Arc-Horn at 47, a half point below the New York Stock Exchange price.

1:04 p.m. Mixteca Hotel. Jim McGowan picked up his ringing telephone to hear the voice of Senator Phil Ireland in New York.

"Jim," said Ireland after the pleasantries, "I'm sitting

in with the Group of Twelve here at the Harvard Club and . . ."

"Just what is the Group of Twelve?" Jim broke in. "You mentioned it Friday night, but didn't explain."

"Oh, I thought you knew. Let's see. Actually the Group of Twelve comprises about a hundred academics, including four or five Nobel laureates, serving on university faculties and in research facilities in twelve countries. The twelve are the big industrial powers, including Russia. The organization is an offshoot of the Club of Rome. They have three main worldwide concerns—overpopulation, pollution and depletion of natural resources. The last is their main target right now and they're presenting papers that I told you about—at Geneva beginning Monday.

"Right now I'm meeting with the Group's executive committee on political and publicity angles. We're informed that your Arc-Horn board on Thursday will be asked to approve two operations that the Group believes will have disastrous results for the world. One's called Green Tree, as we understand it, and the other's Neptune West. Do you know anything about them?"

"Phil, you know I'd help you if I could, but board matters are confidential." Jim hesitated. "Just how important are these supposed to be?"

"So help me, the outcome of Green Tree and Neptune West may determine whether you and I and other humans have enough oxygen left to sustain life."

"That's a pretty big mouthful," said Jim slowly. "Is this some kind of put-on?"

"I'm serious as hell. If Arc-Horn goes into Green Tree and Neptune West, and other companies follow, there's a good chance the world's oxygen supply may be cut below the peril point."

"Two questions. Are you sure you're not falling for some fanatic's far-out propaganda? And what do you want me to do?"

"The oxygen calculations have been made by some of the best brains in science. They're not infallible, of course, but we ignore them at our peril. As for you, all we ask is that you give us a hearing and then decide for yourself whether to use your influence to block the projects."

"How can I give you a hearing before Thursday?"

"The Group has two papers," said Ireland, "about a hundred pages in all, that'll be read in Geneva next week. One of the men here has agreed to fly down with the papers for you today. I'll send along a personal letter giving my own views. . . . How about it?"

"Sure, no problem. As long as it's understood I'm making no commitment beyond reading the papers."

"If you're the man I think you are, you'll break your back to stop Green Tree and Neptune West after you read the reports. That I'll bet on."

"Maybe yes, maybe no. . . . Look, Phil, there's no need for any of them to fly here." He told of Moyer and Meg coming down and gave the hour and flight number. "So just have somebody deliver the reports to Meg and we'll be all set."

"I'll hand-deliver them to Meg myself at the Eastern counter. The matter is that critical. . . . And, Jim, read my letter carefully. I've smelled out some big-power politics in this and some of it stinks, believe me."

"You have my word on that, Phil."

1:52 p.m. Mixteca Hotel. Behind the locked "No Admittance" door of Arc-Horn's specially soundproofed and air-conditioned communications room, Chalmers Davidson and his assistant, Ronald Jeffers, watched the keys of a teletype machine clatter across a moving roll of paper. The message appeared on a printer connected by private line to a room in a huge building situated in a parkland area of Langley, Virginia. Had either man attempted to read the message aloud, he would have uttered gibberish.

When the keys ceased their chatter, Jeffers tore off the sheet of paper, placed it in an adjacent decoding machine and pressed a button marked "Blue Five." Within a minute, the computerized decoder, which switched cipher systems daily, delivered a message in plain English through a slot at the bottom. Jeffers quickly scanned the paper, then handed it to Davidson.

File Series 802-W
No. 7

From: *Mother*
To: *Cedric*
FYI. President and Soviet No. 1 had lengthy phone conversation this morning with our interpreter at this end. Subject: Coordination of U.S.-Soviet strategy for Geneva environmental conference opening Monday. Both agreed they fear UDC's will seize control of conference and demand that diminishing resources be strictly apportioned country by country by population.

Davidson broke off his reading. "What the devil's a UDC?"

"Underdeveloped country," said Jeffers. He was a precise, quick-spoken young man.

"I wish Mother would curb his bent for the unnecessarily arcane," said Davidson with an annoyed frown.

P. and S-1 agreed it vital that no such demand be permitted to surface. S-1 pledged that KGB will derail report of satellite scientists on dangers of further mining of ocean floor. In return, P. pledged blocking of G12 report on possible exhaustion of oxygen in Amazon Basin which both leaders consider to be blatantly false propaganda. S-1 said KGB has already "isolated" a Soviet meteorologist who was providing data covertly to G12.

P. and S-1 authorized close cooperation of KGB and us. They are to talk again Friday on progress.

In view of above, imperative that you:

1. Insure Arc-Horn board approval Thursday of Green Tree and Neptune West.

*2. Take all measures there to carry out objectives
of P. and S-1 as stated above.*

*At the most we hope to smother expected de-
mands of UDC's. At the least, if Arc-Horn board
gives go-ahead, UDC's will be confronted with fait
accompli.*

*Watch your health. Hot sun and cold margaritas
poor mixture.*

Davidson handed the message back to Jeffers. "Usual
disposal."

Ron Jeffers placed both the plain English and the
coded version in a small boxlike machine and flicked
a switch. After a brief whirring sound, a handful of
paper dropped into a metal receptacle. The paper was
shredded as fine as sawdust.

2 p.m. Mixteca Hotel. In a shadow thrown by a tan
nylon tent on the beach to the south of the hotel, Gwen
Piggott lay on the sand beside Steve. Their bodies glistened from a plunge in the ocean and Gwen could
taste the tange of salt on her lips. Propped on her elbows,
she studied the bronzed face of the man beside her.

"You know, I like you very much."

"Ditto from me to you." He grinned. "Maybe we
got something going."

"Please don't stare at my hair. It's a matted mess."

"It's beautiful." He fingered the long, wet strands.
"And so are you."

"I get by okay, I guess, for an old broad of forty-
four." A look of panic slipped across her face like a
fleeing shadow. "How old are you, Steve?"

"Twenty-nine."

"Oh, my God." She gasped. "Couldn't you at least
be thirty?"

"Not until my birthday next month." He cupped her
chin with his hand and looked full in her eyes. "Age
is a useless hang-up, Gwen. I never bother with it.
I've been in love twice, I guess, once a couple of

years ago with a girl of eighteen and once, when I was in college, with a widow of thirty-nine. To me, a woman's a woman at whatever age. We're people, period." He paused. "If you're thinking I'm one of those guys looking for a mama, forget it. I have a mother."

"Thank God for that. I went through the mothering bit not long ago. Ick. I hated it. . . . I get a different feeling with you. I'm not sure just what, but for starters, I'll say, well, excitement."

"Ditto."

"You mean it?"

"When you know me better, you'll know I mean everything I say—unless I hang out a banner, 'Careful. Joke coming.' "

They were silent a moment, savoring their joint confession, then Gwen said with a laugh: "If I'm going to know you better, I ought to start with your last name."

"Cooper. . . . Steven Andrew Cooper."

"Tell me about yourself, Steve. You already know plenty about me, the old chatterbox."

"Okay." He was born in the small town of Eaton, Ohio, played baseball in high school, dreamed a lot, but was a good student. Most people guessed he was a school dropout, but that wasn't true. He was graduated from Princeton with honors in economics and worked a year in New York for General Electric, statistics, plans, etc.

"That's when I did drop out. The whole system bugged me. What they called the GNP was mostly looting the earth to churn out mountains of consumer stuff that put people on a treadmill where they mistook convenience for happiness. I just felt it was all bullshit, but since very few people felt as I did, trying to organize opposition looked like utter futility. So, I decided to walk around the world and I've been at it seven years. One more continent to go—South America."

Gwen ran a finger over the fine blond hairs on his arm. "I think I understand. But I couldn't go that route. I have to be part of my time, whatever it is."

"Yeah. I thought a lot about that." He rolled on his back and stared up at the blue sky, where a lone frigate bird circled. "I do too. But I've got another conception of time. 'My time,' as you call it, is the ancient one of the sea, the tides, the moon and the seasons. . . . I guess I'm walking because I'm human and I want to know the world like men knew it thousands of years ago—and like they'll have to again in a few hundred years, maybe less. You see, I've got a gut feeling that all this industrial civilization will exhaust itself, just wear down from lack of stuff to make it go, and people will live simply again—like the Huichol Indians I stayed with further north."

"My rhythm is different," said Gwen. The tentative lovers were staking out the boundaries of self in advance of the mutual invasion. "I thrive on the stimulation of city life, my friends, the bustle, the shows, business, even some politics from time to time. Then I like to retreat into myself for a while. Back and forth like that." She laughed. "I guess if I could have the ideal, I'd live eight months like Jim McGowan and four months a year something like you do—without the hiking."

"I invited Jim to walk along with me. He acted like I'd threatened him with death by slow torture."

"Jim's okay. I think he'd like to loosen up and break out of his rut, but doesn't know how. But he's solid. And one more thing for sure, you can trust him."

'Yeah. I get the same vibes from him." He stood up and stretched. "How about another swim?"

Gwen scrambled to her feet. "Beat you in."

They ran across the sand, splashed into the water and dove into the first large wave. When they came up for air, they laughed, then kissed.

2:20 p.m. Mixteca Hotel. A bell rang on the teleprinter, one of three in Davidson's communications hub, that linked Arc-Horn's temporary headquarters to the New York office and thence to branches in forty-seven countries. The message came in Spanish and Jeffers translated for the English file copies.

From: *Pedro Gutiérrez, office manager,*
            Gusto Más, Buenos Aires
To: *Antonio Percevale, Gusto Más,*
            Mixteca Hotel, Acapulco
Copies: *H. Praeger, C. Davidson, Arc-Horn*
   Rudolfo Betancourt, Deputy Minister of Public
Works and Services, demands *I relay the following*
to you:
   1. Aquarius, wrecked Sea Routes tanker, has
ruined several miles of coastline by oil spill.
   2. Argentina demands prompt indemnity of twenty
million American ($20,000,000) or government
will consider punitive measures against Gusto Más.
   Privately I've learned that Betancourt checked
this demand with Casa Rosada and has presidential
backing. Apparently Betancourt learned from Capt.
Tanner of Aquarius that tanker carried $20,000,000
of special oil-contamination insurance. So Betan-
court knows Arc-Horn can shift the cost to the in-
suring company.

Jeffers placed both Spanish and English copies in a
hotel envelope and rang for a conference hostess who
would deliver the messages to Percevale's room.

2:25 p.m. Mixteca Hotel. Cal Silliman stood in the
hotel's great tiled kitchen, talking with Henri, the pastry
chef, a rotund, apple-cheeked native of the Loire Valley
in France. Cal's surprise for the final Thursday-night
banquet, his dream to cap a long career managing conventions, was nearing fruition.
  It would be a mammoth Arc-Horn birthday cake, ten
feet in diameter and four feet high, with an Arc-Horn
logo in blue and red icing bursting from the center and
elaborate pastry symbols of each of the nineteen subsidiaries adorning the circumference. The upper half of
the cake would bear a legend in scripted red icing:
"Happy Twentieth, Arc-Horn." The blue-icing script on
the lower half would say: "Here's to Another Smash
Twenty, Hugo."

The two men bent over a large sheet of wrapping paper on which Henri had sketched his design.

"This isn't pastry," said Henri. "It's engineering."

"But think of my problem," protested Silliman. "I have to time the cutting so that five hundred people all get a piece of cake and a glass of champagne within five minutes." He brooded, glancing at the sweep of the second hand on his stop watch. "Actually, if I can get the breaks, I hope to shave that by forty-five seconds."

"I'll have to bake it in sections," said Henri. "It will take four ovens. And the ingredients!"

"Anything you need. This takes priority over everything else in the kitchen. . . . Problem?"

Henri wrinkled his brow in thought. "Only the eggs. I need nine hundred of them."

3 p.m. New York City. Harold Frascella, executive vice-president of First Merchants Trust, took the call in his office high in the bank's towering building in lower Manhattan, where he could see the bleak monoliths of his competitors, Chase Manhattan, Manufacturers Hanover, Chemical New York, shouldering the poisonous overcast.

"Just a tip, Hal." It was First Merchants' vice-president in Paris. "I hear over here that some kind of adverse report on Arc-Horn will be made to the U.N. ecology meeting in Geneva Monday."

"Any specifics?"

"No. That's about it. Reliable source, though. I thought you might be able to follow it up over there."

Frascella rang off with thanks, then renewed his study of the Arc-Horn file he had been perusing. Poor day for Arc-Horn, what with the Doylestown strike, loss of a tanker and now the ticker's latest bulletin that Argentina was demanding $20,000,000 indemnity for the oil spill. Still, Arc-Horn tankers, he knew, all carried that expensive oil-spill insurance. Shouldn't be any static there.

Let's see, as of today, Arc-Horn was about $27,000,-000 above the loan's $150,000,000 cash-reserve requirement. Good chance now the cash flow would tighten next month. He wondered what other difficulties the wily Praeger might be keeping from him. Good time to press Hugo. The bank deserved a seat on that board.

Frascella paced the corner room, then stood by the long window, thinking, while he gazed out at the Manhattan skyline and the tugs curling bow waves through the East River. Then he returned to his desk, resumed his study of the Arc-Horn file and began punching at the buttons on his Nakamura desk calculator.

3:20 p.m. Mixteca Hotel. Scheduled events of Arc-Horn's twentieth annual convention struggled forward through the sultry afternoon despite a growing executive restlessness that could be traced to the unusual number of items about Arc-Horn appearing on the chattering financial and general news tickers in the Toltec Room.

In the Zapotec Room unsmiling John Lindquist gave his yearly lecture on inventory controls to two dozen computer specialists of the subsidiaries. He ordered the room darkened for his prize exhibit, a film on Deutsche-Mannheim's new automated warehouse near Frankfurt.

Nate Berger, his shoulder occasionally twitching, held forth in the Puebla Room with phosphorescent-tipped pointer as he explained the uses of video cassettes and disks at sales distributors' meetings.

In the Quetzalcoatl Room, Pete Quigley, a bottle of beer at hand, explored his favorite commercial mystery, "value analysis," on a platform laden with buttons, balloons, tags, ribbons, badges and other supposed incentives to executive performance. His continued use of the initials "V.A.," for analysis, led some of his yawning auditors to wonder if they were being encouraged to contract some new social disease.

3:30 p.m. Mixteca Hotel. Gilda and her newest lover, Nina Robbins, lolled in Gilda's bed as they talked.

Rumpled linen lay at the foot of the immense bed,
Gilda's flaming hair was in disarray and smoke from a
forgotten cigarette spiraled upward. Gilda had been
extravagant in adulation of Nina's spent ardor and now
she fantasized possessively about the future.

"You're tr'fic, baby." Her voice drawled huskily, but
her eyes shone. "You'll love my pad on the upper
West Side. Too big for one, but cozy for two. Your
own room when you want to use it. I can net a grand
a week when I work hard. Maybe we could work up
an act. God, honey, we'd be a lovin' team."

Nina shook her head. "I'd like that, Gilda, but very
frankly, dear, with me it's a question of money. Hugo
understands. He's generous with me and . . ."

"That big horse's ass!" Gilda exploded. "Baby, you
can have two thousand a month. If that's not enough,
I'll make more."

"Please don't insist." Nina caressed Gilda's face with
her fingertips. "I can come to your place a couple of
afternoons a week. Love's better without possession anyway."

"No. I want you to live with me. I'm tired of going
it alone, the goddam loneliness, the empty rooms."

"I'll be honest with you, sweetheart. When I left
Rock Island, I had exactly six dollars and I made up
my mind I'd never be broke again." Nina's obsession
with money was seldom reflected in her look of vir-
ginal innocence. "Besides Hugo, there's a man who
pays me well for information. . . . Oh, my God." She
pulled herself upright. "I forgot my two-o'clock call.
May I use your phone?"

Gilda pointed to the telephone on the dresser a few
feet away. Nina clambered from the bed. Gilda saw her
dial eight for inside calls, then one, one, two, nine,
before she turned her back to Gilda.

"This is Clarissa," said Nina. "No, I didn't forget. Very
frankly, it was just, well, impossible at the usual
time. . . . How strong is he on what? . . . Green Tree?
. . . And what's the other one? . . . I'll try. Okay, about

six then." Nina hung up and returned to sit on the bed beside Gilda.

"Was that your man?" Gilda's face clouded with suspicion.

"A man, yes. My man, no. I have no man. I'll be honest with you. This is purely business. I make it where I can, Gilda."

"Who is he? Do I know him?"

"Please don't ask. I told you it's only business."

"Damn you." Gilda glared at her, then suddenly seized her and covered Nina's face, throat and shoulders with hungry kisses.

A half hour later, after Nina hurriedly dressed and left, Gilda called the hotel operator.

"Who has room eleven twenty-nine?"

"Mr. Chalmers Davidson. Shall I ring?"

"No, no. Not now."

So that was the man, the tall, smug WASP who looked as snottily aloof as the doorman at the Plaza. The idea of Nina in the arms of that put-down bastard filled her with nausea.

4 p.m. Mixteca Hotel. Jim McGowan and Tony Percevale, both sweaty and short of breath, walked back to the hotel carrying their racquets. They had gone two fast sets, 6-3 for Percevale and 7-5 for Jim, and they were lamenting their weaknesses, Jim's lagging backhand and Tony's tendency to leave his back court open for the long lob, shortcomings that each had exploited in the other's play since college days.

"Nothing much changes, Tony."

"Not us maybe, but Arc-Horn. That oil spill could cause us plenty of hell back home. And it would happen right off Betancourt's property."

"No sweat. I hear there's plenty of special insurance to cover it."

"But you know adjusters. They'll try to haggle the price down. Then the government will start turning the screws on us. Well, we'll see. . . . Anything new at Doylestown?"

"Yeah, Moyer is flying down tonight to see Praeger. Meg's coming with him. And Meg is bringing a report for me from that Group of Twelve. Ireland says there's real doomsday stuff in it. I'll let you and Gwen have it when I finish. Then we can talk about Thursday."

They met Jules Amarel hurrying along the passageway. The Six Flags Insurance president looked distraught.

"What did Arc-Horn close at?" asked Tony.

"Forty-seven. Off a dollar." Amarel was not disposed to chat. "It'll fall some more tomorrow." He walked on without explanation, his head bent.

4:15 p.m. Mixteca Hotel. The vast open lobby was in turmoil. The few Arc-Horn officers who stood in the foyer, bathed by the warm ocean wind sweeping beneath the arches, were engulfed by a swarm of tourists who invaded the hotel as suddenly and as massively as a legion of locusts: overweight males in Bermuda shorts and black city socks, plump women in pink slacks, children smothered by enormous Mexican sombreros, brawny Americans in T shirts. The half-acre lobby quivered with straw handbags, sailor hats that said "Acapulco," cameras, stuffed iguanas, shoulder bags, spangled shirts, psychedelic halters, beach towels, sunglasses, swimming suits, bottles of sun-tan lotion, cigars, candy bars and name badges by the hundred. Outside stood a dozen chartered buses. Inside the din threatened all decibel records. "Where's the ladies'?" . . . "I wanna Coke, Mommy." . . . "Where the hell's the bar?"

Cal Silliman, who had been chatting with Walter Lowdermilk and Lucy Jenkins, looked like a guard on the city walls gazing out over besieging hordes of barbarians.

Cal reached out for the arm of the nearest invader, a grinning, ruddy-faced giant in chartreuse slacks, swung him around and inspected the name tag. "FRITZ . . . Zimmerman . . . HI, BUDDY! I'm from Teamsters Council 708 and proud of it."

"What are you doing here?" Silliman fairly choked on the question.

"It's on the schedule, mac." The giant looked down on the pygmy with instant camaraderie. "Swim, cocktails and dinner."

"You know this is the Mixteca." Silliman had to shout to be heard.

"Yeah. Nice place." The giant surveyed the chaotic scene with paternal pride.

Silliman plowed through milling bodies toward the hotel manager's desk. A small boy thrust out his foot from the haven of his mother's skirt. Cal tripped, started to fall and landed against the abundant breasts of a woman who wore an "Acapulco" sailor hat.

"Oh, pardon me."

"Any time, lover." She kissed his forehead. "I'm in 422 at the Americana." She smelled of sun-tan oil.

By the time Silliman reached the manager's desk, he had lost his name badge and the drag of his left heel told him he had stepped on a wad of chewing gum. A knot of people surrounded the desk and a short, wizened man, holding a battery-powered megaphone and wearing a T shirt that proclaimed, "Dirty Old Men Need Love Too," was screaming at the manager.

"Goddam it, right here, look." He held out an open booklet. "Hotel Caleta. Swim, cocktails, dinner."

"I'm sorry, but this is the Mixteca." The suave Mexican manager sought, not with total success, to maintain his professional cool. "At this hour, according to your program, you're due at the Caleta."

"Where the hell is it?" The T shirt who needed love tried to tamp his fires.

"Other side of the bay. About an hour's drive from here."

More fractured argument ultimately led to the summoning of the chief bus driver, a somnolent, imperturbable man. Ah, yes, the Caleta. He shrugged. One of those errors with which a busy life was fraught. How did it happen? *Quién sabe, señor?*

"Back to your drawing boards," said Silliman tartly.

T shirt leaped to the top of the manager's desk and lifted his bull horn. "Seven-oh-eight! Quiet, quiet. There's been a mistake. We're in the wrong hotel. . . . Please move back to the buses. Back to the buses, please. . . . All right, move it, everybody."

A chorus of good-natured boos greeted the command and a few people turned toward the portico. "To the buses, please!" Slowly the throng began shuffling through the lobby in the direction of the parked vehicles. It required a full ten minutes to empty the hotel of the invaders, for stragglers from the shops, the terrace and the Tarascan Bar had to be coaxed along with encouraging bleats from the megaphone.

At a signal from the manager, a half dozen uniformed custodians manned brooms and began clearing the tiled floor of candy wrappers, chewing gum, empty bottles, bottle tops, cigarette butts, tinfoil from film rolls, tissue, plastic bags and one lost billfold.

The barbarian hordes had passed from the gates. The citadel of the Arc-Horn empire was spared.

4:55 p.m. Mixteca Hotel. Hugo Praeger lay bulbous and bare on the special collapsible table brought down from New York in the Learjet. He was five minutes early for his daily massage and Nina's accommodating fingers began kneading his padded shoulder muscles. The sweet odor of aloe oil mingled with the fresh ocean air near the eleventh-floor balcony.

Hugo grunted with pleasure. "Have a good day?"

"Yes, I did. A nice long talk with Gilda." She bent to her task as she talked.

"Watch out for that broad. What she's after isn't your conversation."

"Don't worry, bunny. Very frankly, I know how to take care of myself. . . . How did it go with you?"

"Lousy day for Arc-Horn. That strike, the wrecked tanker, oil soaking the Argentine shoreline. But we'll manage. We've had worse days."

The phone rang. "Tell 'em to call back at six," said Praeger.

Nina walked to the nearby telephone, answered, listened, then cupped her hand over the mouthpiece. "It's John Lindquist. He says it's important."

"Okay, okay. Bring it over here."

Trailing the extension cord, Nina delivered the instrument to the massage table. Praeger propped himself on an elbow. "Okay, John. What's up?"

"There's a bad development on that oil contamination insurance. I think you ought to talk to Amarel as soon as you can. Since Gusto Más is involved too, you better add Percevale. And Boke-Milgrim, of course."

"All right, you bring the three of them up here at six-thirty. And tell Chalmers I want him here too." Praeger lowered the telephone to the floor. "Always another goddam emergency."

"Work, work, work." Nina stroked and kneaded with her fingers, palms, then knuckles, pressing heavily, up and down the back, along the spine, her oiled hands sliding over the aging flesh. Praeger was silent.

"What is Green Tree, bunny?" she asked after many minutes passed.

"A big project we have cooking for the Amazon Basin. It looks good." He grunted. "Ought to make a bundle."

"And Neptune West?"

"Mining the ocean floor for copper and manganese nodules out in the Pacific. That's another possible big one."

"Have you decided?"

"Not yet. They both look okay, but there are problems. On these, I'd like to hear what the board has to say Thursday. I'm going to allow plenty of time for discussion."

"Sometime you should take a day off."

"Can't spare days. But tonight is a free one on the schedule and you and I are going to hit the high spots. First, we'll go by the shops and load you up with new clothes. Anything you want, Nina. Then dinner at Armando's and a couple of go-go joints, what?"

"You know I'd love that." As she spoke, she felt a tremor of disloyalty, her closest approach to outright guilt. She didn't mind her chores for Davidson—good pay for easy work—but she disliked the man. But then Hugo, for all his generosity, was unpredictable. He could end it all in a moment. She sighed. A woman had to make it however she could.

The heavy back and leg massages finished, Nina began plying her fingers lightly, temptingly, down Praeger's spine. He quivered. She let the tips of her fingers flutter over the small of his back, then move slowly over the crease of his rump and down, gently and softly, between his legs. After pausing a moment, her fingers rippled like tiny waves.

The big man whimpered.

Nina looked beyond the balcony rail to the setting sun, a huge orange ball sinking toward the horizon. She hesitated, sighing once more, then let her hands resume their daily chores.

Tuesday, 6:30 p.m.

Hugo Praeger eyed each man in turn in the heavy silence, his gaze lingering on Jules Amarel and Joyce Boke-Milgrim, assessing blame like weights on a scale.

"Christ Almighty, gentlemen." At last the pent anger burst. "We're talking about a loss of forty cents a share, what?"

The six men sat hunched at the bend of the Arc-Horn conference table in a wedge of light from the overhead chandelier. Behind them the tropic dusk settled on the balcony and probed the open doorway as if eager to fill the vacuum created when the sun wiped itself from the far horizon. With their gold and blue shirts exposing

graying chest hairs, the executives could have been garish
clowns left over from a spent carnival.

"Forty cents a share." Praeger repeated the figure
with mingled wrath and awe as though the apportioning
of $20,000,000 to each unit of Arc-Horn stock somehow
increased the enormity of the offense.

Corporate finance impels a curious inversion in the
emotional impact of language. The mortgaged householder finds the $350 monthly payment to the bank a much
lighter cross to bear than his $40,000 debt. No vassal
of the automobile speaks of the $2,500 owing on his
chrome-flecked charger, but rather of the $189.73
monthly finance payment. The lower the sum, the less
onerous the individual deems his financial thralldom.
In corp-speak, the reverse is true. The smaller the number,
the more baleful the economic weather. The minister
of big business is so accustomed to dealing in millions,
tens of millions, even billions of dollars that the zeroes
jiggle before his eyes like lifeless skeletons. Not until
he translates the loss into a dime or a quarter a share
does the executive perceive flesh-and-blood figures with
the power to ulcerate his intestines.

Hugo Praeger's discovery that the wreck of the Sea
Routes tanker S.S. *Aquarius* would cost Arc-Horn International an additional $20,000,000 beyond the $16,000-
000 insurance loss on vessel and cargo had seemed a
matter of nebulous celestial interest until, dividing $20,-
000,000 by the total number of Arc-Horn shares, he
brought the financial reverse down to earth.

The trouble was, the funereal Jules Amarel had revealed, that the special oil-contamination insurance carried by the *Aquarius* was held, not by some distant,
hapless corporate agent, but by his own Six Flags Insurance Co., and thus the indemnity demanded by Argentina would have to be met by the Arc-Horn subsidiary.

"Let's go over this again, Jules," said Praeger with
a brave effort at civility. His fingers kneading the armrests
of the special oak armchair betrayed his inner ferment.

"As I said, if the *Aquarius* had made a harbor in

the Paraná, we'd have been home free." Amarel folded his hands on the table as though in prayer. "She only had two more voyages scheduled before being scrapped in July and the six-company pool had agreed to take over her oil-spill insurance as of April first."

"But the new pool policy covered all Sea Routes tankers as of the first of the year," protested Praeger.

"Except for the *Aquarius,*" Admiral Boke-Milgrim put in. "Question of her old plates. The insurance pool demanded a premium that Jules and I thought was excessive. Jules bargained the pool down with the *Aquarius* coverage to start next month." Boke-Milgrim shrugged. "I'll take the blame, Hugo. When I was offered a handsome price to bring seventy thousand barrels of crude from Venezuela to Rosario, I called Jules and proposed that Six Flags handle the special oil-spill coverage for one trip only. He agreed." Boke-Milgrim frowned. "And then that unexpected storm. We gambled and we lost."

"Hardly a gamble," said Amarel. "The odds were a million to one in our favor."

"Goddam strange that nobody ever mentioned this to me." Praeger again eyed each man in turn, Amarel, Boke-Milgrim, John Lindquist, Chalmers Davidson and Antonio Percevale. "You know anything about this, John?"

Lindquist shook his head as if to escape the noose of guilt. "Not until Jules told me just before I phoned you."

"Lovely surprise, what?"

Tony Percevale smiled in spite of himself. How like Hugo to imply by the sardonic inquiry that he had been done a grave injustice. Decisions of similar magnitude were daily occurrences throughout Arc-Horn. If each of the profit centers were to refer all such issues to Hugo Praeger, corporate machinery would grind to a halt.

And why did Hugo so resent "surprises"? Was it not because the distasteful surprise, like murder, contaminated everyone it touched? Hugo, despite his disclaimers, was delighted by the tangy surprise when a venture proved more profitable than anticipated. But the vexing surprise implied that Hugo's world, like that of a child, was one of high expectations where the gingerbread man danced without crumbling and every fairyland romance became a love eternal. The vision of Arc-Horn as a commercial Holy Roman Empire still filled the recesses of Hugo's mind, despite almost weekly evidence that the goal would never leave the gossamer world of dreams. For all his surface cynicism, thought Tony, Hugo was a man who lived with illusion.

"Another strange goddam thing is that Argentina demands the exact amount of our insurance." Praeger addressed the remark to Percevale as though, being Argentine, Tony must share responsibility for this Latin oddity.

"They got that from Captain Tanner," said Boke-Milgrim. "He told the Prefectura Naval during the interrogation."

"So why is a sea captain such a blabbermouth?" asked Praeger.

"Oh, that's routine, Hugo." Boke-Milgrim failed in his effort not to sound patronizing. "In case of a marine accident, a captain has to present all his documents, sailing papers, insurance and so forth along with his log."

"All right, all right. Let's get this thing in focus." Once he had plumbed the depths of bad news, Praeger wasted only a minimal amount of time in lamentation. The fact was, thought Tony, that if Hugo were deprived of emergencies by heavenly decree, he would invent some of his own. Arc-Horn's invisible twentieth subsidiary, Crisis, Inc., manufactured adrenalin for the exclusive use of its chief executive. "We stand to lose a wad, but I'll be damned if we're going to cough up forty cents a share just because Argentina's Señor Betancourt asks for it."

Praeger reflected, then turned to Davidson, who had sat impassively silent through the exchanges. "Chalmers, this is your bailiwick. I want you to fly down to Buenos Aires tomorrow and get us out of this fix as cheaply as you can."

"The Thursday-afternoon board meeting," Davidson reminded quietly. "I should be here for Items Eight and Nine."

Hugo nodded. "That's right. . . . Okay, then, you Telex Betancourt and tell him you'll be down Friday, ready to start negotiations."

Percevale protested. "That's not a wise move, Hugo. Chalmers shouldn't go anywhere near Buenos Aires right now. Gusto Más is in a delicate situation as it is—and now with the oil spill . . ." He let the implication hang like a threatening cloud.

"And what do you suggest, Tony?" asked Praeger.

"That we pay without quibbling."

"Just like that? Fork over twenty million dollars? No counterproposal, no negotiations, no nothing?"

"No, no." Tony raised his palms in a disclaimer of such innocence. "A decent counterproposal will be expected. But we ought to compromise quickly at any reasonable figure. I know my government. In today's climate, a fast agreement by Arc-Horn would improve our visibility considerably. But prolonged haggling and a defiant attitude. . . . Well, you could kiss your new Rosario plant good-by and get ready to have Gusto Más harried at every turn."

"What do you think, Chalmers?"

"I know my way around Buenos Aires." Davidson's smile exuded confidence. The aura of the international operations chief was one of affability, discretion, easy charm and a certain understated status. His manner implied instant ability to dissolve all but the steeliest of man-made obstacles. "I understand Tony's fears, but an outsider has, well, ammunition not available to Argentine citizens."

The thought struck Percevale at once. Did Davidson's arsenal include bribery and burglary of the sort visited on Portilla during Ron Jeffers' hooded trip to Buenos Aires? Though it was difficult to imagine such orders coming from a man with Davidson's establishment credentials, the American political-economic hierarchy had been caught in some sordid back alleys in recent years.

"That might be true in any ordinary case," said Tony, "but several factors make this one unusual. For one thing, Rudolfo Betancourt's own personal property has been smeared with oil and Betancourt has as much influence with the Casa Rosada as anyone in Argentina. Second, the Paraná delta has a special hold on the affections of the people who count in Buenos Aires. Almost everyone who's somebody has property on those waterways. They have their summer homes and their boats there. The delta has a special place in their hearts. I can't imagine a worse place for an Argentine oil accident unless the skies were to dump petroleum on the mountain resort of Bariloche or on one of the major football stadiums."

"Do you have a house there?" asked Praeger.

"Yes, I do, Hugo, although not anywhere near the Martín García Channel. And I can judge the probable reaction of Betancourt and others by my own. I actually loathe the thought of oil fouling any of those beautiful waterways. I used to cruise there in a small outboard as a kid. I courted my wife there one summer. I've eaten hundreds of Sunday dinners at restaurants along the shady canals and now my children race around in their outboards. All we *porteños* love the area and the thought of oil killing the water birds and ruining the foliage, well, damn it, my stomach turns."

"I know how you must feel." Praeger's sympathy was genuine. "I can imagine what it would be like to have oil swamping my place on Martinique where I keep the *Arc Hornet.*"

"I grant the symbolic aspect of the delta," said Davidson, "and the emotional repercussion in Buenos Aires. Still, that's an advantage for us. I've always found it easier to make headway when the opposition is largely emotional rather than based on logic."

Tony was quickly embattled. "Are you saying there's no logic in the government's demand?"

"At twenty million, no. That oil can be cleaned up for a couple of million, three at the most."

"Come off it, Chalmers." Tony's temper rose. "How

about the aftermath? Dead birds, a stinking shoreline, grass, shrubs and trees that won't recover for years."

"I think you're letting sentiment influence your judgment." Davidson was courteous but firm. "That's understandable, of course. But if Arc-Horn were to compensate on the basis of sentiment, we'd be liable for half a billion dollars."

"Damn it, Chalmers, that's exactly what we're dealing with—sentiment. And any man who goes to Buenos Aires thinking he can buy off Latin sentiment on the cheap is in for a rude shock."

"I've never found my Latin American friends less interested in money than we are in the United States."

"We put a far higher price on intangibles like honor, pride and sentiment than North Americans do." Tony hesitated. "But that's not the real point. An Arc-Horn accident has ruined some of the most beautiful shoreline in the world and I think we should recompense my country quickly and reasonably."

"And that," said Davidson, "is the very reason the negotiations should not be carried on by an Argentine. With all due respect, Tony, your judgment is colored by the happenstance of your birthplace."

They argued for several minutes, Tony's ire rising as he talked and Davidson playing the role of the cool, dispassionate arbiter. Praeger listened closely, swiveling his eyes from man to man like a mid-court spectator at a tennis match.

"Okay. That'll do it." Praeger turned to Amarel. "Suppose this were just a routine damage case that you were handling yourself, Jules. What would you do?"

"I'd fly a couple of adjusters down there tomorrow with orders to assess the damage and get Six Flags out of it as cheaply as possible—considering all factors, political, legal, emotional."

"All right, that's what we'll do. But we want it wrapped up fast. No prolonged haggling." He shot a finger at Amarel. "That clear?"

Amarel nodded, but Davidson cut in. "Is this a final decision, Hugo?"

"Nothing's final but death." And Praeger's tone indicated that, as for himself, he wasn't even absolutely sure about that. "What's on your mind?"

"I think we should avoid the adjuster route." Davidson spoke with the authority of one who sees both the forest and the trees. "I have some very close friends in Buenos Aires. I'm certain I could get us out for a good deal less than Jules' adjusters could."

"Maybe, Chalmers, but I don't want to run the risk. This time I'm taking my cues from Tony. As he says, we're dealing with intangibles here." As he looked at Tony, Praeger suddenly brightened. "I've got an even better idea. We're in a fuckin' jam, what? So why not turn the mess into a plus for Arc-Horn? . . . Tony, you get Betancourt on the phone soonest. Tell him you're as outraged as he is, which seems to be pretty close to the truth. Tell him if he's willing to settle for twelve, you're sure you can argue me into it. If he sounds interested, wait an hour, then call him back. Tell him I put up a battle, but I finally backed down. Generous Argentine triumphs over miserly Swiss, what? That way Gusto Más will get all the credit, smoothing the way for you in the future. What do you say?"

"Fine." Tony was enthusiastic. "I like that."

"Okay, get down to the Toltec Room right away and have one of the Arc-Horn switchboard girls locate Betancourt. . . . Remind him that a quick settlement will avoid the drawn-out business of adjusters, investigations, hearings, all that crap."

The phone by Lindquist's elbow rang as Tony hurried from the conference room. Lindquist put his hand over the mouthpiece. "Hal Frascella at First Merchants. . . . He wants you, Hugo."

Praeger impatiently took the phone from Lindquist, then swiftly manufactured a smile that creased his face like that of a happy Buddha. "Hi there, Hal. Working late, eh?" His booming voice filled the room. "Yeah, yeah, one of those days. Happens to the best of companies, what? . . . Right. Our cash flow will be cut, no doubt about that . . . Oh, don't worry about Top Court.

Just one of those flash strikes that'll be over in a few days. . . . What's that? No, I haven't heard a thing. I've got some of my team here. Let's see if they've heard anything."

He smothered the mouthpiece with his palm. "God-dam banker's sticking his nose into everything. Anybody here know about some adverse report on Arc-Horn coming out soon?"

Amarel, Lindquist and Boke-Milgrim looked blank. Davidson puzzled a moment, then asked: "Couldn't be the Group of Twelve, could it?"

"I doubt it. I think they knocked that off."

"Then I wouldn't know."

Praeger spoke into the phone again. "No, that one stumps us, Hal. Sorry, no light at this end." He listened for a full minute. "Yes, that's right. Six Flags will have to take a sixteen-million book rap on the ship and cargo. But, Hal, that's not the whole story. I'm going to level with you. Six Flags also holds the extra oil-spill insurance."

Praeger, speaking slowly in the frank, somber voice a banker expects from an indebted client in times of misfortune, explained the bad news in detail. Six Flags' liability ran to another $20,000,000. If the storm had hit just a few hours later, disaster would have been averted. A one-in-a-million unlucky shot, what? But he hoped to get by with an offer of twelve as against Argentina's demand for twenty.

"I know, Hal. This morning we were a big twenty-seven million over the one-fifty reserve requirement. . . . But Christ, man, even so, we're in no danger. I'll stake my life on that. I got six hundred seventy-eight profit centers to draw on, remember, and Uni-Land is coming through handsomely now. Also Thursday I expect board approval of two projects that figure to pay off big. The future has never looked so bright for Arc-Horn. . . . Yes, Sea Routes is an admitted problem. But for the rest, we're in a small, temporary bind. I said small and temporary, Hal. . . . What's that? . . . Well, screw the security analysts. What the hell do they know about my business?

. . . All right, sure. No sweat. I'll bring John Lindquist along with me so we can nail the numbers down tight. Four o'clock Friday at your shop then. And, Hal, give my regards to Lillian, will you?"

After hanging up, Praeger shoved the telephone aside as though it were an instrument of evil. "Damn all vulture bankers. The way Frascella talks, you'd think we were facing bankruptcy instead of a piss-ant little matter of cash flow over a couple of months. Well, he doesn't fool me. This is just more pressure to get First Merchants a seat on the board." Praeger slammed his palms on the table. "I'm not going to have any goddam banker sitting here, telling us what not to do. One banker can dig up more reasons why you can't do something than a whole platoon of lawyers."

Praeger stood up. "Well, that's it, gentlemen." He looked pleased with himself. Crisis did more for Praeger's mental health than all the chess games, early-bird fiestas and massage tables combined. "Nina and I are going out on the town tonight. I advise you to go and do likewise. Good for what ails you." He gathered up papers and stuffed them into a manila folder.

Davidson lingered after the others left.

"Okay, what is it, Chalmers?"

"I'm thinking about Green Tree and Neptune West. After today, they look more important to us than ever."

"That's obvious. So?"

They stood by the head of the big horseshoe table in the wedge of light shed by the chandelier. Through the french doors open to the balcony could be heard the dull pounding of waves on the beach. Early stars speckled the black sky.

"I think we ought to ram those projects through Thursday with a minimum of discussion," said Davidson. "A bare minimum."

"Why the rush? I know you've got a personal stake in bringing both to the starting gate, Chalmers, but we'll need some time to explain the goals, the financing, and how we'll mesh the subsidiaries. We're only talking about an hour or so of discussion."

"I'm troubled." Davidson stood with one hand fondling the back of Praeger's armchair. "That crazy closed-circuit interview stirred the animals. We may get some argument Thursday. Look at Tony today. That's the first time I've heard any officer put environmental concerns ahead of the company. We may get some more flak like that if you allow a free board discussion Thursday."

"You're imagining things. The board will get the hots for both items after a little explanation. You watch."

"How do we know those Group of Twelve fanatics haven't gotten to some board member?"

"Possible, but not likely. I see your point, though. I'll give it some thought, sleep on it tonight. Then we'll see. Okay?"

"Fine. My hunch tells me we should move as fast as we can."

The two men parted, Praeger leaving by the side door which led to his suite, Davidson via the corridor exit.

Ron Jeffers was waiting for him in the hallway.

"Mother," said Jeffers. "He wants the latest word from you."

Davidson and his subordinate walked rapidly down the hall toward the classified communications room.

Tuesday Night

Jim imagined himself an astronaut, speeding timelessly through space yet nevertheless hovering, strangely and silently, a few miles—or was it only inches?—away from this mysterious, glistening planet. Rich foliage covered the great orb. The coloring was as brown as the dusty hills of Mexico, yet deep and lush as if nourished by abundant rainfalls. Here and there he could distinguish greenish flecks, like little tropical isles, and in the center loomed a large black circle, fixed, unwavering, yet living and luminous. A veil of moisture softened the tawny planet, which appeared to be suspended in a vast, milky white sea where curious reddish threads traced exotic patterns. Occasionally, a flesh-colored shadow snapped downward as swiftly as a camera shutter, obscuring the mystery globe for a microsecond. Then the black circle seemed to crest on the curvature of the globe, moist, dark, penetrating, almost hypnotic in its intensity.

Jim was staring into the right eye of his wife.

Meg and Jim were sitting cross-legged on a black-and-tan Indian rug in his opulent Mixteca suite. Their knees touching, they had been gazing steadily into each other's eyes for almost five minutes.

At first Jim found it difficult to focus. He felt a bit ridiculous, conscious as he was of Dave Moyer prowling about the room, weaving a trail of fragrant pipe-tobacco smoke. Then, as he looked full into Meg's eyes, Jim's mind skittered from facet to facet of the woman he thought he knew. Dave asked them to monitor their own feelings as they scrutinized each other in silence. Jim tried his best. He thought he had tagged irritation, fondness, wonder, puzzlement, certainly malaise. And then he noted a kind of fear as though Meg's shining black pupils held nameless power over him and that he must yield a secret piece of himself at her command. Although the secret's nature remained vague and formless, he resented Meg's seeming capacity to beckon it from hidden recesses.

At last he forgot about Meg and himself and concentrated on her right eye as might an ophthalmologist or a student of anatomy. Slowly the apprehension receded and he became engrossed in his scrutiny. He had never inspected anyone's eye this closely before. Intriguing and even overwhelming. Then came the fantasy of himself as a space man making a spectacular approach to the tawny planet.

"Okay. That's enough," said Moyer. "Take a chair and relax."

Moyer himself continued to pace the room in his loose, shambling way. He wore blue slacks, a short-sleeved jersey, beach moccasins, and his body seemed as boneless as his clothes. Something in Moyer's gait triggered Jim's memory and he recalled that weekend at the Westhampton house almost two years ago. They had played a parlor game in which they imagined one another in a sequence of five different forms. As an article of furniture, the consensus had pegged Moyer as a hammock; musical instrument, a harp; animal, an English sheep dog; plant, a sunflower; sport, curling.

"We started off with the eyeballing," said Moyer, "because I felt you two weren't really seeing each other. The eye has magic in it, yet most couples haven't eye-balled, let alone eye-fucked, since they were first lovers. . . . So, let's start with Meg. What went on with you?"

Meg sat far back in an armchair, her long legs drawn up beneath her like an elegant embryo. She had changed into a pink sweater and slacks and white thong sandals after arriving at the Mixteca, yet there was nothing careless about her dress. The cut was modish, the press neat and the vanished price tag from a Manhattan boutique most certainly expensive. Her black hair hung like a bell and her pale lipstick matched the nail polish on both fingers and toes. Meg, a loyal corporate wife in matters she deemed inconsequential, patronized the Fragrance, Inc., cosmetic line exclusively. While neither a compulsive shopper nor a slave to beauty aids, Meg at forty-six kept a close eye on her appearance. Result: a chic, understated exterior.

The inner Margaret Chesley McGowan was less amenable to easy classification by strangers, or even by friends. Arc-Horn executives knew her as a sleekly hospitable hostess with the customary graces expected of a female subsidiary, household division, and only those especially observant noted that she did not quite fit the approved mold. Outside the formalized corporate social circle—where a wife could be giddy but never drunk, saucy but never belligerent, flirtatious but never seductive, smart but never intellectual, reformist but never radical, elegant but never regal, friendly but never intimate, immersed in charitable good works but never in crusades to revamp the system by which the poor remained poor, tart but never bitchy, feminine but never feminist—Meg was almost herself. She could be warm and radiant or coolly withdrawn, depending on the people around her. Moods passed over her like scudding clouds. She spoke her mind, seldom equivocated, but even her best friends were never sure the Monday Meg would match the Meg of Wednesday. There was a restlessness, an inquietude, the lack of a core that stayed fixed. She was like a shining circle without a center, a spinning wheel without a hub. "Sometimes I wonder what I want to be when I grow up," she had said with a laugh to Dave Moyer on the flight down from New York. She baffled her husband at times. A new lover might find her fascinating until his zest for exploration waned in the ageless manner of lovers.

As he looked at his wife now, Jim recalled the consensus on Meg during that parlor game at Westhampton. As furniture, Meg would be a three-pronged modern floor lamp, the angled lights shining in three directions. Musical instrument: banjo. Animal: thoroughbred filly. Plant: dogwood tree in bloom. Sport: badminton.

Now her brows furrowed as she pondered Moyer's question about her feelings. "I guess . . ."

"Just a second before you begin." Moyer loped across the room and halted in front of her. "Notice your posture. You're as far back in that chair as you can maneuver. Your feet are tucked under you and your arms are folded tight to your body. What does that say to Jim?"

She tossed her head. "It says I want to be comfortable."

Moyer swung around to Jim, who sat in another armchair, facing her, a few feet away. "Is that what it says to you?"

"Hardly." Jim flashed a nervous grin. "I hadn't

thought about it, but now that you mention it, maybe she's trying to get as far away from me as she can."

"Does that check, Meg?"

Meg unfolded her arms and inched forward self-consciously. "Not really. I like to huddle in chairs, get comfy."

"You do?" Moyer cocked an eyebrow at her. "How about coming down this evening in the plane? You had plenty of room for curling up in first class, but you had your legs stretched out wide as far as you could. And in the limo tonight, coming from the airport, you practically sprawled from the corner. Then you rolled down the window and said, 'Love that air.' You circled your arms like you were trying to embrace the night. Remember?"

"My, how observant." Meg looked pleased. "Did you notice that in the car, Jim?"

"Not exactly. Well, no, I didn't."

Moyer spoke to Jim. "And you. You've got your legs crossed. Does that say anything to you about your subconscious attitude toward Meg? And what's this palming of the back of your neck? You've done it twice now. You got a pain, maybe?"

"No." Jim knew his smile must appear awkwardly defensive. "I wasn't aware I was doing it."

"Let's try to be aware of everything we do, feel and say tonight. For starters, how about both of you sitting in a way you think says, 'Hi, friend. I'm open to you.'"

Husband and wife looked sheepish, fidgeted, rearranged themselves, then waited apprehensively.

"Hell, you both looked like you were restacking a pile of lumber." Moyer laughed. "Still, that's better, even if Jim seems to be preparing himself for crucifixion."

Jim had slumped in the chair, spread his legs wide and draped his arms loosely over the broad arms of the vivid blue upholstery. Meg sat more primly, but her sandaled feet were on the floor now and her hands rested on her thighs.

"Okay, Meg." Moyer was refilling his pipe from a

tobacco pouch. "So what did you feel while you looked into Jim's eyes?"

"I'm not sure. Lots of things. I was nervous at first and then, well, oh, a string of thoughts . . ." Her voice trailed off.

"Come on," Moyer urged gently. "Try to remember. First nervousness, then what?"

"I felt unsettled, well, helpless, I suppose. Then scenes crossed my mind."

"What scenes? Can you give us a specific?"

"Yes. There was one in particular, a lovely one. . . . Dave, do I have to say *everything* I thought, no matter how intimate?"

"You do as you please. But remember, you and Jim promised each other to be open and candid. If you start holding back, we won't make much headway tonight."

"I'm not used to spilling my insides. But if you say so . . ." She looked to Moyer for reassurance. "There was one special scene that popped up. It was about the night we decided to get married. We were . . ."

"We were—" Moyer repeated slowly.

". . . sitting on my aunt Lil's porch at Southampton." Meg visibly braced herself. Her gaze drifted above the two men. "It was a chilly, cloudy night, and Jim didn't exactly propose and I didn't either. It just sort of happened." Meg's speech speeded up. "I was so much in love with that big Irish—we were Episcopalian and my parents weren't too eager about a daughter's match with a Catholic—with that big Irishman that I couldn't bear it and I could feel the same vibrations from him. All of a sudden, we were all over each other, kissing and hugging, and the old porch swing, one of those creaky, couch-like things on metal standards, began to squeak and clank and carry on and we started to laugh. Before we knew it, we were going to be married in August, two months away. It wasn't just physical because we'd been to bed together four or five times before." A tremor came into Meg's voice. "It was love and we both knew it, deep, satisfying and yet thrilling. It's hard to believe, looking at us now, but I felt glorious that night on the porch and so did he because all of a sudden he . . ."

Moyer swung quickly toward Jim. "What are you feeling? Not back then, right now."

"A tight feeling in my stomach." Jim hesitated. "And, Jesus, the inside of my nose is wet. Like I've got a cold."

"Do you feel like crying?"

"No. . . . It's more like a case of the sniffles."

"All right. So, Meg, all of a sudden Jim what?"

"He picked me up in a big swoop and carried me down the porch steps. Then he set me down and took my hand. We began to run through the chilly mist, running toward the beach like a couple of kids. We threw ourselves on the sand, ripped off our clothes, and began making love, a couple of mad people. We could hear the wind cutting through the saw grass and the waves crashing." Meg halted abruptly.

"And?"

"Dave, I don't want to talk about it any more." She flashed a quick, derisive smile. "Anyway, it was a wild, crazy night and I wound up with sand in my you-know-what."

"No. I don't know what."

"My thing. Vagina sounds too clinical and I can't use the Anglo-Saxon word. I don't mind others using it, but I just don't. . . . My stuffy WASP background maybe?"

"Maybe. . . . .What else did you feel during the eye-lock?"

"I felt good for a while, remembering lots of old scenes in flashes. Then I began to feel afraid. It was weird, as if those big green eyes looking at me had some kind of power over me and were forcing me to give up something important, I didn't know what, but something vital, my own, nobody else's. And Jim's eyes were insisting I surrender it and I hated him for that. Then the hate simmered down to just plain resentment, I guess you'd call it, that smoldered away for a couple of minutes."

"Can I interrupt, Dave?"

"Sure. You come from a free country—more or less."

"That's amazing," said Jim, "because I was feeling almost the same thing as Meg, that her eyes had a power to make me fork over a hunk of myself that I didn't want to let go of. So, naturally I resented the hell out of her."

He glanced at Meg, saw her face soften. He felt a flicker of mutual understanding. He liked the feeling.

"Okay," said Moyer. "Let's just stop here a few minutes and do some brainstorming together. You two are on to something important, and frankly, I'm delighted you got to it so quickly. Some couples take hours to bring themselves to the same space." He grinned. "I knew I had a couple of fast ones this time. . . . Let me try a philosophical question. What about power? Arc-Horn's a power structure, Jim. You deal with it every day. Just what is power?"

Jim shifted in his chair as he thought. "You find it in the master-and-slave bit. No, wait a second. . . . It's the capacity to make other people do what you want."

"Meg?"

"Yes, that's about it. If I wanted Jim to quit the rat race and become a business-school professor, say, and Jim refused, then Jim would have the power to arrange our lives the way he wanted, not the way I wanted."

Jim bridled. "Is that a hint?"

"No, just a for-instance. I'm not so naïve, Jim, as to even imagine you'd ever leave Top Court."

Moyer pointed to the heavy Mexican coffee table which squatted on the Indian rug like a dark toadstool. "Could you have power over that?"

"No, it can't talk back," said Meg.

Moyer settled on the coffee table and blew a smoke ring. "So in our concept of power, we assume a person with influence and at least one other person who can be influenced. Can anybody have power unless someone else yields that power to him?"

"No. When I sold Top Court to Praeger, I handed

over to him a fistful of power in return for lots of financial goodies—I thought."

"Right. But when we come to mates, supposedly two free and equal human beings, why do we think in terms of power at all? Do you want power over Jim, Meg?"

"God, no. I don't even like the idea of it."

"Jim?"

"No, I guess not." He was slower to respond. "Although there are things in life I damn well want."

"Which you have the power to get for yourself." Moyer aimed the stem of his pipe at Jim. "But Meg felt very deeply, she says, that you were exercising power over her, trying to make her yield some part of herself she didn't want to give up. Were you?"

"No." Jim was bemused. "Just the opposite. I was too busy worrying about her influence over me."

"Meg, do you have power over Jim?"

"Me?" She hooted. "Absolutely none."

Moyer laid aside his pipe and dropped to the rug between them. He lay back, propping himself on his elbows. He looked appraisingly first at Jim, then at Meg. They began to smile, tentatively, as if probing each other's reservoir of faith.

"What's up with you two now?"

"You made the point. Meg and I were both assuming something that wasn't there."

Meg nodded, frowning. "Yes. It's peculiar, isn't it? . . . And, actually, I'm flattered that Jim thought I had a hex on him."

Moyer waited through a long silence, then said quietly: "After a lot of years of kicking this sort of psychological stuff around, I've come to only a few definite conclusions. One of them is that we're all in charge of our own lives. I can't change Jim. Meg can't manage or change Jim. Only Jim can manage himself, change or not as he wishes. And nobody can have power over a person unless that person yields the power. I except, of course, those cases where you're imprisoned or tortured. There, you're helpless. But in the main run of life, say ninety-eight percent of the time, the person who surrenders power to another is playing a game, the 'oh, poor me' gambit. Life would be rich and sweet if only it weren't for terrible old Bill or Fred or Henrietta who makes me so miserable. Poor me in bondage. . . . I could go on for hours, but I can see I don't need to sell you two. . . . Jim, what else did you feel looking into Meg's eyes?"

"I felt foolish at first, then that passed and . . ." Jim reflected. "I don't remember definite images like Meg did. Oh, yes. There was one. I could see Meg coming home from the hospital in New York with the baby twins, Carol and Connie, back in fifty-eight. She was riding in a cab with a friend of hers, Janice, and I wasn't there because I was at the office. Top Court was in trouble. I could see that scene and it made me feel guilty and . . ."

"Did you blame him at the time, Meg?" Moyer cut in.

"Yes, I did. I felt neglected. I thought he could have spared two hours to take his new family home."

"How about now? Do you still resent it?"

"Now? Oh, Lord no. I haven't thought about it in years."

"Do you believe her, Jim?"

"Yeah, if she says so." He looked questioningly at Meg. "Yes, I do."

"Okay, then. You've got a hang-up, Jim, that maybe you'd like to work on, perhaps ask yourself if you're doing something now that could be corrected and that's connected with the old home-from-the-hospital scene."

"I'm not sure I get what you mean."

Moyer sat up and reached for his pipe. "Maybe harping on the old scene is a cop-out, a handy substitute for not reminding yourself of something you didn't do for Meg yesterday or today. . . . Any other feelings you can remember?"

"Yes. A loving feeling toward her for a while, then that power business and irritation, I guess. But right at the end, maybe for a minute, I forgot everything except one eye, the right one. All of a sudden, I was an astronaut whizzing through space toward this mysterious planet." He described the floating voyage, the great black center, the veil of moisture and the illusion of rich foliage, curiously brown in color. "Man, that was a trip!"

"Why, that's terrific, Jim." Meg reached out and touched his knee. "I had no idea I had such a fantastic jewel from outer space in my head. I want to see." She left her chair and hurried to the other end of the large room, where the long, gilt-framed mirror hung.

Moyer grinned. "Jim, you've started a new science —astro-anatomy. Two things strike me. One, you got totally absorbed in a discovery. That's like you. I've noticed it in your business, our deal at Doylestown, for instance. But two, was it a way of veering away from the emotions Meg had set off in you? At work in his lab, you know, the scientist doesn't have to worry about other people."

Jim nodded. "It's a cinch I felt more relaxed and comfortable once I fixed on that eye as an object in itself."

"Divorced from Meg as a person?"

"Yeah." Jim pondered. "I see what you're getting at."

"Nothing wrong with getting absorbed in particulars, mind you. But it's valuable to be aware of the difference. A whole person is a helluva lot more troublesome than an eyeball—or a vagina, for that matter."

"You think I don't see Meg as a whole person?"

"Do you? . . . Take that scene tonight at the airport. The greeting and the kiss were perfunctory. Then right away you wanted to get into that letter and report from Senator Ireland. Had we read the report? What did we think? Did Ireland say anything about it to us? Then, in the car, you were itching to start reading it at once. And if you'd had proper light, I think you would have."

"But Christ, that's natural, Dave. It's a big issue right now for Arc-Horn and Ireland has shoved me into the middle of it. Same with Doylestown. I wanted all the news you two could bring me from the employees' meeting this noon. Hell, that's why you're down here—to persuade Praeger."

Moyer was puffing on his pipe again. "All true, but

you also knew that Meg was counting on this three-way session tonight. You'd agreed to it on the phone. That's why she flew down here with me. Yet, your mind was hooked on business."

"I locked up the report and Ireland's letter in the safe until tomorrow, didn't I?"

"Yes, after Meg and I asked you to. What you really wanted to do was dive into that report at eleven o'clock at night."

"The damn thing's on my mind. I plead guilty, Judge." Jim was tart now.

"No guilt and no judges in this room, man. We're just trying to be aware of what we do and why."

"Weird!" It was Meg's voice from the other end of the room. She gave herself a final glance in the mirror, then returned swiftly, her pink slacks flashing. "It is a planet, isn't it? Floating in all that white space with the little red wriggly lines. I must look awful when my eyes are bloodshot." She sank into the armchair. "But didn't you notice the mascara, Jim? One little blob of it on a hair of the upper eyelash. My God, it looked like a great poisonous black ball about to fall from a spike and blot out all life on the globe. . . . Hmm, maybe it's trying to tell me something."

They fell to discussing the wonders of the eye as a machine, a window on the soul, a funnel for information and sensation and as an awesome, inexplicable medium for the transfer of power between human beings. Jim recalled a scene he had witnessed in a shoe-repair shop in Rome. Behind the back of the cobbler, two boys fell to quarreling. One jumped on a stool and glared down at his playmate, demanding that he utter some phrase of surrender. The other boy refused. Slowly the boy on the stool withdrew his belt from his pants and wrapped the leather around his fist. He continued to glare, motionless, for several minutes. At last, the eyes of the other boy wavered with fear. He looked down at the floor as he mumbled the password for defeat. The winner jumped down from the stool, then fixed

Jim with proud, piercing, triumphant black eyes. He was perhaps nine years old.

"We're running on," said Moyer at last. "Let's get back on the track." He glanced at his wristwatch. "It's twelve-thirty now and we've just begun. I know you're both bugged by lots of stuff that will have to wait for the weekend sessions at Doylestown. But I've also got a hunch about you two. I want to try something I've never done before in this sequence. I've got two exercises I'd like to try. They'll take about an hour in all. You game or are you too tired?"

"I'm ready for anything," said Meg. She pulled up her sweater sleeves as if to prove it.

"Another hour's fine with me," said Jim.

"Okay. We need a clean handkerchief." Moyer lifted himself from the floor. "No, wait a minute. It might be better to do the other one first. I'm not sure." He hesitated. "Yeah, let's try the sex bit first."

"Right here?" Meg feigned apprehension with her laugh. "All three of us?"

"No. Just more talk." Moyer studied his pipe, then set it aside once more. "We're all sexual beings. That's why we mate, right? But after the years pass, nineteen in your case, the sex act gets loaded down with more trash than the city dump—husband-wife roles, mommy-and-daddy roles, hang-ups by the dozen, old slights and wounds, boredom, duty, religion, the male's fear of not being able to perform, the female's fear of being used. All of it corrupts and corrodes what ought to be a plain, simple act of love and/or lust." He paused, looked at each in turn. "Now, as difficult as it will be, I want you to pretend that you're not husband and wife who've invested heavily in a marriage, but just male and female. And I want each of you to describe to us, as frankly and as specifically as you can, two sexual fantasies that you've had."

Meg squirmed back in her chair. "I'm not sure what you mean by a sexual fantasy."

"Oh? . . . Fantasy. . . . Not what you do, but what

you think about doing. Didn't you ever think of another man or method when you were in bed with Jim?"

"None of your business, Mr. Moyer."

"Do we have to go into this, Dave?" Jim was aware of a growing tightness in his shoulders. Unconsciously, he rubbed at the back of his neck.

"No, we don't." Moyer lowered his voice. "We can quit now, if you like."

"Oh, we don't mean that," said Meg quickly. "It's just that . . ."

"If you want help from me you'll have to trust me. I'm no genius, but I think I know my business. There's a risk, sure. Living's a risk. I said I had a hunch about you two and I'm playing the hunch."

"Sexual dreams and images can be pretty far-out," protested Jim.

"Men tell them to their mistresses," said Moyer, "and women to their lovers. But husband and wife remain frozen in blocks of ice. Are you afraid to share all of you with Meg?"

"Afraid's not the word. Habit or custom, maybe."

"I'll do it," said Meg in a voice that seemed shrunken, "if Jim goes first."

"Okay." Moyer turned to Jim and waited in silence.

"Goddam it, I don't know how to begin."

"Like this " Moyer opened his mouth wide. "Look, Jim. Let me tell one of my own. Sometimes on the beach, I fantasize that there's a mermaid sitting on a rock. I swim out to her and she welcomes me to her wet, salty-tasting breasts. Then when I run my hand down to her mound of Venus, the tail and the scales fall away, to be replaced by two tanned, beautiful, feminine legs. We start to fuck on the rock, and it becomes soft like a huge downy cushion, and the waves wash over us and we make love, rolling and heaving, in the bright sunshine. We love all afternoon and at last when the sun goes down, a flaming orange ball, we have an orgasm together. We're exhausted and not until it's dark do we have the strength to slip off the rock and swim to shore. Only then, standing on the sand, do I see her face distinctly. It's Peggy Rahn, my cousin. I had a yen for her in the sixth grade, but being cousins, we never made it—except in my mermaid fantasy." Moyer hunched his shoulders. "See? You just think the image and say it aloud."

"You're sure this is okay with you?" Jim asked Meg.

"Well, after that one, I'm dying to hear your secret passions."

"That's just the point, Meg. I don't have any secret passions, only images now and then." Well, there was Gwen, but Gwen herself had labeled him a passionless lover.

"How about it, Jim?" Moyer gently urged him on.

"Sure, I have fantasies too." Jim thought before he continued and when he did, he averted his eyes from Meg. "Not recently, I guess, but some years ago, I remember, I imagined this scene where I was in bed with two woman, one white and one black. There was a great round bed and overhead a circular mirror. The white woman, whose face I didn't know, was very slim and had long blond hair that swished over the three of us. The black woman was curvy with soft, big breasts, very earthy and passionate. We were excited as hell. First the two women made love to each other, kissing everything, all oral, you know. Then I, well, I screwed the black woman while she kind of moaned, then the same with the white woman. Then we were all three together in one big love bundle, into everybody and everything at once." Jim had forgotten his audience. "I'm not sure just how it worked. I guess you don't in fantasies. But I know that every time we rolled or twisted, we watched ourselves in the overhead mirror, and that made us still more excited." Jim paused. "Well, that's it. Went on a couple of hours, the way I imagined it."

There was a moment of silence. Jim glanced covertly at Meg.

"Wow!" She tilted her head as she stared at her husband. "All that in old Jim McGowan."

"Dave said to level. I tried."

"You said the white woman was faceless." Moyer's comment was casual. "How about the black woman?"

Jim was annoyed. Actually, several times the image had been unmistakably that of Lucy Jenkins. "Kind of fuzzy. I've never slept with a black woman since I was in college." And at once, Jim realized that he had slurred the truth as much to protect Lucy as to spare Meg's feelings. After all, it was no fault of Lucy Jenkins that he had snared her into his fantasy and in reality he regarded the warm, volatile Fragrance vice-president with affection.

"Does that scene bother you, Meg?" asked Moyer.

"Not at all. And that's a surprise. I thought it would, but hearing it, I think of Jim as more, well, human."

"That's a helluva word." Jim flared. "Most of the time, I'm inhuman?"

"No, no. More vulnerable, I guess I mean."

"Let's not get into hair splitting. The main thing is that Meg felt okay, not put off, by Jim's scene." He waited, then looked at Jim. "That's one. You owe us another."

"The other one is more romantic. I've had it a number of times." Jim felt easier now, already intent on the image in his mind. "I saw a movie once, I forget which one, where a guy ran nude through a field of tall grass and wild flowers and then threw himself on the ground and rolled around. It was summertime. I guess that gave me the idea. Anyway, in the fantasy, it's a bright day, showers of sunlight, and I'm also lying in a grassy field on a hillside with no clothes on. It feels great, the earth and the grass against my skin and the hot sun. Across the field comes a woman, nude and smiling. She is tall, like Meg, and with the same black hair. She's beautiful, again something like Meg, but not exactly. Actually, I'm not sure of her features, but she is radiant and quite purposeful. That is, we both know that she is coming to me to be made love to. She kneels on the grass beside me, gently takes my head and puts my mouth to a breast. Then we make slow, easy love and afterward we lie in the grass and gaze up at the sky.

It is the bluest of blue and we know we are both very content, although neither of us has said a word."

This time the silence was a long one. Meg broke it softly. "That's perfectly beautiful, Jim."

Moyer too waited before he spoke. "There's a poet in the businessman." He looked thoughtful. "We mesh, Jim. I've had one something like that myself. . . . Meg?"

She tensed. "Funny, but even after hearing Jim, I find it hard. It's like stripping in public."

"We're very private, Meg," said Moyer. "A mate and a friend. And the walls have no ears."

She still hesitated. "The trouble is, mine are both raunchier than Jim's last one." Her eyes brightened. "Okay, here goes. . . . But do I have to look at you?"

"Do whatever you please."

She fixed her eyes on the black gap of the open balcony doors. "Well, I've had one where I'm a real sexual princess. I've been served breakfast in bed, a big royal bed with a canopy over it, and for some reason, I'm feeling very, er, horny." She paused as if to muster courage. "So I ring a bell and pretty soon, about a dozen handsome men, all nude, come into the boudoir and stand in a ring around the bed. They're all ages and races, but no fat ones, and all strangers. They're trim with nice, rippling muscles and smooth skin. Some have hair on their chests and some don't. As they stand there, they all get slowly rising erections and soon there are these dozen or so weapons all poking straight at me and all throbbing with desire. I'm imperious." Meg straightened her shoulders. "I pick out three and wave the rest away. They march out of the room, leaving three men. I beckon to one and he comes to the bed and screws me, tough-like, bruising me and biting my shoulder. Then he leaves. The second one is calm, but firm and passionate. The last one is so gentle and considerate I end up weeping. . . . How about that?"

She glanced at the two men. "I thought I'd be afraid to look at you, but I'm not." There was a touch of defiance in her voice. "I'm outnumbered, you know, two to one."

"So it's not husband and wife with an outsider, but a woman with two men. . . . How do you feel about her story, Jim?"

"I expected to be jealous, but I wasn't. I guess I'm surprised. Yes, plenty of surprise."

"From old Meg, huh?" She was enjoying herself now. "You know, I feel relieved, having told that one. My second one is much shorter, but I have it more often. In this one, I've just seen a bullfight and afterward the matador barges into my room, still dressed in his sparkling, skin-tight costume. He looks stern, lusty, but he's contemptuous of me. He undresses before my eyes, then walks slowly toward me, reaches out and rips off my dress, my brassiere, my panties, zip, zip, zip. Just like that. Then he takes me. I fight back at first, but then I surrender and have a marvelous orgasm. . . . I haven't embroidered the scene much in my mind. It all goes very fast."

"And what's your feeling about the scene?"

"I hate it and I like it. You see, I'm wanted so much the man can't wait. I have no control over anything. Since I'm overpowered by the bullfighter's lust, why not relax and enjoy it, as they say?"

Moyer smiled. "You were aggressive and dominant in the first, passive and yielding in the second, traits we all share. . . . How about Jim's fantasies? Did they make you feel nervous or insecure?"

"Hmm." Meg looked appraisingly at Jim. "No. I thought they would, but they didn't. The first one was a bit much. Still, it showed me a part of Jim I didn't know existed. I was shocked to realize how little I knew about my own husband. . . . But the second one was lovely. While he described the scene in the meadow, I imagined myself as the naked woman who was walking toward him."

"Both scenes are intertwined in Jim, remember. Can you accept both parts of him?"

"Oh, sure." Meg reflected. "Actually, now that I know, I . . . well . . . I feel relieved."

"Jim? How about Meg's fantasies?"

"I can understand the rape better than all those studs standing around her bed, but . . ." He shrugged. "If that's Meg, well, so be it."

"Shock?"

"At first, yeah." Jim nodded. "But now, just surprise —and curiosity about what else goes on in her head."

Moyer puffed at his pipe, letting the silence seep around the room like mist. From another suite came an explosion of laughter, then a muffled patter of voices.

"We don't have to rap much about this," said Moyer after a time. "I can see the meaning is self-evident to you. Just a couple of thoughts. Learning to accept all parts of your mate, and I mean all, is a giant step toward freedom and understanding. We do it as a matter of course with close friends, but with husbands and wives—ah, all those old, adolescent dream-prince and goddess expectations clutter the roadway. As for fantasies, they're as much a part of our lives as the physical acts. On occasion, telling a fantasy is a fast way of revealing what's ticking inside you. The more of yourself you expose to your lover, the richer the mix. Of course, trying to act out a fantasy is another matter. Then, you've got problems."

Moyer walked to the balcony doorway and stood for a moment, looking out at the ocean. Stars glittered in the black dome, the surf rolled methodically and the air had a warm, silky texture. It was another flawless tropic night.

"Okay, one last experiment. This one won't take long." Moyer reached into his hip pocket and pulled out a large white handkerchief. "Here, I believe this one hasn't been used. Meg, you're first this time. You blindfold Jim with this, making sure he can't see, then lead him around the suite, guiding him, helping his hands if you want to explore a wall or a fixture. Anything. You lead. He's the blind follower. Take five minutes. I'll time you. . . . And do it in complete silence, please."

Jim stood still while Meg placed the folded handkerchief before his eyes and knotted it at the back of his head. Then she took his hand and began walking him slowly around in a circle.

Almost at once he felt helpless. He realized as Meg began to lead him in a straight line that he was dependent on her. The thought struck with force and he rebelled against it. He resisted, tugging backward against Meg's hand, which felt warm, large, dominant. She drew him onward with a slight pressure. He noted that he was stepping carefully, then shuffling awkwardly, fearful of what lay beyond. He could feel the edge of the rug and the beginning of the terrazzo floor. It felt hard and slick, even hostile. He shortened his step, tugging backward again.

Suddenly, he felt panic. My God, he thought, this is absurd. My wife is leading me around a hotel suite I've seen at least a dozen times. Why the panic? But logic failed to help. He had no control whatever and his surroundings seemed unknown, threatening. He felt his hand grow moist and he sensed a trembling in his arm. Meg halted, took both of his hands and pressed them slowly. They stood for perhaps fifteen seconds that seemed like many minutes. Gradually the panic ebbed. Meg's firm grasp felt pleasurable, reassuring, even motherly. He too squeezed and felt Meg increase the pressure in return.

Then she released one hand and guided the other upward and outward. He felt smooth wood, then a grooved edge. She moved him a few inches forward, pulled his hand far out. Now he felt a cold, flat surface. No, it was curved. His fingers brushed a seeming imperfection. Oh, sure. He was feeling a bottle and the slight rise was the paper label. Meg moved his hand to another surface. Curved again. Another bottle. His confidence flowered back. Hey, this might be fun.

When they moved off again, Jim gave himself over to Meg's leadership. All reluctance evaporated. He pressed Meg's hand, nudging it forward, trying to communicate his desire to go faster. He found walking easier. Why? Because he was relaxing and letting Meg do the work without resisting? Meg responded by speeding their progress.

She pulled his hand wide to lead him around some obstruction. Then he could feel himself going through a narrow place. It was as though he had radar and sensing waves bounced back from the woodwork. Oh yes, they had gone through the door to the bedroom, for now Meg halted and let him test with his feet, then his hand. The bedstead and the coverlet. They walked faster around the room. He felt a table, a lamp, the telephone, then a cold metal object with a small protrusion. Sure, the wall safe where he had placed Ireland's letter and the Group of Twelve report.

They toured the bathroom, where he felt a half dozen fixtures. Meg moved him into an enclosure. She pressed his head forward and he felt soft fabrics touching his cheeks and nose. What the hell? Oh, yes. She had buried his face into her clothes which hung in the closet. He smiled. He felt completely comfortable now, dependent on Meg, yet anxious for more exploring.

They walked through the doorway again, speeded up, stepping in a straight line. Then he noticed the air had changed. It was fresher now and he could feel a stir of breeze on his bare arms. He could hear the ocean pounding, a distinct, wondrous sound the clarity of which surprised him. They were on the balcony. Meg put his hands on the railing, then moved away from him. Instantly, he missed her guiding hand, felt himself alone, wished she would return. Had she abandoned him? No. After a few moments, her fingertips touched his arm, ran lightly down to his hand, enclosed it. She led him away from the balcony and back to the center of the parlor.

"Time's up." It was Moyer's voice. Meg untied the rear knot and the blindfold fell away. The room looked garishly bright.

"No talking yet, Jim. Just blindfold Meg and lead her wherever and however you want."

Jim tried to vary the route. He led Meg first into the small service kitchen, let her touch the glossy refrigerator, trays of ice cubes inside, then the sink and faucets. He noted that she reacted much as he had, hesitant and mistrustful at first, then willing to be led, easy and responsive to his touch. She pressed his hand many times in the first minute as though seeking reassurance. He circled the living room, let her sit in an armchair and later feel the finish of the painting of the cowled Spanish monks. When they toured the balcony, he placed her back against the iron railing, then let her explore the stone surface of the Mixteca's exterior wall. The five minutes passed much more swiftly for Jim this time.

When they were settled again in their chairs, Moyer said nothing for a while. The man seemed to use the vacuum of sound as a catalyst more effective than speech. Jim and Meg grinned at each other.

"All right. Tell me what you felt—then and now."

Jim and Meg both started to talk at once. Meg's face was flushed. "I . . ." But she yielded to Jim and his fervor.

"Hey, that was out of this world." Jim described his initial clumsiness and fear, the feeling of helplessness, the empty, forlorn sensation that lack of control brought, then the panic and Meg holding his hands to give him confidence. He talked about panic for a full minute, telling how it ballooned, then faded away.

"I guess I finally realized that Meg was in full control, that I was helpless, but so what? I had to trust her. Say, that's it. I learned to trust her. No, that's not right. What I learned was that I did trust her, that I'd always trusted her. . . . For God's sake. . . . Meg?"

He looked at her in wonderment. "I trust you. I've trusted you ever since we first met. . . . Jesus." He stopped, looking at his wife as if through new eyes. "That's a wonderful feeling." He felt his eyes growing moist. "I'm not sure what trust is, but it sure gives off a glow."

Meg rose and stepped to him, put her arms around him and kissed his lips lightly. "Sweetheart," she murmured, then quickly returned to her chair.

"How about dependency? Did being totally dependent on Meg bug you?"

"That's the astounding thing." Jim was bubbling now. "All of a sudden it hit me—how dependent I was. And you know what? Not only didn't I mind it, but pretty soon I began to enjoy the hell out of it, me who likes to be in control every hour of every day. . . . Such a simple exercise, Dave, just a walk through some rooms, but the range of emotions. . . . It still gets me."

"I always said you were a fast study. You're beginning to check your feelings and that's the name of the game. . . . Meg?"

She leaned forward, glowing, tensely exhilarated. "Everything, but everything was just like Jim. Isn't it spectacular that we both felt the same things? First the hesitation, the fear, then the panic. My panic lasted only a few seconds, though. Perhaps, Dave, that's because I'm more accustomed to following Jim, right? . . . And dependent! I loved it. I just yielded to him, every part of me. I knew he'd lead me safely, without even a rap on my knee or a scratch on my hand." Meg was gesturing as she talked. "But the trust! That was incredible. I trusted Jim fully, never a doubt after the first few seconds of apprehension. And better than my own trust was the feeling, when I was leading Jim, that he trusted me. I could feel it in his hand, tiny pulses, and in the vibrations from him. I could sense how much he needed me right then and the awareness of his needing me really turned me on. It was a delicious feeling."

Jim could sense a bond, vibrant, alive, urgent, pulling them together. Meg's excitement made her look beautiful. In a flash, he was back on her aunt Lil's porch, on the clanking, swinging couch, then running to the beach. . . .

"No need to add much," said Moyer quietly. "When you've experienced the dependency within you, woman or man, and when you've sensed the mutual trust, well, then you're into each other." He paused and gestured with his pipe. "You two are special, you know. Why, I've had couples who went through traumas on the blind walk, never got over the fear, couldn't trust, hated the dependency. I remember one man who tore off the blind-fold after about a minute, said he wouldn't take another step with that bitch, his wife. Then a woman who intentionally led a man—who wasn't either her husband or lover, just a friend—into bumping his nose against the edge of a door. When he bawled her out afterward, she said sweetly, 'When you go with me, I promise only that you won't come to harm. I don't guarantee to protect you against every scrape or bruise. You're a big boy, you know.' The guy was mad as hell. I sided with him. Her reasoning was valid, I guess, but would you trust a woman who made you take your lumps on purpose?"

Moyer paced between them. "You've got a lot going for you. You're euphoric now and that's okay. Let it flower. But remember, there's a long way to go yet. We haven't got into the crud—Meg's deep resentment over Jim's absorption with Top Court and Jim's feeling that Meg nags him. Just a couple of the dozen or so obstacles I've noted. But let's see if tonight's rolling start will keep rolling. I've got a suggestion for you after I leave. Are you willing to try?"

"Sure," said Jim. Meg said: "After this beginning, I'll try anything you suggest."

"All right. I want you to promise me that when I leave, which is right now, you won't say a word to each other until you wake up in the morning. But you'll fix a couple of nightcaps to relax you—and then do whatever comes naturally. Have I got a bargain?"

They both nodded. Moyer took each by the hand, pulled them upright and drew them together. All three embraced in a tight circle and Meg kissed Moyer softly on the cheek. "I love you both," said Moyer. Then he pulled away.

"That guy Silliman put me in a damn broom closet," he said as he headed for the door with his loose, shambling gait. "As for business, Jim, I'll see you at nine at Praeger's suite. . . . Good night and good luck."

Meg and Jim held their embrace, kissing each other questingly. Then Meg pointed toward the bar. Jim nodded. He walked over, poured two tumblers a third full of scotch and dropped in ice cubes. When he handed Meg her drink, they both, as with a single motion, began walking slowly toward the balcony with an arm about the other's waist.

They stood there for many minutes, drinking, watching the shrouded, surging Pacific, feeling the night air, a bit cooler now, brushing their skin. Meg huddled against Jim's shoulder. He felt as full of life as first spring.

"And so help me, the son of a bitch had the gall . . ." It was Walter Lowdermilk's voice sounding several floors below. Ragged laughter. A chair scraped on tile and someone rattled ice in a bucket. Then a feminine voice, shrill, frenetic: "And I wasted the whole stinkin' winter in Miami!"

The spell was broken. Jim, his arm still around Meg, led her from the balcony, through the living room and into the bedroom, where the huge beds rested beneath the yellow-and-tan headboards.

They put aside their glasses, stood uncertainly by one of the beds, gazing into each other's eyes. Jim wrapped his arms around her, kissed her on the mouth, felt her tongue seeking his.

Suddenly, he pushed her away, put a hand at the throat of her pink sweater and yanked. Buttons scattered on the floor. He swept the sweater off her shoulders. Meg looked both alarmed and fascinated. She stood without moving. He tore at her slacks, ripped them from her hips and pulled downward. Meg fell backward to the bed. He clawed at her brassiere, broke the snap at the rear, threw the bra across the room. The panties parted at one swipe, a small, jagged cry of protest. Meg kicked off her sandals and lay back on the embroidered bedspread.

A half hour later, lying on her back with Jim's chest and belly pressed against her and with the sensation of their slow, full rhythm as hypnotic as a tolling bell, Meg had a sudden vision. Along with Jim, thirsting for more of her body and clasping her ever tighter, was another man. The features were familiar. Slowly they materialized into those of Dave Moyer. As quickly as it formed, the image faded and only Jim lay beside her, thrusting, powering, loving. Guilt came at her like the stab of a knife, then promptly vaporized. Meg smiled.

They lay beside each other, drained, lax, content. Jim's head was tucked in the curve of Meg's neck and one hand rested heavily on her hip. I love this woman, he thought sleepily. He could feel the rise and fall of her breast and below them the surf pulsed like the breathing of a distant giant.

"Jim, it's not far from morning," she said softly, "so the rules are off. There's something I want to tell you."

"Okay." He stirred, nuzzled her throat.

"I just thought of something. You remember that parlor game we played at Westhampton the weekend you met Dave?"

"Yeah. Funny. I thought of it twice tonight."

"Remember what you were?"

"Something about a horse. I can recall you and Dave, but not much about me. What was I?"

"We decided that for a piece of furniture, you were a thick wooden chest. . . ."

"And?"

"As a musical instrument, a drum. Animal: a horse. Plant: an oak tree. The last was a sport. You were football."

"Heavy all around, wasn't I?"

"Uh-huh. But after tonight, I'd change the last three. Instead of a horse, I'd say antelope. You're not an oak tree. You're a birch. And not American football. You're soccer."

"Sounds better."

"Thing is, I love all five."

"I love you, Meg."

"I think you do."

But in the half-world between full consciousness and sleep, a fuzzy image formed in the torpor of Meg's mind. She had seen it before. A long, purple tennis net stretched to infinity. Jim, in jersey and shorts, stood beside the net. He was being pulled two ways, by a mammoth, perspiring Hugo Praeger, who clutched one of Jim's arms, and by Meg, who held the other. She pulled and strained, but inch by grudging inch, Praeger gained possession. He won. He always did.

Wednesday Morning

Jim sipped at his coffee while Meg slept on. Wearing Wednesday's fresh gold shirt, he sat in a wicker chair, his feet propped on the low wrought-iron, glass-topped table. It was eight o'clock and the balcony, shielded from the eastern sun by the pyramidal bulk of the Mixteca, held the cool, early-morning shade like a cup. The hotel was quiet save for the small, scattered noises of the staff preparing for another convention day. Sunlight glinted on the Pacific and two beach boys plodded through the sand, setting out deck chairs and raising candy-striped umbrellas. To the south, Steve Cooper's tent made a khaki blob on the stretch of shining beach.

The thick photocopied report of the Group of Twelve and the envelope from Senator Ireland lay beside the coffeepot fetched earlier by María, whose brisk salutation was offered with the usual clipped condescension that fell just short of hostility. Jim had yet to look at the papers. Instead he was musing about Meg and, occasionally, Gwen Piggott.

For the first time in months, he felt good about Meg and himself. Sure, as Dave Moyer said, they had obstacles to clear away, old wounds to salve, hang-ups to unkink. Last night's euphoria had dissolved now, but some of the sharp, new insights remained like fresh blazes on a forest trail. There was a time last night—it was during the blind walk—when he suddenly saw Meg as the woman he loved. Wife and mother were forgotten. Instead he sensed a woman of myriad facets, some luminous, some opaque, others merely perplexing, that he hadn't glimpsed in years. He had felt a flowering of excitement, the thrill of discovery, he guessed, that still lingered, bright and beguiling, this morning.

He understood now what Gwen meant Sunday night. He had gone to bed with a female body that happened to house a friend of his. Not until he and Gwen began talking candidly afterward did his sense of her grow, putting out tender shoots of understanding. Guilt about Gwen? No. He had slept with other women sporadically, almost mindlessly, over the span of his marriage and the onetime altar boy's heavy vestments of guilt had worn thin. And he surmised that Moyer's exercises might have met a wall of indifference within him had it not been for the night with Gwen. No, guilt didn't fit. Yet, for all of Dave's praise of openness and his castigation of secrets between mates, Jim knew he would never mention the episode with Gwen to Meg. On the other hand, he would readily tell Gwen all about the session with Meg and Dave. He knew that Gwen would be delighted that her reluctant, transient pupil had gone to school in earnest.

But none of this had much to do with his new feeling about Meg. She was his woman and he wanted, belatedly, to explore her, with her, and have her poke around in this mysterious jumble of desires, feelings, wants and needs that he called himself. Actually, he wished she would come awake right now, so he could go to the bedroom, kiss her and welcome her to another bright, ambivalent day.

He glanced at the envelope lying on top of the report and at once, within a split second, one compartment of his mind slammed shut and another swung open. Now, Ireland and the Group of Twelve—to be followed by Praeger and Moyer at nine. He opened the envelope. While Jim failed to make the calculation, it was exactly

two seconds since the thought of Meg's awakening had
fled from his brain. Now, an instant later, she could
be sleeping thousands of miles away, in Majorca, New
York or Westhampton. Jim McGowan was at work.

Ireland's letter, on Harvard Club stationery, was hand-
written, covering two pages on both sides. As he unfolded
it, a small, tightly wadded piece of paper fell out. Jim
turned it over, frowning, then pushed it aside for the
moment. Ireland's uncrossed *t*'s and cramped *g*'s made
reading of the letter difficult. Jim traced the lines slowly:

March 18

Dear Jim:

*Just a few comments about these two reports from
my friends in the Group of Twelve which I hope
you'll consider carefully before your Thursday-
afternoon board meeting.*

*Green Tree. As I told you on the phone, some
of the Group's specialists believe that Arc-Horn's
proposed huge development in Brazil's Amazon
Basin would imperil the world's oxygen supply.
Among them is the talented Russian meteorologist
A. Barankov, who was, suspiciously, placed under
house arrest last week by the Soviet government.*

*But I do not want to mislead you. Some bota-
nists and men in other disciplines differ radically
with the Group's conclusions on oxygen exhaustion.
These men contend there is no danger of oxygen
depletion from Amazon Basin developments.*

*My own conviction is that, when there is doubt
on a matter of such life-and-death importance, pru-
dence is served by delaying Arc-Horn's Green
Tree until the facts can be established.*

*Regardless of the impact on the oxygen supply,
there is absolutely no disagreement among the experts as to the danger of large-scale "developments" of the Amazon jungle. If Arc-Horn logs
off its vast area, preparing it for farming, ranching
and mining operations, the land will be ruined.
Crop yields would be abundant for a few seasons,*

then the thin tropical soil, shielded for thousands of centuries by the forest, will be leached away by the heavy rains, leaving a barren, man-made wasteland.

Neptune West. Here again there's disagreement among the scientists. Some say the underseas mining already under way has had no discernible effect on the ocean environment. Others, equally distinguished, argue that harmful results on the sea bottom will certainly manifest themselves within a few years.

The Group of Twelve has charted various lines of probable damage, including the doomsday possibility that huge machinery operating from the surface will impair the home of the phytoplankton, the tiny aquatic plants that drift in the upper levels of the ocean and provide the earth with about half of its usable oxygen.

I feel very deeply that these warnings raised by scientists and technically qualified academics should be heeded and that all doubts, weighing further industrial production against irreparable damage to our planet, should be resolved in favor of those sounding the alarms. If they're proved wrong in the years ahead, we can always accelerate production, but if they're right, we might all be dead before we could apply remedies.

With our background of wholesale pollution, poisoning the lakes and wetlands, and huge shortages of petroleum and other minerals in recent years, it's difficult for me to see how any reasonable person could conclude otherwise.

The Group of Twelve's special report on Arc-Horn needs a note of explanation. The Group picked your corporation, not to single it out for criticism, but because Arc-Horn covers a wider spread of industrial and consumer production than most other multinationals. Since Messrs. Prae-

*ger and Davidson refused cooperation, the paper
may have some understandable errors.*

*On behalf of the Group, may I impose on our
friendship to make two requests? First, that you use
your influence within the corporation to delay
Green Tree and Neptune West pending special
ecological studies. If Arc-Horn votes to delay,
the Group would be delighted to announce the
fact at the Geneva conference, citing Arc-Horn's
act as an example of mature responsibility by a
leading multinational corporation.*

*Second, if you see any errors in the special
Arc-Horn study, please call me.*

Sincerely,
Philip Ireland

Jim turned to the wad of paper which had fallen from
the letter. It was a carefully folded piece of stationery
bearing Ireland's handwriting.

Jim:

*You have my permission to show my letter to
anyone you wish in connection with the Arc-Horn
board matter. This note is for you only. Please destroy it when you finish reading.*

*Sources within the government's intelligence
community tell me that the U.S. and Soviet leaders,
together with their intelligence agencies, are working covertly to block third world demands at the
Geneva conference. The house arrest of Barankov in Moscow is seen as one fruit of their joint
endeavor.*

*My own belief is that someone inside Arc-Horn
is working with the CIA, undoubtedly trying to
advance the Green Tree and Neptune West projects.*

*My sources tell me there is solid evidence that
Ronald Jeffers, an assistant to Chalmers Davidson, is a Central Intelligence Agency operator and
has been since he joined the CIA after college in*

*1968. While there is no similar evidence, there is a
strong suspicion among my friends that Davidson
himself cooperates with the CIA, either as a volunteer or as a sworn agent under Agency discipline. It is known, for instance, that Davidson
helped recruit pilots for the abortive Bay of Pigs
invasion back in 1961. Also you'll recall the incident several years ago in Bulgaria when Davidson
was accused of bribing an official on behalf of Arc-
Horn. I'm told the Communists failed to press
this angle against Davidson personally because
of a "trade-off" for release of a Russian KGB
agent trapped by the CIA.*

*I'm giving you this information in hopes it may
help you evaluate any moves Davidson and his
assistant may make with regard to Green Tree and
Neptune West.*

Repeat, please destroy this.
Best,
Phil

Jim crumpled the single sheet of paper, placed it in
an ashtray and lit a match. After the small flames died
away, he stirred the charred bits with his finger, then
emptied the ashtray over the balcony railing. The ashes
scattered on the morning breeze.

Davidson and Jeffers CIA men? The news hardly
came as a shock after Tony Percevale's story of the
burglary and bribery of Professor Portilla. Still, Jim
was surprised. He had always viewed Davidson as the
reserved, poised, occasionally supercilious proper Bos-
tonian who put his extensive knowledge of the world
to use for Arc-Horn. That Davidson's missions, many
of them clandestine and even suspect, involved goals
other than business and profits had never occurred to
him. As had others, Jim had wondered about Davidson's
motives in joining Arc-Horn. The large salary could
hardly have been a lure for a man of Davidson's wealth.
And his life style was so diametrically opposed to Hugo's
as to be laughable. Then that seemingly irrelevant ques-

tion of Praeger Monday by Masuo Sugimoto, who asked whether there were any CIA agents on the corporate payroll. Had the inquiry been prompted by the Japanese's suspicions of Davidson or Jeffers?

Jim turned to the two Group of Twelve reports and began to read swiftly through the general paper. It dealt with more than a hundred of the world's resources. Item by item, it gave total annual consumption for the past half century, predicted swiftly rising yearly consumption in the decade ahead, presented figures on known global reserves and pinpointed the year when the mineral, its last fragment used up, would vanish from the list of the resources available to man. The study covered all minerals in current or prospective industrial use, among them gold, silver, cobalt, platinum, manganese, copper, bauxite, iron, tungsten, molybdenum, in addition to the fossil fuels so much in the news since the worldwide petroleum shortage. Jim found much of the paper heavy going, replete as it was with scientific terms, mathematical formulae and the inevitable rash of footnotes. Like the woman who went shopping in hair curlers, the academic document still bore telltale signs of arduous labors in the workshop.

But the data laid persuasive groundwork for the summaries and conclusions. Based on its findings and amendments to the earlier Club of Rome calculations, the Group of Twelve advanced its convictions that:

(1) Man faced the probability that a wide range of minerals would be exhausted within thirty years.

(2) A few vital minerals would disappear within five years at the current rate of extraction.

(3) Political leaders did the world a disservice by stressing the need for more oil discoveries and exploration for new fuels. Additional energy sources, such as large-scale conversion of solar radiation or the harnessing of the H-bomb's fusion power, would result in an even faster rate of industrial production and a consequent swifter depletion of the raw materials used by industry.

(4) Unless remedial measures were adopted quickly, industrial civilization as now known would grind to

a halt within the lifetime of at least half the people now living on earth.

The Group of Twelve would urge the Geneva conference to adopt a set of resolutions, the most drastic of which would slash production of military weapons systems by fifty percent and civilian production by twenty-five percent. Another would request the United Nations to establish allocations and controls for all those minerals, some thirty in number, whose supply had known, definite limits. The Group conceded that this program would face large and intricate political barriers and would require a revolution in the habits, practices and myths of all nations, particularly the industrial powers. But the political obstacles, no matter how sizable, must be overcome within the next few years, or the world faced a chaos of trade strife and bloody wars, perhaps even the nuclear holocaust itself, as the supposedly sovereign nations battled one another for the fast-shrinking muscles, sinews and bones of the living planet Earth.

The report on Arc-Horn International traced a day in the corporation's working life as a sample of how one multinational company drew on the earth's flesh and juices for a single eight-hour period of production. The final figure startled Jim. When the fuel, transport and materials needed for manufacture and distribution were considered, and the operation of offices, planes, cars, trucks, buildings and warehouses added in, Arc-Horn's one day of production required the extraction from the earth of 165,000 tons of irreplaceable solid, liquid and gaseous minerals. The paper noted that these 165,000 tons of exhaustible resources did not include the paper products, fabrics, plywood, hides, meat and beverages made from reproductive plant and animal life.

Each subsidiary's processes were translated into tons of irreplaceable ores taken daily from the bowels and crust of the earth. Top Court ranked far down the list, but even the manufacture of tennis supplies required the daily extraction of 6,500 tons of ores when transport, heat, light and power requirements were apportioned.

Jim noted a few mistakes in the text, but by and large, he deemed the Arc-Horn example to be fair and free of invidious comparison or diatribe.

Brief descriptions gave Jim his first solid look at the new ventures. Green Tree, said the report, involved logging off 200,000 square miles of the Amazon jungle by Hi-Western Corp. Magna Mines would exploit the area's deposits of mica, beryl, manganese, iron, nickel, chrome and tungsten, while Gusto Más would plant huge tracts to crops and pasture. In Neptune West, Magna Mines would join with the Mexican government in scraping and sucking copper and manganese nodules off the deep ocean floor in the Pacific's mineral-rich area west of Baja California. The way for both enterprises had been cleared by secret negotiations with the Brazilian and Mexican governments.

Though Jim had little more than scanned the two reports, he was impressed. Like thousands of other businessmen, he had coped with material shortages as temporary embarrassments to be overcome by skillful trading, higher offering prices and readjustment of production schedules. Implicit in his every working day was the assumption that any shortage was a transient thing, no more consequential than a rain cloud or a brief hailstorm, soon to pass and be replaced once more by the everlasting sunshine of abundance. Exhaustion of the tools and juices of production had been merely a nightmare of scaremongering futurists, of remote concern only to whoever might inhabit the planet thousands of years hence.

Now the forecast of imminent peril seemed anything but dream-like. Perhaps the new psychic space in which he found himself in the last few days made him more receptive. Was he changing? How? Jim was uncertain, yet conscious of new stirrings within him.

The view from the balcony was of a nature yet unscathed. The sun, still hidden by the bulk of the Mixteca, bathed the rolling Pacific, flashed from the whitecaps and sparkled amid thousands of microscopic organisms that made their home on the wide beach. Pelicans flopped along the waves, seeking another morning meal. A half mile at sea a flock of shore birds wheeled and screamed over a patch of boiling, shimmering water where small fish, forced to the surface by larger species, sought to escape the stabbing beaks of the gulls and terns. Life surged on, savage yet curiously peaceful, prey and predator in natural symbiosis on the heaving breast of the ancient ocean.

Jim glanced at his watch: 8:50. Time to meet Moyer in Hugo Praeger's suite. He gathered in the letter and reports and walked to the bedroom, where Meg still slept soundly, lying on her stomach with her head buried in a pillow. He placed the papers in the wall safe and twirled the combination dial, then leaned over and kissed the back of Meg's neck. She did not move in her sleep. He scribbled a note on the bedside table pad, propped it up against the lamp.

> Meg: Just ring for your breakfast, the white button over the table. Back by lunchtime.
> Love you, repeat, love you.
>
> Jim

Dave Moyer was waiting in the foyer of Praeger's suite.

"Hi, Jim. Good sleep? . . . I thought we got off to a fair start last night. How about you?"

"I feel okay about it. So far, so good."

"I'm glad a few things got unblocked. You two aren't as far apart as you like to think. . . . Did you get a chance to look into the envelope from Ireland?"

"Yeah." Jim grew cautious. "Some interesting stuff on production and the environment, the kind of thing Ireland's targeting these days."

"Meg and I were tempted to take a look at it, what with Ireland delivering the package personally. He's an unusual guy for a politician. One thing, he sure was insistent that we hang on to the envelope and place it safely in your hands."

"Well, there's a matter pending . . ."

Jim let the subject float and Moyer, sensing his reluctance, switched the conversation.

"How do you think I ought to approach Praeger?"

"Come on, Dave. You don't need any tips from me. When you're on your favorite kick, you're a regular evangelist—the Billy Graham of the employee-potential movement."

The door opened and Hugo Praeger filled the space like a giant balloon. Jim sensed his mood instantly. Hugo was distracted, gruff, a man put upon. He looked as if he had been up for hours.

"Good morning, Jim. You're getting to be a regular early-morning customer. . . . So you're Dave Moyer." Praeger thrust out his hand. A fragment of smile slipped on and off. "Heard a lot about you. . . . Let's go down to the conference room. More light there."

They walked rapidly down the corridor, Hugo leading the way. He placed his oak armchair and two smaller chairs just inside the open, sun-flooded balcony, maneuvering them so that he had the sun at his back while Jim and Moyer faced the glare.

No sooner had they settled down than Moyer moved his chair a few feet so that the sunlight angled over his shoulder.

"I don't like to squint when I'm talking to a man," he said.

Praeger looked surprised, but said nothing. Encouraged, Jim moved his own chair away from the direct rays.

"Jim, you'll be a couple of hundred dollars poorer tonight." Praeger wore a fresh blue-trimmed gold shirt, a canopy for the mountain of flesh. "Arc-Horn is going to drop today. Combination of coincidences. Nothing basic, just goddam rotten luck." Talking swiftly, he described his meeting with Percevale, Boke-Milgrim, Amarel and others the night before, ticked off the corporate bad news. "Tony called me a few minutes ago.

He's settling the Argentine oil spill with Betancourt for thirteen million. Better than twenty, but still a hunk of change, what? And Frascella tried to close the vise on our big bank loan. Distorted business, banking. Always figuring out what to do with somebody else's money. I can never understand how a man can reach a workable decision unless his own money's involved."

Like a portly horseman on an early-morning canter, Praeger sailed through a countryside lush with the grasses and shrubs of high finance. He brushed past the thicket of First Merchants, flashed his crop at Chase Manhattan, the Bank of America and Manufacturers Hanover, dug in his spurs at the sight of the iniquitous Rothschilds, Mellons and Rockefellers and gestured obscenely at various tellers, loan counselors, trust officers and vice-presidents who had tainted his visions of commercial glory.

"About Top Court," said Jim when Praeger paused for breath.

"Nothing but a goddam embarrassment right at this time, what?" He wheeled his eyes at McGowan and Moyer, unloading a cargo of guilt. How could they quibble at court over baubles and trinkets for the peasants when outposts of the empire were being assaulted? He lectured his courtiers for another five minutes on the dimensions of peril.

Moyer's eyes glazed. He was hearing more than he wanted to know about Arc-Horn. Jim, while more interested, recognized Hugo's tactic. He was filibustering, eating up precious minutes of the forty-five allotted to Top Court before Summit, Inc., fired the first guns of its final morning salute to new radio, hi-fi and audio-visual lines.

"But no Wall Street banker is going to put me in the switches just because of a couple of bad days," said Praeger. He took more minutes to explain why.

"All right, Moyer," he said at last, "let's hear what's eating those strikers up at Doylestown." Jim's watch now showed 9:26.

"I'd like to sketch in the background briefly," Moyer

began. Praeger shifted massively in his armchair, looked more annoyed than attentive.

Moyer described his initial efforts at the racquet plant, the division of the work force into teams, the gradual involvement of employees in all phases of production and planning, the boosted morale, the payoffs in lower absenteeism, the ideas for new machinery and manufacturing short cuts and finally the major change in the assembly line which completed conversion of the factory to a "happy plant."

"That's all very chummy. But what about the strike?"

"The workers interpreted Jim's phone call Monday as a signal from you that you'd kill the new system and that they'd be forced to return to a way of working which most of them disliked and some of them hated."

"That's not what *The New York Times* story said. *The Times* reported that they walked out in protest against your dismissal."

"That's journalistic shorthand. I'm flattered, but the fact is I'm merely a symbol. If I were allowed to stay on in my consultant capacity, the employees would take that as a sure sign the new system wouldn't be dismantled."

Praeger flicked his eyes over Moyer, appraising him. "I suppose you know I was ready to work out something with Jim, but . . . who's the fool named Elliott Shredsburg?"

"Sheddington," corrected Moyer. "A psychologist, friend of mine. I understand he may do some consulting work for Summit."

"Not on your life he won't. . . . I was ready to bargain with Jim, but the strike changed all that. Now we're dealing with a basic issue—who runs the plant, management or employees."

"I don't agree, Hugo," said Jim quickly. "As I said yesterday, the issue is who runs Top Court, me or you."

Praeger spun the amendment aside with a brush of his hand. "A word from management, McGowan or Praeger, that Moyer stays on and we've surrendered.

The workers win and from then on, management's influence is nil."

"I'm afraid you don't grasp the mood at Doylestown," said Moyer. "They're not in a win-or-lose spirit. They're perfectly content to cooperate with management in the future. Content, hell, they're anxious to. Don't forget, the employees no longer see that big, black dividing line between them and their employers. Old Hank Marks, the curmudgeon machinist, now regards himself as necessary to Top Court as Jim McGowan. It's just that right now, if they go back to work without some assurance from you, they feel the whole new setup is doomed." Moyer leaned forward, his elbows on his knees. "Mr. Praeger, I'd like to suggest a compromise."

"Shoot."

"Terminate my services this week, as you've already ordered, but let the workers know in no uncertain terms that the new system will remain intact and that it won't be tampered with by management."

Praeger eyed Moyer shrewdly, thought for a moment.

"Might have been viable some hours ago. . . . Look, it's obviously no secret that I don't think much of your Doylestown experiment. Charge that off to old-fashioned views about business, if you wish. And maybe you're the one who's right, what? Certainly, when good, sound men like Jim and Masuo Sugimoto side with you, I'm forced to concede there's a chance they're more farsighted than I am. So there's room for maneuvering toward an acceptable settlement."

Hugo, Jim noted, was being eminently reasonable and fair-minded now, occasionally his pathway to an adamant negative. It was not long in coming.

"But my answer is no, no compromise now. Jim rightly limits most of his concerns to Top Court, but I'm responsible for Arc-Horn International. We're in a bind this week, temporary of course, but still a bind. Now, if I suddenly make your suggested pledge to the Doylestown workers, the market will interpret it as a sign of weakness.

So will Hal Frascella and the goddam security analysts. I'm not going to risk that today."

Praeger stood up. Jim and Moyer took their cue and slowly rose from their chairs. Praeger jabbed his index finger at Moyer's coat lapel.

"But I'll make you a counterproposal. A couple of weeks from now, when we're out of the bind, I'm willing to talk this whole thing over with Jim in a spirit of sensible cooperation. So why don't you go back up to Doylestown and just spread the word that if they'll call off the strike, old Hugo will come around, see the light, in a few weeks?"

Moyer shook his head. "I'm sorry, Mr. Praeger, but my whole relationship up there is built on mutual trust. I just can't persuade people to rely on ambiguity. When I give my word, it has to stick—or I'm finished."

Praeger nodded. "I appreciate that. I once committed Arc-Horn to one-twenty-five without a contract."

"Thousand?" asked Moyer.

"Million." He had paid Moyer his respects. "Well, I have to make a couple of calls before the Summit show." He offered his hand.

"And so how do we leave it?" asked Jim.

"The strike goes on, what? But don't worry, Jim. My guess is they'll be back on the job Monday."

Praeger turned and strode to the side door connecting with his suite. He walked briskly, the big body swaying and the arms swinging purposefully.

"Well, now you've seen the great man, Dave."

"I had a feeling that on any other day, if we'd had enough time, we could have persuaded him. He's not unreasonable."

"Sometimes, but mostly not." Jim pondered, then smiled. "You know, with his subsidiaries, Hugo's like me with Meg. Never enough time."

"I doubt Meg would be pleased to be equated with a subsidiary." Moyer refused to pass the remark off lightly. "How about a couple more hours before I leave? I'm on the six-o'clock plane to New York."

"Sure. I have to show at the Summit demonstration

now, but this afternoon's fine. You lunch with us and then we'll go at it."

As they headed toward the door, Jim walked slowly, his head bent, his gaze fixed on the rich maroon carpeting.

"You know, Dave, it just hit me. Three days in a row the man has sat on me, hard. I'm wondering whether I'm nearing the end with Top Court?"

"I doubt it, not the complimentary way he spoke about you. But assuming you're right, how does that make you feel?"

"Awful." Jim paused by the door. "I'd lose between four and five million on stock that won't be vested in me until next year. But it's the company more than the money. . . . Twenty-seven years." He brooded. "I built it up from a damn tennis shop. Just a sixteen-by-twenty clapboard shack near some public courts in Boston."

Jim felt heavy with nostalgia. Abruptly, he grasped Moyer's arm and propelled him through the doorway.

Wednesday Afternoon

As formulated by Jake Apple, the impresario of a hundred convention shows, the rule for human communications was no less valid than Gresham's Law of currency: Bad news drives out good.

He had elevated theory to a governing principle years ago after close observation of his mother and her female cronies. Sylvia Apple, a dumpy, gregarious woman, greeted good news with equanimity and a passing mild interest. It was bad news that galvanized Sylvia and sent her bouncing to the telephone to titillate her friends. Car accidents turned her on like psychedelic drugs, financial disaster, preferably of a close friend, brought the spring of youth to her step, connubial faithlessness enlivened her hours, while death lofted her to heights of spirited misery.

Apple's Law, Jake had noted over the years, had special application at business conventions, where milling bodies and antibodies discharged depressing news of monetary betrayals, bad deals, unloving trysts, market manipulations, gastrointestinal bacteria, rip-offs, dry wells, adultery, worthless checks, stock raids, lagging room service, drunkenness, students, devaluations, the federal horrors of OSHA (Occupational Safety and Health Act), proxy fights, collapse of pension funds, inflation, unions, the FTC, hangovers, antitrust suits, hippies, wage demands, environmentalists, Socialism, peevish wives, shortages, ghettos, bad coffee, sunburn and the slow strangulation of the Puritan work ethic.

Apple's Law held that bad rumors were even more virulent than bad news. Rumors of catastrophe swept through conventions like cholera, contaminating the halls, disfiguring judgment and routing such conversational staples as gossip and flattery.

That morning, when Summit, Inc., exposed its new radio and hi-fi lines to a half-empty Maya Hall, a rumor sped through the loyal auditors that many of the Arc-Horn mercantile army had been felled by diarrhea. Completely unfounded, the rumor nevertheless persisted until well into the lunch hour, when all five hundred Arc-Hornians ate with their usual diligence. Another rumor had it that Arc-Horn stock dropped five points during the first two hours on the big board. This too proved false. Actually, in these initial hours of trading, Arc-Horn slumped from 47 to 46¼, an untimely occurrence since the bulk of the market was rising, yet hardly cataclysmic. A third rumor flashed through the Mixteca like lightning—Argentina had boosted its oil-indemnity figure to $30,000,000. The "thirty" turned out to be a corruption

of the "thirteen" million dollars which Antonio Percevale
pledged to Rudolfo Betancourt in a remarkably amicable
and speedy settlement of Argentina's original demand.

Still another rumor had Alex Rosinski, the imprudent
Summit designer, tortured, robbed and sexually assaulted in the Acapulco jail. Cal Silliman, who had visited Rosinski again that morning, reported that the
prisoner was unmarked, healthy and comfortable—indeed slightly high on pot supplied him by a friendly
Mexican cellmate—but fact never caught up with fic-
tion. Like Mrs. Sylvia Apple, the Arc-Horn merchants
preferred to imagine Rosinski on a dirty concrete floor,
a bloodied, degraded heap over which cockroaches
prowled at will and upon which a scorpion with venom-
ous tail was about to drop from a blackened rafter.

The financial parasites all fed upon a common source
of discontent: Arc-Horn's financial bind caused by Sea
Routes' wallowing in red ink and the simultaneous
reverses in Argentina and Doylestown, Pennsylvania.
Forgotten on the wave of rumors were such glad tidings
as Uni-Land's flourishing real estate sales, quarterly
profit surges by at least fifteen subsidiaries, Nakamura's
bold forays in computer land against the harried legions
of IBM, the Mixteca's excellent cuisine and the generally
decorous behavior of the professional businesswomen
from Miami.

Jim McGowan breasted the tide of rumor without
mishap, chiefly because he was too busy to tarry long
in the Toltec Room or the lobby. After reading the
Group of Twelve reports and Ireland's two letters and
after the fruitless session with Praeger and Moyer, Jim
had attended the Summit show, where he dropped into
a seat beside Tony Percevale. He told Tony of the report
and they left early, going to Jim's suite, where Jim opened
the wall safe and gave Tony the papers. Tony promised
to read them at once, then pass them on to Gwen Piggott,
who would return them to Jim after her own perusal.

While Meg sunned herself on the beach, Jim reported
to Smitty in Doylestown, conferred with Al Bebout over
his ouster by Praeger—whether tentative, or definitive,

neither man knew—heard from Katie, his secretary in New York, that the Polex people were threatening to cut off Top Court's plastics shipments because of Jim's "unacceptable" complaint about shabby quality, took a call from Steve Cooper in the lobby, wanting to know the date of Gwen's birthday, and tried unsuccessfully to reach Phil Ireland in Washington. A final call from Smitty during the noon hour confirmed his hunch—the workers would stay out. Sorry, they knew Jim's attitude, nothing against him, hated to cut racquet production, etc., etc., but no flabby-gutted Hugo Praeger was going to dictate to them out of his bottomless ignorance.

Now, after lunching with Meg and Dave Moyer on the terrace and after instructing the switchboard operator to hold all calls to the McGowan rooms for the next two hours, Jim was seated in the parlor of his suite, ready for the second session of matrimonial guidance. Meg was embullient. She wore an old pair of faded jeans and a yellow polka-dot halter that exposed abundant skin tinted rose by the Acapulco sun. Schooled in easy posture now, she sprawled in a large armchair a few feet in front of Jim. Moyer roamed about the room, digging his pipe into a tobacco pouch and glancing occasionally at his customers, who came seeking, if not marital bliss, at least a viable harmony.

"So how did it go last night after I left?"

"As I told you this morning, great." Jim said it with less than heartiness. He felt ill prepared for further psychological encounter with his wife. He'd rather be playing tennis or working at his desk in New York.

"Wonderful," said Meg. "I haven't felt so turned on in months. The world looks good and Jim was a dear this morning. Believe it or not, he left me a love note."

Meg's rejoicing tended to dampen rather than enflame what little fire Jim had for the afternoon venture. Damn it, what was wrong?

Moyer, who seemed to carry invisible radar, swung toward Jim. "What's up with you?"

"I don't know." Jim puzzled over his feelings. "Somehow it's not the same as last night. My mind isn't in the right place. Maybe it's business troubles."

"I've seen you snap your mind shut against everything but the matter at hand. How about closing off all compartments except the here and now—the three of us in this room?"

"I'll try."

Moyer turned to Meg. "Does Jim's attitude bother you?"

"No. I'm used to it. If he isn't worried about Top Court, he's worried about Arc-Horn. My own regard for Arc-Horn is lower than usual today. Cal Silliman treats me like I've got the plague."

"I told him yesterday you were coming in and would be sharing the suite with me," said Jim. "It's nothing personal on his part, Meg. He's supposed to enforce the rule against wives attending and Cal gets uptight when someone side-steps a Praeger order."

"He could treat me with as much courtesy as he does those call girls from Miami."

Moyer eased himself down to the black-and-tan Indian rug and lolled back on his elbows. "Let's try something upbeat for an opening, see if we can give Jim a lift. . . . Couples are forever harping on the shortcomings of each other. In the gloom of their joint misery trips, they forget all those good days when the world shone and the mate looked terrific. So, each of you dig into your memory and come up with five peak experiences that you shared with the other one. A sea voyage, you know, a birth, a special hour of intimacy. Take a few minutes and come up with five apiece, okay?"

At once Jim's mind, prodded by Meg's recollection last night, centered on the porch swing at Southampton. That was a peak night. Let's see. The week at St. Tropez and Cannes when Carol and Connie were small and he and Meg left the twins home in care of a nursemaid. A great week. Then the cruise on the *QE II* in '73. Too much booze, but a swinging time for both. Hmm. Oh yes, that miracle September morning in Ontario when they rode horses before breakfast and then came back, drank bloody Marys and romped in the sack until noon. . . . A fifth? Well, how about last night? Sure, that was big.

Meg was still wrapped in thought. She stared through Jim for some time, frowned, then brightened. "I've got my five."

"All right. You go first."

"The Southampton porch of Aunt Lil's and the beach at night, of course. That's Number One." Her eyes shone. Meg was enjoying this. "Then my second one I'll bet Jim doesn't even remember. It was our fourth Christmas. Usually Jim gives me a whole swarm of presents, some of which I suspect have been purchased by Katie. . . ."

"Is that right, Jim? Does your secretary buy gifts for Meg?"

"Sometimes—when I get pressed at the office."

"How does that make you feel?"

"One word. Guilty."

"There's an easy out. Never give Meg a present you didn't buy or make yourself. Presto: fewer guilt trips. Who needs them? . . . Meg?"

"Well, this Christmas—our fourth—he gave me just two presents, a lovely pearl clasp and a four-page hand-written letter. He told me how much I meant to him, that he loved me, loved Carol and Connie, the more so since they came from both of us. Oh, it was a beautiful letter. I cried some and we had good friends in that afternoon and at night we made sweet love. It was soupy and sentimental and gorgeous, the whole day and night." She paused, awash in memory. Then her voice took a lilt. "My third big memory is of howling, good fun. I threw a surprise party for Jim on his fortieth birthday. He had no idea that anything was up and you should have seen his face when he walked in that night, late as usual, from work. The place was jammed with the people he likes best, Al and Sue Bebout from the office, Tony Percevale and his wife, Anita, all the way up from Argentina, men in Westhampton he plays tennis with, his favorite professor from Brown, his younger brother, Kevin, about a hundred people all told, and every one of them especially picked. There wasn't a soul in the house that I thought Jim didn't like. They brought goofy little gifts, nothing over a dollar, and we danced until four to a five-piece band and everybody was floating. Actually, Jim got smashed, one of the few times I've seen him that way. It was a terrific party. We had the time of our lives."

Moyer was studying Jim. "You don't look like a man with a happy memory. Did you have the time of your life that night?"

"No." Jim shook his head emphatically. "I don't like surprise parties. I never have."

"How can you say that, Jim?" Meg was indignant. "You were ecstatic, kissing half the women there and dancing with all of them. You gave a funny speech and at three in the morning you staged a diving contest in the pool. You can't fool me at this late date. You had a ball."

"Easy, Meg. Let's hear it from Jim. He says he didn't enjoy himself. Do you know why, Jim?"

"Yeah. Surprise parties put people under obligation. They come whether they want to or not, duty stuff. Take Tony that year. Maybe it was a hell of an inconvenience for him to fly up from Buenos Aires, but Tony, even if he is my closest friend, has too much Latin courtesy to say no. . . . Then, damn it, a guy's fortieth is a tough one to take. That feeling that youth is gone, that he's more than halfway through life, that old age is much closer than it was yesterday. Who wants to be reminded that it's all downhill from then on? . . . Plus the fact that a surprise birthday party is artificial. That night I was the crown prince—for what? What had I done except grow a day older?"

Meg huddled back in her chair, folded her arms and stared at her husband disbelievingly. "Well, I must say, after all the troubles and headaches I went through to keep it a surprise, and now to learn that you despised it . . ." She bit nervously at her lip.

"I take it you don't think much of Jim's explanation?"

"Certainly not. To buy that, I'd have to believe that he really doesn't care about his oldest and best friends—or appreciate all the effort I put out for him."

Moyer let a frosty silence hang for a time, then asked Jim: "Did you ever throw a surprise party for Meg?"

"No. I told you. I don't like them."

"Have you ever wanted Jim to surprise you on an anniversary, Meg?"

"Only every year! I'd have loved a surprise party on *my* fortieth."

Moyer straightened from his reclining position, laid aside his pipe and glanced from wife to husband.

"Get the irony? Sounds like an old O. Henry story. Meg throws a surprise party for Jim because *she* loves them. Jim never gives Meg a surprise party because *he* detests them. Wouldn't it make sense to find out what pleases the other person most and then provide that on an anniversary? In this case, it's simple. On some upcoming anniversary, Jim springs a big surprise on Meg. But Meg, on a similar date, knowing Jim's aversion, gives him a kiss, a bottle of wine and two tickets to the finals at Forest Hills. Right?"

Meg looked unpersuaded. "I can't understand Jim's attitude."

"But you can be aware of it," said Moyer firmly. "Look, Meg, one of your complaints about Jim is that he doesn't take the time to understand you. Well, how about the real Jim? You went, let's see—eleven years, wasn't it?—without picking up a dozen clues that would have told you that Jim dislikes surprise parties. You weren't looking and listening. So you figured that what you like, Jim must also like. Carried to the ultimate, that means you'll never fully accept Jim until he becomes another you. . . . Well, you'll wait through eternity before that happens. Jim is never going to be like Meg, and if he did, you'd hate him for it."

He turned to Jim. "Do you understand Meg's liking for surprise parties?"

"No, but I get the message. I guess it's time I planned

one for her." He smiled weakly. "I'll just have to grit my teeth and go at it."

"If you have to grit your teeth, call the divorce lawyer instead. If you can't get enjoyment thinking of the fun you'll give Meg, better you forget the whole thing. . . . Okay, Meg, you still have two peak experiences for us."

"Peak doesn't seem quite the word now, but here goes. I listed last night among my five. Last night was a special high from start to finish and . . ."

There was a knock at the door. After a pause, they heard a second, louder rap. Jim crossed the room and opened the door.

"Sorry, Jim." It was Gwen Piggott. "The operator said you weren't taking calls, but I thought I ought to return this." She handed him a large manila folder containing Ireland's letter and the Group of Twelve reports.

"Come on in. Just three of us talking." He put a hand on Gwen's elbow.

"No, no. I just wanted to . . ."

"Come on." He gripped Gwen's arm and steered her into the room. "You know Meg . . . and this is Dave Moyer of Doylestown fame."

The two women brushed each other's cheeks with perfunctory kisses, then Gwen faced toward Moyer. "So, you're the man we've been hearing about? What I've heard, I like."

She shook her head at Jim's offer of a chair. "I'll only stay a minute. . . . Meg, you look terrific. Acapulco agrees with you. Jim, the reports made an impression on Tony. Me too." Gwen, usually at ease in any company, appeared to be rattled. "I think the three of us should meet before the board meeting. And how about Masuo Sugimoto? I wish he'd read the material."

"Excuse me a second," said Jim. "I'm going to put this in the safe."

In the bedroom, he opened the wall safe, slid the folder on top of the agenda for Thursday's board meeting and twirled the dial.

"Tonight after the supermarket opening?" he asked

Gwen when he returned. "We could meet in your room or Tony's."

"Yes, well . . ." She glanced toward the door in a moment of hesitation. "Jim, I think we'd better talk outside." Gwen made her apologies to Meg. "Hush-hush corporation business, you know." Her laugh was forced. "Pardon us, please. This will only take a minute."

In the corridor, Gwen closed the door behind them. "Walk down the hall with me and keep your voice low." She looked both ways. "Jim, somebody has bugged all three of my rooms."

"What?"

She gripped his arm. "Steve came up to my place a half hour ago just as I was finishing the reports. He was mixing me a drink when he saw this little metal device behind the bar and a wire leading from it. So we hunted through the place and found another one in the bedroom and a third in the dinette. Steve snipped the wires. He says he fooled around with bugging gear in high school and he knows enough to speculate that this was a professional installation. . . . Come on, let's stand over there." She indicated the foyer near the elevators. "If someone comes, they'll think we're waiting for one. . . . The funny thing is, just before Steve found the bug, he was telling me what María, that snippy hostess, told him. She said she'd heard that some kind of recording system was being run out of that off-limits communications center of Davidson and Ron Jeffers' on the eleventh floor."

They stood facing each other, sharing the alarm. "We've got to assume, then, that whatever we said Sunday night was recorded," said Jim.

She nodded. "But why my place? I'm no big wheel in Arc-Horn. Why would anyone, including Chalmers, want to listen in on my ramblings?"

"Maybe they've bugged the rooms of all board members." The thought seemed preposterous to Jim until he remembered Ireland's burned note. If Davidson and Jeffers were indeed CIA agents, listening devices would not be extraordinary tools. He thought of telling Gwen about Ireland's warnings, but hastily decided against it. Later, perhaps.

"Or the whole damn hotel, for all we know. Jim, what are we going to do?"

His initial shock had turned rapidly to outrage. Was this indeed Davidson and Jeffers' work? Did Hugo know and approve? If not Davidson, who then? Jim had read countless articles on wiretapping and taping since the Watergate affair, but this was the first time in his life he had cause to believe that his own private conversations had been the target of electronic eavesdropping. And, peculiarly, the thought that his talk with Gwen probably had been recorded troubled him less than did a similar recording of last night's long session with Meg and Dave. He became furious at the image of a faceless figure, the head straddled by earphones and features bunched in a prurient smirk, savoring intimate scraps from the bouillabaisse of the McGowan marriage.

"If I knew who it was, I'd beat the hell out of him. I'd like to go right up to Hugo's room, both of us, and demand to know just who's behind this." He could feel adrenalin pumping through him, and he knew from experience, this was a moment for caution. He thought a moment, his mind clicking. "But we don't want to go off half-cocked. Tell you what. Why don't you find Tony, tell him what happened, and get him to search his suite? I'll do the same in my place. Then, I'll clue in Masuo—I want him to read the Group of Twelve reports anyway—and the four of us meet tonight after the Gusto Más opening."

Gwen looked disappointed. "I'd feel better if we met right away. The whole hotel gives me the creeps." She looked about her nervously. "For all we know, this hallway may be bugged."

Jim placed his hands on her arms. "I doubt it. . . . I can't meet this afternoon. I've promised the next two hours to Meg. We're discussing some things with Moyer. . . . Let's not move too fast, Gwen. If this is a Davidson operation, we'll want Masuo with us when we confront Hugo. Sugimoto has more clout than the three of us put together."

"All right." Gwen was less than persuaded. "Where shall we meet? Same place as Monday night?"

"Yes. That far table on the terrace. About ten-thirty after the opening?"

"Ten-thirty." Gwen's eyes roved anxiously as though nothing had been settled. "Jim, do you realize that *everything* we said Sunday night may be on tape somewhere in this hotel?"

"I know. Where is Steve right now?"

"Waiting in my room."

"Look, I'll take Meg and Dave down to the terrace. Then you have Steve search our rooms. I don't know a damn thing about bugging devices." He fished in his pocket. "Here, take my key. Meg's got another one. Then after you find out, let me know. We'll be at one of the shady tables."

They parted, Gwen turning right in the corridor that led to her rooms and Jim heading left. Should he tell Meg and Dave about the recording mechanisms? No. Without the intricate Arc-Horn background of recent days, the story would merely alarm them and probably ruin the rest of the afternoon.

Dave answered his knock. Meg was sitting with her chin cupped in her hands.

"Problems," said Jim briskly. "Give me a minute while I make a call." He dialed Sugimoto's room, but heard only empty ringing. When he queried the switchboard operator, she informed him Mr. Sugimoto was playing golf, would return about five-thirty.

"Say, let's move down to the terrace, I'm too easy to find here." He appealed to Moyer. "Besides, I might do better out in the fresh air." Since a gentle breeze rippled in from the balcony, the excuse seemed a lame one, Jim realized. "I feel distracted up here."

Meg rose from her chair. "We can't have that can we, Dave?" She flashed a knowing glance at Moyer that Jim had noted several times before. It was a look of sharing, as though Meg and Dave were the intimates and Jim the outsider. It nettled him.

"A change of scenery might help," Moyer conceded.

On the long beach-side patio, they settled for a table at the north end in the shade of a sighing palm and a tulipan tree whose huge blooms beamed at them like merry carnival masks. A combination of the late siesta hour and the molten afternoon sun had cleared the terrace of all but a few Arc-Horn conventioneers.

"Where were we?" asked Moyer. "Oh, yes, peak experiences together. Jim, we have five coming from you."

Jim told of the night on the Southampton beach, the week on the French Riviera, the ocean cruise, the September morning in Ontario and last night's experience, noting that two of his memories meshed with Meg's. But even as he talked, he knew that his memory was drained of the original vividness. His descriptions came out flat, spiritless. The fact was, he knew, that Gwen's story had crushed the last fragments of last night's euphoria. Try as he might, he could not snap the compartment shut on Arc-Horn. The corporation kept intruding, hammering for his attention as if Praeger himself were rapping a gavel at the center of the horseshoe conference table.

"Hmm." Meg's disappointment lay like a shadow. "Those are peaks? They sound more like molehills."

Moyer observed him silently. Jim felt an urge to defend himself.

"I'm just not with it today, Dave. It's the same old story. When business problems come up, and we have a mess of them this week, I just can't close my mind on them. God knows, I'd like to, but I can't."

"But you manage the reverse, shutting out everything but business when you're working."

"I know. I know."

"The mind goes where it will." In Moyer's style, it was not an accusation, but a simple statement of fact.

"But I'm willing my thoughts to stay here. The trouble is, they won't." Jim shifted restlessly, waved his hand at the hotel. "Hugo's part of the problem. Every year he brings us to a lush resort like this, where all the surroundings whisper temptingly, 'Relax, goof off, enjoy yourself.' Then he shoves our noses to the grindstone."

"The man's a sadist," said Meg.

"No. It's just that he's more flexible than the rest of us. He can shuttle between business and pleasure without missing a beat and it never occurs to him that others can't do the same. . . . Oh, pardon me a minute."

He saw Gwen hurrying across the terrace, her golden slacks and shirt shimmering in the sunlight. He went toward her and they met by an umbrella-topped table out of earshot of Meg and Dave.

Gwen nodded apprehensively. "Yep. Steve found two bugs, one by your balcony door in the parlor and the other in the bedroom. He cut the wires."

"That means other rooms are bugged too." His stomach tightened as though clutched. "There'd be absolutely no reason for anybody to single out you and me for surveillance. Did you find Tony?"

"No, he's in town, preparing for the opening. Back about six, the desk says."

"Okay. Masuo's on the golf course. I'll get him as soon as he comes back. . . . Just hold everything until the four of us can talk tonight."

When he returned, Meg essayed a playful smile. "What's with you and Gwen? Plotting to take over the empire?"

"I wish we were. No. Just a tougher problem than usual. Actually, this is a nasty one."

Still, they managed to spend more than an hour on an exercise in which they tried to recall themselves as ten-year-olds when parents dominated their lives. They were interrupted once by Pete Quigley, who wanted to buy everyone a drink at the Tarascan Bar, and again by a waiter paging Magna Mines' crusty Damon Kimball. Jim was distracted throughout, his mind veering to Gwen and the recording devices even during one poignant moment when Meg described her father's insensitivity toward her feelings when she was a little girl.

"Dave, I give up," Jim said at last. "I can't hack it this afternoon. Too much going on with Arc-Horn."

Moyer inspected his wristwatch. "I've only got about a half hour anyway before I have to clear my things out of that broom closet and start for the airport. Let's just chat for a bit."

Meg reached out and patted Jim's hand. "I understand. I have my off days too—as you well know. But I feel better about us. We got something good going last night."

"I feel that too and I'm looking forward to the weekend at Doylestown. I'll try to hang loose there."

"I think you will. Meanwhile, I have something to say, an announcement, I suppose." Meg placed her arms on the table and leaned toward them. Her eyes were bright. "I've become very interested in Dave's field. I'd like to get into it seriously myself."

Both men were startled. Jim gazed at her, weighing her intent. "Industrial psychology? . . . Meg, what Dave does is the result of years of training and study."

"I've thought that through." Her smile faded. "You know I've been searching around for something to do, but nothing grabbed me. I'd like to get into psychology, maybe some phase related to Dave's work. I'm exploring, thinking. . . . Perhaps he or some of his colleagues would let me watch them work. I just know it would be right for me. To put it Dave's way, I feel it."

Moyer studied her. Meg's eyes shone and there was a purposeful set to her posture. Impulse or conviction?

"You're talking about five or six years of preparation," he said slowly. "That's a long grind, Meg. Do you think you have the staying power?"

"I think I do, but I won't know until I try. Right now I'm fascinated by what you do and I'm sure I'd get more hooked as I went along. It's all about people and people are endlessly interesting to me." She paused, reflecting. "Besides, I think a woman would have a head start over a man. We're more used to puzzling out motivations of others. Call it our second-class status and the need to manipulate, if you want to take the lib line."

She folded her hands on the table. "Anyway, I've decided."

"How does that make you feel, Jim?"

"Mmm. I'm not sure. Having a career woman around would take some getting used to. On the other hand, I know that the usual round of bridge, gossip, tennis and luncheons bores Meg stiff. And frankly, a bored wife is a pain. I guess what I feel is, well, pleasure for Meg and some apprehension about us."

"What's your overall reaction? Good or bad?"

"Oh, good, definitely."

Meg smiled, a mix of affection and self-assurance. "Jim, I think I've learned something yesterday and today. I kept saying I wanted more from you, more time, more fun, more love, more doing things together. That's true, but as Dave says, I can't change you, and even if I could, I probably wouldn't like it after I got it. Dave said it: We're all in charge of our own lives. I want to be in charge of mine and get all involved in work that I can be proud of and respect myself for. I think I did a good job with the twins. Now it's time for another one."

Jim's feeling was a curious one. Meg's words, tripping along logically, were forming a declaration of independence. There had been but one outside suitor in the McGowan household—Top Court. If Meg followed through, there would be two, Top Court and Meg's work, elbowing each other for attention. He could sense a stir of competition. Meg had always been jealous of his affair with Top Court. Was he already feeling a twinge of jealousy over Meg's nascent interest?

"If you get into it seriously, Meg, it'll mean a bigger change for Jim than it does for you." Had Moyer caught vibrations from Jim's ambivalence? "His friend Tony, for instance, would probably suffer badly—the Latin *machismo* tradition. But we have hidden *machismo* in our culture too. So far, Jim has been the big wheel, father, husband, breadwinner, corporate president. Now we may have two wheels. Suppose Meg became a star in her field. . . . All I'm saying is, Meg, be careful of Jim's pride as you go along."

"I'd never hurt Jim." Her smile was tender, amused. "But of course, it's his life he's in charge of, not mine. Right?"

"Just make sure there's lots of mutual stroking as you go along. You'll need it."

"Promise." Meg leaned eagerly toward Moyer. "Now that it's settled, where should I start, Dave?"

First, he said, she ought to have a long talk with his friend Elliott Sheddington, and his partner, a woman who began her career in her mid-thirties. Then she ought to plan to enter grad school in the fall and . . . They talked for fifteen minutes, Meg peppering him with questions and Moyer gradually becoming imbued with her enthusiasm. Aside from an occasional suggestion, Jim sat quietly with his own feelings. Dave was right. Suddenly there were two wheels, each spinning in its own space. A dependent Meg, picking at him for more time, more energy, more of himself, might be an irritating thorn, but with the thorn plucked out, would he miss it? He could sense two Jims, a generous being near the surface who cheered Meg on, applauded her initiative and sympathized with her yearning, and a deeper Jim who felt challenged, threatened in some dark, shapeless way. Which Jim could he trust for the future? He was still puzzling when Moyer pushed back his chair and stood up.

"It's five-thirty. I'll have to hustle to make the plane. . . . I feel good about you two. A full two days and nights this weekend and you'll be well started. . . . So long. See you Friday in Doylestown." He turned and walked off toward the hotel.

"And I feel great, Jim." Meg hooked his arm as they left the table. "Do you get a big charge of energy like this after you've made an important decision at the office?"

"Yeah. Once the decision is made, good or bad, I can feel more power. It's the wavering back and forth that drains a person." He pressed her arm to his side.

"I'm glad for you, Meg. There's a part of me that resists. I'm not sure what that's about, but I'll give you all the support I can."

"I believe you."

They sauntered toward the lobby in the heat of the lowering sun. "You're on your own until about midnight, Meg. I've got to find Sugimoto now. Then there's the Gusto Más shindig and four of us having a meeting. . . ."

"Don't apologize," she said firmly. "I'm going swimming, then to the hairdresser. I've got lots of things to think out. . . . I'm so excited. It's wonderful." She smiled affectionately. "So you do your thing. I'll do mine."

The lobby was filling with red, blue and gold shirts, a sign the cocktail hour was approaching. Joyce Boke-Milgrim stood beneath one of the stone arches, chatting with Lucy Jenkins.

"What did Arc-Horn close at?" Jim asked.

"Forty-five and a half," said Boke-Milgrim, "off one and a half." He did not look displeased. "Not as bad as I expected."

"Not bad?" Lucy scoffed. "With what he lost today, Jim could endow a hospital. It's easier being poor, honey. Me, I only dropped fifteen hundred since breakfast—in dollars. In pounds, I'm better off. I think I gained one."

Jim and Meg were nearing the elevators when he saw Sugimoto walking up the broad entrance steps. "Just a second, Meg."

"Take your time, I'll be up in the room." She entered a waiting elevator.

The stocky Japanese was still wearing a red golf glove. He peeled it off as Jim approached.

"How'd you do, Masuo?"

"Eighty-eight. Better than my handicap in spite of the heat. But the course isn't hard."

"I need a word with you." Jim quickly described the Group of Twelve reports and Ireland's letter. "Would you have time to read them now? Tony and Gwen and I are meeting here after the Gusto Más ribbon cutting and we wish you'd join us."

"Items Eight and Nine tomorrow?"

"Right. Damn big steps for Arc-Horn and we want to talk them through." He moved closer and lowered his voice. "There are other complications, Masuo. You know the CIA question you asked Monday? Well, there's some evidence that two Arc-Horn officers are working closely with the Agency. And then, we've got some solid proof that somebody is using electronic surveillance in the hotel."

"Where? Here in the lobby?" Sugimoto looked about him.

"No. In some of the rooms. . . . Look, the papers are up in my place. May I bring them around to your suite? Then I'll fill you in."

"Yes, of course, I'm in 929."

Jim rode the elevator to the tenth floor. Meg answered his knock. "I'm just getting those reports for Sugimoto," he explained. He went to the bedroom wall safe, put his fingers to the dial and clicked off the combination: two-five-six-zero-eight. He pulled the small metal door open, then stared.

The safe contained but one paper, the printed agenda for tomorrow's board meeting. He lifted it, peered underneath. Nothing. The thick manila folder, holding Ireland's letter and the bulky Group of Twelve reports, was missing.

"Meg, come here a minute, please."

His note of urgency fetched her immediately. "What's the matter?" She saw him standing, bewildered, in front of the open safe.

"Those reports are gone. Was anyone in here besides us?"

She shook her head. "The maid this morning. No one else."

"I know I locked them up when Gwen brought them back." He frowned as he searched his memory. "I remember spinning the dial."

"I haven't touched them, Jim. I don't even know the combination."

"I know that." He thought hard. "Damn it, somebody had to have entered while we were out."

Gwen or Steve? No. That didn't make sense. She would have told him on the terrace. Also, neither of them knew the combination. Could his memory be faulty? Perhaps he had left the safe open and a maid . . . No again. The image of turning the dial was clear. He knew his recollection was accurate. Who then? What had Cal Silliman said that first day when he handed him the little blue envelope? That only the hotel manager had the list of combinations? Better call Cal right away.

But he dialed 929 first. "Jim McGowan, Masuo. Look, I seem to have mislaid those papers. I'll bring them up to your room as soon as I find them."

"No hurry. I'm resting up here until the motorcade starts for Percevale's show."

Meg was in the bedroom. Jim called to her. "I'm going down to Silliman's office. Back in a few minutes."

"I hope you find them." Meg's voice had a vibrant lilt.

Calvin Silliman's office was tucked in an alcove near the registration desk and behind a miniature waterfall which trickled from the yawning mouth of an Aztec idol into a pool where several goldfish swam. Silliman was on the phone, hacking his labored way through Spanish like a man on a rock pile. *"Muy amable,"* he said at last, bowing at the mouthpiece as though it were a living dignitary.

"That was the chief of police," he said. "He's letting Alex Rosinski out tomorrow noon—as a special favor to Señor Praeger. Hugo doesn't know it yet, but he sent the chief a case of scotch. . . . When in Rome . . ." He sighed. "What can I do for you, Jim?"

"Got a problem. . . . Who besides me has the combination to my wall safe, Cal?"

Silliman frowned, scratched himself under the armpit. "Only Edmundo Monterroso, the Mixteca manager. Why, did you lose something?"

"Yes. Some papers. And I'm a hundred percent certain I locked the safe when I put them in there a couple of hours ago."

"You want to talk to Edmundo?"

"Well, yes. I want to find those papers—and find out who's got sticky fingers around here."

"You wouldn't be thinking of accusing Edmundo, would you?" Silliman busied himself in a desk drawer. "He's a touchy man to handle." He glanced up suddenly with a look of relief. "Oh, I forgot. Edmundo flew to Mexico City today. He won't be back until later. . . . Jim, there's got to be some mistake. Did you look through your rooms?"

"No. I know exactly what happened. I locked up the papers and just now, when I reopened the safe, they weren't there."

Silliman shrugged. "Then I'm at a loss, Jim. The staff here doesn't steal, especially from inside safes. Yours is the first theft complaint of the convention. I'm sorry, I . . ."

His desk telephone rang. Silliman listened a moment after answering, then pressed the receiver tightly to his ear. His glance at Jim was one of apology. He listened attentively.

"No, not right now." His tone was wary. "There's someone with me at the moment. . . . Jim McGowan. . . . Sure."

Silliman handed the phone to McGowan. "It's Chalmers Davidson. He wants to talk to you."

Jim took the instrument with a feeling of surprise. Actually, he had surmised the caller was Davidson. Why? He wasn't sure. Perhaps because his mind had flicked to Davidson several times in the last few minutes.

"Hello."

"I'm glad I caught you, Jim. I was just about to call your room. Something important has come up." Davidson's tone was easy, low-key. "Could you spare me half an hour?"

"When?"

"Right now. There's plenty of time before the motorcade."

"All right."

"I'm in my room. Eleven twenty-nine."

Two minutes later Jim walked swiftly down the

eleventh-floor corridor past the narrow, locked door
with the sign "No Admittance. Authorized Personnel
Only," and past the blue-shirted security guard with the
black holster at his belt. The man nodded to him. Jim
throbbed with curiosity—and with a formless rage that
sought an unknown target.

Wednesday, 6 p.m.

The blue manta cloth shirt of Arc-Horn officers, which
looked merely absurd on such men as John Lindquist
and Bernard Hirsch, fitted Chalmers Davidson as though
tailor-made. His white slacks bore a knife-edge press,
his graying, closely trimmed hair was parted carefully
to the left without a misplaced strand and he walked
to the bar with the same poise and casual air of primacy
that marked all his movements.

"What'll it be, Jim? I'm having scotch on the rocks
with a splash and a twist."

"Fine with me. Add a little more water to mine,
please."

Davidson mixed the drinks and placed them on the
heavy black coffee table, a replica of the United Express
toadstool that dominated Jim's living room. The table
stood just inside Davidson's ocean-side balcony. The
sun was swelling like a balloon as it arched toward the
Pacific for its final plunge. A low cloud bank lay snug
to the horizon and a late fishing boat left a foaming
wake as it skimmed northward toward the harbor of
Acapulco.

"I was sorry to hear about your papers, Jim. Surely you mislaid them somewhere in your rooms."

Jim went instantly on guard. In Silliman's office, he had hung up the phone without mentioning the papers to Davidson. And Cal, he knew, had said nothing of the incident before Jim took the phone.

"I imagine they'll turn up." This was not the time, he sensed, for a fruitless discussion of stolen papers. Nor was it the time to voice a half dozen questions, from burglary to electronic surveillance, that churned inside him and clamored for venting. The first move was Davidson's. He sipped at his drink and waited.

"I've been doing some hard thinking today." Davidson measured his drink with his eyes as he placed the glass on the broad arm of his chair. "Hugo told me of the upshot of his meeting this morning with you and your psychologist—what's his name"

"Dave Moyer."

"Yes, Moyer. That strike is a great pity. No sense to it at all—from your standpoint and mine, that is. This is one time the workers are right and Hugo is a hundred percent wrong. I go along almost in toto with Sugimoto's views. Worker involvement in the planning traditionally reserved for management is, as Masuo says, the wave of the future. No doubt about it. I've kept my eyes open since Lordstown, talked to a lot of employees and done extensive reading. Take the rapid changes in management-worker roles we see in such widely disparate countries as Sweden and Yugoslavia."

Davidson talked for five or six minutes about evidences of the new "industrial democracy"—a phrase he not only repeated but seemed to savor—around the world. His examples were conscise and pointed. As usual, he knew precisely what he was talking about. Jim, who had done but scant reading on the subject, was impressed but increasingly wary.

"I didn't know you were on our side, Chalmers," he said when Davidson finished. "You didn't speak up at the board or during the closed-circuit interview."

"I find I have more influence with Hugo if I hold

my fire for the opportune moment." His smile emcompassed McGowan as a fellow conspirator in the intricate machinations needed to sway the judgment of their leader. "One word in private with him is worth ten in a group. . . . As for the issue at stake here, we both know Hugo is behind the times; deplorably so, in my opinion. Perhaps you share my suspicions that he's looking for a way out that won't lose him face?"

Jim nodded. "He hinted as much this morning." He was tempted to explain Hugo's offer to Moyer, but held off. Question of loyalties. His tie of loyalty to Hugo might be tenuous right now, but there was none at all between him and Davidson. Again he waited.

Davidson took another sip of his drink and leaned back in his chair. "We both know that strike could be ended in five minutes if Hugo merely stated that Moyer stays on and the new system remains as is, untampered with. I strongly believe that is exactly what he should do and as quickly as possible. Long strikes leave ugly scars whatever their solution. And while I don't know Moyer, I believe as firmly in his objectives and his methods as you and he do." Davidson's eyes dwelled on Jim's as if to stress his sincerity. "So I'd like to persuade Hugo this evening to back down, gracefully but unequivocally. I'm confident I can bring him around. I can see the signs. He wants to be convinced. You're not the man to do it. You've had a tussle of wills with him. But as an uninvolved witness, I can give him the kind of advice I know he'll accept."

"Fine!" Jim's exclamation was less than electric. He was held back by a nagging caution, not readily explicable. Why this sudden gift? "I hope you can pull it off."

"I'm more than willing to do it, but frankly, Jim, in return I'd like a favor from you."

Here it came. "What's that?"

Davidson got up, strolled over to a corner desk and returned holding a paper in his hand. "Tomorrow's board agenda," he explained. "I'm deeply committed to passage of Resolutions Eight and Nine. You know about them, I suppose?"

"Yes." Jim was aware of a tightening of his muscles.

"Let me read them anyway." Davidson did so in a slow, measured voice. He seemed to relish the phrases "Green Tree" and "Neptune West," and Jim wondered whether Davidson had invented the names.

"Both undertakings have vast potential, not only for us, but as contributions to the world economy." He paused, eying Jim closely. "Now ordinarily these projects could be considered and passed on their merits, but right now there's a special urgency. Arc-Horn is in a squeeze and the market knows it. Today's drop won't be the end of it."

Davidson talked of the financial bind caused by the oil spill, the Doylestown strike and the cash-reserve requirement of the First Merchants' loan. This prefaced a virtual lecture on the glowing promises, all scientifically buttressed, of the ventures in the Amazon Basin and on the deep floor of the Pacific. He expounded on the roles of Hi-Western, Gusto Más and Magna Mines in exploiting the latent wealth beneath the jungle and told how Magna Mines would join with the Mexican government in sucking a treasure of minerals off the ocean bottom.

"And while this is very much under the hat," he concluded, "I don't mind telling you that both Green Tree and Neptune West have been sewn up tight through extensive, secret negotiations with the Brazilian and Mexican governments. What's more, we've done some detailed planning and purchasing through a classified task force at Arc-Horn headquarters. We have equipment on hand, ready to go April first."

"Where do I fit in, Chalmers?" Jim had listened impatiently, waiting for the other shoe to fall.

"I know there's been some informal discussion on the projects around the hotel."

Jim was tempted to blurt out, "How? By bugging?" But he held himself in. He wanted Davidson to spread his complete hand.

"And I know that you, Jim, are especially influential. You're probably our best-known subsidiary officer, and then there's your friendship with Senator Ireland and all that implies with respect to environmental and resources issues. Also you have several close friends on the Arc-Horn board."

"So?"

"Jim, I want you to make the motion that the board approve Green Tree and Neptune West. On our side, it would be an honor to have the motion made by you. From your standpoint, you end the Doylestown strike and get Hugo out of your hair. Also, you'll have the satisfaction of initiating a major Arc-Horn expansion. You'll be a full member of the team."

Jim ignored the implication that he was now less than a wholehearted team player. "Which would come first, my motion or a commitment from Hugo on Doylestown?"

A fragment of a smile winked on and off like an exhausted light bulb. "I'd wrap up Doylestown tonight with Hugo, freeing you to end the strike by tomorrow morning at the latest. As for the motion, your word is, of course, all I need."

So there it was. The *quid pro quo*. Tidily wrapped and stamped with a sticker that said: "I magnanimously accept your word, McGowan, despite your lack of trust in me."

"And what if you fail to persuade Hugo?"

Davidson waved his hand, sundering bonds. "Then you'd be released from our agreement. But I assure you, that won't happen. I know our Hugo."

And Jim knew his answer, but a hungering curiosity propelled him. "I've heard reports that both the Amazon and Pacific deals risk serious, perhaps permanent, damage to the environment."

"All alarmist mouthings." Davidson thrust a hand downward as if consigning the reports to the trash cans that rattled below rooms allotted to such losers as the Sea Routes executives. "About what you'd expect from people who charge Arc-Horn with taking a hundred sixty-five thousand tons of ores from the earth every day, a wild flight of speculation that nobody can verify and meaningless in any case."

"One sixty-five?" Jim feigned ignorance. "Who came up with that figure?"

"Oh, I understand it's in some document prepared by the Group of Twelve, a bunch of fear-mongering futurists who, for some sadistic reason, want to stop civilization dead in its tracks." Davidson finished off his drink at a swallow. "Same fears being peddled by your friend Ireland. I don't fault Senator Ireland's sincerity, mind you, but the man's an innocent who falls for the propaganda of academics who like to worry about the fate of mankind ten thousand years from now. First Ireland contends the Amazon development would imperil the world's oxygen supply, an utterly unsupported and irresponsible claim, and then says that anyway logging off the area and planting it to crops and pasture would allow the heavy rains to leach away thin soil, leaving a barren, man-made wasteland." Jim recognized the phrases, altered only slightly, from Ireland's missing letter. "Now that's a plain distortion of fact, since it fails to reckon with a whole new tropical technology, including new chemicals and fertilizers."

"Did Ireland say that in a speech?" Jim was pressing now. "I must have missed it."

Davidson returned Jim's gaze without a flicker. "No. I heard it from one of his friends. Ireland has been talking a great deal recently."

Jim sensed that Davidson recognized the essence and the boundaries of this baroque game as well as he did. Obviously prepared for any eventuality, Davidson stood ready to play the game deadpan as long as Jim kept up the charade. He could feel sudden thrusts of anger and frustration. He'd had enough of games.

"No deal, Chalmers. Actually, I intend to move tomorrow that both projects be indefinitely tabled until we can get an independent ecological study by experts." Jim completely surprised himself. His mind had only nibbled at the possibility. "As for Top Court, I'll take my chances without your help."

"And what's your reasoning, may I ask?" Davidson's customary reserve, which had lifted while he sought to persuade, lowered again like a shade.

"Too many unknowns. I want Arc-Horn to increase profits, but not until the doubts raised by scientists and skilled technicians have been cleared away. It's that simple."

"No feeling of responsibility to the corporation, I take it?" In Davidson's arsenal, the weapon of sarcasm had a biting edge. "Here we have two undertakings that could put Arc-Horn beyond financial pinches forever."

"If that's a question, if doesn't call for an answer. At any rate, I've decided to make the motion to table."

"Jim, if you persist, you'll be making a very grave mistake." Davidson managed to infuse his newly paternal tone with warmth.

Jim shrugged. "Well, you know Hugo's percentage rule on errors. Besides, if this is a mistake, it's one I can live with."

Davidson toyed with his empty glass. "I see we differ on the importance to Arc-Horn of Green Tree and Neptune. . . . Naturally you're more concerned with Top Court. Perhaps I can make the trade more attractive." He hunched forward. "Tell you what. I'll also finesse Hugo into rescinding his ouster of Al Bebout. That way you'll have a clear field at Top Court." The sweetened offer floated for a moment. "What do you say?"

"No. Not as part of a deal. I'll handle Al's problem in good time after Hugo cools off."

"No way of persuading you to change your mind then?"

"None."

Davidson gazed at Jim, seeking to probe the depths of resolution. Then he sighed, as if resigning himself to onerous duty, lifted himself from the armchair and walked slowly to the bar. Jim was about to refuse a second drink, but instead of reaching for a bottle, Davidson squatted down behind the bar, disappearing for a moment. When he stood up, a noise came with him, a scratchy, faltering sound, and then a woman's voice.

"But you see, Jim, you didn't have me." Jim started as though struck from behind. It was Gwen's voice, very clear, pleading with a tinge of poignancy. *"You didn't have me because you weren't there. You were off somewhere else, probably with Top Court or Arc-Horn. You weren't with me, with you, with us."* Jim tightened, sat transfixed. *"And neither was I. I wanted to, but every . . ."* An extraneous noise blurred the word. *". . . from you said, 'No, I won't let go. I won't be exposed and vulnerable. I'll keep control.' Except at the end, where nature took over."* Jim's shoulders trembled and he felt a bursting need for movement. His eyes found Davidson. He was standing near the bar, staring without expression toward the balcony doors, where shadows swallowed twilight. The sun must have set. *"Now don't, for God's sake, say you're sorry you weren't a good lover for me. I'm talking about both of us . . ."*

It happened so quickly Jim was unaware of any sensation but the fury. In one great vaulting surge, he left his chair, moved across the room in three half-staggering strides, clutched Davidson's blue shirt in fistful wads, yanked him forward and then struck with all the power of his right arm. With the rim of his knuckles, he caught Davidson just below the cheekbone, a feel of striking a rock padded by thick, yielding moss. Davidson fell backward, tried to maintain his balance by the frantic stamp of one foot, failed, reeled to the left and fell heavily, his head just missing the massive coffee table. He lay crumpled on a patterned Indian rug, staring up at Mc-Gowan with a strange expression of affronted dignity, bewilderment and fright. The look of fear unpenned in Jim a flood of coursing jubilation. He had an overwhelming urge to throw himself on Davidson and smash his face with both fists. He actually took a step forward, then restrained himself by what seemed an immense effort of will. Every muscle tensed like a spring, ready to uncoil and fling forward.

"You goddam filthy bastard." The words, leaping out without volition, struck his own ears as woefully inadequate.

He stood, breathing hard and flexing his fingers, and became conscious of a lust to fight, a ravenous hunger to smash and be smashed. It was a savage feeling, but wonderfully pure and powerful. He could feel vast stores of energy rushing to the ramparts of his body from forgotten wells deep within him. In a flash, he saw an old scene on the elementary school playground when, taunted by a bully, he overwhelmed the older boy in an explosion of flailing arms and might have injured him seriously if Jim had not been pulled off by two of his friends. That was the last time he had hit a person and he had often wondered whether that uncontrollable thirst for violence had vanished from his being. Now he knew. He wanted Davidson to spring up, come at him with flying fists, so that he could reduce him to a sobbing, bloody pulp. He wanted . . . His shoulders ached and his legs tingled. Goddam it, what he really wanted to do was to heave Davidson over the balcony.

". . . *Then there's the thing with Meg.*" The tape was running on, hissing slightly. It was Jim's own voice now. He stepped behind the bar. A thin tape ran slowly between two large, spoked wheels. "*It's the old story. Meg thinks . . .*" Jim broke the tape with a chop of his hand, pulled off the reels and threw them the length of the room. They hit a painting of a doe-eyed Indian child and clattered to the floor.

With that random, irrelevant noise, Jim's fury snapped. He looked down at Davidson and realized that had his head struck the coffee table, only inches away, he might have suffered a concussion or death. Davidson had raised himself to a sitting position and was fingering the left side of his bruised face. One shoulder tilted protectively and the wariness of fear filled his eyes.

"May I get up now?" It was the voice of the vanquished, strangely courteous as though wondering whether the host intended to serve another helping for which he had no taste.

"Do whatever you damn please." Jim walked to the center of the room. "I've heard a lot of things about you, but nobody ever mentioned blackmail."

Davidson said nothing. He raised himself awkwardly, squared his shoulders and brushed off his trousers, the while eying McGowan as if in fear of another attack. He lowered himself into the armchair like precious cargo. The room was almost dark now save for a splash of light from the open door of the economy kitchen, where, apparently, an electric light burned.

"I'm going to ask you some questions." Jim strained to keep his voice under control. "And I want direct answers. . . . How did you get that tape?"

"It was given to me." Davidson was striving to calm himself.

"By whom?"

"That's my business." His breathing was irregular, but the voice did not quaver.

"Goddam dirty business you're in. . . . How many rooms in this hotel have you bugged?"

"None."

"All right, you want to quibble. How many did you order bugged?"

"None."

"Do you think I believe that?"

"I don't know. It's the truth."

"Jesus, who do you think you're kidding? . . . Who stole the Group of Twelve reports and Ireland's letter from my room safe?"

"I have no idea. I didn't know you had such papers. Whether they were stolen or not, I couldn't possibly know. As I told you, you probably forgot where you put them."

"Did you send Ron Jeffers down to Argentina earlier this year?"

"Yes, of course."

"Did you give him orders to burglarize a computer storage and bribe a Señor Portilla?"

"No."

Jim hooked his thumbs in his belt and took a step

closer. "Did you know that he did pull a breaking-and-entering and a twenty-five-thousand-dollar bribery?"

"Of course not. That's ridiculous." Davidson's returning courage brought a cool patina to his tone. "Nobody in Arc-Horn does that kind of thing."

"Who was responsible for buying off a researcher in Bangkok and robbing the apartment of Russell Kirkland in New York?"

"Why ask me?" Now an edge of contempt was back in Davidson's voice. "I never heard of the incidents and have no idea what you're talking about."

"You're a liar." Jim's seething anger boiled up again. "A goddam, conniving liar with all the . . . er . . . morals of a toad."

"And that's in line with your other wild statements." Davidson sought to regain command. "First, you try to break my jaw. Then you malign me with a lot of absurd innuendoes in the form of questions. Perhaps you ought to see a doctor. You need help, McGowan."

"That line won't work." Jim realized that his wasn't working either. "Let's just leave it that at tomorrow's board meeting, before making the motion to table the Amazon and Pacific projects, I'm going to make you face two charges. One, that you have cooperated with the CIA without the knowledge of the Arc-Horn board and to the detriment of the corporation's interests. Two, that your assistant, Ron Jeffers, is an employed agent of the CIA and that his duties for the Agency have your knowledge and consent."

"CIA?" Davidson had sufficiently recovered to manage a short, derisive laugh. "That's absurd." Jim could not measure Davidson's reaction in the darkness. "Do you expect the board to swallow a fantastic allegation like that without any proof?"

"I have the proof." Even as Jim lied, he determined to pump Ireland on the phone for every scrap of evidence.

"It'll be interesting to hear a man try to prove the existence of nothing. An exercise in sophistry. People who try that in public wind up destroying themselves."

"We'll let the board decide that." Jim began to pace. He could feel the anger flooding him like a high tide. "Members will enjoy a field trip through your communications center behind the 'No Admittance' door. You can explain how one installs a recording system and just where one places the bugs for maximum volume and clarity."

There was no response. Silence lay in the room like the darkness. A melting piece of ice dropped to the bottom of a glass, ping. "Does that conclude your fantasy?" Davidson asked.

"No. After the field trip, you can explain the robbery in New York and the burglary and bribery abroad. Then I'll want to quiz you about the opening of my safe."

Davidson arose and stood with his arms folded. Neither man could see the other distinctly in the gloom and Davidson, perhaps protectively, had made no move toward an electric wall switch. The oblong path of light from the kitchenette lay on the terrazzo floor like a frozen beacon.

"If you go through with this, which I doubt," said Davidson, "you won't be an officer of Arc-Horn or the president of Top Court this time tomorrow." There was cold contempt in his tone now. "You'll ruin yourself, McGowan."

"Knock it off. You're wasting your breath." Jim turned and walked toward the door.

He stooped near the painting of the sad Indian child and picked up the metal wheels. A snarl of tape dangled toward the floor, but most of the magnetic ribbon was still wound tightly on the spools. He bunched the tangled tape in his hand and pressed the reels to his side.

"I suppose you have a dupe of this." Jim said it over his shoulder. "It's worthless to you. I can't be blackmailed." But how about Gwen? The thought enraged him anew. "Davidson, you're a prick."

He reached for the doorknob.

"McGowan!"

He turned. Davidson was but a shadowy figure at the other end of the room.

"In a fair fight, I could beat you, you know."

A thousand tiny messengers instantly raced along his nerves, bearing ammunition for prompt battle. He knew in every fiber that he could slam Davidson into unconsciousness. But as quickly, the bravado of the challenge struck him as pathetic. What an odd thing for Davidson to say. The corporate vice-president suddenly became the small boy, boasting of a mythical prowess. And perhaps Davidson's old man could whip McGowan's long-gone father too? Yet, despite the absurdity, Jim groped for a retort.

"You in a fair fight? . . . Who with? A cobra?"

As a parting shot, Jim knew, it was a dud. For emphasis, he slammed the door so hard the woodwork quivered. The noise echoed down the corridor. At the corner, the blue-shirted security guard jerked to attention like a puppet on a string.

Masuo Sugimoto pondered over a sheet of paper filled with scrawled numbers and a gleaming red-and-blue Nakamura pocket calculator. He sighed, blinked at the digits framed in the small windows of the calculator, then glanced at his wristwatch.

Seven-fourteen. Time to freshen up for the Gusto Más ceremony. The motorcade was due to leave the hotel promptly at seven-thirty. Why hadn't Jim McGowan come up with those reports he was so insistent that Sugimoto read? And McGowan's peculiar remarks about CIA agents inside Arc-Horn and some electronic listening devices in the hotel? It had been an hour and a half since he met McGowan in the lobby. Oh well, he'd see him soon at the opening.

The stocky Japanese went to the bathroom, washed his face, splashed fresh water over his damp torso and toweled himself dry. Then from the hangers in his closet he selected Wednesday night's golden shirt.

He stood before his cluttered worktable, pondering. Suddenly he picked up the calculator, snapped the digits back to zero and punched in a set of new numbers. From the scrawled notes on the paper, he put in more

numbers after pressing the button for addition. Instantly
another row of figures popped into the calculator's little
windows.

Yes. It worked out neatly, give or take a million or
two. Hugo, he speculated, would buy the deal as a deft
solution. Not perfect. nothing ever was, but deft. Jim
McGowan would love it. Indeed, who in Arc-Horn would
say no to the trade-off?

Sugimoto slipped the small calculator into a pants
pocket. Not bad for an hour's work after that flash brain-
storm. He felt quite content with himself. In his youth,
inserting the last piece of the puzzle would have produced
an electric thrill, a pulsing halo to frame the young genius.
But experience had taught him the perils of unrestrained
elation. Now it was enough to feel the warm glow of
satisfaction.

A frugal man with his own property or that of others,
Masuo turned out all four lights burning in his suite
before leaving for the executive motorcade.

The lobby, passageways and patio of the Mixteca
were all but deserted. Proconsuls of the troubled Arc-
Horn empire were still in their rooms, girding for the
Gusto Más foray into the heart of Acapulco. Jim Mc-
Gowan hurried toward the ocean. His shirt was tucked
into his trousers and he bulged in the rear. He had placed
the reels of electronic tape beneath his shirt against
the small of his back.

For once the stools of the Tarascan Bar were empty.
Pete Quigley had finally abandoned his post. José, the
bartender, hovered over his platoons of bottles in the
yellowish glow of the overhead lights.

"Got a piece of string, José?"

The barkeeper cocked his head. He had not understood.

"You know, string, cord, anything I can tie." Jim
made a motion of wrapping and knotting.

"*Ah, sí.*" José ducked beneath the bar and came
up with several feet of beige insulated wire.

Jim thanked him, took the wire and walked toward

the dark beach. He slipped the spools of tape from under his shirt and tied an end of the wire around the battered spokes. Now he needed a rock, but the sand in front of the hotel, strained weekly by the beach attendants held nothing larger than pebbles. He searched to the north as he walked. At last, about a hundred yards from the hotel, he found a rusty piece of metal tubing, apparently once part of a beach umbrella. He wrapped the electric-light wire around the tube and the reels of tape and knotted it.

He stepped onto the wet sand in the wake of a retreating wave and heaved the weighted tape over the surf. It plopped in a watery trough and sank out of sight.

Wednesday Night

The motorcade would embrace half a hundred cars and several buses and apparently would straggle over a quarter of a mile of the highway to Acapulco, ten miles to the north. The vehicles stood closely parked in the Mixteca's curving, palm-fringed driveway, glistening in the amber pools shed by the mounted carriage lamps. Each limousine—in its procession tonight, Arc-Horn would make no concession to the gasoline-thrifty compacts—had been newly bathed and polished for the gala opening of the eightieth Gusto Más supermarket.

Protocol dictated the placement of the vehicles. In the lead Cadillac would ride two Mexicans, the governor of Guerrero and the mayor of Acapulco, both loyal members of P.R.I., the long-ruling political party. Next came the Continental carrying a lone passenger, Hugo

E. Praeger, baron of Arc-Horn. The third car, an Imperial,
bore Antonio Percevale, president of Gusto Más. Behind
him four limousines carried the four Arc-Horn vice-
presidents and in line to the rear, ranked by annual
revenues, rode the remaining eighteen subsidiary presidents, each in his own courtesy car. Another score of
automobiles held subsidiary officers, various officials of
Summit, Inc., and such convention personages as Jake
Apple, Gilda and Frankie Fee. The residue, Arc-Horn
pilots, the Broadway dancers, Summit salesmen, the
orchestra, the convention hostesses and several of the
Miami women crowded aboard the three chartered buses
which brought up the rear.

The caravan would roll out to the highway, snake
over the hills to the resort city and move along the broad
boulevard, Costera Miguel Alemán, which circled the
bay. In front of the Hotel Papagayo the motorcade would
halt and, like a caterpillar growing new segments, would
be joined by two boys' marching bands, a gaggle of
portable saints provided by a beer company, a detachment
of sailors from the Acapulco naval base, a flower-be-
decked truck carrying local Gusto Más employees, a police escort, delegations from the Acapulco hotel association and chamber of commerce and, undoubtedly, a
swarm of children and curiosity seekers. Thus adorned,
the caravan would proceed slowly along the Costera to
the center of the city, turn right into a warren of small
shops and pull up at the huge new supermarket, where
three officiating priests waited in a shower of illumination
along with the fireworks *maestro* and his shaky wooden
tower of pyrotechnics. A massive crowd was guaranteed.
After an hour-long ceremony and the snipping of the
red-and-blue ribbon, every opening-night customer who
spent twenty pesos or more was to be given a free bottle of Potosí rum and a Gusto Más T shirt.

All this awaited the Arc-Horn celebrants in the festive
hours ahead, but right now Calvin Silliman was having
trouble tucking his charges into the proper vehicles.
He bustled along the walkway, as distracted as ever,

issuing orders, overruling complaints and imploring everyone to climb aboard for the seven-thirty takeoff.

Jim McGowan trotted down the steps from the lobby with only minutes to spare. After his encounter with Davidson and his hurried trip to the beach, he had barely time for a facial scrub, a change of shirts and a quick kiss for Meg.

"McGowan! . . . You're in car twenty-four," Silliman called as he consulted a clipboard. Jim had the impression that Silliman avoided looking at him. Or was his imagination at work? The conviction was growing that Silliman was involved in the theft from McGowan's safe. "Let's move it, men. We want to roll on schedule."

Jim spotted Tony Percevale among the executives searching for their vehicles. Tony, as befitted a star of an opening night, was resplendent in a golden shirt with intricate embroidery on the sleeves, the silver medallion from Taxco, shimmering tan slacks and white beach moccasins with gilded buckles.

"Where have you been?" asked Tony. "Sugimoto and Gwen are both looking for you. We're meeting right after the opening."

Jim hooked his friend's arm. "Come on, ride with me. I've just had the weirdest showdown with Davidson. Believe it or not, I knocked the son of a bitch on his ass. Wait'll I tell you."

"Knocked him? What? . . . Listen, Jim, I can't ride with you. I'm supposed to be in the car behind Hugo. Silliman's got us pigeonholed, one to a car."

"Screw Silliman." He tugged at Tony's arm as they moved down the line of vehicles. Motors were running.

Silliman bore down on them, brandishing his clipboard like the mace of authority. "Where are you going, Tony? The other way. You're in car three."

"We're riding together," said Jim.

"No, no." Silliman grasped Percevale's other arm. "Impossible. Hugo's orders. The Gusto Más president has to be near the head of the line. We can't have an empty car."

Jim relinquished his hold. A tug-of-war over Tony

in his finery seemed hardly appropriate, especially in plain view of Jules Amarel, Nate Berger and several other executives. Silliman escorted Tony at a fast clip toward his Imperial.

Jim found No. 24, the same Mercedes which carried him from the airport Sunday with the same phlegmatic driver. What was his name?

"Hi! Haven't seen you since Sunday. What's the name again? Miguel?"

"Miguel, señor." The driver held the rear door open with a look of overwhelming disinterest. *"No hablo inglés."* He shut the door and slid into the front seat behind the wheel.

"Okay, move out," came a shouted command from Silliman on the portico steps. The manager watched the motorcade crawl away from the curb, then trotted to the last bus, where he stationed himself in the front stairwell beside the driver and leaned out to monitor the progress of his caravan.

Alone in the rear seat of the Mercedes, Jim felt at once regal and ridiculous in his solitude and he wished that Meg were beside him. But orders limited passengers to those listed on Silliman's official convention list, a ruling that suited Meg perfectly. She would enjoy poking around the big hotel, she said, without being overrun by hordes of male conventioneers. She had met Nina Robbins at the hairdresser's in late afternoon and they'd agreed to have dinner together. When Jim returned, Meg would have the low-down on Praeger's romance with his masseuse. At least that's what Jim thought he heard from Meg as he pulled on a fresh shirt and hurried down to join the caravan.

Since he must ride in lonely splendor anyway, Jim was thankful for the language barrier between himself and Miguel. He could use the time to think out strategy for tomorrow. He still felt a delayed charge from the explosion in Davidson's suite. His muscles retained a vibrancy and his skin tingled. He could see Davidson sprawled on his side with that look of amazement and fear, and he relished the vivid image. But exactly what to do at tomorrow's board meeting? The evidence against Davidson was all circumstantial. To Jim, it was conclusive, but to others it might appear flimsy. Davidson would, of course, deny everything, probably accuse Jim of unprovoked assault and question his mental stability. And how could Jim substantiate the attempted blackmail? He could not describe the recorded conversation of himself and Gwen without revealing the intimate details that made Davidson's play-back such a grotesque offense. And even if he and Gwen should agree to such a joint disrobing before the entire Arc-Horn board, their peers would be offended, would resent being made unwilling auditors of a corporate liaison. Davidson surely had pursued the same line of reasoning before he ever flicked the switch on the recording machine.

The more Jim thought, the more he respected Davidson's ability to shield himself. The blackmail scene, which seemed only gross and blundering at the time, now appeared to have been worked out with finesse. Jim had to confess that a workable strategy for tomorrow eluded him. A showdown with Davidson before Arc-Horn board members, most of whom had no cause to suspect Davidson of machinations inside the corporation, involved complex psychological risks. A wrong word or posture could blow the whole game and make Jim look either idiotic or paranoid. He could only hope that when he met with Gwen and Tony later tonight three minds would prove more fertile than one. . . . Sugimoto was a complication. They needed Masuo. In addition to his quick intelligence, he had clout in the company. With Masuo and his persistent, probing questioning, Davidson would find it difficult to slide off the hook. Yet, so far, Masuo knew nothing of the background. The Ireland letter and Group of Twelve reports were missing, probably locked away in Davidson's own safe. It would take at least an hour to go through the whole story for Masuo.

But there was no other route. They needed Sugimoto. It would be another long night.

More than three hundred tons of automotive armor

rolled along the rim of hills south of Acapulco, squealed around sharp curves, glided past the hillside Las Brisas Hotel with its sybaritic private swimming pools and began the descent to the city, one of the Western world's most durable temples of hedonism. Moonbeams traced a pathway in the great bay. A tourist boat, festooned with lights, coasted the waves. The air was soft, tepid, languorous, and at several spots around the bay, scented with the pungent odor of sewage.

The caravan dropped to the broad boulevard divided by palm trees, and passed the first of the resort hotels which spiked the sky like glittering lances. Leaning from the car window, Jim could see pennants fluttering from the leading limousine and behind him the figure of Cal Silliman canted outward from the last bus like a semaphore.

As a policeman waved the motorcade onward at the fountain of Diana, a traffic circle in front of the Acapulco Royal, Jim's driver, Miguel, vented what seemed to be a string of oaths. He turned to Jim. "Gas." He pointed to his dashboard, then to a large, brightly illuminated PEMEX service station at the right of the circle. *"Momentito, señor."* He held up this thumb and forefinger in the Mexican gesture denoting a forthcoming delay of a few seconds—or minutes or hours, depending on the vagaries of fate. Miguel leaned out and shouted something to the drivers immediately in front and to the rear. Both men nodded in apparent comprehension. Miguel turned out of line, wheeled into the PEMEX station's plaza and halted before one of the gas pumps. He called his order to an attendant, a boy in oil-smeared shirt and trousers. As gas flowed into the Mercedes, Jim watched the rear of the caravan roll slowly past the service station. Cal Silliman, leaning out from the last bus, waved to Jim and pointed ahead, apparently a signal of assurance that McGowan's place in line would be preserved.

After fifty pesos' worth of gasoline had been pumped, Miguel spoke to the attendant, who lifted the hood, pulled out the oil stick, wiped it on his trousers, inserted the rod once more, then studied it under an overhead light. Why the hell does Miguel take the time to have the oil checked now? Jim wondered.

"Está bien," the boy said, replacing the measuring stick and slamming the hood. Miguel handed the boy a fifty-peso blue note without glancing at him. After starting the car, he drove it to the rear exit which opened on Farallon, a street leading into the highway to Mexico City. Instead of turning right, back to the Costera Miguel Alemán, he wheeled the car left, crossed the street and accelerated as they moved up the highway's broad incline. A short cut back to the motorcade, Jim surmised. But after gunning the car no more than fifty yards, Miguel braked abruptly, throwing McGowan forward on his seat. They had stopped in a pool of darkness, midway between two street lamps.

The next sequence of events occurred so swiftly, probably in no more than thirty seconds, that it was over before Jim became fully aware of what happened. Both rear doors were yanked open simultaneously and two men threw themselves onto the rear seat, one on each side of Jim. As they slammed the doors behind them, the car bolted forward, quickly gained speed as the automatic gears shifted from first to second. Jim caught a glimpse of lights, buildings, the macadam surface of the highway, a woman holding two children by the hand and an old man astride a plodding burro. Then the man to Jim's left whipped a pair of dark-tinted glasses to the bridge of Jim's nose and slid the prongs behind his ears. At the same time, a blunt object was jammed against his ribs by the man on his right and a gruff, muffled voice said in broken English: "No talk. You talk, I shoot. *Comprende?*" Jim nodded vigorously. With so little time to react, he felt no fear, only a wondering surprise. Maybe this was a prank, and yet . . .

The Mercedes was speeding now in high gear. Jim guessed they must be hitting fifty miles an hour already. He felt a bulge of soft material before his eyes. He blinked several times, trying to feel the texture. Yes, cotton. Apparently two pads of cotton had been packed inside the lenses, shutting off all vision. He could hear cars and trucks passing and feel the round object pressing against his ribs. A revolver, he decided. The man on his left spoke sharply. *"Sí, sí,"* answered Miguel. The car slowed, swung sharply, pressing Jim against one of his unknown companions. The Mercedes straightened. Jim could feel warm air washing over his face from Miguel's open window at the driver's seat. Apparently all other windows were closed. Jim sensed that the car was climbing in slow curves. Occasionally the tires squeaked as the car tilted. The speed was steady, but not excessive. After a few minutes, the car nosed downward and picked up speed. Apparently they had crested one of the hills that ringed Acapulco.

The air grew warmer as they descended. Once the car braked severely, throwing Jim and his seatmates forward. The man on the right growled an apparent oath. Miguel responded with a placating phrase and they veered to the left. Jim heard some laughter and shouts above him and guessed that they had passed a slow-moving truck loaded with people. The car straightened again, rushing downward.

Now they were on the flat, going very fast, and Jim knew this was no prank. The air became heavily tropical with an aroma of fruits and flowers. Miguel blew his horn twice and Jim could hear repeated clicks as Miguel apparently switched his headlights from bright to dim. Cars swished by, but the intervals between passing vehicles became longer. The object against his ribs was withdrawn and Jim sensed that the men on either side of him had relaxed. He heard a match strike and then the smell of strong, harsh tobacco smoke. The three men began a conversation and Jim could hear relief in their low tones. The man on Jim's right asked Miguel a question. By the pitch of authority, Jim decided he must be the leader. "Cheem," answered Miguel. He laughed. "Cheem, Cheem," repeated the questioner. *"Ah, Jaime, verdad?"* Miguel said, *"Sí."*

"You Jaime," said the man to Jim. "I Chucho. Talk *más tarde."* He emanated a strong, familiar odor. What was it? Barnyard? Yes, an unmistakable smell of manure, whether horse, cow or pig, or all three, Jim could not be sure. From the left, on the other hand, came a city odor, sweet and powerful. Cheap cologne, Jim guessed. It mingled oddly with the harsh tobacco smell. They had been riding no more than twenty minutes, Jim guessed, but already he could feel his senses other than sight growing keener.

The men talked with sporadic gaps, apparently discussing Jim, for he caught a word here and there that seemed linked to his life . . . New York . . . Arc-Horn . . . tennis. . . . *"Muy rico, verdad?"* asked the man who called himself Chucho. *"Sí,"* replied Miguel. *"Millones de dólares."* Jim suspected they were estimating his worth and it dawned on him that the men in the back seat had known little or nothing about him before they sprang into the car near the PEMEX station. The conversation waned, then ceased.

The car was climbing again, hurrying around curves as the tires protested. The air grew cooler, then chill, then cold. Miguel closed his window. There were long intervals now between passing cars. They rode in silence.

I've been kidnapped, of course, thought Jim as he settled into himself. No sooner formulated than the statement called forth a rash of questions. Why? By whom? Being taken where? For how long? A ransom, surely. How much? Who would pay it? Hugo's announcement several years ago that Arc-Horn would never yield ransom money for any executive, employee or relative—a public statement issued during the initial wave of Latin American abductions of industrialists—was unequivocal. Would he adhere to the policy? What about Meg, Carol and Connie? Would they pay? Naturally. But how much? He lost himself in an odd fantasy of numbers, wondering how much he was worth to his family. Up to a million certainly, but what if five or ten million dollars were demanded? He could envision Meg and the twins in a huddle with Mexican security and FBI agents. How did one get large amounts of cash in a hurry in Mexico?

He recalled the conversation with Steve Cooper about the nearby hills of Guerrero. There were guerrillas and plain bandits in the mountains, said Steve, and one had to recognize the difference between political revolutionaries and those who looted as their trade. Which band held him now? That might be important to him later on. Surely, judging by the steady, swerving ascent of the Mercedes, they were in the mountains. And this was the highway to Mexico City, wasn't it? He could recall no sharp turn onto another road. What was that town? Oh yes, Gwen had said that Chilpancingo, home town of the monsignor who gave the invocation at the early-bird fiesta, was about two hours away by car. So, he guessed, they were perhaps a third of the way to Chilpancingo, since they had been traveling about forty minutes.

How the hell did Miguel figure in this? Jim had not seen the man since they rode to the Mixteca from the airport four days ago. Al Bebout, Frankenheimer and Teigert had used the Mercedes assigned to Top Court, but Jim had been too busy with the convention to leave the hotel grounds except to pick up Meg and Dave Moyer at the airport last night. And since Al had the Mercedes then, Jim borrowed Tony Percevale's courtesy car. He thought back to the Sunday-afternoon ride from the airport with the uncommunicative Miguel. That hostess, María, the one with the chip on her shoulder, had ridden with them. She had said she was from the hills of Guerrero. Did María have some connection with Miguel? The hostess role didn't fit her, she was contemptuous of Americans and she had her antennae out. Wasn't it María who told Steve Cooper about recording equipment in Davidson's communications room?

Davidson? No, that would stretch the image of villainy to the point of paranoia. Bugging, robbing, bribery, yes. But kidnapping? Impossible. . . . Or was it? What if Davidson merely wanted him out of the way until the board meeting ended? Why not a quick little snatch, no injury to Jim, for no more than a day or two? Or what if Davidson, in a fit of vengeance after being knocked to the floor, had decided to have Jim killed?

The thought chilled him despite the warm bodies on either side. He had felt surprisingly little fear, merely an enormous curiosity, up to this point, but now the possibility of a revenge slaying became as real as the round object Chucho had held to his ribs for many minutes. . . . Wait, let's see. Did Davidson have time to arrange a contract on him, or whatever the hell they called it in Mexico? Jim thought fast. He guessed that no more than twenty-five minutes had elapsed between the moment he slammed Davidson's door and the time he climbed into the Mercedes in front of the Mixteca. No, hardly possible. A kidnapping like this took planning. The car had to drop out of line, the two men had to be waiting and the route laid out in advance.

Jim could feel the sudden tension drain away. No, this one had to have been planned. What about Silliman's curious insistence that each Arc-Horn officer ride in a car alone? Cal's excuse was that the Mexican public would be impressed by a lengthy, regal motorcade and that Hugo had given orders for solo passengers. Right now, the explanation didn't wash. It seemed more probable that prospective Gusto Más customers, many of them poor, would despise such a display of profligacy. However, the lone riders did provide an ideal setup for a kidnapping, didn't they?

But why McGowan? Assuming Davidson triggered the operation, what conceivable motive could he have had weeks ago when the motorcade plans were made?

Miguel, of course, probably knew the peculiar motorcade makeup for a long while. He had plenty of time to contact confederates and plan the kidnapping. The three men obviously had just discussed Jim's wealth. Millions of dollars, they had said. Once again, his mind swung away from Davidson and back to a routine—he smiled as he thought the word—kidnapping, perhaps political in motive, perhaps with only money as the goal. But the truth was, he admitted, that he had no strong hunch in any direction. The secret, whatever it was, rested with Miguel, Chucho and Señor Cheap Cologne.

A spasm of chatter gripped the three men. Miguel
asked a question. Cologne demurred. Chucho leaned
over the front seat and growled an order. They all talked
at once. Miguel braked and swerved to the right. The
tires skidded on gravel. The car came to a halt. Chucho
threw open his door and pulled Jim out. Cologne ran
around the rear of the car and both men held Jim for
a moment as he stood upright. The Mercedes backed
up in a crackling shower of stones, paused for a shift
of gears, then sped off along the highway—away from
Acapulco, Jim thought.

Chucho and Cologne turned Jim around three or
four times, a spin that made him dizzy, then pushed his
head toward the ground. Chucho pulled off the cotton-
wedged glasses and Jim got a brief, vague glimpse of
what appeared to be a gravel roadbed. He felt a stab
of fear and waited for a blow on his head. The night
was very dark. He could hear both men breathing heavily.

But no blow came. Instead, Cologne swiftly placed
a band of cloth before Jim's eyes and fastened a knot
behind his head. The blindfold felt gritty and smelled
of grease. Chucho took Jim's hand and led him forward.
Jim heard only two sounds, that of shoes crunching
on gravel and the fading whine of a speeding automobile.

Wednesday, 11 p.m.

They had been riding for more than two hours, Jim guessed. His rump felt sore, his legs were chafed on the inside and he shivered with cold despite the rough woolen poncho that Chucho had draped over his golden shirt. His horse was sandwiched between those of Chucho and Señor Cologne, now identified in the occasional whispered conversations of the two Mexicans as Pepito.

His hands were free to hold the reins, but he had long ago looped the frayed rope over the bulky bone pommel and let the horse, who knew the trail, have his head. The blindfold made his eyes smart. Worse, he could smell the dirty handkerchief with its coating of grease. With his eyes covered, Jim's other senses had sharpened amazingly. In the deep stillness of the night, he could hear the metallic echo of horseshoes and pick out individual words in the slur of Spanish when Chucho and Pepito conversed. Occasionally, when a horse shook its head and neighed, the sound reverberated like the trumpeting of an elephant. Once his horse dislodged a large stone and Jim could hear it go banging down a hillside, clattering against rocks, rolling through dirt and ending with a faint, far-off plop in some body of water far below them. From the echoes, Jim surmised that they were picking their way through a canyon. He could feel the presence of a substance, perhaps rock, shielding him on his right and a yawning emptiness on his left.

They had climbed steadily from the point, perhaps
several hundred yards off the highway, where Chucho
and Pepito had boosted him into a saddle. For one awful
moment, when his head was bent, he believed that he
would be struck on the head or shot. But the moment
passed without injury and as the ride progressed and
the horses followed the rocky trail, hooves clanging
methodically, Jim felt danger receding. They obviously
were crossing rugged, uninhabited terrain, ideally suited
for lonely murder, and each mile without assault lent
support to Jim's theory that he was being taken to a
spot where he could be held for ransom without detec-
tion.

From time to time, they dipped into a gulley and
Jim learned to adjust himself in the saddle via clipped
warnings from Chucho in the lead. When Chucho said
"abajo," they went down, and when he said *"arriba,"*
the horses struggled upward. Jim leaned back or forward,
holding to the wide bone pommel with both hands and
pressing his knees tightly to the horse's flanks. The path
was strewn with rocks and the animals picked their way
carefully in the dark. Jim came to know when his own
mount was uncertain of his footing. The horse would
hesitate, occasionally with a great wheezing snort of
displeasure, test gingerly with a hoof, then lurch forward,
his back swaying and his joints seemingly articulating
in various directions. Once the animal adamantly refused
to go forward and Chucho had to dismount and lead
him down a short, steep descent while Jim clung to
the pommel.

It had been several years since Jim had ridden a horse
and he tired quickly because of the extra alertness required
of his muscles and nerves by his sightlessness. Since
he wore beach moccasins, sockless in the Acapulco
fashion, his ankles and the insides of his lower legs
were soon rubbed raw by the iron stirrups. When he
complained, Chucho called a halt while he wrapped
one ankle with Jim's pocket handkerchief and the other
with a strip torn from the poncho. The padding helped,
but the irritation turned to pain with the continuing

friction of the stirrups. Still, despite the aches and the discomfort, Jim experienced a kind of exhilaration, compounded of apprehension, the cold, clear air and a sense of boundless space. He had gained confidence as he adjusted to the rhythm of the horse's gait and became aware of the great stillness of the night, covering the harsh land like a mantle. The air grew crisper and colder as they moved steadily upward. Each sound, a hoof against stone or the creaking of leather, was as isolated and distinct as the clap of hands in an empty hall. Once, when they crested a sudden rise, he heard the distant mooing of a cow, a lone sound that seemed carved from a vacuum. There was an acute sense of peaceful, open space and Jim imagined that the sky above him sparkled with thousands of stars.

Now they were on the flat, a plateau perhaps, and the quickened pace of the horses, a quivering of the flanks and the restless bobbing of heads, hinted that the animals were nearing home. Jim could feel his horse straining to break into a canter. He took the reins in hand again and pulled back gently. A branch flicked against his leg, then a leafy twig brushed his cheek. Chucho stopped his horse and the other mounts halted, switching their tails nervously.

Chucho whistled, a short, two-note sound. They waited in silence. How far had they come? Jim wondered. Eight or nine miles? But he was vague as to the direction. The highway ran generally northward, he believed, but after being spun around by Chucho and Pepito, he could only guess that they had struck off to the southeast. The act of spinning itself, he now realized, augured well for his safety. Why worry about whether a dead man knew where he was at the moment of death?

They heard an answering whistle, the same two-note sound, low, then high. They moved forward at once. The horses walked swiftly, slamming their hooves and straining ahead. They advanced several hundred yards before stopping. A man's voice fired a question, in surprise, Jim thought. Chucho answered with a flood of words. Another question. The man's voice was husky and commanding, but again the touch of surprise. Chucho's response was short. Jim caught the word "Jaime" and something that vaguely resembled "McGowan." He heard Chucho dismount and then both Chucho and Pepito were helping him from the saddle. It felt good to touch the ground again. Jim shook himself, stamped his feet and at once felt pain in his ankles. The husky voice gave an order. Someone grasped his hand and led him forward. It was Chucho. The barnyard odor was fainter now, but still distinguishable.

They entered a structure. Jim could sense the enclosure. He heard and smelled a wood fire, a comforting fact. He was led from the room into what seemed to be a short hallway, then turned right through a doorway. Chucho stepped behind him, untied the blindfold and gave Jim a slight push. "No talk," said Chucho, digging him in the back with his fist as though to simulate a weapon. The door closed.

Jim rubbed his smarting eyes and looked about him. All he could see at first was that the room was small and dark. He stood for a moment, accustoming his eyes to vision after some three hours of being either blindfolded or barred from sight by cotton-wedged glasses. He noted that a patch of dim light fell on the floor from a single window. Paneless, about one foot square at eye level, less a window than a slot in the wall, it was covered by a cloth, nailed to the frame. Was there a moon tonight? Yes, that accounted for the patch of light. Now he saw a narrow bed shoved against one wall. It held an old, torn mattress without sheets or blankets. A squat chair, made of wood strips and cowhide, stood on the floor. A candle and a box of matches rested on the leather seat. Jim lighted the candle and peered about him. There was no other furniture.

The wall opposite the bed held three objects. He stepped closer to examine them. One was a rough board with four protruding pegs. Another turned out to be a plaster, bloodied Christ, nailed to a small wooden cross of shiny veneer. He was a soiled and grimy Redeemer, his beard blackened by soot. One leg was

cocked awkwardly as though He were striving to lessen
the weight on His pinioned, blood-splotched palms.
The third object was a dusty, old color photograph of
John F. Kennedy, obviously ripped from a magazine.
He wore a sports jersey and he was driving a golf cart
loaded with small fry of the boisterous Kennedy clan.
His happy grin, which brushed Jim with sudden nostalgia, contrasted sharply with the expression of the
other martyr who gazed downward with that look of
terrible sadness so characteristic of the Savior in Latin
countries.

Someone opened the door. Jim held up the candle.
He could not recognize the man, whose face below the
dark eyes was masked by a piece of gingham cloth,
but he smelled Chucho. He carried a bucket and a sheet
of dirty newspaper. He put the bucket and paper on
the floor, pointed at Jim and withdrew, closing the door
behind him. The sight of the pail triggered a powerful urgency in Jim. He urinated with relief, splattering the
metal bottom like a garden hose, then promptly became
conscious of the stench.

Jim inspected the walls with the candle. They were
made of adobe, the color of ocher save for the wall
behind the bed, which had been whitewashed. When
he scratched with a finger, a piece of the reddish clay
crumbled into dust and drifted downward. The floor
consisted of hard-packed earth worn into grooves by
the tread of many feet. A large brown insect, momentarily
caught in the candlelight, scuttled for the obscurity of
a corner.

The cloth at the window was burlap sacking nailed
to the frame. Jim pulled back the burlap between two
nails and peered out. Moonlight splashed a small, grass-
less yard, a high hedge of some kind and far beyond
the shoulder of a mountain. The window had no bars,
but was too small for a man to crawl through.

Jim seated himself in the cowhide chair and picked
up the soiled sheet of newspaper. It was a page torn
from a copy of *Excelsior,* the Mexico City daily. The
columns of Spanish meant nothing to Jim, but he recog-

nized a picture of Henry Kissinger and noted the legend in the upper right corner: *"Excelsior 3-A Sábado 14 de Diciembre de 1974."* Hmm. Three months old. Jim realized with a sinking feeling that his exploration was yielding a great deal of utterly useless information. But he was keyed up, still buoyed by the mountain ride in the night air. Apprehension was a constant now, a new way of life, but he felt little fear. The room denoted safekeeping, not imminent peril.

Voices were audible on the other side of the wall where Kennedy and Christ hung in reverence. Jim moved his chair closer. Phrases came through plainly and if he knew Spanish, he could have picked out whole swatches of conversation. He smelled food cooking and later heard a clatter of dishes, then footsteps in the hallway. Chucho, masked, entered the room. He handed Jim a plate of food and a cup of coffee trailing wisps of steam. *"Sabroso,"* he said, nodding at the plate. He quickly withdrew, closing the door again.

The plate was divided about evenly between a heap of warm black beans and a stack of five tortillas. The sight and smell stirred Jim's appetite and he realized he had not eaten since early afternoon. He fell to with the lone utensil, a spoon. The beans, afloat in a thick gravy, tasted good. He found the tortillas, which he had once heard described as "the most melancholy nourishment known to man," to be almost tasteless, but palatable when wrapped around several spoonfuls of beans like a pod with its peas. When the last morsel had been scraped from the plate, he savored the coffee, sipping it slowly, making it last as long as possible. It was thick, black and bitter, but as welcome as a lighted window in a blizzard.

With the poncho outside and the food inside, Jim felt reasonably warm, although the room was cold. Even colder air filtered through the burlap sacking at the window and Jim guessed the temperature at not more than fifty degrees, a drop of about thirty-five from the tropical, ocean airs of the Mixteca. How far had he come? He calculated about thirty miles by car and another eight or nine by horse. He guessed that he was perhaps twenty or twenty-five miles from the Mixteca in a straight line. But he was much higher now and he surmised that several ranges of foothills and mountains separated him from the convention hotel.

The three male voices had risen in volume as time dragged by and Jim could hear the clink of glasses after the men finished eating. Someone switched on a radio. Battery-operated? For perhaps a half hour Jim heard the strains of music beneath the ebb and flow of voices. The tunes ranged through popular ballards, from rock to old-fashioned swing bands to mournful Mexican lamentations in which the word *"corazón"* provided endless opportunities for rhyming. Then the music stopped and a male radio voice took over. By the heave and fall of the cadence and by numerous breaks, Jim guessed it to be a news broadcast. He glanced at his wristwatch: 1:04. Yes, probably the one-o'clock news.

Suddenly the voice switched. Another person began speaking English with an American accent. The radio went silent, but someone—in the husky, dominant tone that belonged neither to Chucho nor to Pepito—gave a sharp command. The radio blared again in English: ". . . this translation for our tourist friends from the United States and Canada. Acapulco—A wealthy American businessman, James F. McGowan, is missing tonight in this city, and it appears possible he may have been kidnapped. This station received an anonymous phone call shortly before midnight, saying that the guerrilla band operating in the Sierra Madre del Sur, a revolutionary group known as Los Hijos de Zapata, had kidnapped Mr. McGowan and was holding him for ransom, the sum unstated. This station does not broadcast information from anonymous sources, but our night news staff immediately began checking. Inquiry at the Mixteca Hotel, where executives of Arc-Horn International are meeting, confirmed that McGowan, president of Top Court, Inc., and a board member of Arc-Horn, the parent conglomerate, had been missing for some time, specifically since the motor parade which preceded the grand opening of a new Gusto Más supermarket here in Acapulco. Mr. McGowan's car, a black Mercedes, pulled out of the motorcade at the Diana circle on the Costera Alemán and neither Mr. McGowan nor the car has been seen since.

"Police then confirmed the news of the missing businessman and automobile. Thus far, the only solid information in the possession of police comes from Enrique Flores Alvarez, sixteen, an attendant at the PEMEX station at Diana circle. He said he sold fifty pesos' worth of gas and checked the oil of a black Mercedes at about eight p.m. The car had Guerrero plates, a Mexican driver in the front seat and a light-skinned foreigner, middle-aged, in the rear, said Enrique. The boy said the car left the gas station and took a left on Farallon, which is the beginning of the highway to Chilpancingo, Cuernavaca and Mexico City. We will bring you further bulletins on the possible kidnapping on the hour and on the half hour, in both Spanish and English, until we sign off at four a.m. . . . London—The British government tonight announced further . . ."

Someone lowered the radio volume and at once a spray of chatter enveloped the three men in the adjoining room. Jim heard occasional bursts of laughter and more clinking of glasses against the low agonizing of Mexican singers caught in the toils of tortured love.

So it was all but official—he had been kidnapped. The news added little to Jim's store of information aside from the anonymous phone call from—what was it?—Hijos de Zapata. He knew Zapata as the "land and liberty" peasant hero of the Mexican Revolution sixty years ago, but what was an *"hijo"*? He sat for a few minutes in the leather chair and became conscious that he was shivering. The cold was pervasive and insistent now. Jim rapped loudly on his door.

Chucho soon stood in the doorway. Black hair, brown eyes, olive-tinted skin on his forehead above the masking bandana. He wore brown boots, old jeans and a gray woolen poncho. He was a stout man to whom the not unpleasant barnyard odor still clung.

"Cold as hell," said Jim, hugging himself to make the point.

Chucho held up thumb and forefinger with a tiny space between them.

He came back soon with two blanket-like serapes. He shook each in turn, raising a cloud of dust that sifted luminously through the candle rays. He tossed the serapes on the bed and then pulled another candle from his pocket and handed it to Jim. An obliging fellow, considering everything.

"You *hijo de Zapata?*" Jim asked haltingly. He pointed at Chucho.

"*Yo?*" He shook his head. "*Me llamo Chucho.*"

"What's an *hijo?*"

"*Niño del padre.*" He pointed at Jim. "*Usted es papá.*" He lowered his hand to a spot several feet off the earthen floor. "*El es su hijo.*"

"Oh. The sons of Zapata?"

"Sons. . . . *Eso.*" Chucho's tone hinted at pride in his ready pupil. "*Pase bien la noche, Señor Cheem.*"

Apparently Chucho relayed the conversation to his friends, touching off several bursts of raucous laughter. The phrase "*los hijos de Zapata*" seemed good for a rattle of hilarity each time Chucho used it. Jim drew the obvious inference. These men were not members of a guerrilla band with that name. But were they other guerrillas, kidnappers-for-hire or just enterprising bandits who chanced upon a good thing? At any rate, he guessed, they did not intend to harm him tonight.

Jim arranged the serapes on the bed, blew out the candle and crawled under the rough blankets. Even with his trousers, moccasins and poncho, he felt the cold. He was bone-tired from the mountain ride, yet not ready for sleep. At one-thirty, the music stopped again and the news announcer took over in Spanish. Someone turned up the volume. The English translation followed. Police reported they had found the abandoned Mercedes beside the Acapulco–Mexico City highway, about seven kilometers short of Chilpancingo, capital of Guerrero. The driver, identified as one Miguel

Espinosa Galván, believed to be about thirty, address unknown, had vanished.

Jim huddled in his mound of wool, tucking in edges where the cold penetrated. He wondered how Meg was taking it, what she was doing, whether the twins knew by now, whether Gwen, Tony and Masuo had met and whether they had linked his disappearance to the bugging, safe theft and other events that began with the computer robbery in Buenos Aires. And Davidson? What was he telling the police? Arc-Horn stock, Jim thought, might well fall again tomorrow.

He dozed off, lulled by the music and the now lowered voices in the next room. He came fully awake again at two o'clock, when the announcer gave a long, more or less accurate biography of James F. McGowan, listing him as a friend of a possible Democratic presidential candidate, Senator Philip Ireland, in the United States. The profile closed with a message. In case Mr. McGowan was near a radio, his wife, Margaret, sent her love and said she was praying that he was alive and well. Jim was grateful for the love, but he doubted the part about prayer. Meg, an agnostic, was not on speaking terms with deities.

He drifted off again, aware that the third man had also gone to bed, for he could hear only Chucho and Pepito now. The two-thirty news made only a vague impression on him. He heard it as though from a great distance. Something from Mexico City about the police widening the search for McGowan.

Outside a horse stamped and whinnied, and seemingly miles away, a dog barked. Inside the room something crawled on the sheet of newspaper, a crackling mini-sound. He fell asleep with aching ankles, a sore rump and the smell of his own urine in his nostrils.

Thursday Morning

Calvin Silliman was having as much success as a man trying to swim upstream in a white-water rapids.

"Quiet!" he called for the third time. "Quiet!" His fevered shouts fell like whispers. He hammered a desk with his fist. The decibels of many human voices, each striving to be heard above the din, were deafening.

The Toltec Room, Arc-Horn's communications hub off the Mixteca lobby, normally held but a few executives who came to use the direct telephone lines or to glance at news bulletins. Now the thirty-by-forty-foot salon was jammed with bodies. Some two hundred people milled about, bumping elbows, spraying the maroon carpeting with cigarette ashes, igniting rumors that raced like sputtering fuses, crowding about the three news tickers—UPI, Reuters and Dow-Jones—and jostling one another for use of the six phone booths where leased wires connected with the Arc-Horn switchboard in New York.

The Toltec Room was no longer a private Arc-Horn preserve. A dozen uniformed Mexicans, ranging from an army major general to helmeted and armed Acapulco motorcycle patrolmen, stalked about in that aura of truculent efficiency which surrounds officialdom when it is long on authority and short on inspiration. Two television crews, fresh in from Mexico City, vied for position in a snarl of cables and a welter of complaints and curses. The journalistic contingent had swelled to

thirty men and women, chiefly from Mexico City dailies
and the capital's corps of foreign correspondents, but
including reporters from major American newspapers
who had flown direct from the United States on post-midnight flights. A sprinkling of hotel employees, curious
tourists from other hostelries and even a few of the Miami
female flock mingled with gold, red and blue shirts of
the Arc-Horn convention forces. While nobody knew
any more about the kidnapping of James F. McGowan
than his neighbor, efforts to transcend the mutual ignorance produced a deluge of noise.

"Listen, please!" This time Silliman had climbed to
the desk top. His foot dislodged a portable typewriter,
which fell to the floor, provoking a scream of outrage
from a reporter. Silliman cupped his hands to his mouth.
"Please, please. Quiet. . . . Pipe down. . . . Just a simple
announcement."

The roar diminished slowly, became a buzz of conversation from groups huddled about the news tickers.

"Mr. Praeger will be down here promptly at ten
o'clock," said Silliman. "He has a statement for the
press."

His "thank you" was overwhelmed by the quickly
renewed clamor. A TV electrician shoved Jake Apple
away from a coiling wire. Lucy Jenkins sought to question
a Mexican colonel in rubbery Spanish. A fight broke
out at one of the phone booths between a newspaperman
and Walter Lowdermilk, who tried to use the telephone.
"It's reserved for the AP," the reporter shouted with
the anguish of demons. Lowdermilk, unattuned to the
primacy of instant communications in the world of
journalism, reached again for the phone, only to be
hurled back with tiger-like ferocity by the Associated
Press correspondent. Lowdermilk fell against Jules
Amarel, who fell against Damon Kimball, who collided
with Frankie Fee in an illustration of the falling-domino
principle. Dominoes might not fall in Asia, but they
toppled readily in the Toltec Room. All two hundred
twenty pounds of Frankie Fee hit Nate Berger, who
crashed into a metal box. The ravaged Summit president

had been consulting an electronic device, which, when
the proper buttons were pressed, yielded instant quota-
tions on any listing on the New York Stock Exchange.

Murmurs of dismay welled from the crowd ringing
the Dow-Jones financial ticker as chattering keys brought
the latest roundup from Wall Street, where Daylight
Savings Time was two hours ahead of Acapulco:

*New York—March's month-long rally suffered
a sharp reversal today.*

*Selling buffeted the New York Stock Exchange
in the first ninety minutes of trading, knocking the
Dow-Jones averages down eleven points and trim-
ming the composite price of all listed stocks by
thirty-one cents.*

*The list sagged in the wake of selling centered
on Arc-Horn International. The conglomerate, usually a favorite of the funds but now suddenly
beset by an expensive oil spill, a tanker loss and
the kidnapping of its best-known subsidiary president, Top Court's James F. McGowan, dropped
two dollars in the first hour and a half.*

*Political implications were seen for other multi-
nationals, many of which were off from a fraction
to a point.*

Another crowd, clustered about the nearby United
Press International teleprinter, learned that politicians
as well as brokers and financiers were reacting to the
abduction south of the border.

*Washington, March 20—Republican National
Chairman Felix Bingham said today the kidnapping last night of Top Court president James F.
McGowan by Mexican revolutionaries showed
"the bankruptcy of the policies being urged us by
Senator Philip Ireland," a leading contender for
the Democratic presidential nomination.*

*"Ireland's 'America last' program," said Bing-
ham, "involving cutting the defense budget, crip-*

*pling the CIA and relying on a visionary hope of
good will among peoples of the world, would leave
U.S. citizens at the mercy of such terrorist bands
as the one which seized Mr. McGowan."*

*Bingham said that unfortunately strength still
counted in today's world and that he, for one,
would fight to the finish to prevent Ireland from
reducing the United States to a "toothless giant."*

Elsewhere on the Mixteca's ground floor seminar
leaders went forward bravely with the task of expanding
the Arc-Horn hierarchy's store of knowledge. John Lindquist had exactly five executive students in the Zapotec
Room for his declamation on "How to Live with OSHA,"
the detested federal act governing the health and safety
of employees. Nicholas Calabrese, the savant of international law, drew a half dozen auditors to the Puebla
Room as he dwelt on legal aspects of the Argentine
oil spill. A Washington lawyer-lobbyist did somewhat
better in the Quetzalcoatl Room. Nine somber businessmen heard him excoriate the warren of federal reg-
ulatory agencies which hampered Arc-Horn in fulfillment of its historic mission: bringing the maximum
amount of goods to the most customers at the highest
possible price.

Fugitives from knowledge who did not head for the
Toltec Room gathered in the vaulted lobby where the
fresh morning breeze vied with dispiriting gusts of rumor.
Joyce Boke-Milgrim held dolorous parley with Helmut
von Weise while Sukit Sukhsvasti, the agile little Thai,
traded conjectural wisdom with Charles Holloway of
Indo Deep Rig.

Steve Cooper lounged in his frayed jeans beneath
an arch near his unpatronized easel. Business was bad
all over. María, the convention hostess, bore down on
him like one of the avenging Furies. Her transparent
slacks flapped to her warrior stride, her look was grim
and no jacaranda bloom graced her ebony hair.

"Qué grosería!" she flared without bothering with
salutations. "We had nothing to do with the kidnapping.

The Hijos de Zapata would never snatch a man who's a friend of Senator Ireland, the only reasonable voice in Washington. Absurd, no?" Despite the tumbling flow, there was the singsong cadence of the Guerrero mountains in her Spanish. "We trust you, Steve, and you know we are but two in the hotel. Neither of us made a move or received an order. Without us, it would be impossible."

"What about the anonymous call to the radio station?" asked Steve. "The caller said the Hijos pulled the job."

"A lie!" María tossed her head in anger. "A ruse, an excuse so that the government can send in the army and terrorize us in the hills. Anonymous calls? Sometimes, yes, but always followed by a card, made up of letters clipped from a newspaper, giving the ransom figure and instructions. It was so in Aguacalientes and in Tuxtla Gutiérrez, no? Where is such a card?"

"Who knows? . . . Who do you think did it then?"

"I'm not sure yet." María could ponder in full vocal flight. "The government has the most to gain. One thing I know. Miguel, the driver, is no Hijo."

"You want to discover the identity of the kidnappers, true?"

"Clearly. I have my duty."

"Look, María. I'm helping Señora Piggott—you know her?—who is a good friend of Señor McGowan and his Señora. We want to find McGowan if we can. It's like trying to find a special grain of sand on the beach, but we must try. Will you help us?"

"I will help *you,* Steve. Always I'm here in the hotel. *Hasta luego.*"

She hurried off in the direction of the Tarascan Bar, skirting Hugo Praeger and party, who had just emerged from the elevator.

Praeger, flanked by Chalmers Davidson and Bernard Hirsch, and escorted by three security guards, swung into the Toltec Room and pushed forward through the heaving crowd. A hush fell with the expectation of a news break. Praeger walked with emphatic step and his eyes glistened in the hillocks of flesh. A man of crisis who enjoyed the spotlight, he threw a salute to the Mexican major general, patted Walter Lowdermilk's arm and glanced about for an appropriate forum. Since there was no platform, Davidson and Hirsch helped him climb on a chair. Reporters stood ready with open notebooks and two television cameras focused on him.

"I'll make a short statement, but unfortunately I'll be unable to entertain questions at this time." His eyes roved the room. "I know you gentlemen of the press will understand. The hours immediately ahead are most delicate ones. None of us wants to do or say anything that would jeopardize the safety of Jim McGowan. His return uninjured is our only concern at this time. All else must give way to that objective. So when I finish, please do not ask questions. Arc-Horn International is always anxious to help the press, but in this instance we must beg off. We solicit your cooperation. So much by way of preface."

He glanced at a sheet of paper on which he had scribbled notes. "We have received from the kidnappers a file card on which are pasted letters, clipped from newspapers, which make up the text of the message. The card was placed in the glove compartment of the courtesy car being used by Mr. Chalmers Davidson, our vice-president for international operations and communications. I can reveal only two items from this message. It sets the ransom at 12,500,000 pesos or one million dollars American. At the end, it carries this slogan—and I will read it in Spanish—'*Abajo los capitalistas monopolistas. Arriba tierra y libertad!*' It is signed 'Los Hijos de Zapata.' "

Praeger nodded to reporters jammed about his chair. "I know you gentlemen want the entire note, but most of the rest involves instructions for delivery of the ransom. On our own common sense and upon advice of the Mexican authorities, we must withhold these details at this time."

He paused, clearing his throat. "Despite our deep concern for the life and safety of Jim McGowan, Arc-Horn International can have only one response

to this criminal demand. We will not pay. I stated unequivocally four years ago that Arc-Horn would never
pay tribute to terrorism. We adhere strictly to that policy.
As for our reasoning, I reply on the simple, eloquent
words of Golda Meir: 'To give in when one life is en-
dangered is only to endanger more. The answer is that
terrorism must be wiped out.' "

Two newspapermen broke for the door. The Associated Press man was dictating rapidly into the phone
wrested from Lowdermilk. Praeger motioned for quiet.
"Just one final word. Mrs. McGowan is in her room,
as you probably know. The kidnapping was a fright-
ful shock to her—she was up most of the night—but
she is carrying on with courage and has been in touch
with her daughters in New York. Please do not try to
contact her. The switchboard operators are keeping her
line clear for emergency calls. When this ordeal is over,
she'll be willing to talk to the press. . . . That's all and
thank you."

Questions flew despite the embargo. Lowering his
head as though ducking a flight of arrows, he climbed
down from the chair and headed for the door in a protec-
tive wedge formed by Davidson and the security guards.
Bernard Hirsch remained behind. One of the public
relations officer's jobs was to fend off journalists, denying
them access to pertinent information without enraging
them. For his systematic and uncomplaining failure at
this implausible task, Hirsch was paid $175,000 a
year.

Silliman pressed closely behind the security forces
as they maneuvered Praeger into the lobby. The convention manager was agitated by a number of problems,
not the least of which was the ten-foot birthday cake
baking in four ovens.

He plucked at his leader's sleeve. "Is tonight's closing
banquet on or off?"

"Let's hold off that decision until late this afternoon.
Meanwhile, Cal, just carry forward with the schedule
as is."

The Arc-Horn ruler moved with his escort into a

waiting elevator and ascended to less cluttered heights. "I'll get off at ten," said Praeger. "Meg McGowan is waiting for me. . . . Chalmers, you handle General Sandoval. And ask him why in the hell his people aren't on the ball. They haven't even questioned the hotel staff yet. You'd think this was a case of overtime parking instead of a kidnapping."

Davidson bobbed his head. "I'll do my best." Unconsciously he fingered a purplish bruise on his left cheek where, so he said, a careless cleaning woman had swiped him with a mop handle.

With a security guard at his elbow, Hugo Praeger pressed the doorbell of the McGowan suite with some trepidation. He had last seen Meg at 3 a.m. and although he had spoken to her twice on the phone recently, he was unsure of her current emotional state. She had gone from numbed shock to tears to a kind of frenetic activity that masked her feelings. Praeger had tried to put himself in her place, but failed. Not since the death of his mother many years ago had the childless entrepreneur felt the pangs of grief. A generous man, he wanted to offer himself in sympathy, but like a cut flower, he lacked the juices of rooted plants.

When she opened the door, he surprised her with a bear-like embrace that left them both embarrassed. Meg's black hair was still neatly coiffed from yesterday's visit to the hairdresser, but she looked drained. There was a weariness about her eyes despite her flushed cheeks. As she ushered Praeger into the living room, she made fluttering, nervous gestures.

"Can I get you something, a Coke or a ginger ale?"

"No, no." He sank into a wide armchair and found it a close fit. "I wish there were something I could do to help." One brought food to the legatees of death, but what did one do for the wife of a kidnapping victim?

"You can, Hugo. I saw you make your statement on television just now." She seated herself on the massive coffee table and smoothed the folds of the white cotton shift she was wearing. "When did you find the ransom note? You didn't tell me about that."

"Just a few minutes ago. Chalmers got an anonymous call telling him to look in the glove compartment of his car. Ron Jeffers went down and found it."

"Are there explicit instructions on how to deliver the money?"

"Yes. . . . Of course, the details are academic in light of our policy." He sought her eyes. "Meg, I'm terribly sorry we can't break our . . ."

"Please don't, Hugo." She held up a hand to block further apology. "Let's not go over that again. It's too painful. You have your policy and I have my ideas about it. I think it's inhuman, no, shitty is the right word, and there we are. But that's not the point right now. What I want are those instructions."

"Why?"

"I've talked to Carol and Connie." She gripped the edges of the table. "We decided to put up the ransom money ourselves. Anything within our capacity. You say the note demands a million dollars. We're ready to pay it."

"They want it in Mexican pesos in small bills."

"I got hold of Hal Frascella. We have our personal accounts at First Merchants, you know. He says it would be no problem. If we pledge securities to the bank in the needed amount, he'll authorize the Banco Nacional here in Acapulco to get the pesos together for payment."

"Have you already done this?"

"No, I told Hal I'd call back after I talked to you. . . . Is there a deadline in the note?"

"I . . . " Praeger hesitated. "I'm sorry, Meg. We have an agreement with General Sandoval that no ransom details will be released."

"Released?" Her temper flared. "I'm not the public, for God's sake. I'm Meg McGowan. Remember me? The wife of a man who may be facing death."

"Please, Meg." His customary booming voice wilted before her fury. "We're under orders from the Mexican authorities. We have the handicap of being in a foreign country. All we can do is cooperate."

"You seem to be able to manipulate foreign officials easily enough when you want to."

He shrugged. "This is different—a criminal act. Not the same type of officials we're accustomed to dealing with."

She fixed her eyes on his. "Hugo, I want those ransom instructions."

"That's just not possible, Meg." He returned her gaze with difficulty. Some wives bent to corporate discipline as obligingly as their husbands. Others, unfortunately, did not. "You know I'd do anything I could for you. But this, I can't."

She stood up and folded her arms. "I have weapons, you know."

"Oh." He was at once intrigued, wary and laden with guilt.

"Yes. For instance, I could march down to the Toltec Room and tell the newspapermen that I'm ready to pay, but the president of Arc-Horn refuses to give me the ransom note."

Could she mean it? The implications quickly wove psychedelic patterns: Arc-Horn painted a villain before the world, the brute Praeger turning his back on the sorrowing wife, deep headlines, moralizing commentators, pictures of the twins in tears. He shook himself free of black visions before answering.

"I know you're going through hell, Meg, but please think this through." He tried to be patient, understanding. "You couldn't conceivably help Jim by that kind of action and you might cost his life. Hearing your readiness to pay and seeing the uproar in the press, they would be sure to escalate their demands. This thing might stretch out into many days, even weeks, with each passing hour more threatening to Jim. Our job is to get him out of the hands of those kidnappers as soon as possible."

"I'm supposed to just sit here, doing nothing?" Her whole body, tense as a compressed spring, argued for action. "Like these Mexican police and army officers? . . . Do you know that not one person in authority has asked to question me yet?"

"I can't understand that either." Praeger wiped his brow. "Davidson is asking General Sandoval about it now. We're demanding a more vigorous, aggressive investigation."

"There are so many leads. . . ." Meg pointed toward the bedroom. "For instance, those papers stolen from his safe. I have a hunch there's a connection. Jim was so upset—and he was kidnapped soon afterward. Then that driver, Miguel. Why doesn't whoever hired him know his address, his background, God, at least something about the man?"

"I know, I know." Praeger boosted himself from the armchair. "Give me a couple of minutes, Meg. I want to talk to Chalmers. May I use your phone?"

"Of course." She walked to the bedroom. "Meanwhile I'll do something about this face of mine."

She returned with fresh, pale lipstick as Praeger concluded a brief conversation with his vice-president.

"Chalmers and I have a proposal to make." He came to her and placed his hands gently on her arms. "Give the authorities until tomorrow morning, Meg. If there's no break by, let's say, nine a.m., you'll be free to take whatever steps you wish. Without giving details of the note now, I can assure you that tomorrow morning is well within the deadline. General Sandoval promises swift pursuit of all leads. In fact, a federal security man is on his way here now to question you. Every person in the hotel, whether staff or Arc-Horn, will be interrogated. I think it's only sensible to give the army and police a decent amount of time."

"That's a whole day and night, Hugo."

"I realize that, but with a million dollars riding on him and the deadline some time away, Jim is in no immediate danger. Your cooperation is the best thing you can do for him right now."

"What about arrangements for the money? If I agree, and Jim is still being held tomorrow morning, I'll want to contact the kidnappers at once."

"You have my promise that you can read the ransom note at nine a.m. tomorrow. As for the money, Chalmers

is putting his car at your disposal. You can talk to
Frascella and then go into the Banco Nacional to meet
with their Acapulco officials. That way you can have the
cash ready. I'm giving you another security guard in addition to the man stationed in your hallway. . . . Please,
Meg. It's only common sense."

"All right." She knew that, without the ransom note,
she had no alternative. Hugo was right. To blow her
top to the press would produce headlines, but no Jim.

"You're solid, Meg." He kissed her on the cheek.
"We'll do everything in our power. You know, I'm very
fond of Jim. We have our differences, but he's my kind
of man."

Suddenly she gave way once more. She threw her
arms around him, buried her head in his chest and began to sob. He held her firmly and wondered at the quick
surge of his own feelings. Could this be compassion?
They stood for almost a minute and when she backed
away, wiping her eyes with the back of her hand, he
knew that his own eyes were moist.

"You'll have Jim back. I feel certain of it." He offered
her his handkerchief.

"Life plays its jokes on us, doesn't it, Hugo?" She
essayed a wry smile as she dabbed at her face. "Like
a lot of couples, Jim and I had our troubles. But then,
Tuesday night when I came down, everything seemed
to change. We had some of that old glorious feeling."
Her voice broke again. "I knew I loved the man and
that he loved me. . . . And now, this."

They stood silently, sharing the ancient mystery of
injustice.

"Well . . ." Praeger pressed her arms again. "I'd better
get back upstairs." The truth was that he felt a twinge
of envy. The richness of love eluded him, always had,
and he felt uncomfortable in its presence. "I'll call you
the instant we have any news."

"You've been kind. I mean tender. I appreciate that,
Hugo."

"You're special, Meg."

He opened the door to find a slight, black-haired man

reaching for the bell. He wore a black suit and shoes gleaming with polish.

"Señora McGowan? . . . Bernardo Figueroa Estrada *a sus órdenes.*" He presented a laminated identity card. "Security, Gobernación. May I speak with you a few minutes, please?"

"Good luck, Meg." Praeger walked off down the hall, trailed by his own security man.

Meg ushered the agent into the suite. She had few hopes, but she would tell what she knew. She dried her eyes again with Hugo's handkerchief. It would be good to talk with someone in authority.

Chalmers Davidson finished his adieus with General Sandoval, a process that consumed almost as much time as their short conversation, then strode to the sound-proofed communications room in answer to the buzzer.

Ron Jeffers tore off a message from the computerized decoding machine and handed it to Davidson. "They're keeping us busy this morning." He said it in his clipped, toneless, professional manner.

File Series 802-W
No. 12

From: *Mother*
To: *Cedric*

Your project TeeCee understood at highest levels as necessary calculated risk.

FYI: President briefed early. At 9 a.m., he took call from Los Pinos, using our interpreter. Mexican president offered all-out army search, involving 5,000 troops in Guerrero. President vacillated, appreciating offer but indicating forces already committed as probably sufficient. Mexican understood at once, said would down-play incident with pro forma effort.

President used opportunity to say that since U.S. and Mexico undertaking joint Neptune West, he hoped Mexican delegation to U.N. Geneva conference would in no way give comfort to

*"ecology extremists" blocking "reasonable indus-
trial progress."*

*Mexican equivocated. Said was under great
pressure from third world countries. In view of
this, he thought U.S. credits to Mexico for Neptune
West should be doubled to $300 million and that
Mexico's take be increased to 40 percent from 25.
At end of bargaining, President agreed to 38 contingent upon Arc-Horn approval.*

*In light of background, imperative you gain
quick adoption Green Tree and Neptune West resolutions.*

"Anything in reply?" asked Jeffers.

"Just tell Mother we're on track for passage soon
after four p.m."

Shortly after noon Masuo Sugimoto conferred with
Hugo Praeger, then rode the elevator down to the lobby
and walked to the Toltec Room, where people went
forward with their business in an atmosphere of confusion. Printers chattered, executives elbowed one another for use of the three direct lines commandeered
from an indignant press, TV crews waited captiously
for action, Mexican officers strolled about with a resolute
air, reporters interviewed one another and white-coated
waiters laid out a table with sandwiches, ice cream and
coffee.

Damon Kimball pressed the Arc-Horn symbol on
buttons arrayed on the electronic device which had sur-
vived Nate Berger's fall without lasting damage. The
machine instantly flashed the latest Arc-Horn sale on
the New York Stock Exchange.

"They got us by the short hair," Damon remarked
to Sugimoto. "We're down to forty-two seventy-five."

Sugimoto mounted the chair which Praeger had used
earlier.

"Gentlemen of the press!" He stood primly, his hands
folded behind his back. "I'm about to make a purchase
that may interest you. I'm phoning my broker in New

York and placing a buy order for two hundred thousand shares of Arc-Horn at forty-three."

"Why?" someone shouted.

"This corporation is not only fundamentally sound," the Japanese replied, "it is a spectacular bargain at today's prices. I'm making the purchase for my own account with my own money."

While the AP correspondent dictated the news to his office in New York, Sugimoto bowed, dismounted, strode to the row of phone booths and stood in the shortest queue behind Jules Amarel of Six Flags and Hi-Western's Paul Chesterfield. Both men respectively stepped aside and waved him toward the telephone.

Thursday, 1 p.m.

They were huddled around the huge round coffee table in the McGowan living room, picking at the sandwiches and drinking too much coffee. They were frustrated, and occasionally irritable. No one knew what to do. They had strained the hunches, clues, tips and rumors as fine as dust without finding a particle on which to act.

Meg, Antonio Percevale and Gwen Piggott had been here since noon. For the moment, after another peevish flare-up, Jim McGowan's two best friends in the corporation were treating Meg as delicately as they might the grieving widow of the deceased.

"Cut it out . . . please," Meg said sharply. "Jim isn't dead and it gives me the creeps to act as if he were. . . . I really feel confident about tomorrow morning. Hal

Frascella has been a big help and Señor Ramírez at the Banco Nacional is going to keep some staff on after the bank closes to assemble the money for me."

"What time are you seeing him?" Gwen marveled at Meg's reserves. Beneath the infrequent displays of nerves was a core of steadiness. And movement, activity, plans seemed to calm her.

"Four o'clock."

"Help yourself to my car. Félix, the driver, speaks passable English."

"Thanks, hon, but I won't need it. Hugo says Chalmers Davidson is lending me his car for the day."

"You can't be serious!" Tony eyed her in amazement. "After all we've told you?"

"Oh, my God." Meg clapped her hand to her mouth. "I forgot for a second. Okay, Gwen. I accept."

They had spent a half hour explaining the corporate background to Meg, from the computer robbery in Buenos Aires to the discovery of electronic eavesdropping in the hotel just before the theft from Jim's safe. They could only speculate about Jim's meeting with Davidson. The lone hint had been Jim's surprising remark to Tony—"Believe it or not, I knocked the son of a bitch on his ass"—just before last night's motorcade left the hotel. All signs pointed toward Davidson, they told Meg, and while neither would flatly accuse Davidson of engineering the abduction, they were deeply suspicious of him. Actually, they had selected McGowan's suite for their meeting knowing that Steve Cooper had neutralized the recording devices.

"I can't imagine what Davidson could have said that made Jim hit him." Meg cocked her head as she speculated. "It's so unlike Jim. He gets mad, sure, but punching people? Never."

"He did a job this time," said Tony, "judging by that swelling on Chalmers' face."

"I know Jim was furious yesterday afternoon when I told him about Steve discovering the bugging." Gwen chose her words carefully. She had no idea who might have heard a recording of her intimate conversation with Jim and the feeling was growing that she should explain Sunday night before wild rumor reached Meg's ears. "Suppose Chalmers tried to blackmail Jim by playing back our talk in my place that first night?"

"Blackmail?" Meg puzzled. "I don't understand. What did you say that . . . ?"

"Oh, our talk would have been perfect ammunition for Davidson if he wanted something from Jim," Gwen broke in. "I gave Hugo a going over and we groused about everything wrong with Arc-Horn. Corporation business, you know. But if Hugo ever heard a tape of what we said, we'd be in trouble."

"I see." How long had they talked Sunday night? Did Jim have something going with this attractive, very female woman? Meg brushed the thoughts aside.

"Meg, please don't count too heavily on tomorrow morning." Tony leaned forward and placed a hand on her arm. "You can exchange money for Jim if the kidnappers are really Los Hijos de Zapata, but Gwen and I don't think that's probable. Steve says he's got it from a trusted source that Los Hijos weren't involved. Also, in previous operations, Los Hijos have demanded release of political prisoners as part of the ransom. No hint of that this time."

"But we don't know what's in the ransom note," Meg protested. "Maybe there is something about prisoners and the Mexicans want it kept quiet for the time being."

"Possible." Tony considered for a moment. He was dressed immaculately as always, fresh golden shirt, expensive, soft lime slacks and white moccasins with gilded buckles. "But how do we know the note is genuine? I find it curious that the card was supposedly found in Chalmers' car. If it were really from Los Hijos, why not in Hugo's car? or mine, since I'm known as Jim's good friend? But the main reason to doubt it is Steve. He swears by his source, whoever it is, who says Los Hijos aren't guilty this time."

"By the way, where is Steve?" asked Meg. "He said he'd be here a little after twelve."

"He's checking out another tip." Gwen looked at her wristwatch. "Still, he should be here by now."

The phone rang. "That may be him." Tony stepped to the bar, picked up the instrument and listened for a moment after giving his name. "No, no, not on the phone. . . . You haven't told anyone else, have you? . . . Yes, right away, please."

He turned as he hung up. "Alex Rosinski, the Summit designer. He's just out of jail. He has some information for Meg. He's on his way up."

"Oh!" Meg brightened at once. She fussed with a stack of magazines, then emptied an ashtray in a wastebasket. She seemed compelled to movement.

Tony walked to the balcony while the women chatted. Meg told Gwen she couldn't understand the attitude of the Mexican authorities. The security man had interviewed her for only fifteen minutes. "And most of that," she said, "was the kind of dreary facts they want in hospitals when somebody's bleeding to death—age, mother's name, residence, date of birth, occupation. Can you believe it, Gwen? Nothing about who I suspect or any clues I might have. A big nothing, if you ask me."

Tony listened with less than full attention as he stood on the balcony, stretching in the sunlight and gazing at the knots of Arc-Horn executives lunching beneath the striped umbrellas. His eyes drifted from the terrace to the beach, where a few people sauntered along the water's edge. He saw three figures on the sand to the south. One was Steve talking with María, the hostess, and a man who looked familiar. They were facing the ocean, apparently in animated conversation. The man turned toward Steve and Tony caught a glimpse of his face. Yes, José, the keeper of the Tarascan Bar. He crouched and began marking the wet sand with a finger.

As Tony left the balcony to answer the knock at the door, he saw Steve and María bending beside José, watching him sketch something on the sand.

Alex Rosinski was a frail young man with curly blond hair and bushy sideburns that made him look oddly top-heavy, like a small sailboat with too much rigging. His red manta cloth shirt and white trousers were splotched and rumpled as though he had slept in them for a week. Actually, it had been four nights.

"Excuse my appearance," he said. "I thought I ought to tell Mrs. McGowan first before I cleaned up."

Tony made quick introductions. "We're not worrying about looks this afternoon."

"Can I fix you a drink?" asked Meg.

"No, thanks. What I have will only take a minute." He declined an offer of a chair. "I got it from the guy who was in the same cell with me, a character named Nacho. It's not much, I guess."

He paused as though awaiting permission to continue.

"Please go ahead," said Meg. "Anything at all is more than we know."

"Okay. Well, this Nacho is a real street operator, pushes drugs, hustles, has a dozen rackets and knows everybody around Acapulco making an illegal buck. Frankly, I liked him." He smiled sheepishly as if his taste in humanity might prove offensive. "Anyway, when the radio carried the name and age of the missing kidnap driver, Nacho said he'd bet that was the same Miguel he knew who used to pimp and now made a living at small-time thieving. Nacho knew that Miguel was working this week at the Mixteca as a driver and he told me that Miguel's cousin ran a small bandit gang operating out of a shack in the mountains.

"When the radio said the abandoned Mercedes was found near Chilpancingo, Nacho said that probably meant that McGowan had been taken to the cousin's hut." He hesitated. "That's all, I guess." He apologized again. "Sorry I couldn't learn more, but that's all Nacho knew."

"The shack," said Meg quickly. "Did he have any ideas of the location?"

"No. Just that it's somewhere in the mountains between here and Chilpancingo."

"That could be anywhere inside three or four thousand

square kilometers," said Tony. "Did he know the cousin's name?"

"No, but they call him El Profanador, the profaner, I guess it would be. It seems that one night he carried a girl up to the altar of some old Indian ruin and, well, violated her there. Nacho is full of stories like that."

"Why wouldn't the police know about Miguel's cousin?" asked Meg. "And about this place in the mountains?"

"Have the police acted at all? That's the real question." Tony turned to Rosinski. "What did Nacho think about the connection with the Sons of Zapata?"

"He thought it was a phony. He said Miguel was about as revolutionary as the owners of the Acapulco hotels. He laughed when he heard about the anonymous phone call."

"Anything else?"

"No." Rosinski shook his head. "I wish there were."

"Do us a favor, Alex," said Tony, "and keep this to yourself, will you?"

"Well . . . I was going to tell Mr. Praeger or Mr. Davidson so they could pass the word along. Of course, I wouldn't want to hurt Nacho."

"Please hold off. I can't go into it now, but we have reasons not to trust the authorities on this. Wheels within wheels, you know."

"I know what you mean. They threw me in the can when actually it was this big Mexican who jumped me. . . . Sure, anything you say. . . . I wish I could help more, Mrs. McGowan. I know it must be rough for you."

"Oh, I'm managing." She essayed a smile, but her expectations had shriveled. "Thanks awfully for coming here first. You must be dying for a bath."

"Yeah, I'm going to let that shower run and run. . . . Well, good luck."

Rosinski's departure left a vacuum of hope.

"Interesting," said Gwen, "but how do we go about finding somebody who knows this El what's-his-name and where his place in the mountains is?"

Meg was puttering again. She picked a speck off her skirt, fussed with her hair.

"Why can't we take that story to the police?" she asked. "At least, it's a lead for them."

"I know how you feel, Meg," said Tony. "But I think that's unwise. Davidson is working hand in glove with that General Sandoval. I know nothing about Sandoval but I don't trust Davidson."

"It's my decision, you know, Tony." She said it quietly but firmly.

"I realize that. I can't expect you to share the suspicions of Gwen and myself about all that's happened in the last month. I can't measure it or prove it, but deep down . . ."

Two loud raps sounded on the door, Steve Cooper's signal. Tony hurried to the entrance alcove.

"I've got something, not much, but something." Steve clumped into the room. He wore his hiking boots and his usual uniform, short-sleeved denim shirt and frayed blue-jean shorts. He greeted Meg and Gwen, centering his eyes fully on each woman in turn.

"I need a glass of water. That sun's hot today." He walked to the bar, found the bottled water and drank deeply.

"Here's the scoop." He squatted near the coffee table, rocking slightly on his heels. "I can't tell you my source, but take my word for it, it's okay. . . . You know, a lot of employees in these Acapulco hotels live in the valley just east of the hills. A few of them live further out, along the highway to Mexico City as it climbs into the mountains. My source has a friend who works—well, around Acapulco. He rides the bus back and forth to his home on the highway near a town called Tierra Colorada. Across the road from his place, maybe a couple of hundred yards off the pavement, there's a run-down stable where some horses are kept by a guy they call El Profanador. This . . ."

"El Prof!" exclaimed Meg. "We know about him, Steve."

"You do? How?"

"Go ahead, Steve," Tony urged. "We'll tell you when you finish."

"This El Profanador," Steve continued, "is known around Tierra Colorada as a shady character. Some think he's a bandit. He uses the horses to ride up to a place he has in the mountains about ten miles away. Last night, the guy who lives across the road heard some noises just as he was going to bed. Brakes squealed and a car pulled off the highway and stopped. He heard some people get out, then the sound of the car backing up to the highway in gravel and driving off fast toward Chilpancingo. He heard people walk on the gravel and then later the sound of horses on the mountain trail. He listened until the echoes became faint and died away. He thought it was unusual for people to be riding that trail at night because it goes along the ledge of a canyon in one spot. Then, when he woke up this morning and heard the radio news, he became suspicious, especially since they said the car had been found on the same highway this side of Chilpancingo. Just to satisfy himself, he walked over to the stable. No horses. Whoever rode toward El Profanador's hideaway during the night hadn't returned."

"Did he tell the police?" asked Meg. Her eyes glistened. Hope enveloped her again.

"Never. The police are bad news." Steve turned his thumbs down. "You got to know these people. An awful lot of Mexicans, especially the poor, won't go near the police. That goes double for the mountain people. They figure the witness gets worse treatment than the suspect. Hell, I know a family of eight near Iguala. The father was murdered, but not a single person in the family, nor any of the neighbors, went to the police. Anyway . . ."

"Steve, listen." Tony hurriedly told what Alex Rosinski had learned from his cellmate. "It all fits. El Profanador, the shack in the mountains."

"Did your source say Miguel and El Whosis were cousins?" asked Gwen.

"No, but I wouldn't doubt it. Every Mexican has

a network of cousins, aunts and uncles. When you're powerless, you need family to survive."

"Tierra Colorada?" Meg questioned. "How far from Acapulco is it?"

"A bit under seventy kilometers," said Steve. "That's around forty miles. . . . No problem finding the town. My sources drew me a map with some landmarks along the highway. Of course, the trail would be tricky to follow."

"Why?" She was excited now. "Once on the trail, you'd just keep going, wouldn't you?"

"Oh, you wouldn't go in by foot or horse. The way to do it in a hurry is by air." Steve's eyes swiveled to Percevale. "One of those Arc-Horn choppers could put us over Tierra Colorada inside fifteen minutes, then with luck . . ."

"I have the use of a helicopter." Tony stood up. "The one assigned for the Gusto Más opening."

Steve straightened from his crouch. They grinned at each other. "It's a long shot."

"What can we lose? Perfect flying weather."

"You ready?"

"Let's go," said Tony.

"Wait a minute. You got any old clothes?"

Tony shook his head apologetically. For once, the man cherished by his London tailors found himself without appropriate attire.

"Well, at least put on heavier shoes. If we can land up there, rocky soil is no place for beach sandals. . . . And guns. We need a couple." Steve frowned. "Christ, I haven't fired a bullet since I was sixteen."

"I do some trap shooting at the gun club," said Tony. "The pilot keeps a pistol in the helicopter."

"Where's the pilot right now?"

"At the airport. Our men are on stand-by duty during the day."

"And money." Steve looked at the two women. "I'd feel better going up there with some cash. How many pesos have we got?"

Gwen dug into a white handbag beside her chair.

"I think I have four thousand. I used my credit card yesterday at the desk. I was going shopping this afternoon—I thought."

Meg produced some nine hundred pesos in bills and coins. Tony had six hundred fifty in his wallet. Steve, emptying his pockets, counted a total of two hundred thirty-seven. He scooped up the money.

"A little over four hundred sixty U.S. Not enough. With more money, we might be able to do business up there. Who knows?"

They consulted swiftly. Tony said the desk's limit for cash on credit cards, boosted for the Arc-Horn convention, was ten thousand pesos. If Meg asked for money, it might arouse suspicion. So Gwen would go down at once and ask for the limit. Tony would do the same on the way out of the hotel. First, he'd change to heavier shoes. Steve would try to find a weapon. He thought José kept a gun under the counter of the Tarascan Bar. He wasn't sure.

"Okay," said Steve. "Tony, you and I meet at your car in ten minutes. What kind is it?"

"Imperial. The driver's name is Raúl."

"Gwen, you meet us at the driveway with money. Keep it casual, like we just happened to meet. Okay?"

Gwen was already halfway to the door with her handbag. She blew Steve a kiss.

"Anything else?" he asked.

"The map," said Meg. "Do you have the map that was drawn for you?"

Steve tapped his head. "It's up here—I hope."

Meg kissed both men as they walked to the door.

"What about my date at the bank? Should I go through with it?"

"Sure," said Tony. "Just do everything normally. Remember, this is a one-in-fifty gamble, no more. Don't get your hopes up."

"And keep this to yourself," said Steve. "If anybody asks for Percevale, you know from nothing, right?"

"Don't worry. . . . For God's sake, be careful."

She braced herself against the door after closing it.

Yes, she would try to keep a lid on her hopes. This escapade was just a bit insane, wasn't it? Flying over the mountains because of what some jailbird and an anonymous "source" had said. Who knew whether this shack of El Prof-something even existed? But she understood the men's need for action. She felt the same way, cooped up here with security guards in the hallway, nothing to do but agonize, conjecture and listen for the ringing of the phone.

She walked slowly to the center of the room and eased herself into an armchair facing the sun-flooded balcony. There was that thought again. What if . . . ? Yes, face it, what if Jim never got out of this alive or was already dead? A week ago, even two days ago, the thought would not have cut so cruelly. But after Tuesday night, those beautiful hours and that powerful feeling—not a mental recognition at all, but an awareness deep within her—of her love for Jim and his for her, well, the thought slashed like a knife.

But she must face reality. Without Jim, what? The work with Dave Moyer? Yes, she truly wanted that and perhaps, once involved and immersed in study and work, the pain would drain away. How would it end for Jim? Would they shoot him? In the head? . . . Carol and Connie. Oh, dear God, this was the road to collapse. Enough of it.

Meg gripped the arms of the chair, tensing herself intentionally. Her eyes lighted on the platter of sandwiches at which they had only nibbled. Suddenly, she was hungry. My God, she hadn't eaten since last night.

Steve was counting the money in his lap as Tony drove the limousine at sixty miles an hour along the highway to the airport.

"I make it almost twenty-five hundred bucks," he said, "what with Gwen's ten thousand pesos, your ten thousand, plus what we had. . . . Hey man, slow down. It's been seven years since I've been in one of these things."

"This *is* slow." Tony did not ease up on the accelerator. "Did you get a gun?"

"Yeah." Steve patted a bulge in his shirt. "José gave me his revolver and a box of shells. How do I load the damn thing?"

"I'll show you in the chopper." Tony kept his eyes on the road. "That was close with the law, wasn't it?"

Gwen had met them at the foot of the Mixteca's entrance steps and slipped a roll of pesos unobtrusively to Percevale. Tony dismissed the driver, saying he wanted to drive himself, but just as they prepared to wheel from the curb, a helmeted Mexican policeman informed them that no one was to leave the hotel without written permission from General Sandoval.

Tony placed a hundred-peso note beneath his left hand on the frame of the car's open front window. The bill peeped from his fingers as he explained in swift Spanish, peppered with slang, that he was the president of Gusto Más, an emergency had arisen at the new supermarket and he must go there at once. The officer leaned against the door, palmed the bill and walked off with the air of a man who has fulfilled his duty.

"Yeah," said Steve. "I hate *mordida,* but that's one cop who won't tell anyone we took off. . . . Jesus, man, is that the best you could do? You look like you're going to watch a polo match."

Tony had changed to a copper-colored turtle-neck sweater by Giovennelli and a pair of cordovans hand-tooled in London. He still wore the soft lime slacks.

"All I had." He shrugged. A friend in Buenos Aires once quipped that when Percevale died, the story of his burial would be carried on the fashion page of *La Prensa.*

Three blue-and-red Arc-Horn helicopters rested like giant toys a few hundred yards from the terminal. Tony drove through the gate reserved for Arc-Horn executives and braked to a stop near the middle aircraft. A man in a white short-sleeved shirt, wearing sunglasses, walked toward them from the nearby wooden building.

"Hi, Pete," Percevale called. "Get Bill, will you? We're going up."

Pete quickened his pace, extended his hand in greeting. "Sorry, Mr. Percevale. No flights today. We're grounded until further notice."

Bill, the copilot, left the building and came toward them, swinging his sunglasses. He was younger than Pete with a ruddy, boyish face and a guileless smile.

Tony made the introductions. "The hell with orders. This is an emergency."

"The call was from Mr. Davidson," said Pete. "He's our boss."

"Not this week he isn't," Tony shot back. "He assigned this helicopter to me and I need it—right now."

Pete made an open-palmed gesture of resignation. "Well, if you say so. Just so you clear me with the front office."

"No problem. Let's go."

The pilots stood aside while Tony and Steve mounted the steps to the aircraft. The cabin was upholstered in dark leather with three roomy seats on each side of the aisle. Between the seats and the cockpit stood a card table with cushioned banquettes fore and aft, built to hold four persons. Bill pushed a button and the steps folded into the fuselage. The jet engine coughed, took hold and soon the long blades above them were whirling. They sat on the ground for several minutes, the craft shaking and rattling while the engine warmed and the pilots went through their checklist.

The helicopter lifted easily into the air, gained altitude and swooped forward on a long slant in the direction of Acapulco.

Pete turned and called over his shoulder. "Where to?"

Tony and Steve went forward and leaned over the seats of the pilots.

"Toward Acapulco, but cut behind the city along the hills," said Steve. "We want to find the highway to Mexico City and then follow it for a while."

"Has this something to do with the kidnapping?" asked Bill, the young copilot.

"Right. And if we find what we're looking for, we may have some action." Tony, raising his voice to be heard above the clatter of the aircraft, described the mission, the highway, the trail leading off to the right through a possible canyon, then a shack and the possibility that McGowan was being held there by men who were undoubtedly armed.

"Better get out my thirty-eight then," said Pete. He jerked his thumb over his shoulder. "It's in that compartment there. Just pull on the tab." He seemed pleased. "It's loaded, but the safety's on."

Tony found the revolver, inspected the chamber, then took Steve aft to the card table. "Let's have yours," he said. "I'll give you a five-minute lecture. Then it's up to you." He demonstrated loading and simulated firing.

"If I aim at a sombrero, I might possibly hit a foot." Steve regarded the weapon with distaste.

He rummaged behind the elegant little bar, found a plastic bag and stuffed the roll of pesos into it.

When they returned to the cockpit, Pete pointed out a black ribbon of road curling over the hills. They flew at several thousand feet, could see cars toiling around the curves like busy ants. Houses made of corrugated metal, stone or adobe swarmed over the hills. To their left was the glistening bay of Acapulco and the ring of waterfront hotels lancing the sky.

"There's your highway to Mexico City," said Pete.

"Okay. Just follow it inland," Steve directed. "Our first landmark is a river, then a few kilometers further on, a village with thatched roofs."

The sky was cloudless, burnished almost white by the intense afternoon sun. The helicopter flew like some clumsy antediluvian creature, shaking and snorting. They passed over a lush valley, thick with foliage and bursting with color, that signaled the presence of water.

They spotted the river, a thin brown rope coiling through a rocky riverbed. Months had passed since the rains and the river had shrunk to a sliver of its maximum width. In a splash of color near the highway, they could distinguish women washing clothes and spreading bright garments over the rocks to dry. Just beyond was the village, a cluster of thatched roofs.

"Okay, our next marker is the highway zigzagging up a mountain, then a series of curves going down."

A minute later, Bill pointed ahead. The ribbon of macadam wound upon itself. Near a sharp curve, four cars crawled behind a truck.

"Yep." Steve leaned over the copilot's seat. "Next, a couple of kilometers further on, a small church with a couple of houses near it."

They saw the white cross almost immediately. "Now no houses near the highway for about ten kilometers," said Steve. "Then we'll see the town of Tierra Colorada. Just this side of it should be a house standing by itself to the left of the toll road. It's opposite a gravel road leading to a barn."

They flew several minutes without seeing a dwelling, then a town spread below and ahead of the aircraft. Tony, looking down to the left, said: "There's the house. We've flown past it."

Pete banked the craft in a slow turn, heading back toward the blazing western sun. They all saw the house now, almost hidden by trees. Opposite, across the highway, the brown soil seemed scarred. Pete circled again, lowering the craft as he turned, and they saw that the blemish was a gravel road.

"There's the barn!" Steve said. "Okay, now the trail. . . . Yeah, there. See it?"

The trail looped and dipped beneath them like a tiny brown thread. The chopper hovered less than a thousand feet aboveground. As they approached a rugged pass with a mountain on either side, they saw a deep, rocky cut. The thread of the trail disappeared.

"That must be the canyon." Steve peered ahead. "Right. There's the trail again."

Southeast of the gorge, the path reappeared, snaking upward in a bewildering series of haphazard loops like a string blown by the wind. Then the trail divided into scraggly lines, one veering ahead and the others twisting off at sharp angles into the embracing mountains.

"Take the middle one," said Steve. "It figures."

The treeless landscape below them looked bleak and forbidding. The harsh sunlight glinted on great boulders, pockmarks of earth lay in shallow shadows and little whirlpools of dust swept across the barren land like dancing funnels. The trail twisted upward, then flattened out. They were above a broad, rugged plateau, perhaps a mile in diameter.

"There it is!" Steve pointed. A small tan structure, roofed in brown tile, appeared as no more than a protrusion on the flat expanse. A cluster of stunted trees and bushes stood near the house. A dusty green line surrounded the house. Within seconds, they saw that it was cactus, planted to shape a fence. In a lean shadow thrown by the cactus hedge stood four horses. They started, rearing their heads and pawing the ground, at the clattering overhead.

"Look." Steve pointed again. "There's a guy standing out front."

They caught a glimpse of a wide-brimmed hat, a blur of an upturned face. Then the figure ran back to the house, disappearing beneath the tile roof which extended beyond the building to form a veranda.

"Okay," said Pete. "Let's wander around and see where we can put down."

He guided the chopper upward again to fifteen hundred feet, then swung into a wide circle around the plateau, the craft tilting inward. The blades thrashed, the helicopter shuddered and shadows flashed through the cockpit as they turned toward, then away from the sun.

"That spot ought to do it." Pete turned the craft into a tighter circle, then leveled off.

The blue-and-red helicopter hovered awkwardly for a moment, then flopped toward the earth like a duck shot on the wing. It bumped the ground as dust boiled upward.

The unpainted adobe house stood perhaps four hun-

dred yards away, its rickety veranda visible from behind
the protecting boulder where the helicopter had come
to rest. The blades revolved slowly, the engine idling.
The sudden heat was overwhelming.

Thursday, 2:20 p.m.

Jim McGowan noticed the difference in sound the moment he heard the first faint droning. He had marked
the far-off whine of airplanes a number of times that
day and surmised that they were commercial jets powering upward for the flight from Acapulco to Mexico City.
This was a single, tentative hum at first, then a slowly
amplifying growl as though a huge bucket of nails were
being swung overhead.

He and Chucho had been laboring through a ragged
thicket of English, Chucho lolling on the bed and Jim
sitting in the leather chair, when they heard the distant
sound. As the volume swelled, they both looked upward
reflexively. When the aircraft clattered overhead in a
narrowing circle, Chucho bolted to the window, tore
a corner of the burlap sacking from a nail and peered
out.

He turned to Jim, his eyes blinking above his mask,
and made a quick, whirling motion above his head.

"*Sí.*" Jim nodded. Juices began pumping instantly.
"A helicopter. . . . Is it painted? You know, colors?"

Chucho looked out again. "*Azul y rojo. Como se
dice? . . .* Blue, no? And . . . *No sé la palabra.*"

"Red?"

"*Sí sí. Eso.* Red."

An Arc-Horn helicopter. Jim's thoughts churned divisively. Rescue or peril? He stared at Chucho through new eyes. Suddenly his new-found friend reverted to his original shape—the enemy.

Jim knew that if he lived, he would remember it as his longest day. He had awakened near eight o'clock to see sunlight brushing the fragile, plaster limbs of the bloody Christ. He had dreamed of Meg, Carol and Connie in an elusive scene beside the Westhampton pool. Meg, in those slippery wisps of recollection upon awakening, had seemed to fade away like a ghost into the shrubbery. A strange posse, composed of Jim, Dave Moyer, Gwen, Meg's Aunt Lil, Tony Percevale and Senator Ireland, beat the bushes in search of her. Jim found her sitting beneath a weeping birch, composed and contented. She resisted his entreaties, shaking her head when he asked her to walk back to the house with him. Then, curiously, they were both blindfolded and Meg was accompanying him willingly, sometimes following, sometimes leading. They returned to find the posse ringed about the barbecue pit, where Carol and Connie were broiling steaks. No one, not even the twins, paid the slightest attention to the couple. Meg and Jim removed their blindfolds and sat apart, musing, eying each other in shared wonder.

The adobe room with the single whitewashed wall was cool and dry at first, dark only in the corners where daylight, filtering through the window sacking, failed to penetrate. Chucho fetched more beans and tortillas, along with acrid black coffee, for breakfast. Later, at Jim's insistence, he emptied the stinking bucket which now held feces as well as urine.

The room became warm, then stifling hot, as the sun climbed, beating directly on the uninsulated tile roof. Jim's hours fell into two distinct segments, one in which he was alone with his pitching thoughts and the other when Chucho, a strangely likable ruffian, used one excuse or another to come in and talk.

When alone, Jim's mind swung like a pendulum between Meg and Top Court, tracing the old, familiar arc. But there was a change that he did not fully comprehend in the first hours. Meg expanded in time and space while Top Court and Arc-Horn contracted. He became aware of a new feeling for Meg, comforting, trusting, yet streaked with tremors of discovery. In the dream, he and Meg had been together, content if still wary, and had shared the feeling of a distance between themselves and their friends. As he paced the packed-earth floor or slouched in the leather chair, he felt Meg close to him, an easy warmth, an aura of fulfillment. Several times the feeling became a yearning, a sharp, almost painful desire to hold her, to stroke her, to swing into the rhythm of love.

On the contrary, the office on Lexington Avenue, the plant at Doylestown, the bustle of business, the coming deal for the tennis ranch, the addictive trappings—power, decision, tension, money, status—all withered in the swelling heat. Meg might be a living presence in this mountain shack but the frenetic, complex world of Top Court seemed eons distant, less real than fantasy. If Top Court was loosening its old grip on him, the cause, he knew, could be traced to his single decision that morning.

It came to him in one lucid flash. If he lived, he was through forever with Arc-Horn.

Whatever the understanding between Praeger and Davidson—and he had puzzled over this to no conclusion—the voice of Gwen, pleading and vulnerable, on Davidson's hidden tape recorder, had snapped his nine-year adventure with Arc-Horn. The theft from his safe, the incidents of bribery and burglary, merely added distaste to revulsion. Gwen's haunting voice blotted out everything, from Hugo's bursts of generosity to the 100,000 additional Arc-Horn shares that would be McGowan's next year under the terms of his management contract. Here in the shack, the four or five million dollars he would give up seemed a small price to pay, especially, he noted wryly, for a man who'd still have about ten million left, counting all his assets. But the fact was, nickels or millions, he could no longer live with the corporation. And if McGowan and Arc-Horn were finished, then his twenty-seven-year love affair with Top Court was over as well. Top Court belonged to tens of thousands of Arc-Horn stockholders, to Praeger, to Sugimoto, to the Bergers, Sukhsvastis and Kimballs, not to Jim McGowan. The realization brought great relief to him in the stuffy room with its faded images of the martyred Savior and President. Like a man who sheds a provocative but demanding mistress Jim could feel a loving weight lift from his shoulders. In every sense but one, he was a free man.

He was, of course, a prisoner in body, a fact that shoved rudely through his thoughts each time that Chucho opened the flimsy door. He came with breakfast, with soap, towel and a tin basin slopping with water. He came to carry out what he had brought, to empty the odorous bucket, to check the time with Jim's watch, to tell him of the next newscast and, finally, just to talk. He seemed obsessed with his charge. He would lumber in, his brown eyes shining above the absurd gingham mask, eager for fractured conversation. The drooping cloth, which Chucho kept knotted behind his head, became Jim's symbol of hope. The mask signaled that Chucho hid his identity against the hour when they released McGowan. If the mask should disappear—who bothers about what a corpse has seen? At each entrance, Jim's eyes flicked instantly to the bandana, dreading that this might be the moment when he would see an unmasked face.

Chucho, it turned out, knew more English than he had hinted at last night. Each time he came into the room, he revealed more of himself. He had worked two years on a west Texas ranch as a *bracero* in his youth and it intrigued him to renew his acquaintance with the barbarous language of the Anglos. He tried out more English words as the morning drifted by, mouthing laboriously at his task. As a pupil, he was more willing than apt, a friendly, naïve, curious man. He had an engaging openness and a desire to please. Jim heard the English translation of the bulletin about Praeger's announcement at the Mixteca—Arc-Horn

would not pay the million-dollar ransom demanded by
Los Hijos de Zapata—through the adobe wall, but Chucho hurried to the room to enlighten him further. Los
Hijos was now a standing joke between them since Chucho had confided, as best he could, that he was a businessman working for his share of the fifty thousand dollars to be paid upon completion of the McGowan
assignment. Just what completion implied, Jim could
only speculate.

By a combination of deft questioning and Chucho's
real or seeming guilelessness, Jim had learned something
of his abduction. It seemed that about a week ago, Miguel,
Chucho's occasional confederate, newly hired as a driver
by some American businessmen who would hold a convention at the Mixteca, came to him with a glittering
proposition. If he and Pepito would locate themselves
at El Burrito, a cantina on the airport highway about
a half mile from the connecting road to the Mixteca,
they would be paid five hundred pesos (forty dollars)
a day to do nothing.

Agreeing with alacrity, they slept in a back room
of the bar and lounged about the premises, day and
night, eating and drinking. The only stipulations were
that they could not leave the immediate area of El Burrito
and they could not get drunk, a stricture that Chucho
thought highly unreasonable. It was understood that they
were ready for any venture, licit or illicit, which their
unknown employers might ask them to undertake, but
the days passed without orders. Every morning at eight-
thirty Miguel came with their wages for the previous
day and soon they quit wondering why they were paid
to amuse themselves with the *chicas* who frequented
the bar. Probably a whim of some crazy gringos, for
who else but Americans would so waste good money
on Chucho and Pepito?

Then, about seven o'clock last night, Miguel roared
up in the Mercedes, spraying dust like a windstorm as
he stopped. Standing behind the car, he informed them
that they were to go at once to a spot on Farallon, about
a hundred and fifty meters up the street from the Diana

fountain, and wait for him. When he arrived in about an hour, they were to throw themselves in the back seat, pinion a passenger who would be riding there and help Miguel take him to an undisclosed destination.

The price for the mission staggered Chucho and Pepito. Miguel promised that when the job was finished, in four or five days perhaps, they would each be paid a hundred thousand pesos, or eight thousand dollars, a fortune. Never in an entire year had Chucho earned that much, even when he worked the bull rings and football games as a pickpocket. Miguel handed them each a thousand-peso note on account—Chucho showed it proudly to Jim as he talked—and then drove away at high speed. Both men went to the back room for their guns, took one of three taxis waiting outside El Burrito, got out about a half a kilometer before the Diana fountain on the Costera Alemán, then strolled to their station on Farallon, a dark place between two street lights.

Jim could not be sure he had the story straight. He pieced it together over several hours while he and Chucho dug out matching English and Spanish words like miners toiling with picks. But whatever the precise details, Jim got the clear idea that Chucho and Pepito became sudden kidnappers after a period of lolling indolence at El Burrito.

If Chucho knew more, he was an accomplished actor, for his ignorance as to future plans seemed unfeigned. Actually, he appeared baffled and at times worried. All he seemed to know for certain was that the third man in the dwelling, the one with the commanding voice, went by the name of El Profanador. He was, so it was said, Miguel's cousin and he eked out his living at animal stealing and thievery. Chucho had only met him twice before and he didn't trust him. But as to the whereabouts of Miguel, when the business with Jim would be "completed," how El Profanador fit into the action or who put up the promised fifty thousand dollars, Chucho had only vague surmises. *Quién sabe, Cheem?* . . . He did know that the business would end when an unknown person or persons came to the hut with the proper password. Miguel had told him the phrase and he had relayed it to El Profanador. That, of course, was a trade secret as such an accomplished businessman as McGowan would appreciate. . . . The smell of the barnyard about him? Ah, that he was happy to divulge to his new friend, Cheem. Behind El Burrito was a pen for hogs and the back room stank day and night of pig shit. Pepito preferred to drown the odor in cologne.

No sooner had he established the colors of the helicopter than Chucho ran from the room. The door swayed, creaking on its hinges. He had forgotten to close it.

Jim could hear the rumble of an engine and the swishing sound of a helicopter's blades. He pulled back the flap of burlap at the window, yanking it free from two more nails.

His hasty glance from the window last night had given Jim a vague sense of his surroundings. Now his sunlit field of vision was fairly wide, perhaps fifty or sixty degrees when he craned his neck in either direction. He saw baking, dusty soil, strewn with rocks, and a fence-like barrier of living cactus plants. Above the cactus, he could see a far mountain and a brilliant white-blue sky that dazzled the eyes. To the left, about a quarter of a mile from the house, stood a huge boulder, shimmering in heat waves. Each fraction of a second the tip of a helicopter blade flashed into view from behind the rock. The chopper had come to rest to the rear of the shielding boulder.

Suddenly, a streak of color, tan and green. A figure, crouched low, ran swiftly from a giant boulder and dove behind a smaller rock about forty yards nearer the house and further to the right. Dust kicked up by the dash settled slowly. For several minutes there was no other movement and only two sounds, a wheezing snort from an invisible horse and the steady grumble of the idling helicopter engine.

Then, from behind the rock, came a splatter of shouted Spanish. Jim felt a surge of excitement. It was Tony

Percevale's voice. No mistaking it. Tony, thank God. And who else?

An answering shout rang from the next room, harsh, commanding, clearly a question.

Silence, lengthening. Jim began to sweat. Heat washed through the window as if from an oven. Then, in a loud voice, Tony asked the oddest question Jim had ever heard from his friend.

"Hey, Jim! What the hell's the password?" A bantering inflection rode a wave of apprehension.

Should he answer? Millions of brain and nerve cells jostled one another, spilling chemical changes from cell to cell in that miraculous chain reaction, surpassing the speed of light, that is called thought. What the mind weighed, selected and discarded in that sliver of time, no computer could evaluate, but it was an instant in which Jim knew he was worth more money alive than dead.

He took the risk, shouting through the window. "I don't know, Tony. . . . I'm okay, but watch it. Three guys here, all with guns." It came out as a weird shriek that left him trembling.

Then Jim could feel energy coursing through him like quick throbs from a pump, the same sensation he had felt just before he smashed Chalmers Davidson in the face. There was wild exhilaration, fear, joy and a sense of being vibrantly alive in every muscle and tissue. He snapped around toward the door and waited with feral wariness.

Boots pounded in the hallway and at once Chucho filled the narrow doorway, dirty T shirt, dust-streaked jeans, the mask oddly askew over the bridge of his nose. He held the weapon in his hand this time. It pointed directly at Jim's chest, a dark circle at the end of a long, thin barrel.

"No talk. . . . You talk, I kill." Chucho's voice was firm, but the singsong inflection might be rendering a mundane report on the weather. Not a hostile warning, certainly. Jim stood tensely, his arms at his sides.

Chucho motioned with the pistol to the clump of serapes at the foot of the bed. "Sit!" Jim took two steps, eased himself down on the mattress. The gun's muzzle fascinated him. He stared at it, noting each blur of movement.

Silence again except for the helicopter engine drumming like a lone irrigation pump in the desert. The heat held the adobe room in a vise. Even the cool earth floor was becoming warm. A fly cruised along Chucho's sweating forehead and Chucho swiped at it with his free hand.

Tony's voice sounded through the window, high-pitched, loud, speaking Spanish slowly, enunciating with care. Each word drilled through space. It was a long speech.

"Jim," called Tony after a pause. "I said that if they'll release you, they will get twenty-five thousand pesos in a plastic sack. If they refuse, we will call in Mexican forces from the chopper's radio. . . . Do not try to answer."

Apparently Chucho had caught the drift of the English. He nodded to Jim as if confirming the translation.

Feet shuffled on the floor of the adjoining room, then El Profanador replied in his curious, staccato half-shout, firing words like a machine gun.

The odd dialogue lasted through minutes that seemed like hours. Tony barked at the house and El Profanador rattled at the boulder, the exchanges cleaving the torpid air and now and then echoing against some nearby rock hill or cliff. Both voices pulsed with command, but El Profanador's seemed querulous at times and once explosively scornful. Jim sensed that negotiations were heading toward an impasse. Tony uttered a single sentence. El Profanador responded harshly: *"No!"*

"No es Mexicano, su amigo? You friend?" Chucho's question evinced genuine interest in Percevale's nationality.

Jim knew that a talkative Chucho was less dangerous than a silent one. Talk disarmed, led into unexpected byways that might be exploited.

"No. . . . What country do you think? . . . Guess."

Chucho shook his head. Jim repeated slowly, Chucho

stepping forward to hear better. He stood inside the room, slightly to the right of the door.

"Ah, Chileno, no?"

"No. Guess again."

Chucho's brow furrowed as he thought.

Outside, Tony's voice again, shouting. A new offer? The answer from the house was wandering, inconclusive. The voices merged.

Chucho cocked his head, first to one side, then the other, attempting to catch the exchange. At that moment, the busy fly dove from the rafters and made a buzzing pass at Chucho's right ear. Chucho involuntarily raised his right arm to brush off the assailant. For a split second, the pistol pointed upward, and in that fragment of time, Jim acted.

In one flowing movement, he pressed his feet against the dirt floor, then uncoiled like a spring. He leaped across the few feet separating him from Chucho and brought him down with a flying tackle. An instant replay would have shown Jim's head ramming into Chucho's groin, his arms encircling the body and both men falling to the floor. As Chucho fell, his hand thumped against the ground, loosening his grip on the pistol. It slid several feet on the shiny, packed earth.

Both men kicked, trying to unscramble themselves and reach the weapon. Jim, on top, had the best of it. He tore himself from the arm that Chucho had flung about his shoulders, wrenched backward, lunged to the side and reached the gun with his right hand. His fingers closed on the butt. With a final kick which struck Chucho in the thigh, he freed himself and heaved to his feet.

Now the pistol pointed down at Chucho as Jim's fingers slid to the trigger. Chucho lay on his back, his brown eyes full of dismay. Once again, trust had been betrayed. He brought his hands up slowly as if to shield himself.

"Get up." Jim commanded softly, motioning with his free hand. Then irony took over with a phrase Chucho could not mistake. "You talk, I kill."

The shouting match in Spanish was still rocketing

back and forth between Tony and El Profanador. Had the men in the next room heard the voiceless struggle? He listened, straining, as he kept the gun aimed at Chucho. Apparently not, for he could hear Pepito talking and a demurring growl from El Profanador. They were arguing. Another burst from Tony. It had the sting of a warning. An ultimatum?

Chucho got to his feet, raised his hands above his head without being asked. What to do now? Jim's mind grappled with the unknown floor plan of the house. It had but two rooms, he believed, with a kitchen to the rear. A short hallway ran from the main room past Jim's door. He was sure it led to a side exit, for he had heard Chucho clump in that direction when he emptied the toilet pail. If he and Chucho moved to the hallway, they could not turn left. That way led to the room where Pepito and El Profanador were talking. Okay, to the right then.

Jim motioned with the gun for Chucho to turn. He grasped Chucho's wide belt in the back. He guided him slowly so that Chucho edged sideways into the hallway like a crab. Jim poked once with the pistol to show he meant business. Chucho started, raised his hands higher. Jim ducked behind his hostage in a half-crouch.

He shot a quick glance over his shoulder. About ten feet away, at the end of the dark, windowless hall, was a door. The only obstruction was a large can resting near it.

"Quiet!" Jim whispered. "No noise. You talk, I kill."

They walked slowly backward, Jim tugging at Chucho's belt. Once Chucho's foot dragged, a scraping noise, and Jim jabbed his back with the pistol. They retreated like clumsy crustaceans. Now they were almost at the door.

Clang! A sharp, clear, metallic noise. Goddam it. He had side-stepped to avoid the can—a five-gallon gasoline tin, he guessed—but Chucho's heel struck it.

An exclamation in the front room. Then a huge shape filled the other end of the obscure hallway. A hand lifted. It held an object. Jim circled Chucho's stomach with his gun arm, aimed the pistol at the figure.

"No, no." A frenzied cry from Chucho directed at the men standing in the hallway. *"No tires. Soy Chucho."*

Jim felt his rump touch the door. He pushed backward, striking the door with his shoulders. It held. He fumbled with his left hand, found the doorknob. The door opened.

They stumbled out backward in the garish sunlight. Jim was blinded for a moment. He blinked rapidly. He heard quick, cautious footsteps. He chanced a glance behind him. The fence of dusty cactus stood about fifteen feet away with a gap to the left. He twisted, trying to line his back up with the opening.

"Tony." He shouted as loudly as he could. "Coming out. . . . Don't shoot. . . . Got a guy with me." The fright in his voice, an eerie, scratchy sound, astounded him. In his body, all he could feel was the furious pumping of energy, a shapeless power.

He pulled at the belt, moving faster now. Their groping feet raised a trail of dust, scraped stones, kicked a rusty tin can, skidded on a decaying melon rind. Something pierced Jim's skin above the left wrist. From the corner of his eye he saw the cactus, veered to the left. They had reached the slit in the fence. He pulled Chucho through after him.

A man was clearly visible in the side doorway, a large, masked man with a shock of graying hair, a ragged, short-sleeved blue shirt and dark trousers. He had a hand gun in front of him. It was pointed at Chucho.

"Pay no attention, Jim." It was Tony's strong voice. "No danger if you keep coming as you are." He managed to sound both authoritative and comforting. "We'll talk you right back to the chopper. It's maybe four hundred meters behind you. . . . Easy does it. . . . Okay, angle to your right now, just a little. . . . That's it."

They were about twenty yards beyond the ring of cactus when El Profanador appeared in the opening. He shouted a new command. Tony yelled back.

"Don't worry, Jim," said Tony. "He knows I've got him covered. I've got a clear line on him."

Now he heard another voice. "I'll take over the directions, Tony." For God's sake! Steve Cooper. Who else was in the helicopter? The noise of the idling engine sounded somewhat closer and he could hear the soft swish of rotating blades.

"Straight back, straight back," called Steve. "Now a bit to your left. You've got a rock behind you. . . . Good, that's it. Only about three hundred yards to go, man."

Jim had the weird sensation that he was a pilot without instruments, being talked down to the runway by voice radio. But there was no soupy overcast to thwart him, only a blazing sun and a wasteland of dust, rocks and seared earth. He saw only a few scraggly trees and shrubs. Chucho grunted. Jim could feel the tremor of fear in the Mexican's body and his own right arm, protruding beyond Chucho's waist, began to tire.

A puff of dust flowered several feet in front of them and at once he heard the crack of El Profanador's gun. He had shot at them! It was the first time in his life that Jim had been a target for a bullet. The irrelevancy and the injustice overwhelmed him.

A second later dust spurted at El Profanador's feet as another gun fired. Tony screamed Spanish toward the cactus barrier. Then silence save for the clumsy backward shuffle of feet and the churning of the waiting helicopter. Fear coursed through Jim as if from an injection. His muscles ached with fright, but he kept moving backward on quivering legs.

"I told him if he did that again, he'd be dead."

El Profanador ducked behind the cactus.

Tony loosed another speech, again speaking with deliberation. After he finished, El Profanador reappeared in the opening. He tossed his gun to the ground. He spoke only a few words.

"That's it, Jim," Tony called. "We've got a deal. . . . Just turn around and walk forward, but keep that

guy with you going backward. . . . Careful. We don't
know about the third man."

Jim turned halfway around, but kept his gun aimed
toward the slit in the cactus. The huge, pitted boulder,
white as snow under the relentless sun, stood about
two hundred yards distant. Long blades revolved above
it and to the left Jim saw the tail of the helicopter, striped
red and blue. Steve Cooper peered from behind the
rock. Jim could see a thatch of wiry brown hair with
sun-bleached streaks, the angular, tanned face, a comforting grin.

"Just walk on home, baby," Steve called. "You've got
it made."

Jim could see that Steve held a hand gun, somewhat
awkwardly, he thought. He pulled hard on Chucho's
belt, dragging him forward like a sack of grain. He tried
to walk faster, bending to his task. Dust billowed in
their wake. When he was less than fifty yards from the
boulder, he saw Tony leave the haven of the smaller
rock and walk cautiously toward the chopper, keeping
his gun trained toward the house.

At last Jim was behind the boulder. He let go of
Chucho's belt and stood teetering, gawking at Steve.
His legs were rubbery and he could feel his jaw tremble.
Suddenly the energy that had powered him rushed away
like water from a broken dam. He felt limp, light-headed
and very weak. He thought he might faint, but Steve
threw his arms around him in a hug of reassurance.

Chucho stood watching them, his eyes above the mask
darting apprehensively from man to man. Then he
glanced downward. On the ground was a plastic bag,
stuffed with bills.

"It's theirs under the deal," said Steve.

Jim gave his gun to Steve, reached down for the bag
and handed it to Chucho. The Mexican accepted the
sack as formally as he might a diploma, bowing and
murmuring his thanks.

"You're not a bad guy, Chucho." Jim turned him
around, faced him toward the adobe house and gave

him a gentle push. *"Adiós.* Next time demand your money in advance."

Chucho walked off, slowly at first, glancing behind him every few steps. Satisfied he would not be shot in the back, he broke into a trot, then began running, holding the money like a sackful of eggs.

Tony backed into the narrow space between the helicopter and the boulder, enveloped Jim in a warm embrace. His gun thumped against Jim's back.

"Okay, up and out!" Tony shouted toward the cockpit. He pushed Jim up the short flight of steps. Steve and Tony climbed in behind him. Bill, the copilot, was waiting. He reached for the button that would fold the steps into the fuselage.

Jim, on an impulse, tossed Chucho's gun to the ground. "I liked the guy," said Jim when Tony started to protest. "Maybe he'll find it." The door closed.

The craft lifted from the ground. The metal shell rattled, the gunned engine rumbled with power and the chopper lunged off in a great upward swoop. Jim bent to a window, eager to see the place where he had been held captive for some fifteen hours. The house appeared to be little more than an angular protrusion on flat, barren land that stretched between treeless mountains. He saw the clump of dusty cactus fence around the house, the horses in the rear. His last glimpse, as the adobe shack shriveled in size like an object seen through the wrong end of a telescope, was of three men running toward the horses.

Tony tapped his shoulder. "This will fix you up." He held out a plastic cup, half filled. Jim sniffed. Scotch. He took a swallow, wiped his lips, grinned. The liquor worked through him quickly, a warm, friendly sensation. The trembling in his limbs eased and then gradually disappeared.

"Cut straight for the airport," Tony called forward over the clatter of the machine. "Full power, Pete."

They were skidding through a pass, mountains looming above them on either side.

"I think I've got it in sight already," Bill said. "We'll be on the ground in about fifteen minutes."

Steve, Tony and Jim all started to talk at once, each bursting with his news. Steve and Tony gave way, let the hostage tell his story. Jim talked fast, scattering facts and recollections like seed. Then Tony and Steve, interrupting each other continuously, told what had happened at the Mixteca—Meg was holding up well—at the airport, on the scorched earth behind that boulder. At first, El Profanador apparently thought the helicopter had been dispatched by his employers, but when Tony failed the password test, the big man with the shock of gray hair turned belligerent and scornful. Tony made a number of offers, all refused. What might have happened if Jim had not suddenly appeared, dragging the captive Chucho, Tony could only conjecture.

In the finale, Tony told El Profanador that if he would not shoot again, they would leave the twenty-five thousand pesos, would free Chucho and would say nothing to the authorities for three hours, giving the men time to make their getaway. Tony surmised that El Profanador knew many exits from the mountains, for they had seen cobwebbed trails from the air during their approach.

"Only Tony knows how to dress for a kidnapping." Jim laughed, his first since yesterday. Save for the dust on his expensive cordovans and soft lime slacks, Tony might have spent the afternoon in the clubhouse at the races. The copperish turtle-neck sweater fitted him fashionably in odd contrast to Steve's faded blue denim. Tony beat at his legs. He frowned at the spray of dust.

Tony straightened and glanced at his wristwatch. "The board meeting begins at four. We're in a squeeze for time. It's three-seventeen now. We don't know what will happen when Praeger raps the gavel, but we'll damn soon find out."

"Your idea is that we both go into the meeting together?"

"Sure. What else?"

"Hold it." Jim raised his hands. "I did some thinking

about that meeting back in the shack. It was just wild daydreaming then, but now . . . Suppose I could just walk in there unannounced at some critical point? And suppose at that moment nobody knew I was free?" Jim's speech quickened. "Anyway, I've got a plan that might work. To bring it off, Tony, you'll have to do some acting. Okay?"

"Anything you say today, Jim. Tomorrow's another story."

Jim leaned over Tony, supporting himself on the quivering metal skin of the aircraft. "All right, here's what we'll do." Tony and Steve listened closely, cocking their heads, straining to hear above the din of the helicopter.

When Jim finished, the chopper swooped into its approach to the Acapulco airport, where heat waves shimmered on the apron and a commercial jet thundered from a runway, fleeing the streaming pollution of its own engines.

The helicopter's steps fell open like a gaping jaw. Tony ran around the craft and to the Imperial, parked near the fence about eighty yards away. He drove the car back to the chopper, which shielded the automobile from the terminal. He unlocked the trunk of the black vehicle. McGowan trotted down the steps and climbed into the trunk. Tony slammed the lid.

With Tony at the wheel and Steve beside him, the Imperial rolled to the gate reserved for vehicles serving the fleet of Arc-Horn planes. Tony flashed his Arc-Horn identity pass for the two men at the gate, a blue-shirted Arc-Horn guard and a uniformed Mexican who doubled as customs and immigration officer.

"Just a hop over town," Tony said to the blue-shirt. He repeated in Spanish for the Mexican. Both men waved the car through the gate.

Tony hit seventy-five on the airport highway, braked for the turn into the wide avenue leading toward the Mixteca. Three motorcycles barred the hotel road. Helmeted policemen chatted beside their mounts.

"*Chingada,*" Tony swore. "We need money. I'm out."

Steve dug into the watch pocket of his sawed-off jeans, slid an American five-dollar bill across the seat.

"That's my last. If it's not enough, we've had it."

Tony placed his left hand on the window frame, the green bill peeping out from his fingers. A policeman strolled over.

"Gusto Más business in the city," Tony explained.

The patrolman inspected Tony and Steve, saw the green bill, palmed it with a crinkling sound, cleared his throat. He kicked up the metal guard rest of one of the motorcycles and wheeled it away, clearing an opening for the car.

Several hundred yards in front of the Mixteca's imposing portico, the service road branched to the left. Tony swung the car into the auxiliary road and drove at reduced speed to an unloading platform at the side of the hotel. No one was around. The siesta hour was not yet ended. Steve slipped out, walked to a passageway that led to the big service elevator. In a moment, Tony heard the whistle. He hustled to the rear of the car, unlocked the trunk. The lid flipped up. Jim uncoiled and reached for Tony's hand, pulling himself up.

Tony pointed the way and Jim walked swiftly past the trash cans and swollen bags of garbage, ducked into the hotel and followed the passageway. Steve waited by the open elevator, his hand on the holding button. Jim stepped in with Steve and the doors clanged shut.

Tony drove the Imperial back to the entrance to the Mixteca and parked it at the end of the long line of courtesy cars. Then, with an easy, leisurely stride, he walked up the steps, through the near-empty lobby.

Gilda, the red-haired entertainer, was waiting for an elevator. She wore a trim black pants suit and she was weaving slightly. When the doors opened, Tony stood aside to let her enter, but she hooked his arm.

"Any old port in a storm." She slurred the words. Her breath carried an odor of alcohol. She leaned heavily against him.

"Do you mind if I press the button for eleven?" Tony asked. "I'm late for a meeting."

"I'm late for life." Her smile sagged.

Tony pressed eleven. The doors closed and the elevator slid upward.

"Who's meeting what?"

"The Arc-Horn board."

"Old fat-ass Praeger, huh? . . . Well, the hell with him. What he doesn't know would fill a book. Maybe I'll barge in there and tell him what his slut from Rock Island is up to. . . . Yeah, maybe . . ."

The elevator stopped and the doors opened. Gilda lurched forward. Tony pulled her back.

"Take it easy," he said. "You could use some sleep before the banquet."

"Hmm. I guess you're right."

As Tony stopped out, she poked at a lower button and the doors closed again. Tony walked off down the corridor toward the Arc-Horn conference room, where two security guards paced on the maroon carpeting.

When the service elevator carrying Jim and Steve reached the seventh floor, Steve peered into the corridor. No one was in sight. He beckoned to Jim and they walked swiftly down the hall. Steve had Tony's key out by the time they reached 740. When the door closed behind them, Steve fastened the inside safety chain. Jim stretched, facing toward the open balcony on Tony's ocean-side suite. God, he felt good, just breathing that free, salty air. He noticed the telephone on the bar and started toward it. Meg. Then he caught himself. For the plan to work, not even Meg should know.

Steve saw him eying the telephone. "She's not in your rooms anyway. Meg's at the bank, stacking up a million bucks, no less. Jesus, if El Profanador only knew."

"Could I use a shower!" Jim saw himself in the gilt-framed mirror. His face and arms were splotched with grime, his golden shirt wrinkled and covered with dirt, his once gleaming white slacks a dismal gray. He hoisted his trousers and saw the flecks of dried blood above his scuffed moccasins.

"You're going to the meeting like that?"

Jim nodded.

"You'll blow their minds."

"I hope so." Jim begain to pace the room, trying to readjust, to order his thoughts, to prepare. As he walked, he became aware of his ankles. They ached, a dull, sickly throbbing.

Thursday, 4:15 p.m.

Tony's air was one of apology as he nodded to his friends on the board and walked briskly to the left of the big horseshoe table and slipped into his seat between Gwen Piggott and Deutsche-Mannheim's Helmut von Weise.

"Sorry, Hugo," he said, "but it couldn't be helped. Intestinal trouble. My first in a long while in Mexico."

The full board was in attendance save for the empty chair at Jim McGowan's place. Large white note pads, sharpened yellow pencils and water glasses, the tools of empire, rested before each director. John Lindquist, the numbers genius who doubled as secretary, was already jotting down notes.

Hugo Praeger, an anxious Buddha in his vast, hand-carved armchair, presided at the center of the horseshoe above the corporate logo, the bright blue earth being rocketed to destiny by the myriad blast-off services of Arc-Horn International. To Praeger's right by the customary protocol sat Lindquist and Nicholas Cala-brese, to his left Chalmers Davidson and Bernard Hirsch. Eighteen presidents of subsidiaries, ranked as usual by the size of revenues, ringed the table in an atmosphere at once somber and tense. A stranger unaware of the kidnapping might think the board's major ally, money perhaps, had just passed away.

"Qué molestia, Antonio." Praeger smiled faintly. "That's one excuse we can understand." In the circumstances, Praeger withheld his usual tart reminder that the first duty of an Arc-Horn director was to be on time for meetings.

"Tony, since Nate Berger also showed up late, I'll just brief you both on where we stand, what?" Praeger folded his hands on the table top. The late-afternoon sunlight poured into the conference room, glinting on his blue-trimmed gold shirt. "We've just been through this terrible McGowan business. We're cut up emotionally, as you are, but as directors we're at a loss as to what steps to take. To put our discussion in a nutshell, we have no new leads and we're not at all satisfied with the vigor of the Mexican investigation. So . . ."

Tony leaned toward Gwen and whispered. "Jim's okay. He's in the hotel. Don't let on. Just follow my lead."

For an answer, Gwen nudged Tony with her elbow.

"So I've promised Meg McGowan," Praeger continued, "that if nothing has happened by nine a.m. tomorrow, she'll be free to read the ransom instructions and take what steps she wishes. As a matter of fact, I understand she's at a bank now in Acapulco arranging for the money."

"What does the ransom note say?" asked Nate Berger.

"Actually not much more than the deadline and where to bring the money." Praeger turned to Davidson. "Nothing else of consequence, was there, Chalmers?"

"No."

"What's the deadline?" asked Tony.

Davidson pursed his lips. "I'm sorry, Tony. As Jim's good friend, you're entitled to the information. However, I've given my word to General Sandoval. We can't disclose details of the note."

Praeger tapped his gavel softly. "Much as I hate to do business without Jim, I'm afraid we'll have to move on to the quarterly agenda. I'll be more than glad to discuss any ideas you may have about Jim and the kidnapping at the conclusion of the meeting. I know Tony will want to talk it over with me, so anyone who has a definite idea to contribute is welcome to join us. . . . Okay, let's go to the agenda now. Number One is the matter of the pension fund. John, will you explain that?"

Lindquist began and ended with a number. Arc-Horn's pension fund was sound, but inflation had ravaged hopes, so that retiring employees had barely enough to live on. It was proposed that contributions be increased and pensions raised. After a desultory discussion, Paulo Hochschild, seconded by Jules Amarel, moved that the boosts be ordered. The motion carried unanimously.

Similar unanimity greeted the next six proposals. The directors were in a mood to move swiftly through noncontroversial items.

"That brings us to Number Eight, Green Tree," said Praeger. "Chalmers has been the work horse on this project, so let's give him the floor for some background."

Davidson, sporting a purplish bruise on his left cheekbone, stepped to a large metal-framed flip chart behind him. He grasped a pointer, took hold of a corner of the first sheet of paper, started to lift it, then hesitated.

"Before going into Items Eight and Nine, let me remind you of the climate in which we consider these attractive projects today." He dropped the paper and stood holding the pointer like a spear at rest. "No need to review our setbacks this week. They all add up to a reduced cash flow with consequent renewed pressure from Hal Frascella at First Merchants for a seat on the board and refinancing of our big loan at much higher interest. As you know, Arc-Horn closed at forty-two and three-eighths today despite Masuo's magnificent gesture at noon. We've dropped almost six dollars during our stay here at the Mixteca."

Davidson did not need to stress the point. The combined personal holdings of the attentive directors had shrunk by tens of millions of dollars since the gala fiesta Sunday night.

"Of course, I've no doubt the market will react in time to the implications of this unfortunate abduction. It's no disrespect to Jim McGowan to consider the financial aspects of his kidnapping. As businessmen, that's our obligation. Now this ugly business has several bright spots, speaking in strict money terms, that I'm sure the fund managers will appreciate in the next few days. The kidnapping of a man as well known as Jim McGowan will force the Mexican government, at long last, to crush the terrorists who have harassed industry with their bombings, robberies and kidnappings in recent years. Stern government measures in the offing will be good for all business in this country, but especially for Arc-Horn. Remember, we have some two hundred million dollars invested in Mexico."

Davidson paused and surveyed his fellow directors. "Another plus for business is the blow the kidnapping deals to McGowan's friend Senator Ireland. Voters won't look kindly on a man who preaches forbearance, good will and a lowered military profile abroad and then sees his own friend seized by reckless revolutionaries."

Gwen whispered to Tony. "Even if he's right, that's frightfully bad taste at this hour."

Tony nodded. "A cold fish, that one."

"And, of course," Davidson added, "much as I regret the thought, we must recognize that Ireland's chances of nomination would evaporate completely if McGowan did not, er, unfortunately, manage to survive."

Tony and Gwen exchanged covert glances. My God, thought Tony, did Davidson expect Jim to be killed? Had someone planned it so that Jim could not "manage to survive"?

Praeger voiced his own discomfort. "All right, Chalmers, enough of that. Let's get to the projects."

"I was just trying to point out," said Davidson, "that the kidnapping news is much less bearish than it appeared at first glance. . . . But, of course, even when the market recovers, Arc-Horn still faces a cash squeeze brought on by the other setbacks. The proposals we're presenting for board approval today will, I firmly believe, eliminate such binds for a long time to come. Gentlemen, these two undertakings hold more profit potential for us than anything Arc-Horn has done since the acquisition of Nakamura, Limited."

He flipped back the covering sheet of the chart to reveal the picture of a tree, lush with green foliage, and a legend in red ink: "Promise of the Future." He flipped again. The next sheet carried the names Magna Mines Corp., Gusto Más, S.A., Hi-Western Corp., Uni-Land Corp. in bold green print. A third display disclosed objectives in gold lettering: minerals, lumber, crops, cattle, real estate sales. A fourth showed an aerial color photograph of the Amazon jungle, dense, impenetrable, darkly threatening. The fifth was an artist's conception of the man-wrought wonders to come: rolling green pastures, trim white houses, browsing cattle, a mining complex, all orderly, bountiful, familiar and snugly prosperous.

Davidson talked inspirationally as the pages flicked by. Green Tree would transform 200,000 acres of useless rain forest into a productive Garden of Eden, giving employment to 25,000 impoverished Brazilians, filling the holds of waiting freighters with iron, nickel, chrome, mica, tungsten, shipping thousands of tons of foodstuffs to the hungry people of the world—and yielding Arc-Horn $90,000,000 a year in profits.

Its companion undertaking, Neptune West, would remedy any number of shortages plaguing the industrialized world by a treasure of minerals sucked off the ocean floor, would benefit Mexico enormously, would advance the infant science of oceanology and each year would net Arc-Horn $40,000,000. While the eyes of his colleagues tended to glaze during the exposition of the glories to be visited on mankind, they snapped at the size of Arc-Horn profits.

"So there you are, gentlemen," Davidson concluded, "two opportunities we can't afford to miss. All that is needed is formal board approval as required under our private agreements with the Brazilian and Mexican governments."

As Davidson leaned his pointer against the chart, Praeger rapped once with the gavel. "All right, let's go to discussion. These are big and expensive undertakings, so I want your candid reactions. . . . First, is anybody flatly opposed?"

"I think the vote ought to be postponed," said Percevale.

"Postponed?" echoed Praeger.

"Impossible." Davidson was immediately embattled. "Any delay would wreck our timetable. Both governments are eager to go ahead at once. If we vacillate now, we could lose out entirely. Our competitors, don't forget, are . . ."

"Hold it, Chalmers," Praeger cut in. "I'm curious, Tony. Do you mean an indefinite postponement?"

"No, no. Just until we find out what happens to Jim. We could delay the vote a week, say, and hold a special meeting in New York." Tony glanced about the table, seeking to persuade. "It's just a simple courtesy to Jim. He's absent through no fault of his own and he ought to be allowed to speak his mind. He took a big interest in these projects and he told me he was opposed to both of them. So let's delay until Jim can be with us or until we get word . . ." He shrugged, leaving the thought unfinished.

"McGowan opposed!" Davidson seemed astonished. "I don't know what he said to you, Tony, but you must have misinterpreted him completely. McGowan favored both Green Tree and Neptune West."

"Oh, no, he didn't, Chalmers," said Gwen Piggott. "He was against them. He told me so."

Incredulity shadowed Davidson's patrician features like a passing cloud. Board members shifted about fitfully in their chairs. Praeger's eyes darted from his vice-president to Tony and Gwen. At a proper wake a dispute over the intentions of the deceased was unseemly.

"I don't know, of course, what Jim said to either of you." Davidson exuded patience and understanding. "I realize the present ordeal has been especially trying for you and other close friends of Jim and that strong feelings often tend to obscure the memory. I can only state that my own recollection is one hundred percent at variance with yours. Jim told me right in my own room on this floor yesterday evening that he hoped the board would give speedy and unanimous approval to Green Tree and Neptune West."

"What was his reasoning, Chalmers?" Praeger put the question as tonelessly as a trial judge.

"My memory is very clear on that," replied Davidson without hesitation. "Jim called me from Cal Silliman's office and asked to see me on a matter of urgency. I . . ."

"Sure." Tony chanced an oblique shot. "He wanted to find out who robbed his safe, didn't he?"

Davidson's sole reaction was involuntary. His fingers brushed the swelling on his cheekbone, then quickly slid away. He stared at Tony with a puzzled frown.

"Safe? I don't know what you're talking about. As for . . ."

"He had just found out," Tony interrupted, "that papers had been stolen from his safe. He was mad as hell."

Davidson wagged his head as if in confusion. "He never mentioned it to me. As a matter of fact, the only things on his mind were these resolutions. He came up to my room right after his call and got straight to the point." He turned to Praeger. "Jim said he thought the projects merited priority action on two counts—Arc-Horn profits and helping to meet the worldwide demand of minerals and food." He paused while his eyes swept around the room. "Actually, gentlemen, Jim McGowan felt so strongly about the undertakings that he asked for the honor of making the motions to approve."

Gwen was dumfounded. "Would you repeat that, please, Chalmers?"

"I said that Jim wanted to move board approval of both ventures."

Tony clutched at his belly. "Oh, no!" He stood up, grimacing. "I'm sorry, Hugo." He turned toward the door. "Please hold off a couple of minutes. I'll be right back."

Tony rushed across the room, yanked open the door and disappeared in the corridor.

The startled directors eyed one another. Gwen laughed. Praeger's chuckle became a guffaw. "Happens in the best of families," he said. "Can't blame the hotel. Our first case all week, what? As a matter of fact, I don't believe we've had a similar incident since the meeting on the *Arc Hornet* off Martinique a couple of years ago. Of course, that may have been ninety percent seasickness. That was you, wasn't it, Nate?"

Berger nodded. "Bad afternoon." The ulcerated Summit president sucked in his hollow cheeks, an act of memorium.

"Okay, let's take a breather until Tony comes back." Praeger hoisted himself from his oaken throne.

The scraping of chairs merged into the buzz of voices and occasional bursts of laughter. The mercantile warriors seemed relieved to substitute Percevale's temporary plight for McGowan's peril. Chalmers Davidson stood gazing through the balcony doors at the lowering sun. Sugimoto called to him from across the room, but Davidson did not hear. He was immersed in thought.

Tony brushed past two security guards, ran to the stairwell and pounded down the steps to the seventh floor. He rapped twice on the door of 740.

"Who is it?" Steve's voice.

"Tony."

The chain fastener slid back, the door opened and Tony walked past Steve. Jim was upending a glass at the bar.

"Don't worry. It's only water."

Tony gaped at his friend. After the washed, combed and scented Arc-Horn directors, Jim looked like an aging wino. Grime streaked his stubbled jaw, his clothes resembled a wad of dirty laundry and he walked toward Tony with a painful hobble.

"Christ, Jim, why didn't you wash up?"

"More impact, I hope." Jim grabbed Tony's elbow, propelling him toward the door. "Let's go. . . . What's the picture?"

As they hurried down the corridor, Tony sketched the scene in the Arc-Horn conference room. "So Davidson has painted himself into a corner."

"Let's keep him there." Jim was tensing himself for combat. "I just hope I don't hit the bastard again."

They walked up the stairs as rapidly as Jim's sore legs would permit. When they emerged on the eleventh floor, the security guards looked at Jim as they might at a ghost.

"Mr. McGowan!" One blue-shirted guard moved to open the door. Jim shoved him aside.

"I'll wait here," he whispered to Tony. "When I hear you say—let's see, er, oh what the hell, Chucho—I'll come in. . . . Chucho. . . . Say it loud."

"Got you." Tony entered as Jim placed himself behind the door.

Tony's colleagues were clustered about the horseshoe table, chatting in small groups. He flashed a self-deprecating smile, waved a circled thumb and forefinger and walked to his chair. Praeger rapped his gavel several times. As the directors settled in again, Davidson confidently grasped the pointer, his lance of battle. He aimed a brief, sympathetic smile at Percevale.

"You all right now, Tony?" asked Praeger.

"Okay." He managed a look of embarrassed relief and Gwen, who had caught his covert nod to her, thought that Antonio Percevale would make a more accomplished actor than some of Jake Apple's professional troupe.

"So where were we?" Tony looked inquiringly at Davidson. "What were you saying about Jim, Chalmers?"

Davidson nodded agreeably. "Yes, just to keep the thread of continuity, perhaps I should repeat." He seemed anxious to oblige. "McGowan yesterday evening asked for the honor of making the motion to approve Green Tree and Neptune West. Now, in view of this . . ."

"Chucho!" Tony raised his head and brought it down sharply. The sound reverberated. Many men thought that Percevale had sneezed and coughed simultaneously.

The door swung open. Jim McGowan walked in.

The silence was so profound that a gasp of astonishment by Sukit Sukhsvasti sounded like a ragged shout. Praeger gaped, then slowly wiped his brow. Davidson stood transfixed, clutching the upright pointer. John Lindquist, who had been scribbling on his pad, looked as if he'd just swallowed an indigestible number.

Jim walked to his empty chair beside Charles Holloway of Indo Deep Rig. He limped, dragging his right foot slightly. He settled deliberately in the armchair, brushed at his filthy shirt, drilled Davidson with a single glance, then looked about the table and grinned.

"Anyone for tennis?"

Jim might have ignited a land mine. An explosion of voices rushed out the balcony doors. Gwen leaped up, rushed around the table and threw her arms about Jim. He was embraced by Chuck Holloway, then Masuo Sugimoto, then Nate Berger. Sukit Sukhsvasti began to clap and soon everyone joined the applause. Hugo Praeger bore down on Jim, wrung his hand, kissed him on both cheeks. Incredulity fastened on Davidson like a sudden plague. He leaned the pointer against the flip chart and sank into his seat as if seeking sanctuary.

It was a full five minutes before Praeger, once again the jovial host of the early-bird fiesta, pounded his gavel. The hubbub slowly subsided.

"Jim, you're one surprise I love." His puffy features were flushed and his voice boomed. "I'm not a religious man, but in this instance, I can say, 'Thank God,' and mean it. Did they hurt you?"

Jim shook his head. "A couple of scraped ankles, that's all."

"What a present for our closing banquet! And for Meg! For all of us, what?" Then Praeger encompassed board members with his Lyndon Johnson look, guileful and conspiratorial. "Of course, in addition to yourself all in one piece, Jim, you've made Arc-Horn a gift of millions. Just your body in that chair solves fifty percent of our financial problems. . . . If you don't believe it, watch our stock tomorrow."

Jim grinned. He could detect no false note in Praeger's jubilation. "I can't perform any miracles for the bottom line today, Hugo, but I'm glad the old bones are worth some money."

"We were working our way through the agenda," said Praeger, "but that can wait. . . . Let's hear the story. Take as long as you like. Personally, I want it with all the relish and spices."

"Okay. It started about a half hour after the motorcade left the hotel." Jim tersely recapped his adventure, the two men seizing him in the back seat, the blindfolded horseback ride at night through the canyon, the long wait, the helicopter, grappling with Chucho, the rescue. He talked for more than ten minutes.

"Tony, how did you find out where Jim was?" Praeger's question was sharp, tinged with suspicion.

Percevale said his information came from "two sources" he was not at liberty to identify. Without mentioning Steve, he told of the flight, finding the hut, the shouted bargaining with the leader and talking Jim back to the helicopter.

"And why didn't you let me or the authorities know before you took off?" Praeger asked. "Goddam it, you might have been killed up there, what?"

"Mostly impulse, Hugo. With my old college friend in danger, I didn't think, I just acted. But, of course, I realized that if I stopped to inform the Mexican officers, they might forbid me to go or else waste critical time deciding what to do."

"But why didn't you bring Jim straight in here from the chopper?"

"There's a special reason. I'm coming to that."

Tony hesitated. The directors all looked at him, waiting.

"I'd like to ask Jim a question," said Masuo Sugimoto. Praeger nodded his permission.

"Jim, is it true you had a talk with Chalmers just before the motorcade?"

"I'll say it is. I socked him one in the face. . . . Look at him."

Davidson flushed, but otherwise his composure remained intact.

"Is that right?" Praeger swung toward Davidson. "Did Jim hit you?"

"No!" Davidson cracked the denial like a whip. "And I can prove it by the cleaning woman whose mop handle struck me."

Jim thought Davidson's protest was too clumsy and vehement for credence, but he sensed that others around the table were suddenly adrift in doubt: the word of the rescued victim of a kidnapping versus that of the corporation's third-ranking officer. Praeger eyed Davidson, then McGowan, his face bunched in perplexity.

"I don't like this one goddam bit," he flared. "A simple fact in dispute, what? One of you is lying, Christ knows why. . . . Jim, you say you hit him. What for?"

"Because the son of a bitch . . ." Jim checked himself. This would never do. Anger only fitfully aided the cause of persuasion. Cool it, he counseled himself. "Because our Mr. Davidson had the damn gall to try to blackmail me." He could not bear to look at Gwen while her pleading, poignant voice filled his mind once again. "You see, Sunday night I had a private conversation with another member of this board. Last night he . . ." Jim pointed at Davidson. "He played me a tape of that conversation on his recorder. I got so mad, I hit him. Knocked him to the floor." Jim could feel the adrenalin pumping anew.

"That true, Chalmers?" Praeger was once again the stern trial judge.

"Of course not." Davidson calmly dismissed the accusation. "Not a word of truth. The fact of the matter was that we had a quiet, frank discussion. Jim wanted to . . ."

"Who's this other board member, Jim?" Sugimoto cut in.

The room fell silent. Jim was about to say he preferred not to name names when Gwen spoke up.

"I am," she said with defiance. "Jim and I talked in my suite after the fiesta. We're old friends and we talked the way, you know, that old friends do. Then yesterday I discovered listening devices, I guess you call them, in my rooms. I told Jim at once."

"Then bugging equipment was found in my own suite," said Jim. "It was only a short time later that I went up to Davidson's place. So when I heard Gwen's voice coming out of his player, I knew who'd made the recording. That's when I hit him."

Directors leaned forward, listening intently, their faces reflecting a strange amalgam of astonishment, confusion, doubt.

Sugimoto bored in again. "Why did he play the recording for you? What happened just before that?"

"He asked me to make the motions to approve Green Tree and Neptune West." Jim fixed his eyes on Davidson. "I refused. I said I had grave doubts about the ecological impact and wanted the projects tabled until our June meeting, giving us time to have a study made. When he saw he couldn't persuade me, he turned on that recording. To me, it was attempted blackmail."

The charges stunned his bewildered audience. Praeger mopped his forehead. Damon Kimball growled something to Joyce Boke-Milgrim beside him. The directors stared at Jim, seeking to assimilate the implications. Had the rooms of board members been bugged, and if so, whose and by whom?

Davidson seemed only slightly shaken. He steadied himself, drumming his fingers on a note pad.

"I think it's about time to end this theater of the absurd," he said deliberately. "I'm not sure what happened to our friend Jim overnight, but he obviously suffered a severe shock of some kind. I think what's needed here is prompt medical attention."

"Is Gwen suffering from shock too?" Jim shot the question.

"Of course not, but we do have the matter of a close

friendship. . . . I'm utterly baffled as to what's behind all this, but perhaps, Jim, you could support your ridiculous accusation by telling us just what you heard on the alleged play-back." His voice dripped with skepticism. "I'm sure the board would like to hear the so-called evidence."

"You *are* a bastard," Gwen snapped.

Directors looked at her uncomprehendingly. Each utterance here, whether calculated or involuntary, compounded the mystery.

Jim slowly twirled a yellow pencil as he struggled with tactics. He must move cautiously, he knew, yet his anger was rising like a tide, sucking his thoughts this way and that. Where to start?

"The conversation between Gwen and me was a private one," he began as carefully as he could, "and I don't propose to rehash it here. Actually what was said doesn't matter and I couldn't remember it in detail anyway. The point is that an Arc-Horn officer had a tape of the private discussion between two board members and that he played back the tape to one member in a clear blackmail attempt." His speech speeded up. "I believe that involves two criminal acts, but whether criminal or not, Chalmers, you violated common decency and, goddam it, I shouldn't have just hit you. I should have beat you to a pulp."

Too strong too fast, Jim realized even before the last hot word had left his lips. He was breathing heavily and he noticed that he was gripping the pencil to the breaking point.

Davidson, after glancing quickly about the table to gauge reactions, leaned forward with confidence. A small, patronizing smile lingered for a moment.

"If I'm to be accused of Mafia and Watergate tactics," he said lightly. "I think you should produce at least one small shred of evidence."

Jim felt a subtle change in the unspoken attitudes about him. The board, ready at first to credit the victim of an abduction, now waited for substantiating evidence. Davidson's request, he could tell by the questioning faces turned toward him, was deemed a reasonable one. His mind groped frantically.

"Your tape recorder," he blurted out. "If we go to your rooms right now, we'll find the reels are missing on that machine behind the bar. I yanked them off."

Davidson folded his hands and looked squarely at McGowan. "I have no tape recorder in my room, never have had. I welcome inspection by anyone who cares to step down the hall."

Now Jim could feel the doubt coming at him in waves, lapping at his frustration.

"By the way," Davidson added. "If you took the reels, where are they now?"

How could Davidson have the nerve to risk that one? Did someone follow him to the beach last night?

"I threw them in the ocean," he said limply, "tied to a metal tube."

"I see." Davidson's triumph was profound.

Hugo Praeger tapped his gavel. Plainly confused, he searched the faces of both men. "Now let's get back on an orderly footing. Jim has made some astounding accusations and . . ."

"He had me kidnapped!" The words leaped out unbidden. Jim shot a wavering finger at Davidson. "The son of a bitch hired Miguel, the driver, and Chucho and Pepito and hid them away in a bar on the highway called El Burrito and right after I floored him with a punch, he sent Miguel out with orders to . . ."

Praeger banged the gavel as Jim's words caromed wildly about the room. ". . . grab me and take me up to a godforsaken shack in the mountains where El Profanador . . ." The gavel fell repeatedly. Jim was bursting with a rage that threatened to consume him. He rose from his chair, was pulled down by Holloway. He saw Gwen looking at him with frightened eyes. Damon Kimball shouted for order. A chaotic jumble of voices assailed his ears. Jim felt the hostility now. Jesus, did no one believe him but Gwen and Tony?

Praeger beat a tattoo with the gavel, finally brought it down with a tremendous blow. "Quiet!" At last the noise subsided, then died away. Praeger let the silence hang for a moment.

"Gentlemen," this cannot continue, what?" He hunched his shoulders and tugged at his shirt as if to remind them of his vestments of authority. "It's plain to all of us that either Jim or Chalmers is lying. Now, in the circumstances, which I must say are extraordinary beyond belief . . ." He was trying to calm with a stream of words. ". . . there are several courses of action. I will state my preference in a moment, but first I must insist on orderly procedure. From now on, no one will speak unless recognized by the chair." He paused, surveying his subordinates around the long horseshoe table.

Tony raised his hand. "May I make a suggestion?"

"Shoot."

"No one can make any sense out of this unless he knows the whole story." said Tony. He spoke evenly in a low, conversational tone. "I know Jim sounds like a madman to many of you, but I happen to know he has been provoked outrageously. . . . What I'd like to do is to take about ten minutes to sketch in the background—in sequence—so that all of you can appreciate what Jim's been up against. May I have the time?"

Praeger glanced at Davidson. "Any objections, Chalmers?"

Davidson's posture was aggressive. "Yes. I think that I should be permitted to answer McGowan's insane charges first. My word and my reputation are at stake."

Sugimoto raised his hand and was recognized. "I suggest we hear Percevale. It's senseless to go ahead without some idea of how this built up."

"But that ignores the possibility," said Davidson, "that there's a conspiracy here to destroy me. For what purpose, I don't know, but I imagine it's linked to the opposition to Green Tree and Neptune West. McGowan, Piggott and Percevale have been seen together repeatedly at this convention and if they've banded together to block our new projects, well then, of course, any sketch of the so-called background would be highly prejudicial both to me and to the two ventures."

"Are you implying this kidnapping might have been faked and then blamed on you to discredit you?" Although Damon Kimball violated Praeger's injunction, his question was on many minds.

"I can't make that charge, no," said Davidson, "but the circumstances are suspect, aren't they?"

My God, thought Jim, is this going to wind up with me being accused of kidnapping myself?

Praeger, who had not taken his eyes from Davidson, continued to study him. He bit his lip, then tapped his gavel. "I for one need some kind of background here, damn it. There'll be plenty of time, Chalmers, for you to speak your piece later. . . . Go ahead, Tony."

"As far as Jim's concerned, this all began Sunday evening in my room when I asked Jim for advice." Tony related the long sequence of events from Ron Jeffers' mission to Buenos Aires to McGowan's receipt of Ireland's letter and the Group of Twelve reports.

"Jim, Gwen and I all read the reports and Masuo was to read them yesterday afternoon, but then came three startling developments." He ticked off the discovery of the bugging, the theft of the Group's papers from Jim's safe, then the kidnapping. "Now the time sequence is important here. As soon as he found somebody had robbed his safe, Jim went down to Cal Silliman's office and . . ."

Something thumped against the corridor door. They could hear sounds of scuffling, a protesting command and a string of obscenities in a shrill, feminine voice, then a loud knock. The door opened.

"I'm sorry, Mr. Praeger, but we've got a problem." It was one of the uniformed security guards.

"All right, all right. What is it?" Praeger was snappish. His tolerance for the unexpected was nearing its limits.

"Miss Gilda. She's intox—real drunk. And she refuses to leave unless I give you a note. We can't get rid of her."

"Let's have it then, for Christ's sake." Praeger beckoned to him.

The guard removed his visored cap, walked stiffly

along the long table and handed Praeger a folded letter. He retraced his steps with the apologetic air of a man who has stumbled upon the College of Cardinals just before its selection of another infallible Italian.

Praeger unfolded the paper and read what was obviously a brief message. He stared at it with growing dismay, then swung his eyes to Davidson. He looked at him hard and long while his hand tightened to a fist on the gavel.

"Chalmers, I think you and I . . ." He hesitated, shook his head, then said bluntly: "I request that you leave the room."

"May I ask why?" Davidson was astonished.

"Serious charges are being made here that involve you. A full board discussion will be freer in your absence."

"I have a right to be here and answer this . . . these malignant fabrications."

"I insist that you leave. That's an order."

Davidson did not move.

"If you don't leave, I'll call the guards and have you ejected." Praeger was taut with anger.

"Very well." Davidson rose slowly, adjusted his shirt, slid his chair carefully back into place and strode to the corridor door. The room was so still each step of his muffled tread on the deep carpeting could be heard as if it were a distinct episode. He closed the door behind him without looking back.

"Okay, Tony, go ahead." Praeger said impatiently. He was trying to contain himself. Little sweat beads formed in the pouches below his eyes.

Percevale rapidly completed his background sketch. Then Jim spoke, followed by Gwen, Sukit Sukhsvasti and Masuo Sugimoto, each of whom corroborated fragments of the story as told by either Tony or Jim.

When they finished, Praeger peered about with an inquiring look. "My own judgment isn't to be trusted at the moment." He shrugged. "A personal matter. . . . What do you think, Masuo?" It was one of the few times in recent memory the commander had sought help in open council.

"There's one small but significant point we could check on," said Sugimoto. "Davidson says Jim called him from Silliman's office yesterday. Jim says no, that he was in Silliman's office, complaining about the theft from his safe, when Davidson called Silliman, then asked to speak to Jim. Why don't we get Silliman up here and see what he has to say?"

"Done." Praeger turned to Bernard Hirsch. "Bernie, get Silliman on the phone. He's to report up here pronto."

Jim saw an opening. "Hugo, I'd like to question Silliman, if it's okay." He had a steady grip on himself now. The clutter of events, from the safe to El Profanador, were sorting themselves, slipping into slots that could be tagged and identified.

"Sure. Just keep it short. We'll have the Mexican army breathing down our necks the minute the rumor starts that you're back in the hotel."

Calvin Silliman's entry was a testament to apprehension. He looked nervously about him, smiled warily, then stood near the door, awaiting instructions. The sight of the entire board, save for one empty chair, overwhelmed him. He plucked at his blue shirt as if to hide the tufts of hair exposed by the low, square cut. If it had been another day, another issue, Jim would have felt sorry for him. Charles Holloway dragged out a narrow banquet chair and placed it at the opening of the horseshoe. Silliman edged into the chair and faced the nobility of Arc-Horn.

"Just a few questions, Cal," Praeger said pleasantly. "Please try to answer as accurately as you can. . . . Jim?"

The name caught Silliman like a blow. He looked at McGowan in utter disbelief. "Jim! . . . I had no idea." He finished lamely. "I'm glad you're safe."

"So am I." Jim felt distaste for his job before it began. Silliman sagged in his chair like a fallen soufflé. "Would you please tell us just what happened when I came to your office yesterday?"

"Yeah, well . . ." He hesitated, probing for McGowan's intent. "You came in right after I got through talking to the police chief and you said your safe had been robbed and you wanted to know who had the combination. I said only the manager, Edmundo Monterroso, knew it."

"And was there a phone call?"

"Yes, Chalmers Davidson called." Silliman glanced involuntarily at the vacant chair. "I told him you were in my office and he asked to speak to you."

"Just a minute. Didn't you tell Davidson, 'No, not now. There's somebody with me, Jim McGowan,' or words to that effect? And then after he found out I was there. Davidson asked to talk to me?"

"Yes, that's right. I recall that now."

"What did Davidson ask that made you say, 'No, not now'?"

"I . . . I don't remember. Nothing important, I'm sure."

Jim studied his man for a time.

"Cal, between the time I left your office and the start of the motorcade about an hour and a half later, did you talk to Chalmers?"

"I'm not sure." He gripped the edges of the narrow seat. "I may have."

"Did you go up to his suite, eleven twenty-nine?"

"Yes, come to think of it, I did. Chalmers wanted to talk to me."

"What about?"

"Something connected with the motorcade, I think."

"And did you then go down to the driveway and speak to Miguel, the Top Court driver?" It was a chance shot.

"No, definitely not." Silliman plucked at his shirt, avoiding McGowan's eyes. "No reason to."

Jules Amarel broke in. "That's not true, Cal. I saw you talking to Jim's driver about a half hour before the caravan started. Then I saw him get out of the car and walk toward the back of the hotel.

Silliman looked as if he had been struck.

McGowan zeroed in. "Isn't it true that later Miguel drove to El Burrito, a tavern out on the highway, and alerted two characters named Chucho and Pepito to be ready to help kidnap me during the motorcade?"

Silliman started. "I have no idea. . . . I mean, no."

Jim stared at Silliman. He could feel the tension in the room. Praeger had been leaning forward, fingering the gavel. Others were following the exchanges with the avidity of spectators at a murder trial. Silliman, taut and wary, glanced again at the empty armchair at the bend of the table. He seemed fascinated by it.

"Cal," asked Jim quietly, "I'd like to go back to our talk in your office yesterday evening. Between the time I left you and the time I arrived in Davidson's rooms, a matter of a couple of minutes, did you talk to him on the telephone about my complaint?"

"Well, I did talk to him about another matter," said Silliman quickly, "but I never mentioned the Group of Twelve papers."

"The what papers?"

"Group of . . ." Silliman checked himself. A look of anguish swept his face, an expression not unlike that which seizes the crouched and ready soccer goaltender who realizes the ball has just passed neatly between his legs. When Silliman added the word "Twelve," It was in a register of humiliation. He stared down at the maroon carpeting.

"When I came to your office, did I mention the nature of the papers taken from my safe?"

Silliman visibly drooped, his eyes still downcast. Would the convention manager risk his word against a president before the Arc-Horn board? Jim waited.

"No, you didn't." Silliman not only accepted defeat, he appeared to have embraced it. When he slowly raised his eyes to McGowan's gaze, he was a supplicant.

"Cal, I have no desire to twist the knife in you." First Chucho, now Silliman. Why this plague of forbearance at times critical to himself? Someday it might kill him. "But an awful lot is riding on my word today and some people doubt I'm telling the truth. Just a few more questions. . . . Did you take the Group of Twelve papers and Senator Ireland's letter from my safe?"

"Yes." The answer was barely audible.

"At Davidson's direction?"

"Yes."

"And you delivered them to Davidson?"

"Yes. . . . But, Jim, believe me, I had nothing to do with your kidnapping. Absolutely nothing. If I'd had the least idea that might happen, I'd have told you." His words spilled over one another. "And I'd have told Mr. Praeger. Honest. I hate violence of any kind." He looked at Jim with pleading eyes, beseeching understanding for the wide gulf between theft and abduction. "You've got to believe that. Even if you don't, it's the truth."

"How about your talk with Miguel before the motorcade?" Jim asked softly.

"All I did was tell him Mr. Davidson wanted to speak to him. I told him where to go. Mr. Davidson wanted to meet Miguel at the back of the hotel."

"Where?"

"Well, actually, it was in the service elevator."

A soundless moment fell on the room as the executives pictured a clandestine meeting in a back elevator of Arc-Horn's third-ranking officer and a shady character who would soon drive, then abandon, the kidnap vehicle.

"I have no more questions, Hugo."

"I have." Praeger's anger boiled like a river in flood. "When it became apparent last night that Jim had been carried off, why didn't you come to me or the police with this story? You must have suspected Davidson."

"Well, yes, I did, but I didn't know who else. I mean . . ." Silliman threw open his hands in a gesture of appeal. "For all I knew, Mr. Praeger, you had some plan in mind. Or maybe it was a decision of Arc-Horn officers or even the whole board. I didn't know." He sought to rally himself. "I'm loyal to the corporation, Mr. Praeger. In my eight years running Arc-Horn conventions and meetings, I've always put the corporation first."

It was the old story, Jim thought. On the altar of corporate fealty thousands of middle managers had yielded both conscience and principle. They wound in a long, gray line through the temple of business, bearing their souls like sacrificial offerings, shuffling dutifully past the saints of unfettered enterprise, Fiske, Vanderbilt, Doheny, Insull, Whitney, Hughes, Cornfeld, Geneen. In the niches candles burned to the memory of Crédit Mobilier, Black Friday, the great corned-beef scandal, Teapot Dome and Watergate. Above in the vaulted arches hovered the presence of the corporate deity, the Holy Trinity of men, money and machines. In its name and service, endless hosts of Calvin Sillimans had bowed in abnegation. And the James McGowans?

Jim turned toward the open balcony, where tints of rose and mauve signaled the coming of sunset. He could look no longer at Cal, for in the crumpled manager he could glimpse a piece of himself. If Jim had not made his decision today in the sweltering mountain shack, he would have made it now. Sadness engulfed him and he wished Silliman would be spirited away.

But Praeger was not finished. "You mean to say you believed this corporation would kidnap one of its own officers?"

"No, sir. I wasn't at all sure it was a real kidnapping." Silliman faltered. "I thought maybe . . . well, I just couldn't imagine Mr. Davidson acting without you and . . ." He broke off, seeming to sense the futility of further talk.

"Your resignation is accepted," said Praeger. "That's all. You can leave."

Silliman stood up shakily. "What about the Mexican authorities?" In his humiliation, he could still value self-protection.

"My advice is to say nothing," Praeger replied, "until I've had a talk with General Sandoval. I intend to see him soon after this meeting."

"But the banquet?" Silliman asked uncertainly. "If

it's still on, I think you'll need me. There's, well, the surprise, and nobody else knows the routine and the timing."

"You're still willing to handle it?"

"Yes, sir." He was not only willing, he was eager. "Without me, it might be a shambles."

"Okay. Your resignation is accepted as of midnight tonight."

"Thank you."

Calvin Silliman marched out as though the stay in his excommunication might have been a pardon.

"Hugo," said Masuo Sugimoto as the door closed, "I have a motion to offer."

"You're recognized."

"I move that Chalmers Davidson be suspended from duty pending an investigation of all charges made here today."

Praeger pointed his gavel at him. "I'd like that motion a helluva lot better, Masuo, if you made it a demand for his immediate resignation."

Directors took the suggested amendment without visible emotion. Surprise had become a way of life this afternoon.

"All right," said Sugimoto. "I move that this board request the prompt resignation of Mr. C. Davidson and that you be authorized to appoint a three-man committee to investigate all events leading to the resignation."

"Is there a second?"

"Second the motion," said Gwen Piggott.

"All in favor, say aye."

The response was less a chorus than a murmuring. There would be no dancing on the grave.

"Opposed, no."

No one spoke.

"Carried unanimously. I'll give the word personally to Davidson when we adjourn." Praeger appeared to relish the prospect. "As our committee to go into this goddam mess, I name—let's see—Masuo Sugimoto, Jules Amarel and Nick Calabrese. The sooner you get to work, the better." Praeger sighed, dabbed at his brow. "Well, at long last, that brings us back to the agenda. Green Tree and Neptune West are up for discussion again. I gather you want to say something, Jim?"

"Yeah. Quite a lot." He suddenly became conscious of his appearance, the stubble of beard, the splotched clothing. "You all know by now that I'm opposed to both projects—at least for the time being. There are solid reasons, highlighted in the Group of Twelve reports which Tony, Gwen and I have read and which I hope all of you will read—whenever we can persuade Chalmers to return my copy.

"You're aware that the Group of Twelve is against both plans. Leaving aside for a moment whether the Group is right or wrong, it must be obvious to all of you now that Davidson has spent the better part of two months trying to sabotage the studies. For those of you who think his methods, some of them actual criminal acts, derive from an excess of zeal for Arc-Horn, I would suggest that Davidson may have another employer—the Central Intelligence Agency."

Jim paused. "I don't make that as a charge. I don't have the facts. But Washington sources assure me that Davidson has been under CIA discipline, perhaps an employee, for many years. Also there's proof, as much as such things are susceptible of proof, that his assistant, Ron Jeffers, is a CIA agent now. In the Arc-Horn context, what Davidson has done seems improbable at best, but in a CIA context, his moves are understandable."

"Jim, let me interrupt," said Praeger. "I want to make my own position clear here. When we ran a check on Davidson before he joined us, we found out that he had helped recruit pilots for the Bay of Pigs invasion. Naturally I asked if he were still connected with the Agency. He said absolutely not, that he'd severed all ties with it. I took his word for it. . . . Now about the Group of Twelve. When Chalmers told me the Group was making a study of Arc-Horn, I blew my top. I told him we wouldn't cooperate, period. Davidson took it from there. I assumed he had closed off corporate sources to the researchers, but it never occurred to me that he'd go in for burglary and ransacking."

Jim nodded. Hugo, he noted, had not included bribery among the offenses. He was still ambivalent about Hugo's precise role.

"My hunch is," Jim continued, "that Davidson's astonishing moves, aimed at gaining swift approval of Green Tree and Neptune West, resulted from CIA orders. There are rumors in Washington that some kind of big-power intrigue, involving the U.S. and Russia, is behind the CIA effort. While I have no definite knowledge, I strongly suspect that Arc-Horn is being used for purposes that have little to do with the business of production and profit. . . . So regardless of the merits of the Group's objections, I think we should postpone both undertakings until we can straighten all this out. As Hugo says, it's a goddam mess."

Praeger looked inquiringly at his counselors. "How do the rest of you feel?" In his newest dilemma, Praeger was veering dangerously near democracy.

"I think we're being diverted from the damn issue here." Damon Kimball of Magna Mines had an air of ferocity in even the mildest of disagreements. Today he was a tiger. "What Davidson did or didn't do is beside the point. And, of course, I sympathize with Jim, but just because he had a tough night is no reason for us to throw millions of dollars overboard. The only issue right now is whether Green Tree and Neptune West are good deals for Arc-Horn. I think they'll be goddam blockbusters. The risks are small and the rewards could be tremendous. I'm for going ahead."

"I'm with Damon," said Hi-Western's Paul Chesterfield.

"The Group of Twelve insists that both schemes may imperil the world's oxygen supply," Jim countered. "When responsible experts raise that possibility, we'd be guilty of crimes against humanity if we lunged ahead without clear evidence to the contrary."

"Oxygen!" exclaimed Sukhsvasti. "What's all this about oxygen?"

"Oh, the usual doomsday crap from a lot of long-haired grad students," said Kimball. "I know a couple of those Group of Twelve types. If we left the world to them, we'd all be back living in the fuckin' caves and gnawing on roots. I don't believe a thing they say."

"I'd like to know exactly what's in the Group of Twelve report," said Sugimoto.

"Every board member should read it," said Jim. "Unfortunately, for the moment, our only available copy is in Davidson's hands."

"Let's go in and get it from him," said Gwen.

"Vote!" demanded Paul Chesterfield.

"For God's sake, give Jim a chance to explain."

"That's enough!" Praeger peered about him. The room quieted. "All right, we'll proceed in orderly fashion. Since I favor the ventures, I'll give my views first. Then Jim can have the floor for the opposition. After that, I'll entertain comments."

Praeger reiterated and amplified many of Davidson's arguments. He was concise, pithy and emphatic. "And so," he concluded, "we nourish the world, we make ourselves a big buck and we get First Merchants off our back."

Jim took longer. He sketched the fears of some scientists that the work might imperil the oxygen supply in the Amazon jungle and impair the home of the oxygen-producing phytoplankton in the upper reaches of the ocean. He noted that not all experts agreed. But there was no dispute over another aspect of Green Tree—logging off a vast tract of the Amazon Basin and planting it to crops and pasture would mean, after the first few fertile seasons, leaching of the thin soil by heavy tropical rains and turning the area eventually into a gaunt wasteland.

"My own feeling is," he said in summary, "that the world is nearing a critical stage. We can gallop ahead heedlessly on production, ignoring the warnings and saying, What the hell, who cares what kind of a world our children and grandchildren inherit from us? Or we can begin prudent, worldwide planning to conserve our resources and live intelligently within the known limits of the planet. The era of supposed everlasting abundance is gone forever. . . . For Arc-Horn, Green Tree and Neptune West put it to us. We can thumb our noses at the scientists and go out and make a fast buck, or we can act like responsible citizens of the world, taking our time, making an exhaustive study of the impact and then deciding whether to go ahead or not."

Praeger nodded. "Okay, Jim, you laid it on the line. Any other views?"

Kimball, Chesterfield and Paulo Hochschild all took issue with Jim. Their main contentions: If Arc-Horn didn't do it, a competitor would. Arc-Horn's business was business, not the formulation of world resources policy.

"There's one point Jim didn't mention," said Gwen. "If we vote to proceed, the Group of Twelve will blast us at Geneva next week. If we vote to kill or postpone, they say a nice word for us. So there's our image to consider."

"Bernie?" Praeger swiveled to Hirsch, the *maestro* of public relations. "What about that?"

"We've taken a pasting this week," he replied. "A little polish on the logo wouldn't hurt right now."

"All right," said Praeger. "I'm ready for a motion."

Masuo Sugimoto raised his hand and was recognized.

"I move to table Items Eight and Nine until the quarterly board meeting in June," he said, "with the stipulation that you name an independent committee of experts to study the ecological impact and report back to us."

"I'll second that," said Percevale.

"You've heard the motion." Praeger tapped his gavel. "All in favor raise your hand."

Hands flew up as Praeger ticked them off, counting with the handle of his gavel. "I make it eighteen in favor. . . . Those opposed."

Five hands went up, those of Praeger, Lindquist, Kimball, Chesterfield and Hochschild.

"Motion carried." The president brought down the

gavel with a single, loud rap. He showed no chagrin in defeat. "I'll try to name the committee of experts next week after consulting with the opposing viewpoints. There'll be no stacking of the committee, I promise you."

Conversation broke out at once. "Just a minute," said Praeger. "Before we adjourn, I remind you the eight-thirty closing banquet goes on as scheduled. . . . Jim and Tony will have to face a press conference downstairs. I know they won't mention anything that took place in this room just now and I trust them to handle questions with due concern for Arc-Horn interests. As for the rest of you, no one, and I mean no one, is to speak to the press or anyone else about this meeting. What with this mucky Davidson business, we're in a delicate spot and one inadvertent word could murder us. . . . I doubt there'll be any more Mexican security interviews after I talk to General Sandoval, but if you're questioned, play it very close to your vest. Understood? . . . All right, without objection, the meeting's adjourned."

Praeger cracked his gavel for the last time at Arc-Horn International's twentieth-anniversary convention. John Lindquist, keeper of the minutes, noted the time, 6:17 p.m.

In the hubbub of departure, Jim was once more the center of attention. Executives surrounded him, congratulating, asking about his health, his treatment in the mountains, the ordeal of the night horseback ride with his eyes covered.

Sugimoto buttonholed Praeger as the chief swung toward the side door. "I've worked out a deal that will solve our problem with First Merchants," he said. "When can I see you?"

"Is it hot?"

"Very."

"Come up to the suite at seven-thirty," said Praeger. "Right now I want to see a former vice-president of ours."

His face was grim as he opened the side door leading to Davidson's office and thence to the communications room.

Chalmers Davidson looked up, his expression a mixture of expectation and wariness, as Praeger entered. He was seated at a desk, reading a dispatch. Behind him a teleprinter clattered. Another hummed softly. Praeger looked about at the complex of machines jammed into the soundproofed, air-conditioned room. It was his second visit here since the convention opened. Ron Jeffers was half hidden behind a boxlike contraption into which he was feeding a sheaf of papers.

"I'd like to speak privately to Chalmers," said Praeger.

"Of course." Jeffers slid the papers into a nearby file drawer and left the room.

Davidson stood up and faced his superior. Praeger folded his arms.

"Why didn't you tell me the truth about you and the CIA?"

"I did. I left the Agency payroll in 1961."

"And there has been no connection of any kind since that time?"

"None."

"I think you're a liar."

"I welcome any investigation you care to make."

"You'll get it. A committee will look into all the charges made this afternoon. . . . Also the board voted to demand your resignation. I want it in writing within the hour."

Davidson took the news without a quiver of emotion. His stance was one of alert composure like a soldier at parade rest. "This is preposterous, Hugo. Not even a chance to defend myself against those absurd lies and distorted half-truths."

"The committee will listen to you in good time."

"Meanwhile, I've been railroaded. . . . What about Green Tree and Neptune West?"

"Tabled until June."

"May I ask how you voted on my firing?"

"The vote was unanimous."

Davidson placed a hand on the edge of his desk. "That hurts, Hugo. With your understanding of the situation, I took it for granted that you'd stand by me."

"Understanding?" Praeger arched an eyebrow. "What I understand is that you've employed Nina Robbins as a household spy."

The silence had a sound of its own. Davidson started, then quickly sought to straighten the dent in his self-possession. "If you're referring to what I think you are, somebody has badly misled you."

"Forget it." Praeger brandished his arm like a weapon. "I'm surprised Jim McGowan didn't knock you unconscious." He turned toward the door, hesitated, then looked back. "Gwen's right. You *are* a bastard."

The door slammed behind him.

Shortly after six-thirty Ron Jeffers tore a coded dispatch from the teleprinter linked to Langley, Virginia, ran it through the decoding machine and handed the result to Davidson.

> *File Series 802-W*
> *No. 14*

From: *Mother*
To: *Cedric*

Your report No. 13 that your Project TeeCee has aborted is bad jolt here. We covering the best we can. What are results Arc-Horn board action on Green Tree and Neptune West? Reply urgent.

Davidson shrugged. "Get out your pencil, Ron. Just a short one to Mother. Make it read: 'Arc-Horn voted to table until June. Regret I blew this one. Am disconnecting now. Will report in person Saturday.'"

While Jeffers busied himself, translating into the code of the day, Davidson walked to the window and gazed down at the swimming pool, the waving palm fronds and the long curl of surf stretching to the south. His first major defeat in twenty years. Well, not even Gus in West Africa or the legendary Frank Baxter won them all. Nobody wins them all. He sighed as he wondered. Would Mother retire him now?

Thursday, 6:30 p.m.

Meg McGowan knew the moment she unlocked the door and heard the drilling of the shower in the ornate, tiled bathroom. Intuition became a certainty that electrified her when she saw the filthy clothes heaped on a chair in the bedroom.

"Jim!"

There was no answer. The noise of the shower filled the cubicle. She pounded on the frosted-glass door with the heel of her palm. A head protruded.

Water streamed from the curly hair, suds lay on the bristle of beard like snowflakes and freckles glistened oddly on the long nose. His grin was wide, wet and soapy.

"Mmm." Meg leaned in to kiss him. A lathered arm circled her, pulled her close while water splattered her white shift and moist kisses lapped her like puppies' tongues.

When he released her and pulled back, she had to raise her voice to be heard over the shower. "Are you all right?"

"Feel terrific—and I love you." He was lathering himself anew. "Meg, do me a favor. Call the house doctor and have him send up some iodine and Band-Aids. My ankles are cut up."

She hurried to the phone in a flurry of excitement, joy and relief. Only ankles! Her world was righting itself again.

She had noted a change in the atmosphere when she crossed the lobby toward the elevators on the way back from the bank. Two rather officious security guards with their shiny black holsters flanked her. "Is it true?" she heard a feminine voice call. Then she saw a man running toward the Toltec Room, ignoring the shout of the thin, spidery woman. From across the lobby, María, that snippy hostess, blew her a kiss and she could see Pete Quigley, standing beneath an arch, waving wildly at her with both arms. As she ducked into the elevator, trailed by the guards, she felt a surge of hope. Could Jim be in the hotel?

The hours at the bank had been dreary ones. Señor Ramírez, assured twice on the phone by Hal Frascella that a First Merchants draft was on the way, tried to be kind, but his solemn solicitude might have been that of an undertaker for the widow. No less than a dozen people scurried about, assembling the money, stamping, counting, checking and chattering in a seemingly endless duplication of tasks. Two young men marked down the serial numbers of the bills while three girls at adding machines verified the results of the manual counters. Meg came to loathe the stacks of hundred-peso notes with Father Hidalgo, a hero of Mexican independence, staring out glumly from the pale-brown face of each bill. At last the final banded stack was placed on a hand truck and 12,500,000 pesos were wheeled into the vault to await Señora McGowan's pleasure on the morrow. Meg left the bank disheartened and weary. It was all a ghastly charade, she felt, for she had come to believe, with Gwen, Tony and Steve, that whoever held Jim—alive or dead—had sent no ransom instructions and had yet to reveal the real demands.

But now! There stood Jim, a towel wrapped around him, his arms wide for her, his smile at once loving and triumphant. He *was* a fine hunk of man for forty-eight. The beginning of a paunch—"executive pregnancy," she called it—was hidden by the heavy bath towel.

They held each other closely, hungrily, nuzzling, kissing feverishly, glad to be alive and together. Then, as they drew apart, the dam burst.

"Tell me, tell me," she pleaded.

He did, talking excitedly and swiftly as he moved back and forth to the bathroom, lathering his face, shaving off the stubble, patting on after-shave lotion, constantly interrupting his chores to illustrate with a gesture. Once he smashed his fist into a pillow to show how he had hit Davidson. Again he feinted and plucked at the air, a reenactment of how he grabbed Chucho by the belt. He was overflowing with himself. Meg had seldom seen him so vibrant, so playful and joyous, and yet so tender. He was forever reaching out to stroke her hair. And when she painted iodine on his ankle bruises and applied the adhesive pads, he leaned down and kissed her head so softly she barely felt the brush of his lips.

His description of Tony's intestinal ruse was hilarious. She glowed with him when Praeger ordered Davidson from the room and she felt his distaste as he quizzed Silliman.

"There are thousands like Cal," she said. "Do whatever the boss says, no matter how slippery, illegal or immoral. Nobody has any guts any more. . . . Company loyalty! It makes me want to vomit."

"I made a decision up at El Profanador's shack." Jim was pulling on fresh white slacks. "I'm going to quit Arc-Horn—that is, if you vote yes."

"You don't have to ask how I feel about *that*." She said it sharply, but within she rejoiced. It was the first time in nineteen years that he had included her in a career decision.

"We'll lose more than four million, you know. I'd have to forfeit those hundred thousand Arc-Horn shares I'm supposed to get next year."

"So we'll be down to our last ten million dollars, right? . . . Really, Jim, what would we do with four or five more? . . . It's not just okay with me, it's beautiful. When do you do the deed?"

"I'm going to tell Hugo before we leave. Effective at the June board meeting, I guess. That'll give us time to break in the new head of Top Court, whoever he is. . . . Jesus, I completely forgot. Is the strike still on at Doylestown?"

"It was when I last talked to Dave at noon."

"I have to get Dave and Smitty on the phone—but first Carol and Connie."

They reached Carol at the New York apartment within a few minutes. She was ecstatic. She knew her father would be freed because she had been assured by a psychic friend of Andy's—who the hell was Andy? Jim wondered—that Jim would be released. Connie would be thrilled when she returned from the drugstore where she'd gone to buy some sleeping pills. Neither of them had slept a wink since a reporter for *The Times* awakened them at 1 a.m. with the terrifying news. Could they go over to J.C.'s tonight to celebrate? They'd be home by midnight, honest. Thanks, Dad. Love, love. And, Mother, it figured, didn't it? With you and us being Libras, no? Libras almost always surmount misfortune from unknown forces.

The call to Doylestown fetched only Dave Moyer. Smitty had gone to Philadelphia to talk to a supplier about increasing the aluminum rod shipments after the strike ended. Jim ticked off the highlights of his adventure once more.

"It's great to hear you're okay, Jim." Dave's warmth flooded the phone. "And how's our girl doing? . . . I knew it. That's Meg. . . . Curious thing. The kidnapping intensified the determination to continue the strike. Kind of a mass feeling that somebody out there was trying to shaft Top Court. . . . Well, I guess we'd better scratch that McGowan seminar this weekend. You two will want to be with your kids."

"Check. . . . Anyway, right now we're both feeling on top of the world." Jim laughed. "Let's leave it that if Meg and I need you, we'll yell."

"Don't call us, we'll call you, huh?"

"Right. . . . As for Top Court, tell Smitty I'll get you both on the phone tomorrow. . . . And, Dave, thanks for Tuesday night. You're the best."

"Me and the kidnapping. Nothing like a good crisis to shake things down between married people. Maybe Fran and I could use one. Kiss Meg for me."

Jim finished dressing by pulling on the fresh golden shirt ticketed for Thursday morning. The phone rang.

"The press is raising hell." It was Tony. "You ready yet?"

"Yeah. See you in the lobby in two minutes flat."

"One thing, Jim. Remember Steve wants to be left out of the picture completely. Matter of his sources. Think you can manage the story without him in it?"

"Sure. I did all right at the board meeting, didn't I?"

"Right. Just keep the story as is—Antonio Percevale, super-hero. Spread it as thick as you like, chum."

Jim had neglected his hair. He stood still while Meg brushed and parted it.

"You do think Davidson's at the bottom of all this, don't you?" she asked.

"Sure. He had me kidnapped. I'm certain of it. But why? My only guess comes from Ireland's note. Davidson was probably acting under orders from the CIA, which, in turn, may have been carrying out some power play by the White House. Phil thinks there's a deal on with the Russians to control the Geneva conference next week. How I figure in that, God knows."

"Are you going to say that to the press?"

"Nope. I've got a dozen theories, but no facts. What I'm going to do is some fancy figure skating on thin ice."

"You mean the CIA gets off the hook again?" Meg was outraged.

"Oh, no. I'm going to tell Ireland all we know and let him carry it through Senate channels. Who knows? As a retired businessman, I may spend the summer on the witness stand."

She fussed at straightening his shirt. "All right, off you go. . . . Tell the newspaper people I'm willing to see one reporter, preferably a woman, as soon as they finish with you and Tony. Don't worry. I won't mention Steve."

Jim sensed a hostile mood when he and Tony walked into the packed Toltec Room. Actually, the press was boiling, cynically suspicious of a kidnapping that had lured many of them from thousands of miles away, only to end abruptly less than twenty hours later with no ransom, no homicide, no injuries and no kidnappers.

Bernard Hirsch met Jim and Tony at the door and escorted them to the lectern that had been placed near the jabbering teleprinters. More than three hundred people had jammed into the room. Journalists ringed the lectern, television crews manned the two camera units, Arc-Horn executives crowded shoulder to shoulder and hotel employees squeezed against the wall. Mexican army and police officers knotted at the exits, fencing politely for position with the Arc-Horn security guards. Jim saw Gwen, Steve and María standing together near the line of phone booths.

Hirsch pulled out an electrical plug, silencing the stuttering news machines, then stepped to the lectern to explain the ground rules. First James McGowan, then Antonio Percevale, would tell their stories without interruption. A thirty-minute question period would follow, reporters to identify themselves. Mrs. McGowan had consented to be interviewed by a pool reporter immediately after this press conference.

"How about Praeger and Davidson?" someone shouted.

"Mr. Praeger will see any of you who are still here after the banquet. Mr. Davidson will not be available. He's been called back to New York by a family emergency and is on his way now to the airport with his assistant."

"What's the assistant's name, Bernie?"

"Ronald F. Jeffers."

Jim began his story with his ride in the motorcade

and Miguel's detour to the gas station. He found the narrative unfolding smoothly in this, his fourth rendition. He let his impressions guide him through the highlights, from the seizure to the rescue. Reporters violated Hirsch's injunction only once. The man from the *Washington Post* wanted the spelling of Pepito, Chucho and El Profanador. A Mexican newsman spelled out the names with thinly veiled contempt for the linguistic talents of the invading gringos.

Percevale's story took less time. He had acted after interlocking tips from two separate "sources." He told of the hurried collection of money, the flight, the exchange of shots, the "talking" of Jim to the safety of the boulder and chopper, the surreptitious return to the Mixteca via the service entrance. He did not mention Steve Cooper.

The first question after Tony finished was directed at Jim.

"Gemmell, *The New York Times*. Mr. McGowan, do you think the outfit known as the Sons of Zapata kidnapped you?"

"No, I don't. The three men in the shack joked about the radio news which told of the anonymous phone call, supposedly from the Sons. Same with the news of the ransom note. A dozen clues from Chucho convinced me this was a straight kidnapping-for-hire at a specific price. In my mind, these were bandits with not the least interest in politics or revolution." Jim laughed. "Chucho sure grabbed those twenty-five thousand pesos in a hurry."

"Roth, AP. Mr. McGowan, why did you sneak into the hotel through the service entrance? And why weren't we told at once?"

Jim did not hesitate. "The annual board meeting, required by our bylaws, began at four p.m. There were several important matters pending and I wanted to be there. I knew if I came through the lobby, it would be hours before you gentlemen let me go."

"González, *Excelsior*. Señor Percevale." He fired his question in Spanish.

Tony answered in Spanish, then translated. "Mr. González asks why I didn't inform General Sandoval of my sources and why I took off in the helicopter without telling the General. My answer: My first thoughts were of Jim. We've been close friends since college days at Brown. Actually, things went so fast I just neglected the Mexican authorities. I apologize for that."

Dwyer, *Chicago Tribune*. Mr. McGowan, the Republican National Chairman said this morning that your kidnapping shows the bankruptcy of the policies advocated by your friend Senator Ireland. He said Ireland, by cutting defense forces and curtailing CIA operations, would leave U.S. citizens at the mercy of such quote terrorist unquote bands as kidnapped you. Do you agree?"

"No, I do not, Mr. Dwyer. While I have some differences with Senator Ireland, I think he's a sincere leader of exceptional ability who's trying to chart a badly needed new course for the U.S. It's pretty farfetched to contend that fewer missiles and H-bombs and Trident submarines would endanger the lives of Americans abroad. I think the reverse will be true. But that comes from a man who opposed the Vietnam war since 1967 and who usually votes Democratic."

"Estrada, *Siempre*. Señor McGowan, how do we know this kidnapping wasn't some CIA—*como se dice?*—ah, *plot* to put pressure on the Mexican government?"

Jim frowned, thought, then cocked his head. "I guess there's no way of knowing, is there? While ten years ago I would have dismissed the thought of the CIA kidnapping a U.S. citizen as ludicrous, today I'm less certain. And when Americans or Mexicans are willing to consider such wild ideas as real possiblities, then I think Phil Ireland's right. It's time to cut back the CIA to the simple business of gathering intelligence."

"McCleery, CBS. Are you implying, Mr. McGowan, that you think the CIA had a hand in your abduction?"

Jim sliced his hands in a cutting gesture. "I'm implying nothing. I just don't know the facts. . . . Look, men, it's only been four hours since I heard that chopper land. Give me time to sort things out, will you? . . . I do intend to have a long talk with Senator Ireland about some of the curious aspects of this thing."

"Mackie, UPI. What curious aspects, Mr. Mc-Gowan?"

"You know them as well as I do. . . ."

"The hell I do," growled the wire-service reporter.

"Well, why me?" asked Jim. "Why not the head of Arc-Horn, Hugo Praeger? Who put the ransom note in Mr. Davidson's car? Was this a spur-of-the-moment seizure or had it been planned for a long time? Why take me to the shack of this El Profanador, who seems to be fairly well known in the area as an unsavory character? There are a dozen puzzles, believe me."

"Dungan, *London Times*. This is for both of you. Are you satisfied with the vigor of the Mexican investigation?"

"I've been too busy to give it much thought," Tony replied.

"I have no basis for complaint," said Jim. "As far as I know, the authorities are doing their job."

"Maxwell, *Miami Herald*. Mr. Percevale, right after you landed on the plateau, what was it this El somebody asked you?"

"He demanded the password. I yelled in English that if Jim was there and knew the password, what was it? Jim took a chance and shouted back, saying he didn't know. He also warned me to watch it, that there were three men with guns in the house."

"Wood, *Detroit News*. Did the leader seem surprised to see an Arc-Horn plane?"

"He was surprised, period," said Tony. "Whether he knew the Arc-Horn logo, I don't know."

"Rockland, NBC. Mr. McGowan, why did you give Chucho the twenty-five thousand pesos? As I understand it, you were already safe by then."

"Right. Well, two things. Tony made the deal with El Profanador. Tony's a man of his word. Also, frankly, I liked Chucho. I just hope he gets his fair share."

"Alpert, *Los Angeles Times*. Mr. McGowan, do you think you learned the real names of your abductors?"

"Miguel, the driver, and El Profanador, the leader's nickname, are real, I think. But Chucho and Pepito? I doubt it."

"Hughes, *Dallas News*. Mr. Percevale, don't all these clues add up to an inside job, either the hotel staff or someone actually in the corporation?"

"My mind's open," said Tony. "It certainly looks as if somebody in the Mixteca was in touch with Miguel, but just who, when and why?" He shrugged.

"Goodman, *Boston Globe*. Mr. McGowan, what's the status of your Top Court strike at Doylestown?"

"Still on." Jim grinned. "But I don't think any of the employees would kidnap me, if that's what's bothering you. Actually, we're on pretty good terms and I hope to work out a solution soon."

The questions ran on. Was he well treated? How about the rumor that Mrs. McGowan was ready to pay the $1,000,000 ransom? When did she first learn her husband was safe? Who contributed the 25,000 pesos? How did Percevale get to the airport without being stopped by the police?"

Bernard Hirsch stepped forward and raised his hands. "Okay, time's up. All of you who don't have to phone or file right away should pick a pool representative—preferably a woman—for the interview with Mrs. McGowan. She's up in her room. . . . One final question."

"García, *Mexico City News*. Mr. McGowan, how do you feel about Mexico after this experience?"

"I love Mexico. I've resolved a lot of things down here since Sunday, personal as well as business. Including the adventure of the last twenty-four hours, it's been one of the best weeks of my life. So: *Viva México!*"

Security guards formed a wedge for Jim and Tony. They moved slowly toward the exit while Arc-Horn associates thrust out hands, patted their backs and called congratulations. Near the phone booths stood Gwen, Steve and María.

Gwen gripped his hand. "Nice going, Jim."

Jim leaned to Steve's shoulder and whispered. "I'll see you later. If it wasn't for you, you know . . ."

María smiled, a proud, covert smile filled with understanding. *"Mil gracias, señor."*

And from the door came a hoarse cry. *"Great job, Jim!"* called Pete Quigley.

Jim waved to him. The banal echo of the tens of thousands of compliments heaped on convention orators and performers was strangely comforting. He was home again with Arc-Horn—if only for a brief reunion.

Thursday Night

Overhead a huge blue-and-red mobile shaped like the corporate logo revolved majestically, subdued lights bathed the long Maya Hall, mellow music rippled from the dinner-jacketed orchestra and the breeze purring from a dozen air-cooling ducts laved the brows of the Arc-Horn troops.

They had gathered to salute the twentieth milepost on the road to empire, but like a medieval army huddled about its campfires after a clamorous battle in which the enemy had been repulsed, yet hardly vanquished, the commercial musketeers were content to feast quietly beside their battered arms. If they had failed to triumph, they had nevertheless attained that secret goal of all fighting men—survival. And for that they were thankful.

More than six hundred celebrants, grouped at tables for eight, faced the dais, which stretched halfway along

one wall to accommodate the twenty-four Arc-Horn directors. Bustling about at a score of tasks as though this
were not his last night before exile, Calvin Silliman had
marshaled sufficient tableware and provender for the
guests—Mexican army and police officers, journalists,
photographers and TV crewmen.

Jake Apple, sensing the mood in the hall, waved his
Convention Dynamics musicians into their "No. 2 banquet" repertoire, bland selections designed to merge
unobtrusively with the hum of conversation while lending
quiet encouragement to the digestive juices in their struggle to absorb invading calories from the *ceviche à
l'Acapulco,* consommé with slivers of avocado, filet
mignon splashed with béarnaise sauce, fresh asparagus,
pomme soufflée, a bibb lettuce salad, mango ice cream,
mocha cake, three French wines, a Spanish brandy and
champagne.

A long blue banner above the stage reminded that
"We Nourish the World," but diners perusing the menu
in the gold-lettered banquet program could feel assured
that the old Arc-Horn priorities were still intact. Only
the foolhardy would attempt to sally forth on an empty
stomach for the herculean task of provisioning the world.
And while the sight of Jim McGowan at the head of
the table comforted those who trembled for the safety
of the dominion, the fact was that Arc-Horn's paper
value had shrunk markedly in three short days, the missing Chalmers Davidson strangely had put a "family
emergency" ahead of the corporation and rumors were
rife that Gilda had torpedoed an Arc-Horn board
meeting with obscenities. In these threatening circumstances, a good square meal was deemed to be a prudent investment.

On the surface all was glitter. In their dinner jackets,
black bow ties and ruffled gold, blue and red dress shirts,
the Arc-Horn merchants presented a splendid spectacle.
The name badges, pinned above hundreds of hearts,
shimmered in the festive lights. Hugo Praeger, seated
at the center of the dais, glowed once more as the conviv-
ial host, beaming, waving, bestowing imperial smiles on

favorites among the coporate family. Nathan Berger, his ravaged features scented with lotion and powder, presided at the rostrum as toastmaster of the evening. White-coated waiters skimmed noiselessly through the hall, collecting the blue banquet tickets and fussing over water tumblers, wineglasses and bowls of iced butter.

The tone of the banquet was set by Monsignor Jaime Morales Ortega of Chilpancingo, who took the lectern on the stage before a red-and-blue curtain where the figure "20" sparkled from a dozen folds. His invocation made note of the safe return of one of God's children and he predicted that while storms still lurked over the horizon, bright skies and calm seas would attend the final voyage of those who humbled themselves before the Almighty. While the blessings of the Monsignor were somewhat hedged as contrasted with those he conferred on the early-bird diners five nights earlier, they were taken as having sturdy upside potential with only minimal downside risk.

As the cleric pocketed the honorarium slipped him by Silliman, the stage curtain parted to reveal the leggy chorines, clad in top hats and bikinis, dancing across the boards while Gilda, her red hair tossing, sang of the glories visited upon Arc-Horn in its first twenty years and of the commercial delights awaiting those wise enough to stay aboard for another twenty. Apparently she had slept off her alcoholic jag, for she hit the high notes without flinching, remembered her cues and never once showed contempt for the cloying lyrics penned by Jake Apple.

She did aim several vengeful glances at Nina Robbins, seated at one of the tables near the stage, but few diners caught the significance.

Frankie Fee mercifully essayed but one kidnap joke. He contended the abductors had actually come for Pete Quigley, but when they poured him into the Mercedes, he trickled out in all directions, forcing them to seize McGowan as a substitute. Fee fed the diners a birthday routine, replete with gags about "Praeger time," the chief's weight, appetite and ambition and John Lindquist's search for the six dollars a share he had somehow mislaid between the Tarascan Bar and the Cihuacoatl Room, den of the serpent lady.

As platoons of waiters swept away the remains of the *ceviche* and served the consommé with its floating slices of avocado, two men in black business suits converged on Table 6. One man leaned over the shoulder of Nina Robbins and said something to her. The second man confided a message to Walter Lowdermilk, seated across from Nina. A few seconds later, after the black suits withdrew, both Nina and Walter excused themselves and walked out to the lobby.

Gwen Piggott took advantage of the change of courses to leave her seat beside toastmaster Berger and go visit the McGowans. She and Meg swapped brushing kisses and laughed about their close-fitting dresses. Gwen wore her clinging gold jersey dress from the fiesta while Meg looked radiant in the gilded formal gown, also with scooped neckline, that Gwen had loaned her. Since Meg was two inches taller than Gwen, the gown fitted snugly.

"What was all that with Nina and Walter?" asked Jim.

"Search me." Gwen looked toward Table 6. "Maybe Walter's the winner of the Golden Globe and Nina will escort him to the head table to receive the award. . . . Anyway, we don't miss Chalmers a bit."

"I suppose I've got his place," said Meg. Silliman's banquet task force had arranged the twenty-four chairs on the dais so that the suspect Davidson gap had been closed and room made for Meg to sit beside her husband.

"How are you feeling now, Jim?" asked Gwen.

"Great. Except for my ankles and my head."

"What's wrong with your head?"

"Nostalgia, I guess. I look at all these people I've known for years and I realize how much I'll miss some of them. Including Hugo. You know, it was just nine years ago, almost to the day, that Hugo and I decided that we had a future together."

"You've made it definite then," said Gwen. "You're going to chuck it?"

"Yeah. I put it up to Meg earlier and she agreed. After all that's happened this week, I just couldn't stay on."

"Then you'll like the little surprise Masuo has for you."

"What's that?" He looked up quickly at her.

"Oh, you'll find out soon enough. . . . But that isn't why I came by. Steve is leaving tonight and he wants to say good-by to you both. How about meeting us on the hotel steps after the spread?"

"We'll be there."

As Gwen returned to her seat, a waiter delivered a small stack of pale-blue envelopes to Jim. He tore them open, read the telegrams and passed on the congratulatory messages to Meg. One came from the National Sporting Goods Association, conveying best wishes "of the entire membership." Another from Carol and Connie, "love, love." Jim's brother, Kevin, wired hearty sentiments, as did the office staff at Lexington Avenue and a dozen friends.

Jim was basking in the warmth of memories when Sugimoto tapped him on the shoulder and handed him a note. Jim unfolded the small slip torn from a notebook and saw Praeger's extravagant handwriting.

Jim: We're going to spin off Top Court. So you'll be your own boss once more. Happy days. . . . Kisses for Meg. . . . Hugo.

Jim looked up in amazement, saw Praeger leaning out from his place near the rostrum. The Arc-Horn chief held a high circled thumb and forefinger as he bathed Jim with an effulgent, although not uncrafty, smile.

"What the hell is this, Masuo?" Jim looked wonderingly at the suave politician of commerce.

"I worked out a deal that Hugo accepted." A wisp of a smile hinted at his pride. "We're going to sell the

Sea Routes fleet at auction—I think we'll net somewhere between one-thirty and one-fifty—and write off the book loss. Then we'll spin off Top Court with a public offering that ought to bring in about a hundred million. The corporation tightens down, cuts off the big loser and takes in needed cash. As for you, you'll have Top Court to yourself again. I can't imagine the new owners not wanting to keep the best man in the tennis industry."

"When does this miracle take place?" Jim fumbled with his thoughts, trying to adjust. He had hardly kissed the mistress of twenty-seven years good-by when she was back again with all her mature, provocative and demanding charms.

"We're going to start with the lawyers next week. We called Hal Frascella and he's all for it. Thinks it's an ideal solution. As for the timing, assuming the strike ends quickly and we don't run into complications, the underwriters should be able to float the issue in May. You ought to have Top Court free and clear this summer."

Jim went on the alert. "What about my stock? Under my contract, I'm to get a hundred thousand Arc-Horn shares next year." The shoe was on the other foot now. Quitting Arc-Horn was one thing, but being traded away quite another.

"Hugo's willing to settle for fifty thousand shares the day the papers are signed for the spin-off. That's a little more than two million dollars as of tonight." Sugimoto smiled. "But I imagine you might be able to negotiate that upward if you hit him on a good day."

"Fair enough. . . . Jesus, this is hard to get used to."

"I ask only one favor in return, that you invite me to Doylestown to see the new methods at work. I'm interested for Nakamura."

"Just name the day and we'll give you the grand tour, Masuo."

The Japanese bowed slightly over the handshake and left with the satisfied air of a man whose financial imagination seldom failed to fatten his corporation's bottom line.

"So now?" Meg had been listening closely.

"I don't know. I used to dream of having Top Court an independent company as it was in the old days. Then today, I decided to cut all ties and felt a tremendous sense of relief. Now . . ."

"Why not let it simmer, Jim? You don't have to decide for weeks yet. When the time comes, you'll know."

"I hoped you might tell me what you'd like."

"What I wanted has already happened—no more Arc-Horn. It never suited you, Jim, and it drained your time and energy like some kind of fatal illness. Top Court alone is manageable, isn't it? But, dear, that's your problem. . . . I'm all set, remember?"

Jim brooded for a time, then brightened. "Well, it'll be good news for Al, anyway." He picked out Al Bebout at Table 18, caught his eye and beckoned to him.

The Top Court vice-president, still under Praeger's ouster edict, made his way to the head table, complimented Meg and waited like a man who expects, if not the worst, at the least nothing promising.

"Good news without any bad, Al." Jim outlined the new plan. "So that means you're back in harness. Since Praeger's cutting us loose, he'll never know whether you're on the job or not. Tell Teigert and Frankenheimer for me, will you?"

"That's terrific. Jim. What about the strike?"

"That's another reason I called you over. I'd like you to slip out to the Toltec Room and call Smitty or Moyer in Doylestown. Tell them the decision has been made: Moyer stays on and the new system will not be interfered with by management."

"Is that from Hugo?"

"No, from me. But I know my man. Once he decided to dump Top Court, Praeger doesn't give a damn what I do. Just tell Smitty the workers have won."

"And that it would be great if he started off with those two shifts again tomorrow?"

"If you like."

"If *I* like? You're the boss, Jim."

"Do whatever you think best, Al. I leave it to you."

"I'm on my way. . . . What a week!"

As Bebout maneuvered amid the closely packed tables, Jim picked his own way through a thicket of feelings. Did he want Top Court back again? Jim recalled his thoughts only five days ago as the Falcon winged southward to Acapulco. He had dwelled on the company as he often did, his mind retracing well-grooved channels: his baby, his son, his flesh and blood. Without his creation, he'd flake away like aged skin. Then this morning in the sweltering shack, beneath the images of the suffering Christ and the slain young President, he had decided that he was finished with Arc-Horn and the cynical manipulations of Chalmers Davidson. And Praeger? As always, his feelings about Hugo were ambivalent—affection, distrust, admiration and distaste all stewing away like some exotic fricassee. But Praeger ruled Arc-Horn and if a Davidson could flourish for years in Hugo's realm, then McGowan could not.

Yet now Jim surmised that a mere divorce from Arc-Horn was less than the final answer. Steve Cooper's cartoon of the imprisoned heart had rankled him. The talk with Gwen Sunday night had set him to weighing anew the old imponderables, life, love, purpose, meaning. And those Group of Twelve papers had troubled him more than his conscious mind conceded. Deep within him had been the certainty, surfacing only in rare, intuitive flashes, that man's plundering of the planet could end only in catastrophe. The Group's report acted as a catalyst to force that deep feeling upward into the more manageable levels of rationality. Tonight, he realized, he could not give the order that would double the production at Doylestown. And should Jim McGowan spend the rest of his life coaxing more and more metals and fuels from an earth that had less and less to yield?

A hundred thought-triggered associations and images spun through his mind within seconds. He turned to find Meg gazing at him.

"I'm trying to let it simmer," he said, "but the pot's boiling."

"With ideas about Top Court?"

"No. Top Court's drifting away with the steam. . . . I guess I'm like you, ready for something new."

"Well, a new Jim McGowan may take some getting used to."

"Rather have the old one back?"

"No, thanks. With a new me, how would I mesh with an old you?"

A gavel cracked. "Honored guests, friends, critics, ladies and gentlemen of Arc-Horn." Nate Berger deployed his crooked smile. "We come now to the presentation of the Golden Globe Award, given annually to that executive who has exhibited the most initiative and enterprise on behalf of the corporation. As you know, the award winner is picked by the outstanding management consultant firm Freer & Mayborn, without any interference or suggestions from any member of the Arc-Horn family . . ."

"Including me!" The shout came from Praeger. He waved his Cuban panatela toward the audience. Berger acknowledged the laughter with an involuntary twitch of his shoulder.

"This is the highest honor the corporation can bestow, given only to those who serve with unusual dedication and self-sacrifice. The Golden Globe honor roll includes such illustrious Arc-Horn names as Praeger, Lindquist, Sugimoto, Amarel and Kimball. Tonight we add yet another name to this esteemed galaxy of service. . . . And remember, this envelope I hold in my hand also entitles the winner and his guests to a two-week cruise aboard the *Arc Hornet*."

He waved aloft the blue-and-red envelope, then carefully tore off one end, fished inside with two fingers and slowly drew out a sheet of paper. "The 1975 winner of the Golden Globe . . ." He snapped the paper and looked for the name. He stared in disbelief. A look of consternation swept his face for a fleeting second, then vanished to be replaced by a contorted smile that could only have been fashioned by an act of will. "The winner is . . . Antonio Percevale!"

Berger crumpled the paper and let it fall to his plate

beside the rostrum. It landed on a leftover fragment of filet mignon and slid into the béarnaise sauce.

He threw a harried glance to his right, failed to find the Gusto Más president, then swiveled and spotted Tony midway along the left arm of the dais. He reached into the recess of the rostrum and drew out a mounted gold ball the size of a muskmelon.

Almost before Percevale could step to Berger's side, the Summit president was thrusting the prize toward him. The scene was less a ceremony than a rapid transfer of assets as though Berger were a thief unloading stolen goods on his favorite fence. Despite cries of "Speech, speech," Berger dumped the glittering globe into Percevale's hands with a gentle pushing movement that forced Tony to retreat.

Berger sank into his chair and looked at Gwen Piggott beside him with eyes stained by recent horrors.

"Congratulations, Nate," she said, "for the worst eyesight on the Arc-Horn board."

He followed her glance to the crumpled paper tilting against the meat like a foundered schooner. The printed name was clearly visible on a centered ridge: "Chalmers Davidson." He grabbed the paper and stuffed it into a side pocket, thereby spotting his jacket.

"Well . . ." Berger sensed the futility of speech. It was enough to embrace the comely Gwen Piggott in a conspiracy of silence.

Praeger's annual address was almost an anticlimax to the convention. For once he spoke candidly, without bombast or guile. The corporation had suffered through a trying week, he admitted, but Arc-Horn was fundamentally sound and tonight it rejoiced in the safe return of one of its most popular officers, James F. McGowan. Next week Praeger would further strengthen the corporate pilings by two moves, one involving appointment of an executive committee to share with him the ever-growing burden of responsibility and the other "looking toward a major realignment of corporate resources."

He praised Meg McGowan, the Arc-Horn board,

Mexico, the Mixteca, the Acapulco police, Gobernación agents. the federal army and all those "who labored to make this twentieth-anniversary convention an outstanding success."

"In conclusion," he said, "I have a special gift for those of you who do not share my enthusiasm for the tropics. Next year the twenty-first annual convention will be held in Montreux. Thank you."

Pete Quigley lurched to his feet at Table 63. "Switzerland! Thank God!" he shouted. He struck his palms to lead the less than unanimous applause.

While Gilda swept on stage, leading the Broadway chorus in a ski-suited salute to the Alps, a waiter leaned over McGowan with a cream-colored telephone and coiled extension cord.

"Senator Ireland in Washington returning your call."

Jim turned his back on the hall and huddled over the phone to hear Ireland voicing his delight at Jim's escape from his kidnappers without injury. They hastened through the amenities.

"Jim, you made a hit with the television interview. People here are talking about it. You handled it skillfully—like a born politician."

"Thanks, Phil. Just between us, it wasn't easy. We had a pretty wild board meeting and wound up canning Davidson. Incredible business. I'll tell you about it when I see you. But your information, I think, was right on the button."

"Oh. The CIA angle?"

"Right. And to our friend's other capers, we can now add kidnapping."

"What? Mr. Establishment? You're serious?"

"Absolutely. And add some bugging and attempted blackmail. Oh, he's a beaut, that guy. Somebody was playing another game, probably the big one you mentioned in your note."

"I've got more on that. . . . But what about Green Tree and Neptune West?"

"Both tabled until June pending a study."

"Great work, Jim. We've got to have a long talk as soon as possible. I've been thinking a good deal about you. It's a damn shame to chain a man of your talents and outlook to business. I'd like to see you step into a larger arena."

"I may be ready. This week sure shook me up."

"Listen, I'm speaking at the Geneva conference. How about coming along with me? We'd have time to talk and I'd like your reactions to the sessions over there. What do you say?"

"Just a second, Phil."

He put his hand over the mouthpiece and swung around to Meg. "How'd you like to go to Geneva next week?"

"The environmental meeting? . . . I'd love it."

Jim lifted the phone again. "All right if Meg comes along?"

"Fine, as long as you and I can have a couple of hours together on the plane."

"Then you've got a customer. I'll cancel next week's business trip to the Coast. . . . Call you tomorrow on the arrangements."

Jim filled Meg in on the conversation. He noted a touch of elation in his voice and then saw Meg shaking her head and smiling affectionately at him.

"Jim, you're incurable." She laughed. "Now that you're a famous man, you're already aiming for vice-president."

"Vice-president? I don't even want to be a president any more."

"I mean the vice-president of the United States, sweetheart."

He was baffled. "Just because we're flying abroad with a candidate?"

She shook her head. "Don't you read the papers? Ireland said the other day that when he makes his formal announcement, he'll also name a running mate who'll campaign with him as a team. No more surprise Agnews, you know."

"For Christ's sake!" Finally he made the link. "You think he's actually considering me?"

"Why else all those talks, asking you to work for the Group of Twelve goals and now this invitation? When you travel with Ireland, you'll be a public character, you know."

The shock lasted only momentarily before his mind began to flick at the possibilities. Meg was undoubtedly overshooting. More likely Ireland's "larger arena" meant advising him on industrial policy. Phil's links with the business community were fragile and perhaps he wanted McGowan to forge stronger ones. A fund-raising role? Maybe. Best bet: Jim McGowan heading a Businessmen-for-Ireland committee.

How did he feel about a year or more of politics with Phil Ireland? He let the question hang, mentally stepping aside to view it. The answer came quickly. He felt damn good about it. Actually, the offer was providential right now. It would fill that restless gap that had been widening by the day. . . . A chance to sell Ireland on the Doylestown worker participation system as a model for industry. . . . A chance to help Ireland try to curb the ravenous hunger of the multinationals for the guts of the earth. . . . A chance . . .

"Well?" Meg scanned his face for clues.

"Vice-president, I doubt. But he probably wants to hook me for some job in his campaign. You want my flash reaction? . . . Yes, positive, affirmative, sure, why not?" The words tumbled out in an eager rush. Then he realized he had not thought of her. "How does it strike you?"

"Let's see." She gazed over the crowded hall. "A week ago I'd have been bitter. No, envious, I guess. There goes Jim, I'd have said, from a twelve-hour business day to sixteen hours a day in politics. But now . . . I'll have my own thing and I intend to work hard at it." She propped her chin on her hands and smiled at him with a touch of wistfulness. "I suppose what I feel deep down is that you're saddled with the old work drive, but I love you anyway. So we're both hooked."

"I'll make you a pledge, Meg. No matter what lies ahead, we'll take plenty of time for just us."

She shook her head. "No promises, please, Jim. Let's just take it as it comes. For right now, I'm deliciously happy that you're safe and beside me."

He leaned toward her to whisper. "I love you. . . . Remember the parlor game at Westhampton? Well, you're not a banjo at all. You're a happy orchestra playing Offenbach."

"As a politician, you'll be a smash." She tossed her head, then broke out with infectious laughter that came rippling back from Jim's friends along the table.

A purposeful commotion at the service doors appeared to be a signal to Jake Apple and his band. The impresario swung around, raising his baton like a battle flag. From the brass section came a blast of trumpets and out from the kitchen walked a bizarre parade. In the lead marched Calvin Silliman, his rubbery features reflecting a wondrous mix of pride and humility. Behind him, stepping jauntily, came Henri, the chef, an immense baker's bonnet flopping on his head. Following Henri came his chef d'oeuvre, the mammoth Arc-Horn birthday cake, measuring four feet high and ten feet in diameter. It rested imperiously on three service carts which had been lashed together and were propelled by several white-coated waiters. Gilda and her eight dancers escorted the creation, exposing gardens of rosy flesh outside their blue-and-red bikinis. Not surprisingly, Jake Apple's musicians gave forth with the melody of "Happy Birthday."

The great mocha cake rolled to the center of the dais, halting in front of Hugo Praeger. A waiter trotted in, perilously bearing a long pole with a cake knife tied to the end. As proud as a boy mayor, Praeger saluted the chef, grasped the pole and managed to carve out a piece of cake the size of a circus poster. People climbed on chairs to read the iced inscription: "Happy Twentieth, Arc-Horn." Beneath it blue icing traced the hope: "Here's to Another Smash Twenty, Hugo."

Silliman and Henri faded to the rear while the chorus

girls scampered onstage to belt out their birthday song. The huge cake was suddenly attacked by the bevy of convention hostesses, all armed with knives like the women of old Paris. They hacked away furiously while waiters snatched each newly cut slice, placed it on a plate holding the mango ice cream and whirled off on their missions of delivery. Another platoon of waiters poured from the kitchen carrying magnums of champagne.

Silliman hovered by a kitchen door, anxiously consulting his stop watch. When the last of the diners had been served with cake, ice cream and champagne, he clicked his watch and turned eagerly to Henri.

"We did it! Four minutes, thirteen seconds."

"They'll give you a raise," said the unknowing chef.

Silliman looked down the long hall on this night of his shame and triumph. "No, Henri. But I'll tell you something. The last time anybody tried that stunt was at a tire dealers' convention in New Orleans. They cut the cake and served it with champagne to six hundred people in five minutes flat. Tonight we had six hundred and twenty-eight bodies and we still beat the tire dealers by forty-seven seconds!"

Silliman paused with a hand on the swinging kitchen door. "At a convention, Henri, always give them what they'll first and last remember." Then he walked sadly toward the service elevator, past the stacked dishes near the sinks, past the shining counters and the empty ovens. He had four bags to pack before his post-midnight flight to New York.

In the Maya Hall, Lucy Jenkins climbed to a snowy table top. "Hey, Walter!" She looked toward Table 6, but Walter's chair was still vacant, as was that of Nina Robbins. Lucy waved at Jake Apple. "Come on, Jake," she called, "let's do Walter's song."

The band swung into the introduction of "Hello, Dolly," and soon hundreds of voices joined Lucy's, soaring on the lyrics that had snatched the early-bird fiesta from the brink of disaster.

Hello, Hugo, well, hello, Hugo,
Arc-Horn's glad to have you here where you belong.
The quarter's great, Hugo,
Like your mate, Hugo.
You're still leadin', you're still feedin',
You're our grand King Kong.
We feel the cash flowin'
From the loans owin'
To First Merchants, Chase and Chem and Guar-
       anty
So:
    Let 'er rip, Hugo,
    One more ego trip, Hugo,
    And we will own both Ford and ITT.

"One more time!" cried Lucy. Now everyone stood. Praeger belted out the words as if he had known them since boyhood. Nate Berger actually grinned as he struggled to adjust his gravelly monotone to the demands of harmony. Joyce Boke-Milgrim locked arms with Damon Kimball and Sukit Sukhsvasti on either side of him and soon the entire Arc-Horn hierarchy was swaying to the melody.

Meg looked at Jim. His head was thrown back and he was singing at full-throated power.

And then, suddenly, it was all over. Hugo Praeger surged along the head table, shaking hands, walking swiftly with John Lindquist trailing behind him. Jim guessed that they were headed toward the eleventh floor for a midnight review of Sugimoto's numbers that would scrap Sea Routes, jettison Top Court at a profit and lead Arc-Horn International into a heavenly pasture where honey bees droned, buttercups nodded and the cash flowed like wine.

As the notables straggled from the dais, Tony Percevale kissed Meg, then embraced Jim.

"I think Anita and I ought to have only two guests aboard the *Arc Hornet*," he said, "you and Meg. How about a couple of weeks in the Caribbean?"

"What do you say, Meg?"

"Terrific. Just so it isn't next week. We're busy."

"Any time, you two," said Tony. "I've got the boat. You set the date."

The McGowans strolled through the dispersing crowd, pausing occasionally to bid good night to friends as they headed for the broad steps leading from the Mixteca lobby to the driveway.

Steve and Gwen were an oddly matched pair as they waited under a rustling palm tree, Gwen in her sleek golden dress and Steve in his opened denim shirt, ragged shorts and hiking boots.

"You won't believe it." Gwen shook her head. "I don't know whether to laugh or cry." A wry smile mirrored her ambivalence. "That Hugo! He's too much."

"What's he done now?" asked Jim.

"Your Hugo's a rough operator, man." Steve propped a foot on his pack resting on the walkway. "You know that security guy from Gobernación that interviewed you, Meg?"

"Señor Figueroa?"

"That's him. Apparently he's a wheel. Anyway, just before your banquet, I was talking to María and we saw Praeger corner Figueroa in the lobby. They had quite a palaver. Then, after the crowd went into the Maya Hall, we see Figueroa talking to two of his men, obviously giving orders." Steve paused, savoring his story. "About a half hour later, these two guys in black suits go into the hall and come right out again. Then Nina Robbins and Walter Lowdermilk came out, both looking sort of confused. Well, this Figueroa walks up to them, whips out some kind of document and reads it to them. Then the two black-suited guys grab Nina and Walter and hustle them out of the lobby and down the steps. . . ."

"Tell them about Walter," Gwen cut in.

"Yeah. We hear Walter ask, 'But can't I even get my goddam clothes?' and Nina is yelling something about being an American citizen. But they're rushed down the steps like a couple of bums. There's a police car waiting here in the driveway. Wham! The Gobernación guys shove Nina and Walter into the car and it takes off and hits maybe sixty by the time it passes the golf course."

"Thirty-three'd, huh?" Jim chanced a guess.

"Right on. Later María got the word from another Gobernación officer. Nina and Walter were deported under Article Thirty-three as undesirable aliens, put on the first available commercial plane, a nine forty-five flight to Dallas—with Walter in black tie and ruffled shirt and Nina wearing her slinky dinner threads."

Meg struggled to understand. "Why, that's incredible. Couldn't they demand a hearing or something?"

"No way." Steve shook his head. "If you're a foreigner and you're thirty-three'd, you've had it. Nina and Walter will play hell ever getting back into Mexico again."

Between them, Steve and Jim explained the simplicities of Article Thirty-three to Meg. Jim then recalled what Tony Percevale had told him of the elevator conversation with a drunken Gilda.

"Gilda's note to Hugo must have accused Nina of some involvement with Davidson," he said. "As soon as he read it, Hugo threw Chalmers out of the board meeting."

"I knew Hugo would get even with Walter somehow," said Gwen. "As for Nina, whatever she did, it's back to the old massage and nude modeling routine in L.A. . . . The elephant never forgets."

"As I've said before, Praeger's a sadist." Meg was fuming.

"No, but he never fails to even the score." Jim grinned. "In a way, it's funny . . . after all, neither Walter nor Nina were actually harmed, were they?"

And once again the baffling enormities of the chief's character engrossed them—the lord of grand visions, the Machiavellian juggler of governments, allies and subordinates, the benign, generous father figure, the vindictive predator, the vulgarian and the sybarite, the ludicrous chronometer of Praeger time.

"Enough of Hugo," said Jim at last. He clasped Steve's hand in both of his. "I don't need to say again how much I owe you. Just remember, whenever you need help, call the McGowans in New York."

Steve looked him full in the eyes. "If you think you're in debt to me, pay off to somebody else. That way we'll get a good chain going and someday maybe it'll get back to me."

"Why in heaven's name are you starting out at eleven-thirty at night?" asked Meg.

"In the hot countries, I'd rather walk in the cool of the night. That sun can murder you. . . . What's next with you, Jim?"

"Senator Ireland has invited Meg and me to go with him to the Geneva ecology conference next week. After that . . ." He shrugged.

"Hey, that's great for you, man. Get in a few licks for old mother earth, will you? They're treating her rotten these days."

"How about coming along with us, Steve? We could use the advice of a man who knows the world at eye level."

"You kidding? Get in one of those jets that burn two thousand gallons of fuel an hour? No, thanks." He reached down and hoisted his pack to his shoulders. "I'm not knocking you, Jim, but I don't put any faith in those high-level palavers. By me, the world will never be safe again until each man decides for himself that he'll treat the earth like the wild thing it is—wih respect and with as little harm as he can manage and still survive."

"That'll never happen. There just aren't that many Steves in the world. . . . For myself, I'll try the road to political persuasion."

"Now who's the utopian?" Steve laughed. "To each his own. You go your way and I'll go mine. Someday let's meet and compare notes."

"It's a date."

"Time to go." Steve kissed both women, held Gwen in a lingering embrace and shook hands once more with Jim. Then he turned and ambled off toward the highway, his boots beating out an easy cadence. His friends stood watching until the darkness swallowed him and only a faint tapping of leather could be heard.

"Your man's a loner, isn't he?" asked Meg.

"Not really." Amber lights of the driveway carriage lamps bathed Gwen's smile. "You see, I'm meeting him in May at Lake Atitlán in Guatemala."

"And then what?"

"I'm not sure, but just to play it safe, I'm going to buy a pair of hiking boots and start practicing in Central Park."

"What about Fragrance?" asked Jim.

"Don't know, Jim. Do I want to spend the rest of my life dreaming up new gimmicks—that use up God knows what precious materials—just to hook women into buying more war paint?"

"Do you?"

"After this week, I don't. But tomorrow, who knows?" Suddenly she was blinking back tears. "You know me, Jim, still the adolescent who wants it all." She brushed at her eyes. "Good-by, you two." She turned and ran up the stairs.

"You know what I'd love, Jim?" said Meg. "To go walking on the beach in our bare feet."

He knew she was thinking of the night long ago in Southampton, while his mind was on that walk along this beach just a few nights past. "All right, let's go." He saw Gwen disappear into the lobby and felt sadness touch him like a falling leaf.

Above them they could hear the first sounds from the Summit hospitality suite, where the blast would go on until dawn. The tinkle of a piano, Gilda's throaty plaint, a gabble of voices, Lucy Jenkins' distinctive laughter, silence for a moment, then the damp monotone of Nate Berger: ". . . and we will own both Ford and ITT."

Workers were already aloft over the portico dismantling the "Bienvenidos Arc-Horn" sign. Along the driveway came a crew carrying another huge sign. As they halted near the steps and looked up to gauge the progress overhead, Jim read the legend: "Bienvenidos New Jersey Bankers Association."

Several Arc-Horn conventioneers hurried down the steps, trailing bellmen with luggage crammed under their arms. Already the managers were fleeing back to work.

A stranger strolled along the walkway circling the hotel. On his orange sport shirt he wore a triangular name badge just over the heart. He nodded politely to the McGowans, gazed about him and breathed deeply of the sultry air.

A taxi drove up and disgorged a perspiring passenger who carried a suit coat draped over his arm. He paid the driver, looked up at the looming pyramid of the Mixteca, then spotted the orange shirt.

"Hey, Art!" His shout was exuberant. "When'd ja get in?"

Jim took Meg's hand. They walked slowly toward the beach. The moon was high and the lone cloud that veiled it was not a large one.

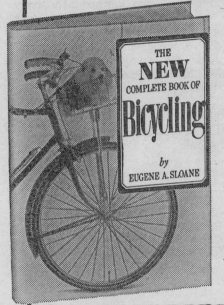

LOOK FOR THESE GREAT POCKET BOOK BESTSELLERS AT YOUR FAVORITE BOOKSTORE